Assassin of the Cross

Holland Timmins

Published by Holland Timmins, 2021.

The Author Holland Timmins would like to thank the following people:

Robert Fitz Odo

Matilda Fitzwalter

J. Stephen Roberts

J.C. Holt

Shad M. Brooks

Galatea Tao

Orrin "Jonas" McClellan for helping me brainstorm

Josie Donnely for introducing me to the works of J.R.R. Tolkien

John Clark for focusing my writing skills

My Mother without whom you would not hold this in your hands

and Jenna Moreci's Black Soul

Assassin of the Cross

Written by
Holland Timmins

Edited by Orrin McClellan and Cathy Mcgreevy

U.S. Copyright 2021
Case #: 1-10164763981
LCCN NUMBER
2021919824
ISBN NUMBER
Hardback 978-1-7367031-0-6
Paperback 978-1-7367031-5-1
E-book-EPUB 978-1-7367031-3-7
MONSTER OF THE MIST PUBLISHING LLC
2950 NEWMARKET ST STE
101-163
BELLINGHAM, WA 98226
Fiction/Historical Adventure/Fantasy/©2021
FIRST EDITION

11 10 9 8 7 6 5 4 3 2 1 0

Assassin of the Cross

Written by
Holland Timmins

DEDICATED TO MARLYSE WELCH
GENIUS, BUSINESSWOMAN,
SUCCESSFUL MOTHER

This book was written using feedback from readers of the groups depicted.

No funds were exchanged for feedback.

This book is a piece of fictional entertainment. While it portrays Robin interacting in historical events, and meeting and interacting with Historical figures, it should not be inferred that this is an accurate portrayal of History. People, dates, events, and locations are sometimes not in alignment with actual history.

This book <u>should not</u> be used as a historical source of information. It is meant to inspire the reader to pursue learning about the subjects for themselves.

Premise

IT'S A STORMING NIGHT, you're safe in a back alley Grind House Theater while everything outside is getting drenched or zapped.

The theater is dingy, sparsely populated, there is too much purple haze, the film starts, It's an old film titled Assassin of the Cross.

The film quality is shit, the color is washed, image flares, snow, grain, scratches, cigarette burns and frame tears permeate this experience, despite that this experience is one you will not forget soon.

Table of CONTENTS

Citation
page

p.461

PART ONE

IN THE PAGES OF HISTORY LEGENDS ARE BORN
E PLURIBUS UNUM

Dramatis Personae

Robin-Archer
   Robert Hode-A minor lord
King Richard-King of England. Hero Warrior
Berengaria-She was there
Joan-sister to King Richard
Eleanore of Aquitaine-Mother to King Richard
Philip the Second of France-King of France
Conrad of Montferrat-Lord of Tyre
Henry of Champagne-Nephew to King Richard
Geoffery of Lusignan-Brother to Guy
Guy of Lusignan-Former King of Jerusalem
Queen Sibylla-Former Queen of Jerusalem
Balian of Ibelin-Lord of Ibelin
Priest-One of Robin's Team.
Bishop-One of Robin's Team.
Pope-One of Robin's Team.
Sigerson-A high ranking Crusader.
Tancred of Lecce- Husband to Joan
Isaac Komnenos-Emperor of Cyprus
Saladin-Muslim General
Abdallah al-Aladil-Brother to Saladin
Saif AdDin-Brother to Saladin
Sultan Ali al Ad-din-A great hero. Distant relation.
Abubu-Servant to Sultan Ali
Sinbad-A sailing legend
The old man of the Mountain-Leader of the Assassins
Agony-Robin's Mentor
Isabella-A freed captive
Sir Orlock-A lost knight
Marshall-A knight
Baldwin-A knight

Walter Fitzwater-A knight
Archer-Leader of the archer squads on Richard's ship
Mercardier-A french Mercenary
Blondel-A minstrel favored by King Richard
Christine-Daughter to Isabella

Unnamed

Peasant
Peasant Woman
Dungeon keeper
Woman at docks
Priests
Falconer
Assassins
Yeoman Archers
Templars
Hospitallers
Town Crier
Friar
Robin's Woman
Women Folk
Bartender
Templar Banker
Templar Traitor
Damsel of Cyprus
jihadis

CHAPTER I

Holy War Declared

ENGLAND, JULY 1189 A.D.

"Jerusalem has fallen!" A Town Crier stands in the town square raised above the crowd; The sky is filled with dark clouds. The Town Crier shouts as he continues reading from his parchment. "King Richard heads to the Holy Land to reclaim it. All of England's sons are asked for help."

A peasant looks to his wife. "How could this happen? God protects Jerusalem."

"I don't know. Now the Saracens have the Grail." The peasant woman says.

Robin is walking through the village to enter Nottingham Castle. He has long brown curled hair flowing to his shoulders. He has a date with a lovely lady. Robin has such a relaxed attitude his girlfriend often remarks he has a jovial tone to his voice. It's always the nice ones you don't want to piss off. He wears rather nice blue clothes over his lithe frame. Robin is just passing by to go meet her until he overhears the local peasant's conversation. He must know what they are talking about. "The Grail?"

"Yes. There is a rumor it resides in Jerusalem. Possibly in one of the towers." The peasant woman responds.

Robin heads to the local church immediately. Robin walks inside the church to meet his local Friar. The church is large, made of stone. There are many stained-glass windows within the church. Robin meets with the Friar in between the dark wooden pews.

"Friar. I must look at one of your stained-glass windows."

"Which one?" the Friar asks.

"Sir Galahad and the quest for the Grail."

The Friar takes Robin to the stained-glass window. The Friar stands next to the window gesturing towards it.

"This is one of our oldest windows."

Robin kneels gazing upon the window. Robin looks upon a knight holding a chalice.

The Knight is offering it to an angel.

"And so, Sir Galahad, having obtained the Grail took it to Jerusalem where he ruled until he ascended to Heaven." The friar says.

"Is that what the Grail looks like?" Robin asks the friar.

The friar looks at Robin. "That is what the artist thought it looks like. If you wish to look upon the Grail you must go to Jerusalem to look inside yourself. "

Robin makes the sign of the cross, he leaves the friar. Robin runs into a forest. He arrives at a combat practice area in the woods by a river. He pulls an arrow out of a quiver. He shoots the first arrow into a painted target on a tree. He hits the outer ring, then after that, he hits the second ring, he hits the first ring, finally, he hits the bullseye. He walks to a stump with a sword embedded in it. Robin looks as if he is staring back in time.

ROBIN IS IN THE CASTLE study, quarreling again with his father, Robert Hode. There is a red rug on the floor, a desk, a chair facing towards a wall. Robert stands in front of the fireplace. He has a long brown beard with bushy eyes. He is a rather bulky man wearing his usual red robe.

Robert Hode points at Robin. "You are going to stop seeing that girl. I order you to."

"You can't order me, Robert. You are not the king!"

Robert Hode's face grows red with fury. "I am your father; I served the last king. You are a spoiled brat who does not know what it means to serve your king."

Robin storms out. This was not the first time he had fought with his father over the woman he loved, but it would be their last. Robert Hode sits down in his armchair. He falls asleep as the fire burns. Robin creeps back in, His Father's sword is resting against his father's favorite chair. Silently, Robin tiptoes towards his snoring father; his heart skips a beat every time there is a slight creak on the floor. He extends his arm, slowly, He grasps his father's sword. The fire pops, starting to crackle. Robin leaps back a bit as his father's sleep is slightly disrupted. Robert snorts, grunts, then nods off. Robin takes his father's sword.

Exiting the room, Robin dances his way out of the castle.

Once outside, Robin sprints to the forest travelling far into the green, he slows himself to a stop as he arrives at a stump by the river. The crashing of wetness echoes through the trees.

Robin slides the sword from its scabbard. "I will serve the king one-day father, but until that day I am taking your best sword, I'm keeping it safe in a stump. I hate you father."

Robin thrusts the sword into the stump. The resistance of the wood reverberates through his arms. He leaves the sword embedded there to go see her in secret. He will spend his time with her in secret until he can eventually marry her.

ROBIN RETURNS TO THE present. He goes to the stump, he be-gins pulling on it, twisting it, he pulls the sword out of the stump. Robin strolls over to his woman's house. He knocks on the door.

She opens her door poking her head outside. She looks upon Robin. He has a boyish charm about him. Robin looks at her, she is so slim, so feminine. Her hourglass figure is complemented by her large breasts. Robin looks upon her face. She has elbow-length hazel hair; Her milky skin is even more noticeable by her red bee-stung lips.

Her green eyes shine brightly as starlight, divided by her ski-slope nose. She's the most beautiful woman alive as far as Robin is concerned.

Seeing who it is she is kind of annoyed by Robin, but she is also confused about why he is here. She stares into his brown eyes "What do you want?" She asks.

Robin lowers his head. "I am afraid I'm going to be gone by to-morrow."

"Oh my god. I had no idea."

Robin's head is still lowered. His girlfriend grows annoyed. She points to her face.

"Robin, my face is up here, not down there."

Robin looks up into her green eyes. "Do you love me?"

"Yes, of course."

Robin motions to her. "Follow me."

Robin picks her up by her waist, setting his woman down on her tan horse, he walks her to his castle for the night.

"I've never been in this room before." His woman says.

"This is my father's room." Robin replies.

She lays down on the bed of Robin's Father.

"How soon will you leave?" she asks.

"I don't know how long I have." Robin says.

She cocks her head sideways. "Have you quarreled with your father?"

"No. Yes. Not recently. I love you."

She grabs Robin's head staring him in the eyes. She kisses Robin on his clean-shaven face. She takes his hand, kissing each of his five digits. She lays Robin down rubbing her hands over his chest, he has a gymnast's body. She lays her head down onto his chest, she listens to his heartbeat. She takes off his shirt revealing tight muscle, Robin does the same for her removing her dress. Robin undoes his trousers; they make love while a framed picture of Robin's Father watches them.

Robin's lover is underneath him; she closes her eyes tilting her head back to let out a roar. She begins clawing at Robin's back becoming the first to draw his blood just as he is the first to draw hers. She begins to pant heavily. Robin grabs her thigh raising it. She then climbs atop Robin. Robin grabs her by the waist, caressing her flanks.

Robin looks up at her. "I want to remember this night."

She places Robin's hand over her chest. "Remember this. It belongs to you. Take it with you wherever you go."

Robin smiles. "You have a stronger heart than mine. I will need it."

Robin climbs off of the bed. His girlfriend takes the sheets covering herself with them.

"Robin! This is so sudden! What has brought all of this on?"

She puts on her dress. Robin puts on his trousers. "I intend to join the Crusade to reclaim the Grail in Jerusalem. I head out tomorrow."

"I have been afraid a day like this might come. You scorn me Robin, but I shall be strong. Allow me to arm you for combat."

Robin is armoured by his woman. She slides a coat of mail over his body. She clothes him in a black tunic with a green cross. She sheathes his sword for him. Robin takes his archetypal bow and quiver from her. If he had the time; he would marry her right now. Slight pain from mail digging into his back.

Robin rubs his back. His fingertips are red. "You are the first to cause me to bleed from pierced flesh."

"You are the first for me as well."

Robin looks concerned. "Did I hurt you?"

She smiles. "Yes. But it was in a good way. I am now a woman."

"Are you angry?"

His girlfriend tilts her head down then looks up at him. "No, it is what I wanted. It was my choice. I chose you. I am glad of it."

"I am off to war. I will return."

"God wills it, Robin."

Robin grabs her, pulls her close, kisses her, then runs off. She stands there, looking off to the horizon. "Try not to kill anyone."

CHAPTER II

Occupation of Messina

ROBIN JOURNEYS TO AN archery area at the English port. There is a massive fleet of ships rocking in the waves off the coast. He walks past Knights Templars who wear white tunics with red Templar Crosses over chain mail. Many are in different circles, some are training, others are laughing it up. He travells past Knights Hospitallers who wear black tunics with white crosses. They are all gathered by a blue tent silently standing there. One Hospitaller comes out of a blue tent caked in crimson. He shakes his head. The other Knights Hospitallers ram their swords into English soil in frustration before kneeling to pray to the makeshift crosses.

Robin passes through a crowd witnessing a Knight Templar duel a Knight Hospitaller. The Knight Templar has the advantage, he knows what he is doing, he just keeps advancing, his enemy is off-balance.

The Knight Templar bats the sword out of the Hospitaller's hand.

"Yield." Says the Knight Templar.

The Knight Hospitaller rolls beneath the sword quickly pulling his knife, he presses it to the Knight Templar's neck as he stands up.

"Yield." Threatens the Knight Hospitaller.

"I yield." Says the Knight Templar.

Robin claps for the brilliant demonstration of combat. Everyone applauds. Robin continues onwards to the archery area. The target is a post set up by the ocean's shore near an anchored ship. He meets the Captain of the Guard. He has a pointed nose with blue eyes along with flowing blonde hair. He wears a white tunic with a black cross. He has mail underneath the tunic, Robin notices he wears black boots with black gloves. The Captain of the Guard looks at Robin. "What is your name?"

"Robin."

"Position."

"Archer."

The Captain gestures at the target down the range. A small piece is missing on the right edge.

"Try to hit the target at fifty paces. Anyone who hits the bullseye serves on our king's ship. You get three arrows to hit the target."

Robin stands fifty paces away. He draws his bow turning the wheels, then fires an arrow.

There is a loud THUNK as the arrow hits the bullseye.

Robin looks at the Captain of the Guard. "There."

The Captain is stunned. "You hit the bullseye!"

"Do I serve on the king's ship?"

"Nobody has hit the bullseye. Do it again."

Robin draws another arrow turning the wheels, then fires it. The arrow hits the bullseye again. The Captain is in disbelief. "Again!"

Robin hits the bullseye a third time.

Robin turns to the Captain. "Did I do well?"

The Captain of the Guard pulls out a paper, he starts scribbling furiously. "Go to the archer's quarters below deck. You are leading a team of our finest archers. Take this parchment."

Robin is handed a parchment. Robin boards the large ship floating off shore. Robin steps below deck. He enters a wooden room with many bunks. He spots a redhead wearing a green tunic with a black cross. "Is this the archer's quarters?" Robin asks the man.

"Do you see any bows or quivers laying around?"

Robin nods his head. "Yes."

"Then yes. This is the archer's quarters."

"I was told to give you this."

Robin hands Archer the parchment. Archer opens it then reads it. Archer examines Robin. "So, you're the one. Let us find you your team."

Robin follows Archer. They arrive at a bunk. It has four hammocks with a banner of the Orion constellation hanging on the wall. Archer swings his hand towards three men. "These are your bunkmates. Meet them. Know them. They are your team now."

Robin watches as Archer leaves. "I didn't even get to know his name."

The man with black hair wearing a white cross on his blue tunic speaks, "That's Archer. He's like that."

Robin stares at him. "Who are you?"

"Pope. The other two are Priest and Bishop."

Pope is the eldest, followed by Priest, and then the youngest, Bishop. Priest is not so much a man as he is a mountain of muscles.

The muscular redhead has many small red crosses displayed upon his white tunic. He wears one black glove. Bishop is the blonde one with the black cross on his red tunic. Pope and Bishop are about Robin's height, they all rise to around Priest's shoulder.

"Who are you?" Pope asks.

"Robin. Are you of the church?"

"We are brothers raised by the church. Now we are archers in King Richard's army.

We are brothers raised by the church. Now we are archers in King Richard's army." Priest says.

"Technically we are not brothers by blood, but we were raised as brothers." Bishop says.

"You are here to make a pilgrimage to the Holy Land too?" Robin asks.

Priest tugs on his tunic three times.

"We must make our pilgrimage.

We must make our pilgrimage."

Robin raises his right hand with his index finger half raised. "Did you just? Anyway, I am here to lead you."

"Did you hit the bullseye?

Did you hit the bullseye?"

Robin stamps his foot. "Stop repeating yourself!"

"I can't.

I can't."

Pope waves his hands. "It's all right. Priest has a demon mirroring his speech. We three are all going to the Holy Land so we can exorcise it out of him. We are all sinners in need of cleansing, that is why we all seek forgiveness in the Holy Land, that is why Priest was spared from the fire."

"They say the light of the Holy Trinity fills those who visit the Holy Sepulchre." Robin says.

"Why do you have wheels on your bow?" Bishop asks.

"Power." Robin replies.

King Richard leads his army across Europe to Italy. The army sails boats to Sicily.

28th of September 1190 A.D.

Arriving in Sicily King Richard leads his army into the city of Messina. Riding on a horse Richard the Lion Heart is a large man around six feet tall with blonde reddish hair. Three golden lion buckles glint in the daylight. Chain-mail creases and folds underneath his crimson gambeson, blinding light bounces off a steel helmet with a golden crown upon it.

As the army marches down the road; Robin bounces repetitiously.

"What are you doing?" Pope asks.

"I think I see some green men." Robin says.

Bishop, Priest, and Pope snicker.

Richard's horse gallops across a group of peasants practicing falconry. A raptor cries as it lands on the arm of the peasant.

"Magnificent bird." Richard says.

"Thank you, sir." the peasant says.

"Give me the raptor." Richard says.

"Why?"

"Because I want the bird." Richard says.

"Well, I want a dirty limerick about my life." The peasant says.

"Give me the bird!" Richard shouts.

The peasant flips the bird at Richard. Richard takes his sword and lops off the offending finger. The peasant screams as he drops to his knees. He clasps his tiny stump. Richard takes the falcon. The other peasants begin to grow angry. They all extend their middle fingers towards Richard. Richard hands the falcon to Mercardier, who takes it and bows. Richard rides off in annoyance.

There are several screams heard, Robin marches by a patchwork of bloody fingers on the side of the road. Robin slides his thumb against his draw fingers.

Richard is on horseback leading his army towards Messina where he unsheathes his sword.

King Richard stabs his sword in the air. "We go to war with the usurper King Tancred of Lecce! By God's calves, I shall reclaim my sister!"

Richard's army invades Messina. Robin marches with the army on King Tancred's castle led by Richard. The castle is located within the center of Messina. King Richard shouts upwards to the castle.

"Tancred! Release my sister Joan, only then will my army leave Sicily."

Tancred walks out with Joan. Tancred has a fit body, short hair, with a moustache. Joan is a small feminine woman wearing a silken blue dress. Her golden hair cascades over her shoulders.

Joan grows excited. "Richard! You have come for me!"

"I am taking Joan with me along with her dowry. Try to stop this from happening, and I will slay you myself."

Tancred lowers his head submissively, then waves his arm.

"Take her. Go."

Tancred releases Joan.

She rushes over to Richard quickly hugging him.

"I demand Joan receive her rightful inheritance." Richard says.

"Very well." Tancred replies.

Three wooden chests overflowing with Byzants are brought out by six Sicilians.

"This is a pittance of her full inheritance." Richard says disgustedly.

"It's all she deserves." Tancred sneers.

Richard angrily storms off with Joan in tow.

"Raise the English banners, we occupy Sicily!"

The English banners are raised. Robin and his men spend some time with the locals. Robin spends most of his time at the local Pizza Inn run by Mario. One day Robin is bringing his men to try Mario's Pizza when screams ring out nearby.

Four of Richard's knights are sexually assaulting the local noblewomen.

"Let them go.

Let them go." Priest demands.

"Mind your business archers!" Yells one of the knights.

Priest looks to Robin; Robin nods his head. Priest, Robin, Bishop, and Pope fire their arrows narrowly missing the knights.

"What the shit!?" One of the other knights screams.

"We're not any archers. We're the best." Robin says.

The noblewomen escape the knights.

Robin along with his men wind up in the stockades for a day.

"Well. That just happened." Robin says.

"Shut up." says Bishop.

4thof October 1190

Robin is with his men attending mass in a local church. Robin spots a stained-glass window of Joseph of Arimathea capturing the blood of Christ with the Grail. Joseph is wailing in tears as the crucified Christ's tongue hangs outside of his mouth.

The Clergyman is giving a sermon. The Clergyman is clean-shaven, has silver hair offset by black eyebrows. He wears his black frock with a certain disdain.

"... and on the third day, Christ rose from the dead. This miracle was witnessed by Christ's most devout disciple Mary Magdalene. In the name of the Holy Trinity, Amen."

"Amen." Robin says.

The Blood of the Saviour seems like Pizza Sauce. Joseph of Arimathea in his red and blue robes resembles Mario. Mario is winking at Robin, while Jesus licks his lips. Robin makes the sign of the cross then leaves. He goes into the city with his team. It's pizza time. The locals are taunting Robin and his men.

"The Crusade will be over by the time your army reaches the Holy Land. Why don't you give up?" The local says.

"Veni, Vidi, Vici." Robin responds.

"You Crusaders will be remembered as monsters." says the second local.

"We will be remembered as the men who saved western civilization.

We will be remembered as the men who saved western civilization." Priest says.

"What was that?" asks a local.

"Sounds like English double talk." says the second local.

The locals start laughing. A tear rolls down Priest's eye. Bishop loses it, he fires multiple arrows into the crowd.

"Damn." Robin remarks.

Richard's army uses the provocation to begin sacking Sicily. Mass chaos and looting erupt.

"What do we do now?" Pope asks.

Robin realises where they are, so he begins ordering his men, "Take everything purple that you can find."

Robin and his men start taking all the purple items in Sicily. Robin rushes into a garment store. He grabs many bunches of purple silk. He stuffs it all into a chest then carries it out.

Robin sets the chest down in a nearby alley. He glares down the street. A caravan of chests is being driven through the streets out of the city. Robin spots purple silk hanging from one of the chests. "More purple than most kings can afford!"

Robin shouts. "Bishop. Guard this chest with your life! I am going after the motherload!"

Robin takes off down the street climbing on top of a building. Robin starts shooting the caravan drivers. The front driver realises what is going on then takes off fast. He begins making serious distance.

Robin peers across the rooftops at the distant driver. "I gauge the distance as about a mile."

Robin gets on his back, putting his feet against the bow. He draws an arrow back with his hands, straining the wheels while aiming with his feet. He releases the arrow. The arrow sings for a mile then pierces the driver through the back of the head. Robin drops onto the street, moves it over to a cart, He observes the dark red liquid dripping off the arrowhead sticking out of the driver's neck. Robin twists inside as he opens the wooden chests. Inside he finds twenty thousand gold ounces, Purple silks, along with other treasures. He realises he is alone; he must guard the treasure by himself. Robin listens as an army coming down the street echoes in its call for blood. The shadows of the massive army dance across the walls.

"I'm dead."

Robin grabs an arrow drawing his bow. It turns out to be an army led by King Richard.

King Richard looks upon Robin. "I see you seized Joan's dowry as it was being transported out of the city. Well done archer!"

Archer pops out from the crowd. "I did it!"

King Richard turns to Archer. "I wasn't talking to you."

"Oh."

Men from the army grab the chests, pulling them off the carts. Richard begins shouting orders. "We construct my fortress now!"

The massive wooden fortress Mategriffon is constructed on a hill overlooking Messina. Its assembly is amazingly quick. As Richard occupies Mategriffon, Robin finds himself on sentry duty.

It begins to rain. Philip the Second of France marches towards the fortress with his army. Philip the Second has short wavy brown hair a pronounced nose wearing blue robes covering chain mail. Robin fires an arrow that lands in the mud near Philip the Second's feet.

"That was a warning shot!" Robin shouts.

"I am King Philip the Second of France! I demand to speak with your king!"

"Wait a few moments. I shall bring him."

Robin hurries away to seek out his king, the pattering of the rain drops smashes against Robin's Hood. Everything sounds wet. A hundred archers are gathered at the walls of Mategriffon, itching for an excuse, while Richard walks out in front of his fortress to discuss things with the French King.

"Why are there only English banners flying over Sicily, Richard? I arrived nine days before you did." Philip the second says.

"We only carry English Banners." Richard says.

"I demand that French banners should also be displayed."

"Feel free to raise them." Richard answers.

"I do not approve of your occupation of Messina."

"I do not need your approval." Richard says.

"Regardless, I have sent my cousin the Duke of Burgundy to warn Tancred what you are up to."

"Do what you want, for now, I shall do the same." Richard says.

The two kings part ways. Richard re-enters his fortress. He addresses his men in the fortress, "Behold! We have a view of all the city of Messina below! We have my wooden fortress, Mategriffon! We have an Army! We head to Messina!"

11th of November 1190 A.D.

King Richard organizes his Army in a way that surrounds Tancred's castle. Tancred hesitantly walks out the front gates then stops. Richard walks up to Tancred. "I suggest a separate peace be made between our two countries."

Tancred is shocked by this. "A separate peace? But what about the pope?"

"Oh. Fuck that guy!"

"I agree."

A single tear rolls down Pope's eye as he watches them from the crowd.

"I guarantee Joan's twenty thousand gold ounces, I also promise a similar sum to the Lion Heart contingent on a betrothal." Tancred says.

"A betrothal between who?" Asks Richard.

"When your three-year-old nephew, Arthur comes of age, he will wed one of my daughters." Tancred answers.

The two kings shake hands. Documents are signed. Joan puts her hand on Richard's shoulder. "What now, dear brother?"

"We wait out the winter in my wooden fortress, Mategriffon!"

"Richard! Wait!" A woman's voice rings out.

Queen Eleanor of Aquitaine marches up to Richard with a younger woman in tow. Eleanor has red hair with striking blue eyes. She wears a white dress concealing her small bust. The young woman has long brown hair, she has green eyes complimented by a lovely smile, she is slender with long legs, gifted with a large bust. She is wearing a green dress accentuated by a purple cloak. The beautiful woman stares at Richard, while King Richard is bewildered by this turn of events. "Mother? What are you doing here?"

Eleanor presents the young woman to her son. "Richard, Meet Berengaria of Navarre. I have chosen her for you as a wife."

Berengaria presents herself to Richard by curtsying.

"Mother, I am on Crusade. I do not have time for this."

"The marriage with Berengaria will bring a dowry that can help you finance your efforts in the Crusade. You will wed her, bed her, then sire grandchildren for me, therefore for England."

King Richard looks at his mother, then to Berengaria. "How did you even get here?"

"I have travelled over the Pyrenees to escort Berengaria to Sicily. You will do this for me,"

King Richard lowers his head in defeat. "Very well. As you wish it, mother."

Berengaria approaches Richard to take his hand. Richard clasps Berengaria's slender fingers in his rough grip. Richard's focus is on her hand, he slowly raises his eyes to hers.

"So, Berengaria, do you know I can build a wooden fort out of sticks and blankets?"

King Richard's army spends their time holding jousting contests, archery tournaments, hand-to-hand combat, the games include all of Richard's men. They make camp during winter.

25th of December 1190 A.D.

A feast at Mategriffon on Christmas Day seems to seal the improved rapport between the two lovers. Robin serves goose to Richard and Berengaria. They sit at a table with a Christmas Tree in the room. Richard and Berengaria can't take their hands off of each other. Robin takes a bite of the goose.

Berengaria addresses Robin, "Soldier, have you ever been in love?"

"My woman is back in England." Robin responds.

"Do you miss her?" Berengaria asks.

"Every day I ask, why. Why am I here when she is there?"

King Richard is somewhat provoked by this statement.

"Then why are you here?"

"Because I remember why I fight." Robin responds.

Richard and Berengaria clap then Robin's motioned away. Robin grabs a metal cylinder from the pantry. He heads back to his barracks returning to his men. Bishop notices the metal cylinder in Robin's arm. "What's in the container?"

"Sherbet ice cream." Robin responds.

"What's sherbet ice cream?" Pope asks.

"Delicious.

Delicious." Priest replies.

"Sherbet ice cream is something Alexander the Great once ate," Robin informs his men. They grab their spoons beginning to eat the cold ice cream. Robin addresses his team, "Merry Christmas, men."

"Merry Christmas, Robin.

Merry Christmas, Robin."

"Merry Christmas." Pope remarks.

"Merry Christmas. I can't think of a better way to spend it." Bishop adds.

10th of April 1191 A.D.

Richard burns down his wooden fortress. The burning fortress roars like hellfire. His Army boards two hundred ships at Messina. [1] Richard is standing on deck as he strings a note to the falcon's leg. Richard allows the raptor to soar.

The ships take off to sail to the Holy Land. Priest, Pope, Bishop, huddle together with Robin in their quarters.

"What do we do with our riches?

What do we do with our riches?"

"We divide the purple in four ways. If anyone in our squad dies, we distribute the remainder evenly among the survivors." Robin says.

"Good enough for me." Bishop says.

"Me too." Pope adds.

"I like this arrangement.

I like this arrangement."

Archer enters the quarters, his footsteps noticeably creaking on the floor.

"You four. What did you manage to sack? I raided a chest of silver coins myself. Everybody else took the gold before I did."

Robin stands up. "We took neither silver nor gold."

"Then what did you take?"

"We took silk, pillows, bracelets." Robin replies.

Archer strokes his chin. "Couldn't get anything very valuable huh?"

"We took purple!

We took purple!"

Robin opens his wooden chest revealing his purple silk. Archer's face has a look of astonishment. "Purple! You have purple!"

Robin nods his head. "Yes."

Archer processes this for a moment. "My God. You four are the richest soldiers in the army now."

The sound of thunder crackles in the sky. Robin looks up to the ship's ceiling. "Lightning! We are entering a storm."

CHAPTER III

The Damsel of Cyprus

The ships enter a storm, lightning crackles everywhere, rain is smashing against the ship's crew like wet projectiles. The Crusader's ships are rocking and rolling like toy sailboats; they can be smashed just as easily. Robin has the stunning realization he may not make it to the Holy Land. Twenty-five ships are blown off course. One hundred and seventy-five ships reach Crete, they slingshot off of the island. Robin and the archers are nearly knocked over as they experience a massive rocking of the ship. Robin clambers up to the deck. The archers, knights, then Templars gather on deck too. The Captain of the Guard stands at the head of the gathered masses. "Some of the king's ships have landed in Cyprus, including the one carrying his sister Joan, along with his wife-to-be Berengaria."

The ships gather off the coast of Cyprus. There is a castle atop a cliff-side above them. King Richard is staring upwards towards a castle at the top of the cliff. "I need a skilled Archer. I have a note."

Robin steps forward, "What is the message?"

"'I demand the release of my men, women, and money.' That is my message."

The briny spray of the ship's surf hits Robin on the face. Robin wipes the saltwater out of his eyes, then he steps up firing an arrow with the note attached into the window. An arrow hits the knight standing next to Robin. Robin hands the note to the Captain of the

Guard. The Captain of the Guard reads the note, "The note says, 'I refuse.'"

King Richard draws his sword pointing it to the shore. "Prepare for invasion!"

One hundred and seventy-five ships flounder off the beaches of Cyprus. Fifty knights led by King Richard launch an amphibious assault by skiff. Richard leads his knights to storm the beaches braving a storm of arrows. Robin fires his arrows as archers rain death on the enemy. There are arrows flying back and forth while the skiffs land. The knights on horses leap off the skiffs led by Richard the Lion Heart in full armour. They fight Isaac's forces on the beach driving off the army. The rest of Richard's forces land on the blood-soaked beach. Richard is squatting on the sand; his armour soaked in a bloody mess.

King Richard turns his gaze to the Captain of the Guard, "Exercise the men along with their horses for twenty minutes, then we ride! We go to war with the false emperor Isaac Komnenos who dares to deal with the enemy!"

The archers set up targets, The knights duel with the Templars. They ride the horses for twenty minutes. The Crusaders take off on a lightning dash to catch up with Isaac. They ride five miles past the citadel. Richard and his army quickly surround Isaac at night, surprising Isaac's forces. Richard seizes the camp with little bloodshed. Isaac takes his horse to try to escape but Richard rides after him.

Richard catches up to Isaac, dismounts him, then kills Isaac's standard bearer. Isaac is a decently tall man. He has long brown hair with a moustache accented by a short beard. He has fair skin as does his forces. Richard duels Isaac. Richard beats the crap out of Isaac. Robin watches the duel with the other archers. The two opposing armies watch the combat side by side. Everyone is taking bets. Richard clashes swords with Isaac. Richard swings but Isaac ducks beneath the blade saving his head. Robin turns to one of Isaac's men, "I bet on King Richard."

"Sic Semper Tyrannis!" Richard shouts.

Isaac swings his sword horizontally. King Richard parries the blow. Isaac thrusts his sword.

Richard parries the thrust to his left, gets in close, he strikes the butt of his sword across Isaac's jaw. Richard bats the sword out of Isaac's hand. King Richard grows angry. "Pick up your sword!"

Richard throws Isaac to the ground. Isaac crawls away. Richard rams his foot into Isaac. King Richard shouts, "Get up!"

Isaac is cowering on his knees. "Show mercy!"

"Don't be a bitch! Do something!"

Isaac crawls towards his sword but is kicked again.

"I said pick up your sword and get up!"

Richard clashes swords immediately as Isaac stands back up. Richard kicks Isaac's shin causing him to lose his balance. Isaac stabilizes himself with his sword, but Richard uses his own to bat the other out from under Isaac. Richard has disarmed Isaac again. Isaac falls to the ground.

King Richard points his sword at Isaac's throat. "I offer terms."

Robin collects his money. Pope looks to his team leader. "How far can you fire, Robin?"

"If you do it properly you can fire an arrow a mile away."

"Can you hit anything a mile away?" Bishop asks.

Robin shrugs his shoulders. "I don't know... can you hit anything five feet away?"

Everyone laughs. Robin continues, "King Richard is not a bitch. King Richard gets things done."

King Richard stands before Isaac. "Come with me to the Holy Land with your army. Together we can fight Saladin."

Richard holds out his hand in friendship. Isaac holds up his index finger. "Hold that thought."

Isaac runs off to a mountain fortress in the distance.

King Richard strokes his red beard. "I think I have been tricked."

Robin chimes in, "You were tricked, my king. You were."

"Ah! Ha! Ha! Ha!" Isaac laughs in the distance.

Richard is wroth with anger. "I am going to burn this shit-hole to the ground!"

Richard sieges the coastline of Cyprus. The people of Cyprus love Richard. One of the ship's projectiles hits a castle wall cracking it open, the forces go ashore. Robin leads his team of Priest, Bishop, with Pope following from the rear up the hillside path. Reaching the top, they file into the castle climbing into the castle over the fallen stone.

The team starts killing all the mercenary forces inside the castle walls. Robin makes his way to the top of the tallest tower.

He finds a well-dressed woman in the top room. She is slender, has long flowing brown hair. She has sharply arched eyebrows, elongated facial features that make her even more desirable.

"Who are you?" Robin questions.

"I am the daughter of Isaac. I am the Princess of Cyprus."

Robin smirks. "Correction. You were the Princess of Cyprus. Now you are my prisoner."

"If you treat me well, I will show you what is stored in this castle."

"Agreed. Show me."

The Princess of Cyprus leads Robin to the treasure hold.

The Princess of Cyprus motions her arm. "Behold the Treasure of Cyprus."

Robin looks to Pope who is standing next to him. "Pope."

"Yes, Robin?"

"Go grab the other forces. They need to see this."

"I understand. I will take only a moment."

Pope leaves. Robin turns back to the treasure. "You all understand what this means right?"

"No. What does this mean?" Bishop asks.

"We are all getting paid." Robin quips.

The Treasure of Cyprus is brought onto the ship. Robin takes the princess back to the boat. Robin presents her to King Richard.

"Who is this?" Richard inquires.

"The princess my king."

The princess is dreading her fate, she looks it. "What are you going to do with me?"

King Richard puts his hands on her shoulders. "I will take you to your father."

Richard spins around to his men. "We march on Isaac's fortress!"

King Richard marches his army to Isaac's mountain fortress. Richard stops outside the front door. The princess is displayed by Robin. King Richard's voice booms.

"Isaac Komnenos! Surrender, or I will personally rip your doors down then throw you to my army!"

The Mercenaries of Isaac lower the door to surrender.

King Richard marches his soldiers into the fortress. King Richard marches into Isaac's personal quarters with several knights.

"Isaac. We have your daughter, the Damsel of Cyprus. Surrender to me now!"

Seven sword-points press upon Isaac's neck. Seven points of blood trickle down his throat as Isaac's eyes behold his terror of Richard the Lion Heart. Richard has Isaac's back literally pressed against the wall.

"Do not put me in Irons."

Silver chains are quickly forged and clasped onto Isaac. Richard, Isaac, Robin, along with the Knights Templar are together in a circular room with a throne in it. Over on the wall to the left is a mural of a shooting star surrounded by several round silver saucer-shaped stars.

Isaac asks Richard, "What are you going to do with my country?"

"I am going to add it to my war chest. Templars!"

A Knight Templar arrives. "What do you need?"

"I need 100,000 Byzants for Cyprus."

The Knights Templar discuss this among each other, then the Knight Templar Richard is negotiating with turns back to him.

"We can give you 40,000 upfront; we will give you the rest once we reach the mainland."

Robin watches King Richard shake hands with the Templars. King Richard turns to Mercardier. "Bring me the archer that captured the princess!"

Robin is brought before the Lion Heart. Richard speaks to Robin, "You are the one who captured the Damsel of Cyprus."

Robin kneels. "I secured Joan's dowry in Sicily, I recently shot your message into the castle window, as far as the princess is concerned, I had a team of archers behind me. They follow me, I follow you."

"That window was a small target in a high far away cliff. You are truly skilled with a bow."

"I am skilled with bow and blade." Robin says.

"A large boast for an archer. Shall I see how skilled?" Richard asks.

Richard motions for a Templar to step forward. Robin fights a Knights Templar. They duel with their swords.

This Knight is skilled, I'm better.

Robin sheathes his sword, grabs the Templar's arm, throws the Templar to the ground pressing his foot on the knight's back. Robin wins.

Three more Templars attack. Robin is put through his paces this time. Robin sweeps his first opponent's legs. He grabs the arm of the

Second Templar using it to sword fight the third. Robin shoves the knight he holds into the knight he combats.

Both opponents crash onto the ground.

The first knight rises. The second and third knights rise. Robin backs up as the three foes coalesce. The three combatants brandish their blades, Robin reaches for something next to the wall. The swords are quickly knocked out of their hands by Robin's arrows. Robin wins again.

Robin senses a small bit of him was betrayed in all this nonsense. Robin stands passively as a squire runs up to him, kicks him in the shin really hard, then runs away. The pain is sharp, throbbing, twisting.

"Impressive." Richard remarks.

A messenger walks into the room. "Geoffery of Lusignan arrives with his brother Guy of Lusignan, King of Jerusalem."

Guy of Lusignan egotistically enters the room. He is a large man with a large forehead, long brown hair, sporting facial hair. He wears a black tunic with a purple cross over his mail.

His brother, Geoffery, is not quite as big, but not small by any means. He has short black hair complemented by a goatee. He wears a black tunic with a golden cross over his mail too.

The two kings meet to discuss things as Robin tends to his shin. The women are reunited with Richard.

Richard is wed to Berengaria in the chapel of St. George. Robin is standing in close attendance to the bride and groom.

Joan is the bridesmaid. The Chapel Priest stands at the head of the church. Richard and Berengaria stand before the Priest with their hands held together.

The Chapel Priest performs the ceremony.

"We gather together today, in the Chapel of St. George the Dragon slayer, to see the marriage of Richard the Lion Heart to Berengaria of Navarre. Marriage is not to be taken lightly. It is a unification of two souls bound together for a lifetime. There is nothing Holier than matrimony. It is not easy; you must put in the work for the marriage to be successful. But the love between husband and wife is by definition: a joyous cause for celebration, which is what brings us here today. Richard, do you take Berengaria to be your wife and queen, to have and to hold, to cherish and protect, in sickness and in health, for richer or poorer, for as long as you both may live?"

King Richard nods his head. "I do."

The Chapel Priest looks to Berengaria. "And do you Berengaria, take Richard as your husband and king, to have and to hold, to cherish and obey, in sickness and in health, for richer and poorer, for as long as you both may live?"

Berengaria looks into Richard's eyes. "I do."

"Then by the power invested in me by the Holy Church of Rome, I pronounce you king and queen. You may kiss the bride."

King Richard kisses Queen Berengaria. Robin begins clapping followed by everyone else in the chapel. King Richard addresses his men in the church, "The others wait for us in Acre. We set sail now."

Queen Berengaria shouts, "To Acre!"

Robin shouts, "To Acre!"

The entire chapel shouts, "To Acre!"

The forces set sail for Acre.[2]

June 1191 A.D.

Robin is in his bunk when the king's messenger arrives. "The Lion Heart wishes to see you."

Robin meanders to the king's quarters. There is a large bed with silk sheets. Robin notices there is a prodigious amount of alcohol along with several empty bottles strewn about the floor.

Robin expected to meet the Lion Heart but finds Berengaria in his stead. Robin immediately bows. "My queen."

"I saw you in attendance at my wedding."

"It was a privilege to be there."

Queen Berengaria uncomfortably turns her back. "I feel Richard only married me to please his mother."

Robin stands up. "The Lion Heart turned the entire fleet around and conquered Cyprus for your freedom. If that is not a gesture of love, I do not know what is."

Berengaria turns around and faces Robin again. Robin lowers his gaze to the queen.

"I suppose you are correct. Richard is a courageous man and I know I could not do better for a husband."

Queen Berengaria looks at Robin and grows annoyed. She points to her face.

"Robin, my face is up here, not down there."

Robin raises his gaze and looks into his queen's eyes.

"Queen Berengaria, may I be so bold as to inquire something?"

Queen Berengaria smiles at Robin. "It depends. What do you wish to know?"

"What are King Richard's goals for the Crusade?"

"The three main objectives are regaining the Holy Cross, the capture of Jerusalem, then reopening the spice routes. However, Richard considers those to be prizes. The true goal is freedom."

Robin is puzzled. "Freedom?"

"During the fall of Jerusalem, the brave hero Balian of Ibelin defended the city for five days. He managed to negotiate the ransom of many people in Jerusalem. Richard's father, Henry the second, paid most of the ransoms. Balian promised payment for the rest of the people in Jerusalem but Saladin refused. He took fifteen thousand people, making them slaves.

When Crusaders take cities, they allow the people to leave with their belongings. Saladin demanded payment, fine, whatever, but then he enslaved the rest. Richard tells me the mission in the Holy Land is to free slaves. The problem is that Saladin has near-complete control of the Holy Land."

King Richard steps through the door behind Robin. "That is where we come in."

Robin bows again. "My king."

Richard points to the door. "Get out. Now."

"As you command." Robin swipes a bottle of wine along with half a wheel of cheese. He goes into a different cabin with its own bed. The Princess of Cyprus has her back against the wall.

Her eyes are wild, she is clearly frightened. "Are you going to rape me?"

Robin shakes his head. "No. I am going to feed you. I have some cheese and wine. I wanted to dine with some female company tonight."

Robin sets a plate, a knife, and two cups onto the floor. He cuts the wheel of cheese then pours his purloined bottle of wine.

"It looks delicious."

"Nothing but the best for a princess. I am treating you well."

"You honour our deal."

"Let us say grace."

Robin and the princess bow their heads.

Robin says grace, "Please bless this food and drink. May it give us continued strength to continue the Holy Crusade. May the princess and I return to our homes safely. In the name of the Holy Trinity, Amen."

Robin dines with the Princess. Robin bites into a slice of cheese. The Princess has some cheese as well. They drink their wine. The Princess chews her food. "This is good cheese."

Robin smiles. "I am glad you are enjoying this meal. I am enjoying your company."

"When will I be free?"

"When your ransom is paid."

Robin finishes his wine. The Princess grabs the bottle. "Have some more wine."

The princess pours some more wine for Robin. Robin raises his glass. "Don't mind if I do."

Robin drinks more wine. The Princess lifts her gaze upwards. "I miss Cyprus."

"What do you miss about it?"

"Swimming naked during sunset."

Robin's shocked face betrays his cool front. "You did things like that?"

"Being part of royalty does not remove one from humanity. I like having fun every-once-in-a-while. Don't you?"

"Yes."

"What do you do for fun?" The Princess asks.

"Explore."

"I want some more cheese."

Robin cuts another slice of golden cheese for the princess. Robin cuts another piece for himself too. Robin asks, "Do you need more wine?"

"Maybe later. Why are you on Crusade?"

"We fight the enemy over there, so we don't have to fight them at our home." Robin says.

The princess looks sideways at Robin. "That sounds like dubious logic to me."

"We have been invaded then enslaved by Muslims for four hundred years. Why do you think Cyprus has had to build so many castles?"

"I didn't realise that's why so many castles exist. It makes so much sense now."

Robin and the princess eat more of their dinner.

"Here is another cup of wine for later."

Robin pours more wine, handing the cup to the princess when full.

The princess takes the cup.

"Thank you. You can have the rest of the bottle if you want."

Robin clasps onto the bottle then drinks it down, before he passes out drunk. The princess grasps the knife from the plate, she raises it to stab her captor in the head.

Unexpectedly, Robin begins to speak, "Mariazzz. I will return. I lovezzz."

The princess puts the knife back onto the plate and pushes it away. She sets Robin's head onto her lap then cradles it as she brushes his scalp. The next day, Robin wakens. He raises his head from the Princess's lap. The Princess wakens as well.

The princess leans her face over Robin's, "You're awake."

Robin's eyes shift right to left. "I must have passed out."

"Who is the woman who you speak of in your sleep? Maria?"

"Maria? Oh. Her. She gave me something before I left."

"What did she give you?"

"Her heart." Robin sits up.

"She must be a strong woman to do that. She must worry for you."

Robin stretches his arms. "I believe she does."

"Do you love her?"

Robin thinks for a moment. "I do."

"Does she love you?"

"She must if she gave me her heart."

Archer walks in on them.

"King Richard says that the Damsel of Cyprus will stay in Joan's company until you are able to ransom her."

Robin stares at Archer then looks at the princess. "I understand. Farewell princess. Thank you for providing me company."

Archer gestures to the door with his thumb. "Return to your quarters, Robin."

CHAPTER IV

Holy War

JULY 1191 A.D.

The Crusader camps are in between the walls of Acre and the forces of Saladin. The sky is red with a blazing orange sun bearing down on them.

Richard meets with Guy of Lusignan, King Philip of France, and Duke Leopold of Austria at Acre. Leopold has a long yellow beard with a moustache. He wears a white tunic with the red cross over his own chain mail. Philip wears his royal blue cape. King Richard wears his chain mail under his red gambeson with three lions. Robin is close to the king's circle.

"How close are the walls to being brought down?" King Richard asks.

"Now that you are here, not long. We have been between this wall and Saladin's forces for too long." King Philip says.

His dark brown hair nearly reaches his shoulder, sweat is dripping off his square jaw.

Duke Leopold scoffs as his blonde mullet flows in the gust of wind.

"I don't get why we waited for Richard. We have been besieging Acre for two years."

King Richard glances sharply at Leopold. "And what were you going to do once the walls go down? Go inside then defend it from Saladin's forces?"

"You have no idea how strong our forces are." Leopold replies.

Richard is growing annoyed with Leopold; He notices the Austrian Duke's white tunic has a sun-faded cross covering his own chain mail.

"Not mighty enough apparently, or else you wouldn't need the ten thousand volunteers in my army." Richard retorts.

Guy of Lusignan is surprised by this news. "You did not order any of these men to fight?"

King Richard smugly replies, "An army of volunteers is the strongest army in the world."

Conrad of Montferrat arrives. King Philip points to Conrad. "Look. It's Conrad of Montferrat, The King of Jerusalem has arrived."

Conrad of Montferrat arrives on a horse outside of the circle. He is a well-built man with black short curly hair along with facial hair. There was something behind his eyes. A cunning intelligence.

Conrad dismounts then walks past Robin, shoving him aside. He enters the circle of kings. Conrad winks at Guy. "I hope things are coming along."

Guy of Lusignan stares scornfully at Conrad. "I am King of Jerusalem. Not you."

Conrad rolls his eyes. "The only claim you have to the throne of Jerusalem is your wife Sibylla. Where is she?"

Guy lowers his head in defeat. "Not here."

Leopold of Austria plants his banner next to Richard's. Richard shows his contempt for this by taking the banner then throwing it down. As the siege continues, the foundations are dug into so the wall inevitably falls. The armies of Kings Richard, Philip, Guy, and Duke Leopold flood into Acre. Robin notices a man watching from the distance. Robin can swear he has skull war paint on his face. Robin disappears into the breach. Robin witnesses many knights killed by Saracens wielding scimitars. Muslim jihadis battle Christian Knights; blood starts to fill the streets. An enemy soldier rushes Robin.

Robin parries the blade, slicing his opponent's torso open in such a way that the wound looks like the top of a tissue box. The man falls dead. Robin observes many other knights fighting for their lives.

Robin begins to lose it in the middle of the chaos.

"Will anybody. Try. Not to. Kill!"

Robin sheaths his sword then takes out his bow. He finds a private corner from the battle. He strings his bow then pulls an arrow from his quiver. Robin is firing his arrows in battle through men's wrists to disarm them of weapons. After the Christian Knights in the surrounding area decide to take their prisoners, Robin heads to the next street. Robin stumbles across more enemies; he shoots them in the leg to disable them from moving far. More prisoners are taken in several acts of mercy.

Soon Robin only has three arrows left. An archer shoots at Robin narrowly missing him. The Archer retreats into a nearby building slamming the door shut. Robin kicks the structure's door in, he quickly checks the corners before he moves through the room, bow drawn. Robin spots the archer run past the door frame. Robin shoots his arrow at the enemy soldier; but the soldier is gone before the arrow gets through the frame.

Two arrows left.

Robin draws another arrow. He walks through the hallway. He enters through an open door to find a Mameluke arched over a knight trying to shove a knife through the skull of the unfortunate Crusader.

"Hey! Think fast!" Robin shouts.

Robin puts an arrow through the Mameluke's wrist. The knife clanks onto the sandstone floor as the Mameluke screams. Robin is back out in the hallway before he can see what happens next.

One arrow left.

Robin hurries to the end of the hall, he rounds the corner. Travelling through the kitchen area, Robin finds a large number of jihadis in the next room. Robin shoots his arrow using a trick shot, extinguishing the flame that provides the only light inside the room. Robin slams the door shut, then uses the rope from a hanging basket to bind it. Robin curses.

"None of them were him... He's still in here." Robin says to himself.

Robin spots the pantry. He slowly enters the pantry keeping alert for any sign of danger.

He observes the grapes, onions, wheels of cheese, sacks of grain all sitting on the shelves, but most importantly he notices the feet standing behind the hanging slab of beef. Robin rolls his eyes.

"Gee... I guess there is nobody else. I must have killed them all."

The jihadi inside the pantry steps out from behind the slab of beef to ambush Robin. The enemy archer shoots an arrow straight to Robin's face. Robin snatches the arrow out of the air then sends it through the archer's draw hand. The Archer is on his knees screaming.

The nearby soldier cries out, "Archers!"

Robin grabs the extra quiver from his captured enemy. Robin barrels through the kitchen towards the exit. Robin somersaults from the doorway to the wooden boxes in the street for cover. Three archers are killing many knights from a perch on the wall of Acre. Robin takes out three arrows from his quiver, popping up from behind the boxes he sends arrows straight through the necks of the three archers.

One arrow misses Robin. Robin realises there is an archer with high ground. Robin climbs to the roofs of Acre, he spots many archers taking out Crusaders. Robin uses his new arrows to shoot all of the archers through the shoulder of their drawing arms. The Crusaders achieve victory. Robin crawls down from the roof as all the archers are taken prisoner. King Richard walks by, putting his arm on Robin's shoulder. "Well done, Robin."

King Richard walks past Robin into the large crowd. "We have taken Acre! Find any prisoners taken by the Saracens!"

Robin takes his team to the dungeons. The wail of imprisoned women was the chorus from hell.

Robin orders his men, "Find the skeleton key! Do it now!"

Robin goes through the dungeon. He runs across the Dungeon Keeper. The Dungeon Keeper spots Robin, and he tries to run. An arrow sings past his ear so his feet screech to a halt. He spins around facing Robin. He notices Robin staring at his chest.

"Oh, come on, I only make three silver pieces per month doing this." The Dungeon Keeper says.

Robin's head tilts down and when it rises Robin's face has transformed, He has a smirk.

"I want the girls..." Robin says ice cold.

Robin points his arrow straight between the Dungeon Keeper's eyes.

"Sir, I will personally escort you to the cell and give you every girly girls girls you could ever hope to see." the Dungeon Keeper says.

The Dungeon Keeper leads Robin down a staircase that spirals underneath the streets. They stop at the cells at the bottom. The Dungeon Keeper pulls out his keys. He puts the key into the lock. Then the Dungeon Keeper breaks the key in the lock.

"Damn!" Robin curses.

"...Oops. Heh. You will never free all the slaves, Christian, inshallah!" the Dungeon Keeper says.

Robin puts an arrow through the Dungeon Keeper's left thigh. The Dungeon Keeper falls onto one knee.

"You shot me!"

"I'm sorry,"

"You asshole!"

"I said I'm sorry."

"Curse your' black heart!"

"Hey, that hurts."

Priest, Bishop, and Pope arrive at the bottom of the dungeon. Robin has his hands on the lock. "He broke it in the lock! He broke the skeleton key!"

"No way to open the cells now!" Pope laments.

"What do we do?" Bishop asks.

The prisoners wail. One female prisoner sticks her arm out of the bars towards Robin. "Help! Help! Dear God, don't leave us!"

Priest steps up.

"I can unleash the demon.

I can unleash the demon."

Robin is trying to process what Priest is trying to do. "Uh. What?"

Pope walks behind Priest whispering, "Priest, not now. Not in the Holy Land!"

Priest grabs the cell grating, beginning to pull. "RRRRRRRRRRRR..."

Priest looks to Bishop.

"...Do it now!

Do it now!"

Bishop smacks Priest across the back of the head really hard. "The power of Christ compels you!"

"AAAAAAARRRRRRGGGGHHH!"

Priest's muscles ripple as he rips the grating out of the wall with his bare hands. The Dungeon Keeper's eyes widen. "I just bought five hundred Gold Dinars worth of new shit too."

Priest slams the grating downwards cutting the Dungeon Keeper in half. A man of the cloth arrives as this act is committed. Women spill out of the cell thanking Priest, Robin, and the others. The Clergyman points at Priest. "demon!"

Pope closes his eyes; he knows they have been caught. "Aw shit! I knew this would happen."

"demon!" The Clergyman shouts.

Bishop tries to reason with the Clergyman. "You don't understand! He came here to be saved!"

"He is possessed."

"Priest is not possessed by a demon! demons do not free slaves!" Robin says.

"The devil uses lies!" Shouts the Clergyman.

King Richard appears behind the Clergyman. "Robin is right, demons do not free slaves. Dare call me a liar."

The Clergyman hunches over. "I... I can't."

King Richard orders the Clergyman, "Leave me with these men. Now."

The Clergyman leaves. King Richard smiles. "I see you four have been keeping a secret from me."

Priest tugs on his tunic four times. Robin puts himself between his men and King Richard. "My king, Priest is part of my team, I take responsibility for him."

"The four of you fight like demons. I am not surprised that one of you has one." Richard quips.

"Will he be burned?" Robin asks.

King Richard grows more serious. "Every man in this army is here to be saved. Do not think me capable to deny a man salvation."

Robin nods his head towards the cell. "The skeleton key was broken."

"Then you will have much time practicing how to pick locks, Robin."

Robin walks past King Richard, grabs a lock pick from a bag, then sets to work. King Richard emerges from the dungeon. "Round up the prisoners!"

The prisoners are rounded up then put in bondage. The Christians are also rounded up as they are freed. King Richard speaks to Guy of Lusignan. "How many are there?"

"About 2,600 Muslim prisoners plus 5,000 women." Guy answers.

"We accomplished a nice bit of rescuing at Acre."

"Richard. The women were separated from their children."

Richard gazes upon the sad faces of the former slaves. Both the white Christian women along with the darker complexioned Byzantine Christian women cry the same tears.

"Fellow Christians, I free you from enslavement. I promise to reunite you with your loved ones. But for now, let us celebrate victory, let us celebrate freedom."

The Crusaders celebrate with the former slaves. Robin, Priest, Bishop, and Pope are inside a building purchasing wine taken from Cyprus. The Bartender stands behind a table. "The finest wine from Cyprus. All yours; if you have coin."

The group of archers pay coin to have their cups filled. The bartender takes their glass and fills them in front of a large stack of barrels full of quickly diminishing wine.

Robin sits at a corner table imbibing with his men.

"Don't get too drunk Bishop. You always walk diagonal when you're drunk." Robin says.

Pope, Priest, and Robin laugh.

Pope speaks, "So Robin."

"Yes?"

"Every man has a reason for being here. Many are here to make a pilgrimage to Jerusalem. Some wish to visit the Holy Sepulchre. Others like Priest are here to save their souls. Others are here to serve the king."

"Your point?"

"You have never told us why you are here." Bishop says.

Robin takes a sip of wine. "Oh. Well... You would laugh."

Priest slams his cup onto the table spilling some wine.

"Tell us! Tell us!

Tell us! Tell us!"

"I am here for a more divine reason." Robin says before taking another sip of wine.

Bishop stares at Priest. "Is he trying to tell us he was sent by God?"

Robin smiles, half chuckling as he says, "No. That's not... Listen, there is no way to say it correctly, so I am just going to say it. I am here to recover the Grail."

Priest, Bishop, and Pope are silent for a moment then begin to laugh.

"The Grail is just a legend.

The Grail is just a legend."

"Every legend has a basis of truth!" Robin shouts.

Pope scolds Robin, "You're a fool, Robin. Sent on a fool's errand."

Robin defends his motivation for joining the Crusade.

"If the Grail exists someone must recover it."

"So, you think you are Sir Lancelot? You think you are worthy enough to recover the Grail?" Bishop asks.

"Lancelot was not worthy to recover the Grail. It was his son Sir Galahad who was worthy enough to obtain the Grail." Robin retorts.

"You must be well-read to know this, Sir Robin.

You must be well-read to know this, Sir Robin."

Pope spits out his wine. "Sir Robin! AH. HA! HA! HA! HA! HA!"

Bishop starts to sing.

>*"Sir Robin! Sir Robin! He wears his heroic mail.*
>*Sir Robin! Sir Robin! He seeks out the Grail.*
>*Except the Grail's a fable so he shall fail.*
>*He will turn to drink then puke up his ale!"*

Robin grabs the bottle. "I'm leaving."

Robin winds his way out of the makeshift pub.

"But why is he really here?" Pope asks.

The three brothers sit in silence as they contemplate the enigma of Robin.

An attractive woman walks up to Priest. "Was that the Hero of Acre?"

ROBIN SITS OUTSIDE his tent getting drunk. Priest shows up at Robin's tent with Isabella.

"Robin, this is Isabella. She wishes to personally thank the Hero of Acre for her freedom.

Robin, this is Isabella. She wishes to personally thank the Hero of Acre for her freedom."

Isabella is a tall but slim woman who has an hourglass figure. She has long auburn hair with green eyes. Isabella addresses Robin, "Thank you, Robin. You along with the Crusaders have freed us all from the bonds of enslavement. Is there anything at all I can do for you tonight?"

Robin stands up. "Yes, this is my good friend, Priest. He has come to the Holy Land in order to be saved. If you want to do something for me, do something for Priest, and save him tonight."

"I understand. Priest, allow me to accompany you tonight."

Isabella curtsies before Priest then takes his hand. Priest tugs on his tunic five times. Priest and Isabella walk off. Priest looks back at Robin; Robin gives him a thumbs up. Robin grabs his alcohol then walks back into his tent. Robin is drinking straight from the bottle. King Richard's messenger walks into Robin's tent. "The Lion Heart wishes to see you."

Robin stands up then is brought to the quarters of royalty. There is the swirling smoke of incense pungent in the air. There is a large circular bed in the room.

The blanket upon the bed has the sun and the moon decorated onto it. Beaded curtains are hanging from the ceiling, a few chests lay around. Robin spots someone by the hookah

"You summoned me, my king?"

"Not quite, Robin."

Robin is taken aback by the beauty and adornments of the woman before him. She has blonde hair, piercing blue eyes, flat eyebrows, pale skin, with an exotic beauty about her. Robin realises he shouldn't be here. "Who are you? How do you know my name?"

"I am Sibylla, Queen of Jerusalem."

Robin begins to panic. "Where is King Richard?"

"Richard told me of how you ensured our victory at Acre. He also told me of your other deeds. I wanted to meet you to see if there was such a thing as nobility in an archer."

"What do you want from me?"

"You cannot keep the Damsel of Cyprus. How much do you wish for her ransom?"

"2,000 gold coins."

"Consider it done." Sibylla opens a chest of gold coins for Robin. Robin takes a gold coin then bites it. "I release her. She is no longer my prisoner."

Queen Sibylla takes several gold coins into her palm, dropping them back into the chest.

"Men. They only want gold and death. My Kingdom of Jerusalem is lost, all of my children are dead, all because men want to kill one another." Sibylla closes the chest.

"I... don't know what to say."

"I don't expect you to say anything. Just listen. Here. Look at this." Sibylla takes out a black square presenting it to Robin.

"What is this?" Robin asks.

"The Assassins call it hashish. You smoke it. It is rumored that the Assassins were named after hashish."

They begin smoking from the Hookah.

"Who are the Assassins?" Robin asks.

"Very dangerous players on the chessboard. Men relish in the glory of war. They crave the adulation it gives them. Years from now no one will remember that I was instrumental in launching this Crusade."

"Trust me, my Queen. Nobody could ever forget you."

The Queen smiles. "I want to know something."

"What is that?"

"Even if you didn't have to, would you still kill a man?"

"Truth is, I only kill when I have to."

Queen Sibylla is surprised by this revelation, she was not expecting this answer. "Oh. I guess archers are noble."

"Why do you want to know that of me?"

"I am dying. I shall never sit on the throne of my fallen kingdom ever again. Thanks to you I am still Queen of Acre. I want to know if there is such a thing as a king without a crown...."

Queen Sibylla moves in to kiss Robin. They make out. Robin rips off the top of her dress. Sibylla grabs Robin's head pressing it into her bosom. Robin kisses her breasts. Queen Sibylla tilts her head upwards in ecstasy. "Tonight, I shall be your queen."

Robin feels something dark twisting inside of him. Robin spins Sibylla around, bending her over. "No. Tonight, you will be my whore."

Robin lifts her dress then screws the life out of the infamous queen. After sex, Robin is putting on his clothes. "I want to know anything I can use to locate the Grail. Sibylla, you have knowledge of Jerusalem. Do you know where the Grail is?"

Queen Sibylla lies naked on the floor looking at the wall.

"It has been moved."

Robin looks down at Sibylla. "To where?"

"Mu..." Sibylla dies right in front of Robin.

Robin begins panicking.

"No! Help! Somebody Help!

CHAPTER V

The Sword of The Lion Heart

Robin is dragged into a tent by guards; He is promptly thrown down to King Richard's feet. Berengaria is laying on a red sofa behind Richard to the right. Behind them is a painting of the stars. There is a barrel to the left. King Richard looks down upon Robin. "Do you know the men are saying that you killed Sibylla?"

Robin gets up onto his knees, he lowers his head in atonement. "Men like saying a lot of things. Doesn't make any of it the truth."

"So, what is the truth?"

Robin is fighting back tears. "Sibylla was impressed with the way you brought me up in discussion. She wanted to see me."

"And you accepted? She has a husband."

"I was informed you wanted to see me. I was as surprised as you are that Sibylla was there. We spoke to one another, we made love, the next morning she died."

Queen Berengaria speaks up, "You fucked Sibylla to death."

Robin raises his head staring in disbelief at Queen Berengaria. "Yes. No! Maybe?"

King Richard folds his arms. "So that's the truth?"

"As far as I know it."

King Richard is furious.

"I should nail you to a fucking cross right now for what you have done, but Sibylla's death has demoralized our troops, it has also thrown the politics of our goals into chaos. Unfortunately, Guy is the man I am supporting to head the throne of Jerusalem, but without his wife, his legitimacy is thrown into question. If this got out, there would be scandal. You just signed your death warrant, Robin." The Lion Heart growls.

Queen Berengaria stands up; she walks over to her husband. "No. Spare him, Richard."

King Richard looks to his wife. "Why do you say that?"

"He's under the influence of hash and wine. Sibylla obviously wanted something from him, so he gave it to her. Look at him. He is really hungry right now."

Robin is eating fruit from a barrel to his left. He is dragged away by a guard then put on his knees before Richard. Robin chomps onto Richard's big toe.

"Ow! I will not dishonour Sibylla's memory. We are changing Sibylla's death date to the previous year to avoid scandal. As far as anyone else knows outside of royalty, she has been dead for a year. Did you miss anything?"

Robin kneels before Richard. "Do you know what I miss? The May Games, where through sheer skill even a man like me can be a king without a crown."

King Richard is amused by this. "You really think that?"

"I'm sorry. I did not mean to offend. The crown belongs to you."

"No. You are right. The greatest men can be kings without crowns."

"I hope to one day be counted as great."

"You are skilled Robin."

"I have many skills. A lot of them end in death."

"Too true. But if you are to serve me now, I cannot be accompanied by an archer. You must be a knight." King Richard pulls out his sword, knighting Robin. "Rise, Sir Robin."

Sir Robin rises. "I am your sword, my king."

"Do you want to know how negotiations are going regarding the prisoners?"

"How are things progressing on that front?"

"Saladin keeps stalling on exchanging prisoners."

"He sounds like an opportunist to me, my king. He keeps stalling while outmaneuvering you."

"What would you do?" King Richard asks Robin.

"You don't want to know what I would do."

Duke Leopold enters the tent. "Richard, Conrad has agreed to be the heir to the throne of Jerusalem. Geoffery has been promoted to Count of Ashkelon."

"We don't have control of Ashkelon." Richard scowls.

"We are leaving that to you. Philip and I are leaving tonight."

"Leopold," Richard remarks.

"Yes?"

"Remember that cowardice is a hindrance to courage."

Duke Leopold becomes enraged. "You had better pray we never cross paths again."

Duke Leopold exits with haste.

"You're a knight, you may go." Richard states.

Robin bows and trepidatiously steps towards the exit.

"Sir Robin..." Richard calls.

Robin spins and salutes His Sovereign.

"...A wise General knows to never waste opportunity." The Lion Heart imparts.

Robin practices his archery skills at King Richard's camp well into the night. Priest, Pope, and Bishop arrive. Robin bull's-eyes the target.

Pope is relieved to see his commander, "We thought you would be dead for sure, Robin."

"It is Sir Robin."

"What do you mean?" Bishop asks.

Robin smirks. "I was promoted."

Robin bull's-eyes the target again.

Priest is confused by this.

"How did that work?

How did that work?"

"I can't tell you that."

"What can you tell us?" Pope asks Robin.

"I collected the ransom for the Princess. Everybody gets 500 gold coins."

Robin bull's-eyes the target.

Hat trick!

Robin distributes the money. In the morning the prisoners are gathered then put onto their knees. Gigantic waves crash against the orange stone walls of Acre. Seagulls cry damnation in arid heat. King Richard's army unsheathes their swords.

Robin pleads with King Richard. "You can't be serious."

"The enemy shall see how serious I am." King Richard says.

"We can still ransom them."

"Saladin seems unwilling to pay."

"They are soldiers. They are only following orders like me. Now we are going to execute them in cold blood?" Robin asks.

King Richard spins around to growl at Robin. "Now you know what it means to be my sword. DO IT NOW!"

The massacre at Acre unfolds at the speed of one swing of the sword. King Richard looks around him. "What a bloody mess... well, I'm not cleaning it up."

King Richard sashays off. Robin is twisted with disgust.

"We just martyred all of these men."[3]

CHAPTER VI

Man Down

Richard's army gathers before the Clergy in the town square of Acre. King Richard is brought out before his men. The Clergy makes an announcement.

"For the crime of sinning, we sentence Richard the Lion Heart to ten lashes."

Richard is put on his knees, his shirt is stripped off, the lash is brought out. Richard begins to serve his penance.

"I am not worthy of God's love."

Richard is given his first lash. A large red gash tears across his back.

"I am not worthy..."

Richard is given his second lash. The blood splashes into the sand swallowed by it.

"...to serve..."

Richard is given his third lash. There is blood, the sound of wet meat.

"...the living God,"

Richard is given his fourth lash. Robin and his men are watching their king lashed before them. Robin feels inspired because his king does not put himself above his men. The fact is not lost on the army that Richard is experiencing far worse than any of his men would for the same indiscretion.

Robin notices a woman's hand grab his own, the hand belongs to Berengaria, she puts her other hand to her mouth. She is deeply concerned as she watches her husband being lashed right in front of her. She squeezes Robin's hand the more upset she is. Robin considers removing his hand from her grip but decides against it reasoning he must be there for his queen. Richard is finished being lashed then collapses to the ground. Berengaria rushes over to him. Robin rushes over to Richard right after his Queen, Robin and Berengaria are by Richard's side, Blondel rushes to Richard's side as well. The two of them glance at Blondel then quickly turn their attention back to Richard.

"Hospitallers! Attend to the king!" Robin shouts.

The Hospitallers carry Richard off to the hospital. Berengaria and Blondel follow, Robin stays behind. Robin spins around to the army barking, "The king expects no less from us as he does from himself."

Two knights named Marshall and Baldwin walk up to Robin. Marshall is a young man in his early twenties, he is clean-shaven with short red hair. He wears plate armour. Baldwin is in his early thirties he simply has gambeson on.

He has short blonde hair with a moustache.

"So, Sir Robin, is it true you used to be an archer?" Marshall sniggers.

"No." Robin answers nonchalantly "I still am an archer. If I weren't still an archer, I would be a sitting target. Like a knight."

"You little cunt!" Marshall screams as he draws his sword but quickly finds an arrow pointed straight at his face by Sir Robin.

"Put down your toy, child." Robin says on a completely higher level than Marshall can respond to. Marshall drops his sword.

"Run along now."

Marshall is backing away then bolts. Baldwin steps towards Sir Robin.

"With such skill and confidence, I can see why the king made you a knight. Are you a friend to the king?" Baldwin asks.

August 1191 A.D.

King Richard's army is now 40,000+ strong. Richard's army has the fighting infantry on the outside with the cavalry behind them facing the enemy. Richard has the wounded on the inside facing the ocean. The army is moving down the coastline while all the ships keep pace in the water.

King Richard's army marches down the coast for seventeen days. The sun beats down on the army, Robin would have burned on day one if he didn't have a hood on his cape. He looks up into the empty skies above. He feels Sibylla is looking down on him.

3rd of September 1191 A.D.

The Army is in the forest of Arsuf located in the grass desert. King Richard is hit with an arrow. His hand grabs at the arrow stuck in his neck. Robin rides up, pulling it out. King Richard tilts his head over. "Is it bad?"

Sir Robin pulls out the arrow, then he examines it, there is a crimson point on the tip of the arrowhead. "The mail stopped the arrow. You are untouchable my king."

"I wish that were true. There have been two reports of Saracen archers attacking our rear flanks. Go to them to prepare them for attack."

Sir Robin rides to the back in the forest of Arsuf, the shade cools him.

"While it's not an English forest, I am grateful to be out of the sun, it's cool, it feels... like home."

Marshall spots Robin riding up. "Why are you here Sir Robin?"

"Marshall, Baldwin, I am here to prepare the rear for attack. King Richard suspects an attack in the forest. The men in the rear have given reports of occasional attacks. I am here to get you ready for a massive one."

"What shall we do?" Baldwin asks.

Sir Robin points to the trees of the forest. "Put all of your archers in the trees; gather up any Templars to group with the Knights Hospitaller."

The battle of Arsuf is waged. Muslim archers on horseback ride through the woods. Some are shot by arrows while other archer's horses are going wild. The Muslim archers dismount their horses. Robin seizes a valuable opportunity. Sir Robin speaks up. "Marshall, Baldwin, they dismounted."

Marshall rears his horse. "All of them dismounted. Knights! Charge!"

Baldwin draws his sword. "Hospitallers! Charge!"

The rear of the army attacks Saladin's forces made up of Saracens combined with the Mamelukes. Richard's rear army charges, the middle follows, Richard realises what is going on.

King Richard rears his horse drawing his sword. "Men! Into the battle!"

The cavalry charges out of the woods crossing a grassy field to the enemy. Richard's Army swarm Saladin's forces like armoured hornets with stingers of English Steel. Saladin's forces take a severe beating by Richard's army, the enemy retreats. After it is over Robin sits on the branch of a tree observing the aftermath. A single knight is found dead.

The forces of Richard gather as the knight is given a Christian burial.[4] King Richard walks over James of Abbott's grave addressing his men on the battlefield, "James of Abbott died on the field of battle today. He was a pillar of my army. He has achieved salvation and has left us to enter Heaven. Our forces are that much the lesser because of it. James, you will be remembered for your heroism today at Arsuf. None shall forget your sacrifice."

A cross is planted at the head of the grave. The army of King Richard moves on.[5]

Richard's forces finally reach the outer walls of Jaffa. Richard gives Robin a note. "Tie this note to your arrow then send it over the wall," Richard says to Robin as he hands him the parchment.

"What does it say?"

"My forces offer the enemy safe passage from the city, so they may take their belongings."

Robin attaches the note, firing it over the wall. An arrow sings back over the wall hitting the guy next to Robin. Robin takes the note handing it to Richard. Richard unfolds it. Robin leans over to Richard. "What's written on it?" Robin asks.

"It says you'll never take us alive." Richard grows short "Breach the walls!"

Richard's forces quickly throw sacks of flour in front of the wall doors. Robin and his team fire flaming arrows at the flour.

The resulting explosion is as loud as thunder. It shatters open the damaged wall doors of Jaffa, Richard's army storms in.

Robin is leading his team through the damaged city. They move quickly through stone streets. Buildings have broken walls, doubtless a result of the conflicts of earlier warfare. The team cross through a nice section of palm trees and shrubbery. They make their way to the top of some stone stairway. They make their way to the bottom. Riders on horseback attack.

The enemy cavalry is shot off their horses by Robin and his men. Large waves of jihadi on foot attack Robin and his team. Robin lays his quiver of arrows onto the ground quickly followed by Bishop, Priest, and Pope. They start firing arrows into wave after wave creating a wall of flesh. Soon after the last arrow is plucked by Robin the enemies are all corpses. Robin and his men gather arrows before they start to take in their surroundings. Crumbled walls, wet crimson earth. Robin can feel his brains twisting.

"The city is in ruins." Bishop remarks,

"War damages everyone. No exceptions." Sir Robin says rather bluntly.

A lost knight rides across the band of Archers. "Archers. My name is Orlock. I have been turned around from my company. I will accompany you until I can rejoin Richard's real forces."

Sir Robin looks up at Sir Orlock. "Follow us. We will protect you."

As the knight rides forward, the bowmen bunch around him for protection. Sir Orlock is a bald man with a scar across his eye. He wears plate armour. There is a quick whizzing noise by the knight's head.

"What was that?"

Sir Robin shouts, "Orlock! Get down!"

Robin launches upwards, tackling Orlock off of his horse. Robin lands on his feet, crouching as he aims his bow. There is another whizzing sound. Robin's hit in the shoulder.

"Robin!" Bishop screams.

Sir Robin clutches at the arrow embedded in his shoulder. *It's inside me! I can feel it in my meat. Feels wet... Pain! PAIN!* Robin is bleeding but he begins shouting orders, "Priest, Bishop, the broken wall! Flank it from both directions! Pope, cover me and Sir Orlock!"

Priest and Bishop flank the enemy from both sides.

Bishop kills the enemy archer. Pope breaks the arrow in Robin's shoulder pulling it out. Robin screams. Sir Orlock stands off to the side saying, "You saved my life, Robin. You shall be knighted for this."

"Sir Robin is a knight." Pope responds.

"A knight and an archer. Very curious. Sir Robin may have my horse. Let us carry him to the hospital."

Robin is brought to a tower. Robin is screaming on the operating table. A Knight Hospitaller is stitching up Robin's wound.

"I know. I know. You are in pain. Here, smoke this. It's called hashish. It will numb the pain; put your mind at ease."

Sir Robin begins smoking the hashish. Robin lays against the tower wall healing while he listens to everybody below his window celebrating the fall of Jaffa. The Crusaders celebrate with women and children. Many are dancing, others are conversing. Crosses have been raised. Robin's men gather around a bonfire. The fire crackles.

Pope raises a glass of wine. "A toast to the best of us."

The fire snaps.

"To Sir Robin! Hero of Acre. The archer knight! May he return to his duties soon.

To Sir Robin! Hero of Acre. The archer knight! May he return to his duties soon."

Bishop turns to a nearby minstrel. "Blondel! Sing us a song!"

The fire pops.

Blondel begins playing his lute; He begins to sing,
> *"Back in England, there is the Count of Mortain*
> *he sits on his horse but the steed is lame.*
> *Lady England misses her sons*
> *by the end will Richard have won?*
> *Everything changes yet stay the same*
> *who knows the rules when you play this game?"*

Robin falls asleep in the tower. He dreams of rain.

CHAPTER VII

The Mission

October 1191 A.D.

Sir Robin wakes in pain, he finally gets out of bed. Sir Robin puts on his mail, it feels cold, hard, metallic, it digs into his flesh. Robin pulls on his Black Crusader tunic. The cross now seems red rather than green to Robin. The messenger of the king arrives.

"The Lion Heart will see you now."

"Are you sure it's King Richard this time?" Sir Robin sneers.

"This time."

"It had better be!"

Robin is brought before King Richard. Robin finds himself inside a room filled with many tapestries of lions and constellations. Abdallah al-Aladil is there. He wears a shiny golden turban, he has large puffy cheeks and looks rather well fed. Abdallah al-Aladil continues pleading his case, "It is a good deal, Richard. Give Joan to me as a wife so your voice will be heard in the Kingdom of Jerusalem. You can return to England successful in your glorious Crusade while Salah Ad-din will rule Jerusalem with your voice in his ear."

Sir Robin speaks up, "Hello?"

King Richard significantly perks up upon spotting Sir Robin. "Ah! Here is Sir Robin! Sir Robin, meet Abdallah al-Aladil, Saladin's brother."

"What is your answer, Richard?"

"I will consider it."

"It is a good deal, Richard."

King Richard suddenly becomes more assertive surprising Abdallah al-Aladil. "Here is my deal, I want the entire Kingdom of Jerusalem to the furthest extent of its borders, then Saladin must pay homage to the King of Jerusalem for Egypt."

"You must be jesting."

"I am a king, not a jester! Saladin made that mistake at Acre! Take my message to Saladin and remove yourself from my sight."

Abdallah al-Aladil exits King Richard's tent.[6]

Sir Robin addresses his king, "What are you doing with the brother of our enemy?"

King Richard gives more notice of Robin. "Negotiating. What does it look like I am doing?"

"Giving the enemy hell on the battlefield."

King Richard speaks more softly to Robin, "Robin, this may be hard to fathom but there are other ways to win without killing your opponent. But diplomacy is only one option for a king. I sent for you because I need you."

"What do you require of me?"

"Sir Robin I am sending you on a mission to kill Saladin. End the war while we rebuild the Kingdom of Heaven."

Sir Robin bows to his king. "I will kill Saladin for you, but I will not make him a martyr."

November 1191

Sir Robin, Priest, Pope, Bishop, Fitzwater, with three others, trek through the grass desert in hammering rain. It feels cold. It feels wet. Fitzwater feels miserable. He is forty with greying hair. He wears chain-mail underneath a red tunic. "How much longer?" He asks.

"Until we reach Jerusalem." Sir Robin replies.

"What's the plan?" Fitzwater asks. Wet sand covers his boots, they travelled beyond the grass.

"Infiltrate the walls. Kill Saladin."

Fitzwater begins to bitch, "Even if this plan were to succeed, and the Lion Heart retakes Jerusalem, what then? What are the king's plans for Jerusalem?"

"King Richard told me that once Jerusalem is retaken, we will fix it up then hand it back over to the Jews." Sir Robin answers sharply.

There is a long moment of silence. Everybody picks up on Robin's sarcasm.

"Ah! Ha! Ha! HA! HAH! AHA! AAH!"

Fitzwater wipes a tear from his face. "My God, that was funny! I love this job!"

Lightning strikes. Sir Robin and his knights are attacked in the rain. Robin shoots the attackers with his bow, then one of the assassins gets close enough to Robin to tackle him. Robin tumbles in the mud with his attacker. A knife is seen, pierces flesh, then the bloody knife is pulled out.

Robin stands up, he begins assessing the dead.

"Four dead knights. Three left not including me. Wait, is that the body of Walter Fitzwater?"

Sir Robin rolls over the body of Fitzwater.

Sir Robin stares into Walter's eyes. "Fitzwater."

Fitzwater starts coughing up blood. He manages to form his dying words, "Protect. You must protect... hrrrrr...."

Sir Robin takes Fitzwater's sword, piercing it into the ground. Robin kneels before his makeshift cross. "I will honour your final wish Walter, even if it means my life. I swear it."

Sir Robin makes the sign of the Cross then pulls out the sword. Priest tugs on his tunic until it rips. Sir Robin solemnly turns to Priest handing him the sword. "Priest. Take Fitzwater's sword, return it to King Richard's camp, the rest of you march with me to Jerusalem. I hear that Saladin sleeps in a wooden tower. He is afraid."

"Of what? Us?" Bishop asks.

"No. The other players on the chessboard."

Priest takes the sword to return to Richard. Priest begins swinging the sword wildly. The storm breaks. That night Pope and Bishop are sitting around a fire with Robin.

"You know boys, I don't think it's necessary to even fight this war."

"What do you mean, Robin?" Bishop asks.

"Sausage, Bacon, and Eggs will defeat the enemy. They are just too damn good for anyone to resist for eternity."

Robin serves the Sausage, Bacon, and Eggs. They begin to eat and reflect in the firelight.

"The fire is warm tonight. How in the hell does a place so hot get such cold nights?" Bishop asks.

"I don't know. I want to get drunk." Pope answers.

"We don't have any wine with us." Robin informs his men.

"Sobriety sucks hard." Bishop states.

Robin jogs his memory. "Wait. I think I have something." Robin pulls out some hashish.

"What is that?" Pope asks.

"The Hospitallers gave it to me. It's called hashish. I've had it before. It's better than wine."

"I want some." Pope says.

"Me too." adds Bishop.

Robin looks at his hash. "This is all I have left. I'll divide it."

Robin divides the hashish. They all start smoking around the fire.

Bishop looks up at the sky. "So many stars out there."

"Do you believe that angels dwell up there?" Pope asks the others.

"They call it the heavens for a reason." Robin responds.

Bishop looks to Robin. "Do you believe we'll ever reach the stars, Robin?"

"The Greeks from the late Hellenistic era believed that mankind came from the stars then one day that is where we shall return."

"So... you believe we will make it to the heavens?" Pope asks.

Robin smiles. "I don't know."

Bishop points up to the sky. "What is that?"

Pope looks upwards. "What's what?"

"That. In the sky. It's moving."

Robin grows excited. "I see it! It's moving all over the place."

Pope starts, "Yeah! I see it! It's starting to change colours it..."

The campfire is attacked by Assassins. Bishop and Pope are assassinated. Swords protrude from their abdomen before quickly vanishing. Robin is taken by surprise. He is grabbed by many men who try to wrestle him to the ground. Robin is being a difficult sonofabitch about it. He is bound then abducted from the mission.

CHAPTER VIII

Assassins of the Cross

Robin has a black bag over his head. He listens to people speaking in Arabic. They keep saying something repeatedly, Alamut. Something they say over and over again is Alamut. *Alamut. Alamut must be found at the top of a mountain because my feet have been dragging up a steep rocky trail for a long while now.* Robin is carried to the Assassin's fortress. The Assassins knock on a door. There is a wall guarding Alamut.

The wet green grass rubs in between Robin's toes. It feels nice. Within the grass-filled courtyard, there are four structures including the three-story castle with two places of worship. Robin's black bag is taken off in the gardens. There is a rather old Saracen man sitting in front of him cross-legged. He has a balding head with grey facial hair. He wears black clothing. Robin listens to the old man of the mountain in the gardens. "Allahu Akbar. God is great."

Unafraid Robin responds, "Deus Vult. God wills it."

"Are you here to kill in the name of God?"

"Everybody here has a purpose. My purpose is higher than slaughter."

The old man of the mountain lets out a sigh. "The fact is these used to be Christian Lands; now few Christians are left under my tutelage. I am willing to work with the Crusaders, but I am willing to train few of them."

"Why am I here?" Robin asks.

"Because you managed to kill nearly all of my top assassins. You have moved to the head of the class. Someone as talented as you must be trained."

"What training?"

"Something new."

The man with the skull painted on his face appears behind Robin as if he were there the whole time. The man has black clothing, long black hair, a muscular body, with a white skull painted on his face. He brings Robin to a room. "Sir Robin, you will be taught secret techniques to kill people with the sword."

He leads Robin into a large empty room. The walls are sandstone. Several wooden posts with targets at the top are posted. "What are those for?"

"You are going to behead them. Go on, try."

Robin unsheathes his sword; He is attacking the dummies by running towards them. Skull-Face unsheathes his blade; He spins 360-degrees, throwing his sword in a spinning motion. The sword beheads the dummies before Robin even reaches the first one. Robin halts, then he stares at Skull-Face.

Targets are posted again. Robin unsheathes his sword; He spins 360-degrees throwing a spinning sword trying to behead practice targets. The weapon falls to the ground before it can behead the first target.

"The targets are too far away. The sword can't reach them." Robin says.

"The targets are not too far away. You are too weak to reach them."

Robin begins to do a lot of push-ups. Three days later Robin is back in the room with the man with the painted skull. He hands Robin his bow and quiver. "Try to hit the target."

Robin fires his bow and arrow hitting the small target dead center. The enigmatic Skull-Face pulls out his knife, he throws it splitting the arrow. "Try to hit the target with your knife."

Robin throws his knife. It completely misses the small target. Skull-Face smiles. "Ha!"

Robin takes out his sword, spinning in a 360-degree motion, throwing his spinning sword beheading the target. Skull-Face puts his hand on Robin's shoulder. "There is hope for you yet."

Robin practices throwing his knife at the target. He gradually gets better at it over three days. Finally, he begins to bullseye the target with his knife. An archer pops up from behind shooting an arrow at Robin. Robin dodges the arrow by moving his body out of the way while standing in place. Another archer shoots at Robin. Robin knocks it out of the air with his sword. Over the next two months, Robin trains with the sword until he can cut arrows out of the air. Eight archers shoot arrows at Robin. Robin spins his sword in a figure-eight motion cutting all of the arrows in half. The man with the painted skull begins clapping. "Well done Robin! It is time for the final stages of your training. It is time for you to learn how to bake a cake."

Robin starts learning to bake a cake. Robin keeps messing with his formula until his cake is as delicious as Mrs. Bakker's. Robin and Agony stride into the center of the courtyard. The old man tastes different cakes. The old man of the mountain tastes the cake of Robin's instructor.

"Well?"

"You have outdone yourself this year. The prize will surely go to you after I taste Robin's cake."

The old man of the mountain tastes cake that is exactly like Mrs. Bakker's cake. The old man of the mountain's eyes pop. The old man of the mountain places his hands on Robin's shoulders. "Where did you learn to bake a cake like this?"

"I spent several days trying to remember Mrs. Bakker's cooking lessons from when I was a boy."

"You win this year."

The man with the painted skull shouts, "Hey! What about my cake?"

The old man of the mountain stares at him for a moment. "Oh. Your cake sucks."

ROBIN NODS OFF ONE night, He dreams of Gardens in the desert sand, he is awakened by female laughter in the garden of delights. This secret garden is a paradise beyond all compare. Thin streams of wine, milk, and honey run on its green slopes. Beautiful young women appear. They are not quite Saracen, yet not quite English either. They have slender figures with perky breasts. Their hair is long, they have killer smiles, they look like Angels and they laugh like them too.

"Welcome to the garden of delights. We are the Angels in Paradise. Please, sit down."

Robin sits down on a couch. Robin is fed grapes by two beautiful women that look like sexy Victoria's Secret models. "Can I have some hashish?"

"We only have the best hashish. Anything for you Robin! You are our number one guy!"

The women in the garden provide him with hashish. He smokes a lot of hashish while drinking wine from a pool. Robin is hot-boxing so much that the women start to cough.

Sir Robin lights a joint. "Who holds top rank?"

"Agony is the top Assassin. He wears skull war paint over his face. Cough. Cough. Cough."

Robin remembers the figure with skull paint at the walls of Acre. "So, Skull-Face, he's called Agony. Say... Can you two Angels massage my back?"

The two women massage Robin while Sir Robin smokes hash. Sir Robin becomes relaxed, he begins smoking too much. Sir Robin passes out, awakening with the old man of the mountain standing over him. "You have experienced Paradise. It is what awaits all who give their life for a higher purpose."

"What happens next?"

"Agony will take you on your first assassination."

Agony escorts Sir Robin into a field mission.

28th of April 1192 A.D.

Agony and Robin overlook a desert camp from behind a sand dune. A gust of wind blusters a few flaps loose on a white desert tent. Out of the dozen tents, Robin and Agony are looking only for one. Agony turns his gaze to Robin. "Watch and learn, Robin. See the bandits over on the edge of the hill?"

Robin nods. Agony continues, "We pay them a small sum to ravage the camp to confuse the enemy with numbers. Then we go in for the kill."

The attack begins. The bandits overwhelm the camp with their numbers. Agony and Sir Robin move in. It's madness, bandits and the enemy are chopping each other to pieces. Robin sprints past the blood to the blue tent with the green interior, Robin shoots a knight. The knight clasps the arrow stuck in his abdomen. He falls to his knees then collapses. Robin enters the tent with his bow drawn. Robin realises who his target is, then stops. "Conrad?"

Agony enters the tent behind Robin, throwing his knife into Conrad's heart.

"NO!" Sir Robin shouts.

Agony drops a cake then leaves. Robin's soul is twisting in all sorts of knots.

Robin and Agony are walking the outskirts of the marauded camp, finally, Sir Robin punches Agony. "You just assassinated Conrad of Montferrat! He was most qualified for the throne of Jerusalem and you just executed him in cold blood!"

Agony rubs his jaw. "Don't go softhearted now, Sir Robin. We are assassins. The murder of high-profile targets is part of the job. In this line of work soft hearts are bleeding hearts."

Robin and Agony climb the mountain. Both enter the walls of the fortress. Agony slams Robin against the wall. "Never disobey me again!"

An Assassin walks up to Robin and Agony addressing them. "The old man of the mountain wishes to converse with you in the afterlife."

Robin and Agony enter a small dark room. They lay down onto two small cots on each side of the room. The two assassins smoke hashish before they drink a potion. Sir Robin is growing a bit sick. "Why do we have to smoke all this hashish?"

Agony tilts his head towards Robin. "Assassins smoke hashish before a mission to put them into a trance-like state. It makes killing people seem less real."

"That's funny. We didn't smoke hashish before we killed Conrad of Montferrat."

"I know."

Sir Robin registers what Agony did. "You sniveling little pimp!"

Robin and Agony pass out from drinking the potion after smoking hashish. They awaken in the garden.

In the garden, the old man of the mountain speaks, "I take it that the task has been done?"

"Tell me, why did you send me to assassinate Conrad?" Robin asks.

"The Assassins often work with the Crusaders. Conrad attacked the Crusader states after making a deal with Saladin. We were paid to take him out. Paid by who does not concern you. The fact you have both returned to me means that my training has paid off."

"No one else has returned to you after a mission?" Robin asks.

The old man of the mountain points to them. Robin looks at Agony beside him. Agony is not wearing his warpaint.

"The two greatest Assassins I have ever trained are you, Sir Robin and Agony. Robin and Agony, I give to you the silent death class Assassin rank."

This is the one-time Robin can observe Agony's true face. Robin walks to his quarters, His twisted mind finally snaps, "Conrad betrayed us! He attacked his own side, and I didn't kill him!"

Robin storms through the meandering halls to the armoury. He grabs two quivers of black arrows. He slings a quiver over his back attaching a quiver to his thigh. Robin raises his compound bow above his head. "I am going to kill every lowlife son of a bitch who ever had it coming!"

Robin leaves the room.

He sprints towards the old man of the mountain, hell follows.

"Give me a target."

"There is a true believer in Saladin. He is known as a hero across the vast desert ocean. His name is Sultan Ali al Ad-din He is Sultan Salah Ad-din's cousin. He is in a desert encampment. He resides in the largest tent. He is somewhat of a military genius. He is too dangerous to live. Kill him, Robin."

"Okay, I am on it. Oh, and please call me, Sir Robin."

Robin bakes a cake then goes out on a mission. A true believer of Saladin is in the white tent with red decor settled by an oasis. Sultan Ali al Ad-din is a tall man with boyish features, with a rock-hard body, who wears a black turban complemented by red clothing. He has a rather pissed off face tonight. His companion Abubu wears green clothing with a white turban. He is short with a few too many pounds.

Ali addresses his second in command Abubu from behind a table. "Richard has rebuilt Jaffa. We shall flank Richard's army from both sides. We attack during the time his forces are busy rebuilding Ashkelon. What do you say Abubu?"

"It sounds risky Sultan."

"Yes, but they won't expect it during the rains."

"Boo."

Ali looks towards the opening of the tent. "What was that?"

"It sounded like a bird." Abubu replies.

"Boo."

Ali stares at Abubu. "It calls Boo."

"A desert bird most likely."

"Boo."

Ali al Ad-din heads towards the noise coming from outside the tent. "It sounds human."

Ali peaks his head out of the tent. A black arrow enters right between his eyes coming out the other side. Ali al Ad-din falls over dead. Abubu starts screaming as he runs to grab a scimitar but is cut off by the appearance of Robin in the tent. Robin glares at Abubu, he raises his bow, aiming his arrow.

"Boo."

Robin fires his arrow straight into Abubu's screaming mouth, he falls over dead. Robin leaves a cake in the tent then departs quickly. Robin returns to Alamut in five days, Robin walks unnoticed into a room with Henry of Champagne and the old man of the mountain. They are sitting down on a couch discussing things. The clear night sky is visible from the windows. Robin moves behind a green curtain to observe; for they are not alone.

"Coeur de Lion sends his regards... and gratitude. Your men are as deadly as they say. But how loyal are they?" Henry asks.

The old man of the mountain points to two nearby assassins.

"You two! Leap out of those windows."

The men stare at their master.

"Imshi!" The master commands.

The two assassins leap outside to their deaths.

"I'll admit, they're certainly dedicated."

"How would you like me to order the deaths of all of your enemies? They shall choke on their own blood." The old man of the mountain offers.

"Hmmm. A very tempting offer. I shall contemplate this." Henry replies.

Robin backs out of the room. The next day Robin meets with his master intending on taking another mission.

"Give me another target."

The old man of the mountain checks his scrolls. "There is a Knight Templar who is exchanging troop movements to the enemy."

"When and where?"

"They meet during the night at Ashkelon."

Robin bakes a cake then takes his leave from Alamut. Robin rides to Ashkelon. Robin joins a group of knights coming back from patrol. He stays up at night, inside of Ashkelon observing a child running across the front of the walls, the child goes to his mother who picks him up then carries him inside. The wind picks up; it starts to rain. His eyes twitch at the flash of lightning, he takes to the crackle of thunder. "I'm wet and miserable. Oh, but I can hate."

Robin watches as a Knight Templar emerges from a doorway, a Muslim Spy arrives, they meet. Robin notices a series of large stones hanging from a winch overhead. Robin shoots a black arrow dropping the large stones onto the spy along with his confederate. They both look up at the sky witnessing flashes of lightning and they see the stones falling onto them. They are crushed. Robin runs up, drops a cake by the crushed bodies, then disappears into the grass. Robin returns to the old man of the mountain. "Give me another mission."

"This one is a suicide mission."

"I'll take it if there is a chance for a high body count."

"There is an army being raised somewhere. Find it, stop it, die if you have to."

Robin bakes a cake. Attaches a quiver to each leg then one to his back. He attaches four sheaves of arrows onto his new horse. Robin mounts the horse galloping off. Robin rides by two Templars practicing combat. Robin strolls up to the Templar's bank. Robin gets off his horse. He walks inside to speak to a Templar Banker. The Templar Banker sits behind a desk cluttered with paper. He has rather long red hair, looking like a bear of a man.

"I would like to know my holdings."

The Templar Banker stares at his records. He shuffles some papers, then he tilts his head back up at Robin. "You have more purple than I have ever seen in my life,"

"Can I buy horses from you for my men?"

The Templar smiles.

"Equine and equity. That's what we Templars specialise in."

The Templar looks at his horse documents.

"The horses?" Robin asks.

"This is strange. Brother Logan has been selling more of our horses to Jerusalem."

Robin tries peeking over at the document. He is in danger of falling over.

"The Equines are at Jerusalem?" Robin asks.

"I was never told any of this. Something is wrong. We haven't taken Jerusalem."

"Thank you for your help with the accounts."

Robin takes off travelling on horseback. Robin rests his steed outside the walls of Jerusalem. Many horses ride out of Jerusalem into the desert. Robin joins the cavalry as they ride across the grass. The horsemen ride to the middle of the desert sand but suddenly they disappear. Robin simply stares as the surrounding cavalry travell through the mirage. Robin gazes upon a giant five-story castle in the middle of the desert. The small cavalry of jihadi fighters ties the horse's reigns to the posts. They join a small army inside the building.

Robin closes his eyes and watches his woman by the fire. Orange flickering light dances around her silhouette.

Sir Robin walks up to her. "Hey."

"Hello. Why are you here?" She asks.

"I wanted to let you know I will always love you most." Robin answers.

She smiles. "I know that. Why are you here?"

"I think I am going to die."

She runs over to Robin, hugging him. "Give the enemy a taste of hell, then send him to it."

Robin kisses his woman before the roaring fire.

Robin opens his eyes and walks into the five-story castle. A person runs out the door but falls over dead with an arrow in his back. A guy is thrown out the window with a large wound across the abdomen. The second-story windows begin to shatter next. A guy shot in the heart falls out of a window. Another guy is just thrown out the window. The third-story windows start to shatter. More guys fall through the windows full of arrows. The fourth-floor windows start to shatter. A severed arm holding a scimitar crashes through the window. A severed head follows soon after. In another window, two enemy soldiers with scimitars through their stomachs fall out the window. The fifth-floor windows start to shatter. A guy with no arms nor legs is thrown out the fifth-story window. A THUNK is heard.

"Really? You use your last arrow, and you miss? Are you for real?"

"I didn't miss..."

"No! WAIT! AAAAAH!"

The unknown soldier is flung out the window fourteen yards away. The Templar traitor is on the roof. He is jacked. He has a strong square jaw, blue eyes, short black hair, with a Jheri curl. Robin follows him there. "I have been sent to do you."

The Templar traitor smiles. "It's fine, baby. It's all fine."

"Be ready to taste hell."

"You have no arrows left Assassin. Prepare to taste Templar Steel forged by years of vicious battles."

Robin unsheathes his sword. Robin holds his sword out in front of him. The Templar traitor unsheathes his sword, then separates the weapon in two. The two opponents stand opposite each other on a circular roof. The desert sun begins to set. The traitor rushes Robin swinging his swords down towards the left. Robin rolls right. Robin kicks the back of the Traitor's knee making him fall onto one leg. Robin strikes but his blow is blocked by the traitor's swords. The traitor stands then begins swinging both his swords downwards in a circular motion. Robin keeps out of reach of his swords. Robin nearly falls over the edge but uses his sword to push him back towards the Knight Templar. The traitor swings his swords downward but Robin rolls underneath the traitor's blades slicing upwards. Robin chops the traitor's hands off. "AAAAH! My Hands!"

Robin sheathes his sword, picks up the traitor's swords then gives them back to him through his abdomen. The traitor falls five stories down dead. Robin leaves the cake on the roof. Robin returns to Alamut. Robin speaks to the old man of the mountain. "Give me another mission."

"There is no mission right now. All work to be done has been done. Get some rest."

Robin is resting in his quarters when he begins to smell something familiar. Robin wanders out of his room; he follows the smell of hashish. He follows the odour down the lower levels of the castle until he finds his way into a secret basement. Robin finds the Garden of Delights. Robin smokes all the hashish in the garden until the old man of the mountain arrives.

"Did you know the one trail leading to this fortress makes an assault nearly impossible?" The old man asks.

"How did anyone decide to put a castle here?"

"This fortress is named Alamut. It means the eagle's teaching. The legend is that there was a king in the past who wanted to build a fortress. He let an eagle soar free, the fortress now stands where the eagle landed."

Robin smiles. "That is a beautiful story."

The old man of the mountain bends over with his hands on his knees. "Do you want to smoke any hashish?"

"I would love to."

"You smoked it all. Get the hell out of my place."

Robin is thrown out a very short distance from the entrance door. An Assassin pops his head out of the door. "...And don't come back!"

The door is shut and locked. Robin journeys back to King Richard's camp at Ashkelon.[7]

CHAPTER IX

Desert Storm

A garrison of knights is cracking wise and cracking up. They should be rebuilding the wall. A knight stares into the desert, he squints into the distance. He points at a small figure emerging from the horizon.

"Hey! What's that?"

The knights turn their collective stare towards the desert at which point, everyone becomes silent. The knights gaze upon a dead man, they stare at Robin. Robin treads past the knights. Archer scampers up.

"You're alive? We all thought you perished in the desert. Did you experience the divine? Did you have a vision?"

Robin just walks past Archer and retires to his quarters. Robin continues eating his last hashish cake, but is interrupted by a large series of crashes. Several soldiers rush past Robin's room.

Robin clambers outside following the soldiers towards the commotion. Robin looks upon Priest trashing his quarters. Several knights try to stop him but are easily thrown off.

"My brothers are dead!

My brothers are dead!"

Priest flips his bed over. Robin steps into Priest's quarters.

"Priest, calm down, please."

Priest grabs Robin, then he pulls his arm back ready to take his superior's head off with one punch. Priest looks into Robin's eyes then he falls to his knees, he begins to cry. Robin walks over putting his hand onto Priest's head.

"I wish it had been you, Robin.

I wish it had been you, Robin."

"So do I." Robin somberly replies.

Several soldiers burst into the quarters. Robin hands Priest the rest of his cake.

"Eat this. It will help you endure the stockade. Trust me." Priest consumes the cake as he is taken away. Outside the quarters, Archer shouts, "The French Army is arriving!"

June 1192 A.D.

King Richard's forces march from Ashkelon across the desert. They raid a sizable supply caravan heading to Jerusalem from Egypt. The Caravan is attacked by Richard leading his knights. Richard is killing just as many of the enemy as his best knights. The army grabs everything from the caravan.

They all ride off as Sir Robin is on his horse figuring it out. "Tyre, Acre, Jaffa, Ashkelon, now a caravan."

Robin's horse gallops up to King Richard. "Attrition. You are fighting a war of Attrition."

"So, you finally figured it out. I do not even need to siege Jerusalem. We have cut off all of its supplies."

KING RICHARD SELECTS a Jury of five Knights Templar, five Knights Hospitaller, five Native Syrians, with five French Chiefs to decide whether to march on Jerusalem. Sir Robin speaks to King

Richard as he leaves the Jury to deliberate. "Why do you not partici-
pate my King?"

"Twenty honest jurors with diverse ideas and outlooks on life
coming to a unanimous agreement is the best way to know how to
correctly go about things."

Robin practices shooting his bow and arrows at a target while
the jury arrives at a decision independently.

A man walks up to King Richard. He is clean-shaven with flow-
ing brown hair. He is in his forties. Richard looks to Sir Robin.
"Robin, this is Balian of Ibelin, the Hero of Jerusalem. Balian, this is
Sir Robin, Hero of Acre."

Balian of Ibelin addresses King Richard, "We agreed that marching on Jerusalem would be too costly and ill-advised.[8] I see Sir
Robin is back again. Is he still failing his mission? Does he continue
to do nothing but smoke hashish during the Crusades?"

"Hey! I spent the last few months learning to bake cakes for people!"

"Does Sir Robin eat his own cakes?"

"I'll bake you a cake, I will bake you the deadliest cake you will
ever eat!"

King Richard loses his cool. "That's enough!"

Balian of Ibelin has had enough as well. "I challenge Sir Robin to
a duel."

King Richard smiles at Robin. "What do you say, Sir Robin?"

"I accept."

Balian and Robin draw their swords. The swords clash. Robin
steps back dodging a horizontal strike by Balian. Robin clashes steel
with Balian. Balian sidesteps a vertical strike by Sir Robin. The
swords clash once more. Robin begins to move forward putting
Balian on the defensive. Robin makes sure Balian is off balance. Desperately, Balian stabs at Robin. Robin ducks underneath the blade

moving in close to Balian. Sir Robin knocks Balian over. Robin has his sword to Balian's neck. "Yield."

Balian sweeps Robin's legs knocking him onto the ground as well. Robin gets his sword back to Balian's neck but Balian has his sword pointed at Robin's heart. "Let us call it a draw."

"Fine by me." Robin answers.

Sir Robin and Balian get to their feet. Robin shakes Balian's hand.

"I can see why you are called the Hero of Jerusalem."

"And I can see why they call you the Hero of Acre."

Sir Robin walks back to King Richard as the gathered crowd begins applauding. King Richard puts his hand on Robin's shoulder squeezing. "Bloody good show, Sir Robin! I never thought you could go toe-to-toe with Balian."

"You look as if something troubles you."

"I have news that my brother, John has kicked Longchamps out of power, at the same time the Templars have lost control of Cyprus. We may have to leave sometime soon."

"If we stay, you could be King of Jerusalem."

"Yes, that is true. But I value the crown of England more. I have questions about where you have been for the past few months, but you look like hell. You could use some rest."

It is late at night. Robin is sleeping in his tent. Sigerson arrives at Robin's tent. Sigerson is a tall yet slender man, with short black hair, eyes like a hawk, with a rather sharp nose. Sir Robin awakens.

"Sigerson. What do you want?"

"I heard a rumor that Saladin is keeping Christian Scholars as slaves in Damascus."

"And?"

"I hear that Saladin is there as well."

Robin takes a small group of knights to a building in Damascus. They are inside a large sandstone hallway with several doors. Sir Robin stands before Sigerson and the other knights.

"Thank you for joining me on this secret mission. I plan to free some Christian Scholars as well as give cake to Saladin, ending the war."

Sir Robin leads the knights down the sandstone hall. They start breaking down doors. Robin breaks open a door then two women run outside screaming.

Robin takes charge of the situation, pointing to two of his men. "You two! Get these womenfolk out of here."

Two knights take the hysterical women outside. Robin breaks down another door, walking inside he observes a hundred frogs sitting on top of chicken eggs. He doesn't understand what's going on but rather feels a cold dread. Robin exits the room slowly, the two knights rejoin the group, Robin and his men climb the stairs to the top floor.

A knight looks at the circular empty room. "There are no scholars."

Sir Robin remarks, "There is no Saladin."

A Knights Templar looks to Sir Robin. "Is this a trap?"

"Why would this be a trap? Who could possibly want to... Oh shit!"

Agony jumps out of darkness having been sent to kill Robin. Robin's former master kills all of Robin's companions in quick succession before they can get in a blow. Agony growls to Robin. "I would kill you right now, but currently we are surrounded by a cult who worships Death. Unfortunately, you are the only one who I can rely on to hold his own with me. To tell the truth you are not what I would consider Assassin material."

"Hey! I am a merciless Assassin! Not a stoner who eats his own cakes. I will prove it."

Robin and Agony take out cult members who enter the room to see what the commotion is. Luckily, the cultists were wearing robes that fit them. They enter a large room with a pulpit, blending among the gathered members of the cult. People just start dropping wherever the two disguised Assassins go. Robin kills the cult leader but Agony changes sides revealing his skull war paint.

"Behold! I am Death incarnate. I have killed countless men! I shall kill countless more! I have been brought before you for that treacherous mortal who has killed your leader."

Sir Robin is storming with fury, "You evil little gremlin!"

Agony leads the remaining cult to kill Robin. Agony rises to cult leader status.

Agony points at Robin. "Grab him! I want to kill Robin myself."

Robin is fighting his heart out, people are dropping right and left, blood is spilt everywhere to the point that the floor quickly becomes a pool of blood. Robin is in the zone. "I swear to God, I'll kill all of you! Come on! Get some! We're going to play a game called, 'you lose!'"

Robin paints the room with blood.

"You lose! You lose! You lose! You lose! Oh, yeah. Guess what?... YOU LOSE!"

The remaining cult members start towards him, but Agony stops them. "He surpasses my expectations. Men; follow me. There will be another time."

Robin finishes cutting men down. Hewn corpses lie dead everywhere; but Agony along with an unknown number of his new followers are gone. Robin walks out of the room, His feet are wet, He marches out of the castle into the desert, His bloody footprints are swallowed by sand.

Robin eventually meets a group of travelling Assassins.

"Assassins."

"Robin. What are you doing here?"

"I am here to give cake to Saladin."

"We are travelling to Jerusalem to give cake to Salah Ad-din as well. You are welcome to join us."

"Why do you wish to give cake to Saladin?"

"Salah Ad-din is going after the Assassins with a vengeance."

"It seems we want the same thing, but for different reasons. Okay, I'll join you."

The Assassins file across the desert. The Assassins are ambushed by Saladin's forces. Robin and his caravan face off against an overwhelming force. They fight their hearts out; the battle is small but tremendous. Robin engages in mass bloodshed but the winds pick up; a raging sandstorm finishes the battle. Every Assassin is murdered in sand except Robin. He manages to make it upwind of everyone.

Great! I have sand in my crack. Now I'm pissed.

He pulls out his bow, he starts shooting arrows downwind in a 180-degree maximum kill zone. Robin spots someone coming for him, so he shoots him with an over-the-shoulder trick shot. Robin must have missed because the figure keeps charging. The figure grabs Robin. Robin tries to get away but only ends up struggling with him.

Whoever this guy is, He's stronger than me! I'm going to die, and I won't even know my killer's face!

The sandstorm dies down, it turns out to be someone dressed in a knight's tunic. Robin removes the helmet.

"Priest? You've been promoted!... Oh, no, no."

Robin finds the arrow protruding from Priest's abdomen.

"Sir Robin, you are my friend. King Richard waits for you at Acre.

Sir Robin, you are my friend. King Richard waits for you at Acre."

"Okay. Just know that this is going to hurt."

Robin breaks the arrow to pull it out. Priest is in blinding pain.

"AAAAAAAAAAAAHHH!"

July 1192 A.D.

Robin travells to Acre with Priest. Robin's friend barely survived the arrow; Robin is unsure of the trip. "Priest, we are in Acre. I'll have to leave you in a doctor's care because of the severity of the wound."

Sir Robin takes Priest to the hospital. They walk over to a Knight Hospitaller. The Knight Hospitaller folds his arms. "What do you want?"

"I have a wounded man here. It would mean my soul if you could save him."

Robin sets Priest down on a bed as the Knight Hospitaller examines him.

The Knight Hospitaller looks at Robin. "It will take some time."

"I entrust his wellbeing to you."

Robin exits the hospital, he glances at the women that they freed a year ago who are reunited with their children.

They are much happier, it's almost as if the trauma is no longer there... No. No, that's not right, the trauma always remains... in some form or another.

Robin runs into Isabella. Isabella is surprised to see him. "Robin!"

"Isabella!"

"Have you seen my husband?"

"You're married? To who?"

"Priest."

"You don't mind his demon?"

"Something is definitely wrong with Priest, but it is not a demon. He is a good man."

"I can get behind that."

"You haven't answered my question. Have you seen my husband?"

"Priest... was wounded."

Isabella's face drains into an alarming pallor.

"What? No! God, No!"

"He is in the hospital recovering. You should go see him."

Isabella grabs a young girl by the hand. "Come along, Christine. We must go to see your father."

Isabella leads her daughter inside the hospital. People begin dashing to the ships. Robin dashes up to one of the men. "What's happening?"

The yeoman faces Robin. "King Richard is loading the boats. We set sail for Jaffa!"

CHAPTER X

Mission Accomplished

Robin follows three hundred men onto the six wooden ships. They set sail down the coastline to Jaffa in a lightning run. The leader of Richard's mercenary forces spots Robin. "You!"

"Me?"

"Yes, you! Are you an archer?"

"Yes, but I am also the sword of King Richard."

"A protector of the king? What are you doing out of uniform?"

"What uniform?"

"Protectors of the king must wear their uniform, don't worry, we have an older uniform in back. Go change before we arrive at Jaffa."

Robin changes into green clothing common for a yeoman. Robin's green tunic has a solid red diamond cross on the front of it. Robin spies the letters RH embroidered on the back inside. Robin attaches a quiver to his back along with a second quiver to his thigh. Robin walks out onto the deck observing the others dressed in green, but their diamond crosses are black.[9] The man Robin spoke to is addressing the Yeoman archers. He is a grizzled soldier with black hair, a five-o-clock shadow, with a distinguishing scar over his eye.

"My name is Mercardier, I have unfortunate news, Jaffa has nearly fallen to twenty thousand of the enemy. We are but six ships, so there are only three hundred of us, the rest of the army is heading down the coast. We are the only prayer that the remaining Christians at Jaffa have, we cannot count on immediate reinforcements. It is your job as the king's personal bodyguards to keep the Lion Heart safe."

1st of August 1192 A.D.

Richard's ships arrive, the artillery is let loose. Boat catapults and arrows bombard the land. King Richard leaps off the rocking boat onto a skiff armed with a war axe and a crossbow. Richard launches an amphibious assault with crossbowmen on the boats providing cover fire. The skiffs move towards a storm of enemy arrows. Arrows are flying back and forth whistling past Robin's Head. Richard leaps off the skiff onto the beach.

"By God's calves, they will not capture the Christians!"[10]

Richard fires his crossbow. Sir Robin is the first one to follow him off the boat.

"Deus Vult!"

Richard storms the beach with three hundred men against twenty thousand soldiers. Richard leads his forces, cutting their way through an encampment of soldiers on the beach outside the walls of Jaffa. The three hundred soldiers burst through the makeshift barrier at the entrance and pour into the streets of Jaffa. The Crusaders are making their way to the citadel.

Richard along with his knights begin cutting down enemies in the streets. Any group of enemies that tries to overwhelm Richard is killed by Sir Robin working with the other green-clad bodyguards. King Richard is going beast mode on the enemy, cutting down any poor sonofabitch in his path. He starts going off on a completely unhinged, righteous, and Holy speech.

"To serve the living God we too have accepted the sign of the cross to defend the place of Christ's death that have been consecrated by his precious blood and which the enemies of the Cross of Christ have hitherto shamefully profaned, and we have taken upon us the burden of so great and so Holy a work."[11]

Robin shoots an enemy sniper in a partially destroyed building. "Keep the faith!"

Robin spots Agony standing over the dead sniper. Robin escorts Richard to the citadel.

Robin journeys back to the partially destroyed building. Robin dodges an arrow, quickly cutting another one out of the air with his sword. Robin hurls a knife into the face of the archer at the top of the tower. The archer topples. Robin takes his quiver of arrows.

Agony addresses his followers, "Robin is separated from his king. Kill him."

Several of the death cult members rush Robin, but his lethality has increased dramatically after he completed his Assassin training. Robin unsheathes his sword then cuts down the entire group in rapid succession. Ultimately it boils down to Robin and Agony in the battle of Jaffa. They fight with their weapons. Agony tries to open up Robin's stomach by cutting across the side but Robin leans back to avoid being split open. Agony strikes his sword diagonally, but Robin is inside the swing. Agony thrusts his sword so Robin spins around the sword clashing it with his own steel.

"We are both Assassins of the Cross. We will therefore burn in eternal hellfire unless one kills the other in atonement." says Agony.

"That makes no damn sense, and nobody has to die." says Robin.

"Too many have died at our hands already just to see who is the best Assassin between us."

Robin clashes blades with Agony. Robin dodges a killing blow to his chest. Robin parries a swing by Agony. Robin gets in close. Robin uses the pommel of his sword to strike a long-deserved blow across Agony's chin disorienting him. Robin kicks Agony's shin with fury, causing him to lose balance. Agony stabilizes himself with his sword.

Robin swipes the sword out from under Agony with his own blade. Agony falls to the ground laying on top of the rubble.

Robin gets his blade in close to Agony's neck; There is wild fear in his eyes. Robin motions downwards with his. Agony peers down as Robin nuts him. Agony is writhing in agony on the ground. Robin takes out his bow. "Tell me if this seems real."

Robin pierces Agony with many arrows, Robin strolls off leaving him to die at Jaffa. Richard's banner flows over the citadel. Richard's forces have retaken Jaffa. Richard's archers retrieve more arrows from the dead. Going outside the front gate the knights attack Saladin's camp. Saladin is already riding away.

Robin pulls out his archetypal bow then draws his arrow, straining the wheels to the near breaking point, aiming with his feet. The arrow sails for a mile across the desert striking the sand, right behind Saladin.

King Richard puts his hand over his face. "You missed."

"He's out of range." says Robin.

"Let's set up camp here."

That night Richard sits beside the crackling campfire with Robin. Richard's army is working in darkness while Sir Robin converses with his friend, The King, "We lost some men. Luckily a boat of reinforcements just arrived led by Henry of Champagne. We are back at full force."

"Robin, wearing that green tunic with the red cross and hood, you remind me of your father." Richard remarks.

Sir Robin is in disbelief. "You knew my father?"

"Why, yes. Robert Hode was instrumental in stopping my coup against my father." Richard says.

"He did say he had served. I hate that I remind you of him." Robin says bitterly.

"Robin."

"Yes?"

"You are far more than your father. Never forget that." King Richard tells his friend.

In the morning, the army is assembled, a kite shield wall is formed made up of three hundred knights. Nine knights are on horses out in front led by Richard.

There are many pikes alongside spear tips pointing skywards, spike pits, and many other delightful obstacles set up on the battlefield between the shield wall and their enemies. The knights growl.

One thousand jihadi fighters attack the kite shield wall.

The kite shield wall knocks them down with driving force, Crusader swords impale them on the ground. One thousand of the enemy collides against three hundred shields, English steel pierces enemy armour. Forces as large as the first wave attack again. One thousand men collide against the shield wall then instantly experience the taste of the English Broadsword. One thousand more Saracens and Mamelukes attack the shield wall. They are approaching as if they are a flood of humanity. It proves as effective as the first time they tried it. The knights stab them dead repeatedly. The knights begin to growl again. Saliva hurling from most jaws.

The Saracens and Mamelukes ride their horses towards the shield wall; but then some of the shields go down. Lances are shoved into the ground causing many horses to retreat. The cavalry rears their horses. As the cavalry starts to dismount their horses, the enemy is struck dead by a blizzard of whizzing arrows. The shields are raised again as arrows hit the battlefield. Crusader swords start beating against Crusader shields.

Enemy archers on horseback approach the shield wall; they begin shooting arrows at the wall. The arrows hit the shields. The wall disassembles as the men rush the horses on foot. Richard, along with his knights on horseback, is hit with so many arrows they begin to look like hedgehogs. The horses rear throwing off the enemy archers. The men keep advancing, they swallow the enemy on the ground, screams are heard but are quickly cut short. The wall is reformed back at the gate. More dead bodies lay on the ground.

Enemy arrows fly as the Crusader shields are raised. The arrows land on the shields. One hundred shields are put away so that one hundred archers pull out their bows and crossbows. They are led by Sir Robin.

Sir Robin shouts, "Archers, show them we can still shoot!"

All the archers lift their middle finger to the enemy.

Sir Robin shouts, "Archers! Return fire!"

Robin leads by example as all the archers grab arrows from their quivers, thrust them into the sand, returning volley after volley into the enemy across the battlefield. Death rains down onto the enemy. The shields are raised again, and swords start beating against the Crusader's Shields. King Richard grabs his lance, mounts his horse, then rides across right to left in front of the enemy army.

Saladin's forces watch this display. One of Saladin's men speaks. "Who is that man who leads them from the front?"

"That is King Richard. He always leads in the front." the second jihadi says.

"Where is our leader?"

"In the back, far away from here."

"Then why am I here? I'm leaving." says the first jihadi.

"Me too! This is some pure shish kabab."

The two jihadis take their leave of the battlefield.

A third jihadi spins around. "I owe Salah Ad-din nothing. I grow tired of death."

The third jihadi exits the battlefield. A fourth jihadi speaks his mind. "Salah Ad-din would not let us take our loot out of the city. I fight no more!" The fourth jihadi takes his leave.

Sultan Salah Ad-din is pleading with his men to stay and fight. "I offer a great reward for anyone who attacks!"

A jihadi named Al-Janah speaks to Salah Ad-din. "Your Mamelukes who beat people the day Jaffa fell and took their booty from them. Tell them to charge."

"Bah!" Saladin walks away in disgust. The demoralized forces of Saladin retreat.

King Richard shouts, "They are retreating!"

King Richard's knights begin to chant, "Deus Vult! Deus Vult! Deus Vult!"

Saladin's emissary arrives. He is of average height with long black hair, a goatee, possessing the devil's charisma. "I am Saif adDin, brother of Salah Ad-din. Salah Ad-din sues for peace."

"I sue for peace." King Richard responds.

King Richard and Saladin go over the terms of peace by messenger.

Saif adDin speaks on behalf of his brother.

"Salah Ad-din agrees to release the remaining slaves taken as well as allowing Christians to enter Jerusalem."

"What about the spices?" Richard asks.

"The spice route will flow as a river does, for all this Salah Ad-din demands that Ashkelon shall not be rebuilt."

Richard makes some demands of his own. "Saladin must agree to recognize the Crusader States then cease hostilities for three years, I shall do the same. After three years' time, warfare will resume. I shall return to take Jerusalem."

Richard signs the document then it is given to Saladin. Saladin signs the document. Saif adDin returns.

"My brother says with his Holy Law and God Almighty as his witnesses, he thinks King Richard so pleasant, upright, magnanimous, and excellent that, if the land were to be lost in his time, he would rather have it taken into Richard's mighty power than to have it go into the hands of any other prince whom he had ever seen. Inshallah! We give you the sweetest grapes in Jerusalem..."

Saif adDin presents purple grapes to King Richard. King Richard picks some grapes, he proceeds to eat them.

"Sweet!"

Richard watches as the horses are brought before him. "...and the fastest horses in the Holy Land."

King Richard has his green archer bodyguards handle the horses. Saif adDin leaves.[12] King Richard eats another grape.

"SWWWEEEEEEEEET!"

Robin leads a horse near King Richard. "Your negotiations have paid off! You were right, there are other ways to win a war."

Richard motions his hand to the Yeoman Archers. "Bring him."

Robin is seized by the other green-clad archers. He is dragged kicking and screaming before King Richard in the citadel. Richard is sitting in his makeshift throne room. The room is filled with green garbed archers. They all have black crosses on the front of their tunics. Robin is put on his knees before Richard. "Robin, your mission is killing Saladin. Have you done this to end the war early? No! You go off mission, then you wind up creating dead knights followed by mass hysteria instead."

"Sorry Sire, but these cults seem to be popping up everywhere worshiping death. These bastards need to be wiped out. Besides, Sigerson said..."

"Sigerson does not give you orders! I do! Your mission is killing Saladin, not wiping out cults! I say again, why have you not completed your mission?"

"The task is proving rather complicated. Perhaps if I can assemble a team of people like me."

King Richard grows angry. "There is nobody like you! You are unique, that is why I have given you the title of a knight to be my personal Assassin!"

"Let me bring in Fitzwater's child as a protégé Assassin."

King Richard snaps. "Get out of my sight! I need time to figure out how to deal with you!"

A bodyguard rips the red cross off Robin. There is a red outline of a cross left on Robin's chest. "For as long as you deem fit, my king."

Robin complies then makes his exit. He steals the fastest horse, vanishing into the desert. An eight-month reign of terror strikes the Holy Land. They say a man was shot dead through a tent window, no archer was found nearby, it is rumoured three Muslim cavalrymen rode out chasing Robin across the desert. All were hit by three arrows in 2.25 seconds, in .75 seconds the first one was struck in the chest, in 1.5 seconds another cavalryman was struck in the heart, in 2.25 seconds the final arrow landed in the abdomen of the last cavalryman. All three fell off their horses. Some say dozens of people were thrown out of multiple windows of the same castle.

One merchant claims he witnessed Robin launch from the ground to tackle a rider off of his horse. Robin travells to Alamut. Robin pounds on the door. The Assassin pops out. "I thought I told you to never come back!"

"I need to see the old man of the mountain." Robin replies.

There is a silent moment between them. "Wait there a moment."

The Assassin exits then two Assassins return. The dynamic duo seizes Robin dragging him by the shoulders. He is taken to see the old man of the mountain. The old man of the mountain pierces Robin's ego with his gaze. He scowls at Robin. "Why have you returned? You killed Agony. Why should I not have the same done to you?"

"I need to kill Saladin. I know you can get me into Jerusalem. Right now, I am the best person for the job. I know you need me," Robin says.

"You are going to have to prove your loyalty by taking a job. First, there is a woman in Acre you must take care of, she is trading our secrets."

Robin bakes a cake then journeys for Acre. A few days later a woman is standing on an old wooden plank dock staring at the sunset. She has brown eyes with long black flowing hair. She has a rather dark sun-drenched complexion with a fit body. She wears a brown cloak. Sir Robin walks up beside her. "Nice sunset."

"It is. It is at this time I am reminded that one day the sea shall take us all." she says calmly.

"Let's enjoy this sunset together, hmm?"

Sir Robin observes the sunset with the woman. The sun disappears beneath the Horizon.

"Twilight has come."

"You are here to kill me, aren't you?"

"I'll make it quick."

"Thank you."

Robin shoves his blade through the nerve center of her brain.

She lays dead on the dock, a small river of blood pouring from her head. Robin shoves her body into the ocean. Sir Robin leaves a cake on the dock next to her floating body. The Nightwatchman charges towards the dock drawing his sword. "Hold it!"

Priest runs up to Robin spinning him around. He recognizes Robin's face in the moonlight. Robin looks feral. He has a grizzled beard, long hair, and feral eyes.

"Robin! What happened to you?

Robin! What happened to you?"

Robin stares blankly at Priest then hugs him. "Priest! It is so good to see you well again!"

"It's good to see you too."

"Priest! Your demon seems to be going away!"

"It's funny ever since you took me to the Hospitallers they gave me hashish to calm me down. Apparently, the smoke subdues my demon. The Hospitallers are selling me really good hashish now."

"And to think that hashish cures what a whole church could not exorcise."

Priest looks at the bleeding corpse. "What could that poor woman have done to deserve that?"

"She was a traitor dealing in secrets she had no business of knowing. All I know is that she deserved it."

"Well, as long as she deserved it her coldblooded murder is alright with me. What's with the cake?"

"Honestly, I have no idea; but I think it adds a nice touch to murder."

"Can I eat some?

Can I eat some?"

"Leave it."

"Done. Come with me, Sir Robin. We must divide our riches."

Robin finishes shaving. He washes in Priest's house. Robin putters into the living room. Two tan couches sit by the door. Priest has two pizzas on the coffee table along with a metal cylinder of ice cream. The presence of the coffee table is rather mysterious since the two friends do not know what coffee is.

"Do I look different?"

"You look like an earl's son."

Priest brings out two chests, Robin looks at them. "What's in the chests?"

"A fortune in the colour of kings."

Priest opens the two chests. In each chest is purple silk, jewelry, alongside pillows.

"Purple! So much purple!" exclaims Robin.

"We get to split it two ways. I haven't forgotten the agreement." says Priest.

"Priest, we are now wealthy men. I still need to hunt for the Grail. We should team up to search Acre."

"It is already done. When you revealed your goal to us, Bishop and Pope helped me comb through Acre for the Grail. It isn't here."

"What about Jaffa?" Robin asks.

"While you were wounded, we searched the ruins of Jaffa but could not find a trace of it."

"Ashkelon." Robin says.

"I searched it while you were presumed dead. I knew you would be back though. You are way too good to die like that." Priest replies.

"So, the three of you searched the cities for me?"

"We wanted to do anything to make you happy. You seemed to be missing something from back home." Priest says.

Robin smiles. "Thanks, Priest."

"Robin. You may have to face the reality that the Grail is still in Jerusalem."

"Impossible! Sibylla said the Grail had been moved."

"Robin. Queen Sibylla has been dead for nearly three years. Robin. Queen Sibylla has been dead for nearly three years. "

"Yes. Yes. Of course."

"Do you want to smoke some hashish with me?"

Robin's eyes bulge at the suggestion.

"Why, of course." Robin answers.

Priest and Robin get stoned together and eat pizza. Robin is on the floor while Priest is laying on the couch. Robin smells the swirls of smoke in the air. The whole house is hotboxed.

"What are you going to do with your fortune?" Priest asks.

"I have been thinking of buying some land on the shores of France."

"Good idea.

Good idea."

Isabella walks into the room, she starts hacking. "What are you doing?"

"We are trying to locate the Grail." Robin answers.

"Why?" Isabella questions.

"So that it will purify our souls." Robin answers.

"My soul has been purified more than most men could stand." Priest says through gritted teeth.

Sir Robin looks rather mystified to Priest. "What are you talking about?"

Isabella turns to Priest as well. "He doesn't know, does he?"

Priest shakes his head.

"Know what?" Robin asks.

"Show him." Isabella tells Priest.

Priest takes off his shirt, revealing the branding of the cross all over his body.

Sir Robin's eyes widen in horror. "My God..."

Priest shakes his head. "No. Our God..."

"Priest, I put Christine to bed. You need to come to bed with me."

"I am talking to Sir Robin. Can it wait?"

"Let me put it this way. I need you to come to bed with me. Now!"

"I see. Robin, make yourself at home. My wife needs me. You know Robin, you should really try to find yourself a good woman."

Robin waves to Priest as he is being dragged away. "Bye, Priest."

"Bye.

Bye."

Priest goes to bed with Isabella, Robin smokes hashish until he passes out. Robin walks outside of Priest's house the next morning. The sun is rising in the east, Robin has a whole new day to kill.

"Over three years of searching for the Grail. Enough is enough. Saladin gets his cake tonight."

SIR ROBIN BAKES A CAKE for Saladin. Robin returns to the old man of the mountain. They meet in the desert, the walls of Jerusalem on the horizon. Sir Robin speaks to the old man, "It's time that you get me into Jerusalem."

"I will hold up my end of the bargain. Behold. My men have brought back a dead jihadi."

Sir Robin looks at the stiff then spins back to the old man.

"Is he somehow going to rise from the dead to show me how to infiltrate Jerusalem, or am I just staring at a corpse?"

"You are going to wear his clothes, you little jackass."

3rd of March 1193 A.D.

Robin is dressed like a jihadi fighter in Saladin's army. He enters Jerusalem. Robin walks through the streets at night. There is practically no one in the streets but when a large patrol walks nearby, Robin melts into the shadows.

Robin makes his way through the streets of Jerusalem so he can visit the Holy Sepulchre. It is a large round room with many pillars. There is a beautifully violent painting of the War in Heaven. Angels are battling each other swirling upwards towards the top of the Dome. Their spears pierce each other's naked frames. The top of the Dome is unfinished, there is an opening at the top. Moonlight illuminates The Tomb of Christ.

Robin is brought down onto his knees before the Holy Sepulchre then he projects his hands upwards to God. Robin opens himself up for the first time, He stares in childish wonder toward the moonlight. He reaches for the Heavens until he breaks down. Robin collapses onto the floor. "I do not feel the light of the Holy Trinity inside me. Have I been damned? Have I lost faith?"

Robin weeps on the floor of the Holy Sepulchre. After he regains his composure, Robin exits so he can sneak into the wooden tower in Jerusalem. He waits for the guards to shift. He presents the cake to the new guard. Robin quickly knifes him in the belly using the dagger he held beneath the cake. Warm wet blood pours down cold metal.

The guard tumbles over dead. Robin dumps him onto the ground. Robin lets himself into the tower.

Robin sets the cake down next to Saladin's head. He has greying hair, arched eyebrows, a moustache with a goatee. Robin rummages through the wooden tower finding a paper underneath Saladin's pillow. Robin looks at the drawing of the Grail on the paper then stuffs it into his shirt. There is a picture of the star and the crescent moon.

Robin raises his knife but remembers the women of his life. He remembers Queen Sibylla.

"Even if you didn't have to, would you still kill a man?"

Robin remembers his true love.

"Try not to kill anybody."

Robin plunges the knife. Robin leaves a cake with a blood-soaked knife in it next to Saladin's head. Robin walks to an old wooden dock in Jaffa. The water is choppy, waves splash onto the wood, Robin can tell it's starting to rot. Robin pays for a boat to take him home. The Captain has a toned form, a square jaw, with a large black beard hiding his boyish face underneath. Sinbad sizes him up. "Crusader, huh? Did you get left behind? Doesn't matter. Where are you headed?"

"I am headed for England. Nice ship, What's her name?"

"Hari Hazzin" Sinbad replies. "Did you hear the news? Saladin died of a heart attack."

Robin's eyes pop.

"So he died anyway?" Robin asks.

"His face looked as if he had seen death. He was scared of something."

"Even in death, he is no martyr."

"So. Did you manage to save anyone?" Sinbad asks.

"I managed to save my soul."

"This place can do that sometimes. I think that is why so many men spill blood on the Holy Land. What is your name?"

"Robin, or rather, Sir Robin of Locksley. I am finally going home."

Robin sails for England. Waves crash against the Harri Hazzin's Bow. Wet brine splashes against Robin's face. Having tasted enough wet Hydroaqua, Robin crouches down against the Aft before he eats his own cake. Robin collects his thoughts.

I wonder if she will even recognize me?

PART TWO

IN BETWEEN THE PAGES OF HISTORY LEGENDS ARE TOLD
E PLURIBUS UNUM
FROM MANY, ONE

Dramatis Personae

R obin Hood-Outlaw Hero
        Maid Marian Fitzwater-A Spy
    Little John-Robin Hood's Lieutenant
    Friar Tuck-Spiritual guide to Robin Hood
    Alan A Dale-A Minstrel
    Will Scarlet-A Court Jester
    Sheriff of Nottingham-A prick
    Sir Guy of Gisbourne-Snivelling Assistant to the Sheriff of Nottingham
    Prince John-Count of Mortain
    Lady Nirvana-A Royal
    Tom O'Brian-An Irishman
    Lord Willy-A Royal
    King Richard-King of England, Hero Warrior
    Lady Feathersoft- a Royal
    Lord Fogweather a Royal
    Sarah-Servant to Maid Marian

                        Unnamed

    Nottingham Guards
    Merry Men
    Peasants
    Priests
    May Games Carnies
    Sexy cook
    Sexy waitress
    Disillusioned
    Nottingham Guard
    Templars
    Black Knight
    Piano Man
    Quack Doctor

Baker
Baker's wife
Boy

CHAPTER XI

The Birth of Robin Hood
Ballad of Robin Hood
Many long years ago lived a man named Robin Hood,
he used to rob from the rich and gave to the poor most every chance he
could,
his buddy was little John another was Alan Dale,
there were a hundred and fifty more and together they hit the trail,
now you mustn't get me wrong because he was no square,
with his trusty bow and arrow, he could part your hair,
They took from the rich man and gave to the poor man,
he was a friend to no man except a maid whose name was Marian.
Marian Fitzwater Bio
Birthdate: 1171, A.D.
Death Date: 1220, A.D.
First Contact with Robin of Locksley: 1182, A.D.

Marian Fitzwater is the daughter of a knight named Walter Fitzwater, the bastard brother to the previous king. She grows up in Nottingham castle. One day Marian is playing in Sherwood Forest when she happens upon a ten-year-old boy practicing his archery skills. "Boy, what is your name?"

"I thought I was alone! I am Robin, Robin of Locksley."

"My name is Marian. Marian Fitzwater. Teach me to shoot a bow, Robin."

Robin spends weeks with her teaching her how to shoot like an expert. One day they go to the beach. While wading neck-deep Marian is caught in the riptide. She thrashes. "Help! The sea is swallowing me."

Robin catches her hands pulling her out. Robin puts his hands on Marian's cheeks. Her body is quavering.

"Are you alright? What's wrong?"

Marian stares into Robin's eyes, so Robin does the same. Marian feels Robin's gaze penetrating through her eyes into her very being. He stares at her with his eyes never breaking contact. Then she shatters. She passionately kisses him for the first time. Marian feels a wave of energy shoot down her spine when she kisses him; jolts of sensations explode throughout her body. Robin has a shocked look on his face. Marian smiles at him.

"I realised the boy who saved me would be the man I will marry."

England, 1193 A.D.

A mysterious hooded traveller roams through the English countryside. The hooded figure is dressed in green with a red outline of a cross on the front of his tunic. The hooded figure visits the Knights Templar. He produces a parchment.

The Templar looks at it. "You have served your country well. We will add this to your account."

The hooded figure takes his leave of the Templars, He wanders through a local town. He stops at a bakery. He plans to unwind.

The hooded figure pays for a pastry. He notices the brand on the Baker's arm. He grabs the Baker by the arm pointing at his brand. The Baker explains, "I was late on a payment to the Sheriff of Nottingham. If you are late on a payment his new man Sir Guy of Gisbourne brands you. Three brands mean a quick death afterward."

The hooded figure picks up the money then drops the coins one by one. The baker grows flush with anger. "The economy is crashing due to the expense of the King's Crusade! People are starving! Most of us can't afford the high taxes put upon us. Many of us are close to three brands. Many more have already had three!"

The hooded figure points to his wife. She speaks up, "They don't brand the women, nor do they kill us, they do much worse."

"Hode." The hooded figure says.

"Hode?" The Baker is shocked to hear this. He hadn't thought of The Earl of Huntington for over a year. "The Earl died of grief when he learned his son went missing in the Holy Land. I think his son is dead too."

The figure leaves. As the hooded figure cuts through the forest he stops, crouching, he picks a blade of grass, the hooded figure plays a haunting melody. When he finishes his performance for the wood, he witnesses seven armed men on horseback chasing a young boy no more than sixteen. A Nottingham Guard leaps off his horse tackling the boy.

The guard wrestles with the boy on the ground. "Brand him! I'll hold him!" The Sheriff has the guards pull back on the boy's sleeve. The Sheriff examines the arm. "No point! He already has two brands."

One guard grabs a rope from his horse saddle then fashions a noose. As the men on horseback raise the boy's legs off the ground, the hooded figure draws his bow then fires, cutting the noose with a well-aimed arrow. The Sheriff of Nottingham becomes aware of this hooded newcomer.

"You dare interfere with justice?"

"You are attacking your own side. Only traitors attack their own side. Why do you wish to kill a helpless child?"

"This helpless child has killed one of the Prince's deer."

"No man or child deserves to be hanged... especially for something as trivial as killing a deer for food, many in this land are hungry."

"Well, I have no problem killing you as well as the whelp."

The hooded figure lets fly six arrows in 4.5 seconds hitting all six men on horseback in their faces. The Sheriff flees like the coward he is. The boy walks over to the hooded traveller. "My thanks to you stranger, I owe you my life. Who are you?"

"I am a traveller in a strange land. Tell me, boy, what has happened to my beloved England while I was away?"

"Have you not heard? While good King Richard has been away in the Holy Land, his treacherous brother Prince John (boy spits) has run England into the ground. If that were not bad enough, he has the Sheriff of Nottingham working for him. A vicious bastard he is, his lackey, Guy of Gisbourne is no better. Taxes have become so high that the common man is starving,"

The hooded traveller speaks in an ice-cold tone. "I have seen what has come of my beloved home. Unfair taxes, people starving, the Economy is collapsing. This is not how man is meant to live. All I have seen has made me livid with anger."

"Yes, but what can one do about it?"

"I shall tell you what I intend to do. I will go to Nottingham to have words with Prince John himself."

Sir Robin arrives at the May Games. There is an archery range. There is a maypole. Men are fighting with quarterstaffs, to the left men are wrestling. Men and women are dressed as King Arthur, Queen Guinevere, Sir Tristan, Isolde, Sir Lancelot, and Elaine of Astolat. Families are throwing wooden balls at milk bottles. Everyone is merry.

Sir Robin remembers the Holy Land. He remembers speaking to the king. "Do you know what I miss? The May Games, where through sheer skill even a man like me can be a king without a crown."

Sir Robin is back at the May Games. An Archery Judge is speaking to him. "Sir? Do you want to shoot in our archery contest?"

Robin takes notice. Robin shoots three arrows into the air, they land, the targets are raised, Robin has hit all three bull's-eyes. Everybody at the archery tournament is astonished by this feat of skill.

The Archery Judge points at Robin. "We have a winner."

Robin is back in the Holy Land. "I'm sorry. I did not mean to offend. The crown belongs to you."

"No. You are right. The greatest of men can be kings without crowns." King Richard replies.

Robin is back at the May Games. He picks up a staff challenging the biggest man. The large mountain of a man reminds Robin of Priest, but Robin thinks it likely he hasn't killed as many men as Priest has. The man looks at Robin, who dares to challenge him at quarterstaffs. "Make way, big man. You don't have a chance," Robin spins his staff.

"You're a plucky one!"

"What's your name, big man?"

"Little John."

"Let me get this straight. Your name is Little John?"

"I am aware of the irony. You have my name, what is yours?"

"I am the king without a crown."

Robin and Little John begin fighting. Their staffs strike swiftly. Little John swings horizontally but Robin blocks it. Robin smashes Little John's toes knocking away his weapon.

Robin is back in the Holy Land. King Richard addresses Robin. "You are skilled Robin."

"I have many skills. A lot of them end in death."

"Too true. But if you are to serve me now, I cannot be accompanied by an archer, you must be a knight. Rise, Sir Robin."

"I am your sword, my king."

Robin is back at the May games. Robin is walking to the hand-to-hand combat arena. Little John is furious. "You owe me! You cheated. You owe me a rematch!"

Robin uses Little John's momentum to throw him into the ring. Little John throws a mean right hook. Robin ducks under the right hook grabbing it, he puts Little John in an arm-bar. Robin forces Little John to his knees.

"Yield." Robin growls.

"Nay!"

Robin lightly pressures the arm at the correct point.

"I yield!" Little John screams.

The Combat Judge looks at Robin, then shouts. "We have a winner."

Prince John is on a wooden platform observing the May Games. He stands up making a royal announcement. "Presenting the Queen of the May Games, the fairest in the land, Marian Fitzwater."

Marian Fitzwater is brought out from behind a silk curtain onto a large multi-level platform. She is clothed in green wearing a crown of plants. Prince John continues, "Now it is time for the winners of the May Games to compete for the hand of Marian. Where are the champions?"

All three judges point to Robin. He smiles and waves. Prince John narrows his eyes. "Who are you beneath that?"

"That is Robin's Hood." Maid Marian says with annoyance.

"It is Sir Robin."

"What?" Marian asks.

"I have been knighted."

"But you are an archer."

"Well, now I am a knight."

Prince John is confused by this. "Do you two know each other?"

Maid Marian smiles in annoyance at Prince John. "No. We are practicing our verbal sparring skills with one another."

"What? Really?"

"Of course we know each other. We grew up together."

The Sheriff of Nottingham whispers in Prince John's ear.

"That man, Sir Robin of Locksley interfered with justice by killing six of my men."

Prince John shouts back to Robin."Knight, you serve me well."

"I don't serve you. I am the sword of the Lion Heart."

"Very well, I dub thee Robin Hood, King of the May Games. I also dub thee murderer and outlaw. Seize him!"

"I am Robin Hood. I can do two things. You do not know what those two things are yet. But I do."

Robin barrels out of the May Games, he hoofs it into Sherwood Forest. It starts to rain violently as Robin tries making his way through the thick forest for hours. He hikes through old-gnarled trails leading to a river until he finally arrives at the pass. Robin stops. He gazes upon Little John standing on the cliff-side waterfall blocking his path. "I really don't have time for this."

"Robin Hood, King of the May Games; I am going to crack your crown so I can claim the reward."

Robin Hood picks up two sticks. "Have at you."

Robin Hood delivers a flurry of attacks towards Little John.

Liquid roars as loud as lions. Robin and Little John are rapidly exchanging blows while staff fighting with furious martial precision. Robin Hood and Little John begin an insane exchange of strikes and counter strikes. Robin keeps smacking his sticks into Little John's face making him angry.

Little John finally manages to jab Robin in the solar plexus with his staff. Robin drops his sticks falling onto his knees.

"HA!" Little John exclaims.

Robin Hood manages to swing his legs in a circular motion, he steadies himself with his hands, using the flowing momentum of his legs, Robin sweeps his legs around knocking Little John onto his back like a milk bottle. Robin spots a dozen archers on each side of them. Robin leaps onto Little John then rolls them over the side of the waterfall. Dozens of arrows hit the edge of the waterfall. Robin

Hood and Little John are washed down the river by the current. They end up deep in the heart of Sherwood Forest.

Little John looks around. "Where are we?"

"We are in a place I haven't been to in a long time. This is my secret place. Nobody can find it. Well, one person found it... but that was a lifetime ago."

"I thought we were dead for sure. You saved me."

Robin Hood starts laughing "You beat me. But if you would like to help, I think I have a good plan to change things."

CHAPTER XII

A New Occupation

Maid Marian is in the castle courtyard. She stares into her reflection in the rain puddles. Marian continues feeding the pigeons.

"Why do you do this to yourself?" Sir Guy of Gisbourne steps forward.

Maid Marian puts her hand to her mouth. "Oh. Sir Guy... you startled me..."

Sir Guy of Gisbourne bows his head quickly. "I beg your lady's forgiveness... you were quite close with Sir Robin of Locksley when you were younger, am I correct?"

Maid Marian nods her head. "You are correct Sir Guy..."

"I have watched you for a year now feeding the pigeons in this courtyard while Locksley was away playing the hero. Denying yourself the company of better men."

Maid Marian smiles wryly. "You would be surprised how good company pigeons are to keep."

"Locksley is gone forever now, Marian. He has turned outlaw; in due time he will be hanged. I just want you to know that I am here for you, if you may need me,"

Maid Marian brushes his hand away. "Thank you, Guy. Your consideration is touching. If you please, I am going to continue feeding the pigeons."

Sir Guy bows. "As you wish, Lady Marian." Sir Guy takes his leave splashing his boots across the courtyard puddles. Marian continues feeding the pigeons.

IN COMPLETE DARKNESS, two figures arrive at the Royal Tax Treasury of Nottingham. The two shadowy figures are Robin Hood and Little John, they have brought a cart with them. They walk up to the outside of the wall. Little John looks at the treasury then he glances back at Robin. "That place is guarded like a fortress, Robin. We can't get in."

Robin smirks. "Even the mightiest knight can be felled by a single chink in the armour." Robin snaps his fingers, pointing. "There we go. The overgrowth in the southwest corner."

Robin removes a vine from a stone in the corner, then with the help of Little John, they remove the stone. Robin Hood climbs into the hole, he quickly pushes out a sack of gold, then two more sacks, and so on. The cart is filled with sacks of money. Robin squirms out of the hole in the wall. Little John is staring at the money they have stolen. "We are rich Robin! We can live like dukes for the rest of our lives."

"It sounds tempting, but I have a better idea of how it can be used. Little John, go out! Find every decent knight and archer who has fallen on hard times and have them gather in Sherwood. I have someone that I must speak to."

MAID MARIAN IS IN HER bed sleeping when a rock crashes through her window. Robin is standing outside.

"Marian, wake up!" Robin shouts upwards.

Marian stands at the window above Robin Hood with an incredulous look upon her face. "Did you just seriously throw a rock through my window?"

"The window had it coming!" Robin shouts back.

"What do you want?"

Robin has to think about this momentarily. "I just wanted you to be the first to know that I robbed the Nottingham Tax Treasury!"

Maid Marian is in disbelief. "Are you out of your mind? Why would you even do that?"

"To give it to the poor!" Robin responds loudly.

"Are you out of your mind? Why would you even do that?"

A guard walks around the corner of Nottingham Castle checking in on all the noise. "My Lady, Marian...are you consorting with the known outlaw, Robin Hood?"

"NO!" Maid Marian and Robin Hood shout back in unison.

The Castle Guard waves his hand. "Fine. Whatever... I hate my job."

THE SHERIFF IS IN HIS stone room pacing. He is occasionally looking out of the window.

"Robin Hood. Robin Hood. Ha! I love it! Robin Hood, it rolls off the tongue. Post a fifty-coin reward."

PRINCE JOHN HAS A DESK next to the window in his quarters. There is also a bed by a smouldering hearth. A tapestry of the stars hangs in his room. Prince John is entertaining Sir Guy's company.

"As I was saying Sir Guy, Nottingham Castle has been my favourite summer retreat since I was a boy."

The Sheriff of Nottingham bursts into the room unannounced. This greatly annoys Prince John.

"Prince John! The royal tax treasury has been raided!" The Sheriff shouts frantically.

Prince John has a puzzled look upon his face. "What? How?"

The Sheriff has a slightly embarrassed look upon his face. "We don't know, it's as if they struck like shadows. We think it was Robin Hood."

"And what pray tell makes you think that?" The Count of Mortain asks his subject.

"We found a black arrow in the treasury room," The Sheriff replies.

Prince John throws his goblet of wine at the Sheriff.

"I want Robin Hood found and executed! I don't care what it takes! Send the Black Knight!"

The Sheriff begins to speak. "Sire, I..."

"Send him I say!!!" Prince John shouts at the top of his lungs.

AT DUSK, EVERYONE IS gathered at the great rock. People are holding flickering torchlight in the darkness. Robin Hood looks to Little John. "Is this everyone?"

"Every decent thief and outlaw in England. All former knights or archers."

Robin Hood clambers atop the great rock to address the massive crowd.

"Fellow thieves, outlaws, I ask you a question, why do we steal?"

"Because we are all natural-born kleptomaniacs!" A thief shouts from the crowd.

"Hear! Hear!" The crowd shouts.

"No! We steal because taxes have become so high, we can no longer buy what we need to survive. So now we take what we need..." Robin says.

"Hear! Hear!"

Robin Hood continues, "...But fellow outlaws, we are not the only ones who suffer. Our entire country is being bled dry and the economy is collapsing all around us... I say to you we pool our skills. Not only to help ourselves but to help our fellow man as well... and I promise you all, men of Sherwood Forest when good King Richard returns you will all be pardoned. But in the mean-time; we will plunder the hell out of England so badly history shall forever remember us as Robin Hood and his band of Merry Men!"

"Uhhhh... can't we be Robin Hood and his band of vicious blackguards instead?" A thief in the front asks Robin.

Robin Hood replies, "No! I like Merry Men better..."

THAT EVENING THE BLACK Knight is brutally terrorizing the countryside. Robin Hood appears with his bow drawn, aiming a flaming arrow.

Robin Hood shouts, "Yield!"

"Nay!" The Black Knight shouts back.

Robin Hood lets his arrow fly. The arrow hits the Black Knight's shield. The Black Knight begins chortling, "Ha! Ha! Ha! Ha! Ha! Ha! Ha!"

Suddenly the Black Knight's shield catches fire bursting into flames. The rest of the Black Knight catches fire quickly. The Black Knight runs off burning alive shrieking into the distance.

BACK AT NOTTINGHAM Castle, Marian is feeding the pigeons in the courtyard. The Sheriff walks into the small castle courtyard. "Lady Marian, I hope I am not intruding..."

Maid Marian shifts her attention to the approaching Sheriff. "Not at all, Sheriff... what brings you here?"

"I know you were quite close with Robin Hood when you were children."

Marian looks away. "We were."

"I hope you realise that he is an outlaw now. Marian... if you know anything that could be of service or should he try to contact you... well... I just hope you do the right thing."

Maid Marian looks back at the sheriff. "Is that all Sheriff?"

"No."

Marian cocks her head sideways. "No?"

The Sheriff arrests Maid Marian's hands. "I fancy you, Marian... You are the most beautiful woman I have ever seen. Your eyes are like starlight. These are dangerous times my lady, thieves are working with outlaws everywhere. Criminals who wouldn't think twice about harming a helpless young woman such as yourself. Even a woman who's as radiant as you, needs a strong man to protect and provide for her. Should you ever want it, my sword, my title, they are yours."

Marian smiles. "Would you like to help feed the pigeons, Sheriff?"

The Sheriff releases Marian's hands. "My duties require me elsewhere my lady."

Marian nods. "Very well... you can show yourself out."

"As you wish."

BACK IN SHERWOOD FOREST, it is evening. Robin is pacing back and forth among the trees as his Merry Men are practicing with the sword. Robin starts instructing with his sword. "Remember men, give your enemies no quarter until you see an opening for an offensive blow...then strike and strike hard. Remember there is no such thing as a cheap shot."

Little John approaches Robin Hood. "Robin, Maid Marian is here. Though how she found us, I haven't a clue... perhaps we should move base camp. If she found us, what will stop Guy of Gisbourne or the Sheriff from finding us?"

Robin Hood clasps his hand onto Little John's shoulder. "Something neither Sir Guy nor the Sheriff possess...a woman's intuition, don't worry my friend, we're perfectly fine where we are. Go help drill the men, Marian and I am overdue for a chat..."

Maid Marian and Robin Hood stroll among the fireflies talking to one another.

"Only you, Robin, would set up your base where we played as children..."

"...And only you, Marian, would be smart enough to figure that out. You are the most intelligent person I know Marian... that's why I need you to be my eyes, you must be my ears inside Nottingham castle."

Maid Marian abruptly stops walking then glances towards Robin Hood. "You want me to be your spy?"

Robin smirks. "Yes."

Maid Marian waves her hand brushing off the proposal. "Forget it..."

Robin Hood ratchets up his boyish charm. He gives Maid Marian a look that only he can give.

"Come on... Come on... You know you wanna... Come on... Come on..."

Maid Marian rolls her eyes. "Oh, very well. But why all of this killing?"

"I never killed a man that didn't deserve it!" Robin Hood exclaims.

"Let's try to keep it that way. I want to know why you have returned home? Why are you not serving in the Crusades?"

Robin Hood lowers his gaze to the ground, he speaks in a low tone, "On my last mission in the Holy Land, things got messy... too messy. King Richard said I needed to clear my head to get back to my old self again. I was supposed to be on leave, but I stayed instead. I remained in the Holy Land for nearly eight months after the Crusade had ended."

Marian is blank.

"The Crusade is over? But where is the king?"

"I thought he was here. I soon learned otherwise. I saw the oppression going on at home in our king's absence. I could not sit by and do nothing about it. Marian, I want to show you something..."

Robin leads Marian away from the encampment into Sherwood Forest. Robin brings Marian behind a bush. Marian follows Robin, she finds that they are entering into a dirt burrow. There is a rack with three bows on it. The banner in the burrow has a tribal fox hanging upon it. Marian looks around her. "What is this place?"

Robin rotates his head towards Marian. "This is my private arsenal. What little I have from the Crusades. The top one is a standard Yew Bow, reliable for any yeoman, but for accuracy you want the

English Longbow, below that is the recurve bow, technologically speaking it is an improvement."

"Do you use it?"

"No. I hate the goddamn things. Too many have been used to shoot at me. I have this rare Mongol bow at the bottom. It is a cavalry weapon only able to pierce Western Armour from a close range. That makes the archer susceptible to a sword."

Marian points to a banner with a red tribal fox. "What does the fox on the banner stand for?"

Robin looks at Marian. "That is the family crest; a tribal fox has been representing my family for centuries. It dates back to when England was less civilized. I'm not really sure of its original meaning."

"If it has any indication on you, it probably means your family is as crafty as a fox."

Robin Hood leans over towards Marian's ear whispering into it, "A crafty fox is a dangerous fox."

Marian smiles then she whispers back, "Dangerous and deadly..."

"Foxy..." Robin goes in for the kiss. Robin begins making out with Marian.

FOUR NOBLES IN A HEAVILY decorated carriage, carried by two white horses, are riding through Sherwood Forest.

Lord Fogweather is telling a somewhat amusing story to his fellow nobles.

"And then he puts the trousers on anyway even though I already told him the cat had finished peeing on them!"

Lady Feathersoft is cackling. "HA! HA! HA! HA! HA! How delightfully irreverent!"

Lord Fogweather notices that the carriage has stopped. "Say, why has the carriage stopped moving? Driver! I say, driver! why has the...."

Lord Fogweather sticks his head out; He realises the carriage is surrounded. Robin Hood swings in on a vine. "Good morning my lord, my ladyship. Your carriage seems to be a tad heavy on account of all the gold you are transporting. It seems to be slowing you down. My Merry Men and I can help lighten your load."

Robin's men start taking the gold. Robin notices the necklace the lady is wearing. "My what a pretty necklace you are wearing my lady."

Lady Feathersoft lurches back covering her necklace.

"You wouldn't dare take a lady's necklace away!"

"Come now my lady, such a small trinket is insignificant when compared to the remarkable radiance of one such as yourself." With that Robin Hood causes Lady Feathersoft's heart to melt.

"Oh, you charming rogue."

Lady Feathersoft gives Robin her necklace willingly.

INSIDE NOTTINGHAM CASTLE, the Nottingham Court Jester is pulling rabbits out of his hat for Prince John, the Sheriff of Nottingham, Sir Guy of Gisbourne, with their guest the Lady Marian. They are in an enclosed room. There are four wooden chairs on a stone dais. The Sheriff turns his attention to Prince John.

"Robin Hood's assets have been frozen as per your request your highness."

"Excellent." Prince John says.

The Court Jester pulls a rabbit out of his hat.

Sir Guy of Gisbourne stands on his feet to point accusingly at the Court Jester. "He pulled a rabbit out of his hat! He's got the devil in him!"

The Sheriff catches the Jester as he heads for the exit. The Sheriff is grappling with the Court Jester "I'll hold him, Sir Guy! You beat on his legs!"

The Sheriff of Nottingham holds the Court Jester while Sir Guy beats on his legs.

BACK IN SHERWOOD FOREST, a carriage adorned with many jewels is travelling through the forest. Lord William is very uncomfortable.

He has short black hair, a decent build, and bugged-out eyes. He rubs his fingers across his moustache, sweat pours from his forehead. He is running late for an important meeting with Prince John. Lady Nirvana wears black silks complimented with long black hair and arched eyebrows. Lord William is looking out the carriage window. "I don't care much for travelling through Sherwood Forest, what with all these bandits about."

Lady Nirvana is applying powder to her face as she talks very droll. "I dare hope we don't encounter that naughty scoundrel Robin Hood ... why the very thought gives my heart the flutters."

"Why have we stopped moving?"

"Driver, my husband demands to know why we have stop-"

Lady Nirvana sticks her head out the window finding that Robin Hood's Merry Men surround the carriage. Robin Hood swings on a vine. "I'm terribly sorry but my Merry Men and I couldn't help but notice how terribly slow your carriage seems to be moving on account of all those jewels encrusted on the wheels. We thought that we might be able to help you move a bit faster. My, my, what pretty silver you are wearing my Lady...You wouldn't mind donating it towards a good cause would you?"

Lady Nirvana starts to Panic. "No! Not my silver! You can't!"

Robin Hood winks at her. "Come now, my ladyship, such trinkets are incomparable to the beauty of one such as you."

Lady Nirvana loudly proclaims. "Oh, you thief of hearts!"

Lady Nirvana hands over her silver necklace willingly then wraps her arms around Robin Hood. Lady Nirvana starts making out with Robin Hood. Lord Willy pops his head out the window. "That's my wife!"

Robin Hood shoves Lord Willy's head back through the window. Robin continues making out with Lady Nirvana.

An Irishman clothed in green is strolling down a trail. Suddenly Robin Hood swings in on a vine. Robin Hood holds up his hand. "Yield. To safely pass Sherwood Forest you must pay a fee."

The Irishman bolts for it.

"You can run and run as fast as you can. You'll never catch Tom O' Brian the Irishman!"

Robin Hood takes an arrow out of his quiver, aims his bow, then fires an arrow through Tom's left kneecap. Tom O' Brian lies on the ground screaming his head off.

"AAAH! AAAH! AAAH!"

Robin Hood looks down at Tom. "Give me your pot of gold!"

"What pot of gold? I'm an Irishman not a leprechaun."

Robin snaps. "Bull! I know the rules! I caught you so now you have to hand over your pot of gold!"

"Caught me? You damn well crippled me!"

"Hand over your pot of gold already."

Robin Hood kicks Tom O' Brian while he's down.

"Here! Here is my pot of gold! Take it and go!" Tom hands over his pot of gold to Robin Hood.

"Curse your black heart, Robin Hood!" Tom shouts at the figure merging with the forest's green.

Robin Hood is strolling with Little John through Sherwood Forest. The sun is shining through the trees in Sherwood. Robin Hood breathes in the clean pine-scented air. Robin spins his head towards a rosebush.

I should pick a rose for Marian.

Robin reaches towards a red rose when the laughter from a group of knights stops him. Robin and Little John stroll by Crusaders who are drunk from binge drinking a keg of ale.

A drunken knight who is sitting on a fallen tree trunk starts to laugh at Robin Hood and Little John. "Ha! Look at that cheap wooden bow and those rickety arrows."

Little John loses his cool. "Don't you know who this is? This is Robin Hood! He is the finest archer in all of England! They say he can hit a target a mile away."

The drunken knight sweeps his hand in the air. Bull! Nobody is that good! I bet a hundred gold pieces you can't hit anything!

Robin Hood perks up. "I'll take that bet."

Robin Hood takes an arrow from his quiver. He holds the bow with his feet, drawing back the arrow he aims carefully. Robin lets his arrow fly so the arrow travells through Sherwood Forest at extreme velocity.

The Sheriff of Nottingham is in front of some houses with straw thatching as he is hitting on Maid Marian.

"I tell you, Maid Marian, there is nothing like having authority. I'm the boss applesauce!"

Marian is both bored, while at the same time contemptuous of the Sheriff as of late.

"And yet you still can't lay your hands on Robin Hood." She replies rather sarcastically.

"Because he's scared of me. I'm too much man for him to handle. Heck, I bet I am too much man for you to handle."

An arrow pierces the Sheriff in the crotch.

"AAAAAAAH!"

The drunk knight looks in disbelief at what happened a mile away. "That shot was bloody impossible! Do it again."

"A bet's a bet. Give me my money." Robin rubs his thumb against his draw fingers.

"I am a little shy of a hundred gold pieces. Can you guys help me out?"

The drunken knights pool their money so they can pay Robin Hood.

"Have a nice day, gentlemen." Robin Hood says as they part ways.

An elderly man is driving a cart of gold through Sherwood Forest. Robin Hood swings from a vine out in front of him. "Give me your gold old man."

The elder is a rather old salt. "I refuse to hand over my gold to a common hedge robber."

"I am no common hedge robber. I am Robin Hood."

"Robin Hood, eh? I've heard of you." The old man pulls out a knife then begins swinging it crazily.

"Come on punk, let's dance, You and me!"

The old man swings the knife crazily.

"Come on old man, hand over the knife. I don't want to hurt you." Robin goes to take the knife but the old man stabs Robin in the shoulder.

"AAAAAAAH!"

Robin Hood is giving money to the poor. There is a family of three standing outside of their circular hut. Robin Hood gives the poor man money. "Here is twenty coin."

"Bless you, Robin Hood. It's hard to raise a family these days. But I do have a roof to repair."

Robin Hood gives him more money. "Here is an extra ten coin for the roof."

The Poor man's wife speaks up, "Thank you, Robin Hood. We shall not go hungry now. But we have no pots nor pans to cook our food."

"Here is fifteen coin for pots and pans."

A little girl runs up to Robin, holding out her hand.

"Ahem."

Robin takes out a single coin, the little girl kicks him really hard in the shin. Robin drops the bag of coins. The little girl catches the bag then runs off.

ROBIN IS WALKING THROUGH Sherwood Forest. He is in a foul mood.

"Steal from the rich, give to the poor. Steal from the rich, give to the poor. You know what? Screw the poor. Let someone else give to the poor. Now, where is that church?"

Robin Hood enters a local church not far from Sherwood Forest. Friar Tuck kneels before the Crucifix.

"Lord, I have served you many long years, I have never asked anything of you until now... please help us."

A large voice echoes through the church from behind Tuck.

"Ask and ye shall receive!"

"Who is that?"

Friar Tuck spins around to look upon Robin Hood.

"Really Friar Tuck, I know I have been gone for many years, but has it been so long that you have forgotten me?"

Friar Tuck stands up, he walks steadfastly towards Robin Hood. "There is no place for you here anymore! I was so proud of you the day you left for the Crusades... little did I know you would betray every principle I have taught you to become a thief! An outlaw! Robin! My Robin!"

"It's ironic. I went to the Holy Land to find God, but instead, I have only lost faith. I still retain the philosophies combined with the ethics you instilled in me as a boy. Those I stole from could afford it, but I still need a way to give to those in need without arousing suspicions."

"You dare ask me to be a conduit for your stolen goods?"

Robin Hood plays the innocent. "Why, perish the thought, Friar Tuck! I expect you to help me distribute my stolen goods to those who are truly in need. The people outside of Nottingham. Sort of like a charity. But that is only half of what I ask of you..."

"What else do you ask of me?"

"I have one hundred fifty fellow outlaws who desperately need the same ethical and moral guidance you gave me as a boy. I can't do it on my own, I am asking you for your help."

"You ask me to give charity to those in need, as well as to help save the souls of over a hundred sinners?"

Robin nods his head. "Yes,"

Friar Tuck puts his hands on Robin's shoulders.

"As a man of the cloth, how can I refuse?"

CHAPTER XIII

An Unwelcome Reunion

Maid Marian sets a pie on the Nottingham Castle windowsill to cool. She heads back towards the kitchen. A bush picks itself up, tiptoes towards the pie, Robin Hood pops out of the bush cutting himself a piece of the pie. As Robin Hood is eating his ill-gotten pie, Marian pops out of the window grabbing Robin Hood.

"Gotcha!"

Robin Hood screams like a little girl, throws the pie into Marian's face, running away. Marian's spitting out pie. "A pox on you and your house Robin of Locksley! I'll get you yet!"

THE SHERIFF OF NOTTINGHAM is in his quarters.

The Sheriff is standing, looking at a Robin Hood Wanted poster hanging on the wall. Sir Guy is standing behind him.

"Why hasn't anyone turned in Robin Hood?"

Sir Guy looks downwards to his feet. "The people love him. He served in the Crusade, so he is still widely considered the King of the May Games."

"He is king of nothing! If anything, he is just the Prince of Thieves. Hmmm... Robin Hood, Prince of Thieves... That would make a great wanted poster. Steal from the rich, give to the poor. What in the hell does he think he's doing? Increase the reward to one hundred coin."

Sir Guy follows the Sheriff as they are brought before Prince John who sits behind his desk near a window.

"Why have you not caught Robin Hood?"

"I am dealing with him in my own way." The Sheriff replies.

"I have seen your way. It leaves great room for improvement." Prince John says rather coldly.

"I have to deal with Robin Hood and his Merry Men."

Prince John has a look of horror upon his face. "You mean to tell me that Robin Hood has men now-and they're merry?!"

"Yes, Prince John. Robin Hood now has Merry Men. Each one is merrier than the last." The Sheriff replies.

"I don't get it. Robin Hood steals from us, the people love him for it. Robin Hood robs from the rich, the rich love him for it."

Sir Guy of Gisbourne is examining his nails. "You see Prince John, some guys they steal your money. These guys, they steal your heart..."[13]

"Take four guards, go into the forest!" Prince John commands.

"Why?" Sir Guy asks.

"To kill Robin Hood, Sir Guy! That is what you are good for, is it not?"

THAT AFTERNOON SIR Guy enters Sherwood Forest with his men. Sir Guy leading his four men arrives at a fork in the road. Sir Guy starts barking orders, "You two take the left path. The other two, follow me. This is the place Robin Hood is most active. We should run into him eventually."

The two guards take the left path separating from the group. Going along the path one of the guards is lifted off the ground upside down by a snare. "Well? Don't just stand there. Cut me down!"

The other guard falls over with an arrow in his back. Robin Hood steps out with his bow drawn.

"What are two Nottingham guards doing this far out in Sherwood Forest without any taxes to guard?"

"Go to hell, Hood!"

"You first."

Robin Hood shoots an arrow at the guard narrowly missing.

"AAAH!"

"Tell me what's going on!"

"No!"

Robin Hood shoots another arrow at the guard narrowly missing again.

"AAAAAH! Jesus Christ, Hood!"

"Missed again. Now tell me what you are doing out here because the third time is the charm."

"We are out here with Gisbourne! We were sent to track you down then kill you! Now let me down!"

"Kill me, huh? As I said, the third time is the charm."

"Wait! No! AAAH!"

Robin Hood shoots an arrow into the snare holding the guard. Robin takes off. The two remaining guards are in the forest led by Sir Guy. The Third Guard shows up. Sir Guy of Gisbourne is furious.

"Where have you been?"

"It was Robin Hood. I thought he was going to kill me, but he let me go instead." The surviving guard replied.

"You moron. You have led him right to us!"

The survivor falls over dead with five arrows in his back.

The two guards on either side of Sir Guy are shot dead with arrows. Sir Guy slices an arrow out of the air with his sword. Robin Hood appears with his bow drawn.

"Gisbourne!" Robin Hood shouts.

Sir Guy takes an Assassin's fighting stance. "Hood!"

Robin does a doubletake. "Agony?"

Robin Hood removes his hood. Sir Guy is delighted but furious at this revelation. "You!"

Robin Hood is just furious. "You!"

Beat his ass!

Robin Hood looks Sir Guy in the eyes. They throw away their weapons. They begin hurdling towards each other to beat the spit out of one another with their bare hands.

"How did you survive the Holy Land, Gisbourne? Or should I say, Agony?" Robin Hood asks.

"When you shot me full of arrows you failed to realise I was wearing gambeson. I just played dead. You were fool enough to fall for it." Sir Guy says.

Robin kicks the crap out of Sir Guy.

"You allied yourself with the wrong faction. You are a traitor to the crown." Robin Hood says.

Robin stops beating on Gisbourne.

"Robin Hood, the way things are going it will be John's crown soon enough."

Sir Guy punches Robin in the face. Robin falls to the ground. Robin tastes warm liquid filling his mouth. He spits out some blood.

Robin has to talk through a split lip. "What do you mean?"

Gisbourne grabs Robin by the scruff of the neck. Sir Guy of Gisbourne glares straight in Robin's eyes giving an evil grin. "None of us have a full picture. Very soon change shall be upon us."

Robin hits Sir Guy with his head. Sir Guy stumbles back. Robin spins his legs on the ground tripping Sir Guy. Robin rolls over elbowing Sir Guy in the diaphragm knocking the wind out of him. Robin gets on his knees, pulls a knife out of his boot, then puts it to Sir Guy's throat.

"I'm not going to kill you. The knife is to show you how serious I am. I want you to give all of your conspirators a message, this is it, 'I will find you then I will assassinate you.' Now get the hell out of my forest."

IT IS NIGHTTIME AS the tax carriage is driven through Sherwood Forest. It is being driven down the road passing through the many rows of dark trees.

"I hope Robin Hood does not rob us this time." The tax-driver comments.

"Even Robin Hood has to sleep sometime. The outlaw does not worry me so much as the forest itself." says the co-driver.

"What do you mean?" asks the driver.

"Have you not heard? Sherwood Forest is haunted. People have reported strange green lights floating through the forest. They say that if you get too close to the lights you shall be whisked away to never return."

The tax-driver strokes his grey mustache. "Sounds like superstition mixed with fairy tales to me."

The taxmen drive by a sign that the driver reads, "Beware of the forest monster Moonfang! Uh-oh. There is a forest monster on the loose. We had better be careful."

"I can't believe you buy into the existence of forest monsters. Are you four years old?" asks the co-driver.

"My cousin said he saw Moonfang while he was travelling through The Holy Roman Empire."

"Well, your cousin is a bleedin' four-year-old too then. Besides, how can you believe in forest monsters but not believe in strange green lights?"

"You can't touch light; light can't touch you. Forest monsters can not only touch you, but they can also eat you." The driver answers.

"That is the biggest crock of..."

Midway through the debate green lights appear in the forest, as the wagon continues rolling on the road, the lights follow. When the driver turns his attention back to the road, he is shocked to find a large bipedal wolf standing in the middle of the road. The giant wolf holds a two-sided war axe. The wolf hurls the axe at the carriage. The drivers bolt. They hoof it quickly to Nottingham Castle. The two taxmen are telling their incredible story to the Sheriff of Nottingham while Sir Guy listens intently.

"It was huge!

"Fourteen feet tall at the least!"

"It was a beastly-looking mother..."

"It carried a war axe."

"Then there are the green lights."

The Sheriff snaps. "Enough! Guy, gather ten of your best men, head out to Sherwood Forest to search for the missing gold."

Sir Guy leads a search party through the forest at night. The search party listens to the sound of beating drums in the night. The first man raises his lantern to the foliage, he sees nothing. He swings the lantern around; the wolf is standing before him. The guard screams. The second guard arrives but can find no one. The wolf emerges from the bush in slow motion behind him as he spins around. Another guard is crawling through a thicket of twigs when he hears a scream.

The arms of a giant wolf emerge through the thicket grabbing his waist pulling him backwards through the thicket. Three of the search party stumbles across a broken-down carriage.

The first man in the squad screams at the other two. "Is that it? Is that the carriage? What happened to the treasure?"

"You two look for it." The third guard says before he steps out into the forest.

The two scared guards inspect the carriage. They hear a scream.

"He's dead!" The first guard screams.

"I didn't hear anything. Let's find that treasure." says the second guard nonchalantly.

They find the treasure a small way from the cart. They open a chest but two huge paws with huge claws shut the lid on their hands. They look up to quiver before a huge wolf. There are two more screams. The seventh guard spots someone signaling him to a tree. The guard goes to the tree, but the person runs off. Then two huge paws clamp-on from above pulling the guard into the trees. The branches rustle then there is screaming. The eighth guard runs up to the tree, but the seventh guard flies out of the tree landing on top of him. The eighth guard steps into one of Robin Hood's snares, luckily, he is only hanging upside down.

"It's okay! I'm all right! It's just one of Robin Hood's snares!"

The wolf walks out of the darkness towards him.

"Aw. Hell."

The ninth guard hears the scream. The ninth guard hears something behind him he spins around but Robin Hood covers his mouth so he can't scream. Robin slams him to the ground whispering to him,

"Monsters aren't the only deadly thing that is in Sherwood tonight,"

Robin spins his cape covering them both. The tenth guard runs up to Sir Guy.

"We're dead! We're dead! We're all dead!"

"Where are the others?" Sir Guy demands to know.

"Didn't you hear me? They're dead! We are all dead!"

The tenth guard points behind Sir Guy with an expression of pure terror. Sir Guy spins around to witness a wolf on two legs run down the road toward them in slow motion. The wolf hits the guard onto the ground as it runs by. The tenth guard is knocked onto the ground then blacks out. Only Sir Guy is left. Sir Guy calls out into the dead of night.

"Robin! Robin Hood! I know you are behind all of this! It is no use pretending."

A whistle is heard above Sir Guy, so he tilts his gaze upwards. Robin is sitting in a tree.

"You are a braver man than I, Sir Guy, hunting monsters in the dark."

"You know as well as I do there is no monster, Robin. It's just another one of your tricks."

"Then what is that behind you?"

Robin points behind Sir Guy of Gisbourne. Sir Guy slowly turns around, he trembles before a giant bloodthirsty wolf standing next to him. The paws clamp-down on Sir Guy of Gisbourne's shoulders, he screams like a little girl running off into the night. Little John takes off his wolf costume laughing heartily with Robin.

"Where did you get that sign, Robin?"

"Marian wrote it for me."

The green lights appear again.

"The strange green lights are back. What do they mean, Robin?"

"I don't really know, John. They could be forest spirits. What I do know is we are not alone out here. That I do not like one bit. Come. We are heading to Nottingham Castle."

TWO GUARDS ARE PATROLLING down the castle hallway on the second floor. The first guard speaks to the second over his concerns,

"I always thought that someone could enter the castle using the ivy on the south wall."

"Pshaw! That only works in children's puppet shows." the second guard responds.

Little John and Robin Hood are standing by the bottom of a castle wall that is overgrown by ivy.

"How will you enter the castle, Robin?"

"I think I will climb the ivy on the south wall."

"Is that even possible?"

"Don't worry... I saw it work in a really cool puppet show once."

Robin Hood climbs the thick jumbled ivy growing on the wall. He climbs inside to steal all of the valuables under the Sheriff's very nose. Robin stops at Marian's room, rummaging through her things when a voice cries out from behind him.

"Freeze, you Hood...."

Robin Hood spins around to find Marian in her bed with a crossbow aimed straight between his eyes.

"Did you honestly think you could break into Nottingham Castle?"

"Marian, I can explain...."

"...Without giving me a goodnight kiss?"

Marian shoots the arrow right next to Robin Hood's head; She motions him to step closer. Robin Hood begins a midnight make-out session with Marian. After a while, Robin ceases kissing Marian. He gives her a silver necklace.

"I just robbed a Leprechaun a little while ago. I am not sure how much longer I can take this occupation."

"Leprechauns don't exist, Robin. They are a figment of your imagination that you brought back with you from the Holy Land."

"I have the pot of gold I took stored in a tree-house. I have not been able to bring myself to give it to the poor."

"Have you checked to see if the gold is made of chocolate?"

"What is chocolate?"

"Delicious."

"Marian, do you know how to sew?"

"Yes,"

"Do you know how to sew well?"

"I am regarded by my peers as the best seamstress in London and Nottingham."

"I need you to make me something."

"What do you want?"

Robin whispers into Marian's ear.

"I can do that." Marian says.

"When I left for the Crusade, I thought I would be remembered as a hero. Instead, I will be remembered as a thief and outlaw until I am eventually forgotten."

Marian looks to Robin taking his hand.

"You will be remembered as a great hero. A champion of the oppressed."

Robin kisses her hand.

"I am the Sword of the Lion Heart. I am trained to kill, nothing more. I foolishly thought I could use my skills to fight for good."

"I did not understand what you hoped to achieve when you told me what you were doing for the poor. Now I understand it. What you fight for is not only necessary, but it is good."

"I cannot fight for something I know I am not."

Marian puts her head onto Robin's chest.

"Robin, I know you better than anyone. You have your faults like any other human but deep down you are a good man. You fight for justice in a time that has forgotten it. That is why England believes in you; that is why I will always believe in you."

"Marian. Something is gravely troubling me."

Marian lifts her head, turning it towards Robin Hood.

"What is it, Robin?"

"I was in the Holy Land. It was my 1001st night of senseless violence. My party was ambushed. We fought for our very lives. I saw dear friends of mine killed right in front of my eyes. This was the most savage battle I had ever been in. Our numbers dwindled, so we increased the savagery with which we fought. Just as we made our final stand, a sandstorm hit us. In the storm I saw an attacker, so I shot him with an arrow. It was one of my own men. He barely survived. Nature ended the battle, I carried my wounded man to seek out help."

"What was his name?"

"Priest."

"You shot a Priest?"

"No. His name was Priest. I'll tell you later."

Robin puts his head in Marian's lap then begins sobbing. Marian holds Robin stroking his scalp with her fingers.

"The elders always warned us that war was haunting when we were children. I think I have something that might help you."

Marian writes on a piece of paper.

"What does it say?" Robin asks.

"You still can't read?" Marian says in astonishment.

"I was busy fighting in the Crusade." Robin replies.

"This will be your lesson tonight, the sixth commandment. It says 'Thou shalt not kill.'"

As Robin exits the castle a guard spots him, so the guard fires an arrow, wounding him.

Things Robin Hood can do:

1. Robin Hood can get shot by arrows.

Though Robin is wounded he makes it back to the forest. He stumbles through the forest bleeding until he collapses. Back at Nottingham Castle, the alarm has been raised, news has spread that Robin Hood has been wounded. Marian quickly walks through the castle halls but notices that someone is following. She rounds the corner so that as soon as her pursuer follows around the corner, she knocks him out with her elbow. As it turns out, the one following her was the Court Jester. Marian finds a doctor then takes him through Sherwood Forest. They find an unconscious Robin Hood on the ground.

Marian faces the doctor. "Can you save him?"

The doctor cracks his knuckles. "Don't worry; I'm a Medieval Doctor. I'm the best there is. He's lost some blood. The first thing we need to do is get all the bad blood out. Let's bleed the patient."

The doctor bleeds Robin.

Marian wears a worried expression upon her face. "He looks worse than before... what should we do?"

"Let's bleed the patient some more..."

The doctor bleeds Robin further. Robin Hood, deathly pale, speaks to Marian.

"Marian, bring the doctor closer."

Marian brings the doctor closer. The doctor lowers his head near to Robin Hood on the ground. "Yes?"

Deathly pale, Robin grabs the doctor's throat with an unnatural strength.

"LET'S BLEED THE PATIENT?!?"

CHAPTER XIV

Beneath the Mask

The next morning the Sheriff of Nottingham bursts into Prince John's chamber.

"Prince John, the royal treasury has been looted! We found a black arrow!"

Sir Guy of Gisbourne bursts into the room.

"The entire castle has been burgled of its valuables! There has been a report that Robin Hood has been wounded fleeing the scene."

A Castle Guard enters with Maid Marian.

"We found a black arrow in Maid Marian's room."

Everyone gasps at this announcement.

"What did he do to you, my lady?" The Sheriff politely asks.

Maid Marian's face blushes red.

"He... He stole my panties."

Prince John has an indignant tone in his voice, "The Cur! I will see him hanged for this! Now, my lady; if you will excuse us, we have business to discuss."

"What's a Cur?"

"What?"

"You said Robin Hood is a Cur. I want to know if you know what a Cur is."

Prince John is confused which leads to anger. "Get out! Get out, now!"

Prince John points to the door. Maid Marian seemingly exits but remains outside the door to eavesdrop.

"My brother Richard has been captured by Duke Leopold of Austria, he is being held for ransom in The Holy Roman Empire." Prince John announces.

"How did you find this out?" The Sheriff asks.

"Blondel found my brother then came to inform me...the little bastard," Prince John says.

"What do you intend to do my Lord?" Sir Guy asks.

"We shall dance. I have decided to hold a masquerade ball here in Nottingham Castle. We shall invite all the lords, barons, all the like. We shall dance decadently. I shall let it be known that now I am king."

Maid Marian is listening to all of this behind a slightly open door.

"NO..." Maid Marian whispers under her breath.

Marian rides to Robin Hood's camp. Marian finds him.

"Robin. King Richard is being held for ransom in The Holy Roman Empire. Prince John is holding a masquerade party to proclaim himself king."

Robin Hood grows visibly excited. "Party? I love to party!" Robin Hood becomes visibly animated.

Maid Marian is in disbelief. She realises she is trying to reason with an unreasonable Robin Hood. "Robin! Haven't you listened? King Richard is being held for ransom. Prince John is becoming King!"

"I have this costume I have always wanted to wear."

Robin goes behind a bush to change. Robin comes out in a black cape, a red vest, green tights, black boots, black gloves, flashing a black domino mask. Robin presents himself to Marian.

"So, what do you think?"

"It looks quite litigious." Marian says wryly.

A hundred lords with their ladies arrive at the masquerade party. No one even notices that Robin Hood is among them. Every noble is dancing or otherwise is being entertained. Robin is laughing it up with a large crowd of nobility.

"What I most love about masquerade parties is that everyone is completely anonymous. Say, is that King Richard come back from Holy Crusade?"

Everyone Robin is talking to spins around while Robin Hood throws several purses out of the nearby window.

"Must have been my imagination... but as I was saying, you can mask anything but one's own true nature at these festivities...Look. Look. Isn't that the Pope?"

Everyone paying attention to Robin Hood spins around, He starts throwing several more purses out of the nearby window.

"My mistake, it must have been someone else."

Guy of Gisbourne spots this interesting display from a distance, he is about to step in when a strong arm grips his shoulder. The arm belongs to a figure in a black cloak with the face of the devil.

"Follow me." the devil says to Sir Guy.

Guy of Gisbourne leaves the disguised Robin Hood to his antics, he follows the devil in disguise down to the lowest dungeon. There are other figures in black robes. They wear different masks, one wears a bat mask, one wears a wolf's mask, another wears a goat's mask, one follower wears a boar's mask, the last follower wears a duck-billed platypus' mask because there is no creature on earth as evil as the duck-billed platypus.

The devil in his disguise raises both of his arms. "We have chosen you, Sir Guy of Gisbourne, to join our ranks. We are a clandestine group of lords who worship the Dark Lord. We now join-together in darkness. Hear our call, Lord of the Darkness, Herald of the Day of Reckoning. Come to us to usher the Ragna Rok, the end of all things. Oh, Dark Lord, spawned from The Gorgolac, come to imbue us with your strength, your might, to make the dark ages darker. Sir Guy of Gisbourne, it is time to begin your initiation."

All the black-robed figures begin kicking/stomping the living crap out of Sir Guy of Gisbourne in some good old-fashioned hazing.

A storm brews. Black hail starts to fall as lightning strikes with ever-closer proximity. Finally, lightning strikes Nottingham Castle. Everyone at the masquerade party is stunned by the booming thunder. Then, at the top of the stairway, a blood-red hooded figure appears.

The hooded figure descends the stairs as the entire party's eyes are transfixed on this newcomer. The figure points its finger at Robin Hood, approaching him to offer a hand. Robin cannot see into the eyes of this red-hooded figure but catches the sight of a deathly pale but eerily beautiful mouth with blood-red lips. Robin kisses the hand then begins to dance with the figure cloaked in scarlet.

The violent storm outside is only a pale reflection of the storm raging in the hearts of these two costumed dancers, everyone at the ball stops dancing to watch the display of passion between these two anonymous figures. Finally, the dance is finished, Prince John claps his hands before everyone else follows suit. The two figures take their bows then vanish into the crowds. The Sheriff appears atop a balcony in front of a red curtain looking down upon the crowd.

"My fellow lords and ladies: remember, Jesus saves, but Prince John saves you more with his tax cuts for the rich!"

Prince John steps forward onto the balcony.

"Everyone, I have an announcement. My brother, King Richard, has been taken prisoner by Duke Leopold of Austria. I will not pay the ransom asked of me; but will now declare myself King of England."

The glass windows shatter, cold wind blusters through the halls of Nottingham Castle as all candlelight goes out. Darkness has come.

Atop the castle turret, Robin is counting how much he has stolen this time when Sir Guy of Gisbourne appears sporting a black eye.

"Robin. I knew it was you... all along I knew it was you!"

Guy of Gisbourne goes to draw his sword, but by the time he reaches it, Robin Hood is on top of him, hitting him really hard every time he utters a syllable.

"AS-SAULT-AND-BAT-TER-RY-AS-SAULT-AND-BAT-TER-RY-AS-SAULT-AND-BAT-TER-RY-AS-SAULT-AND-BAT-TER-RY!"

After Robin Hood assaults Gisbourne twenty-four times, he collects his booty then leaves Gisbourne on the roof with another black eye, a split lip, a broken nose, plus the memory of receiving the beating of his life. Robin Hood begins to walk away from Nottingham Castle towards Sherwood Forest with his ill-gotten gains when a voice cries.

"Robin!"

Robin Hood spins around. "Marian, I thought I missed you at the party."

"I wanted to talk to you about our relationship."

"What is it, Marian?"

"You know as well as I do long-distance relationships rarely ever work."

"Then come with me. Be with me in the forest. Be by my side. It will be like old times." Robin says. He is charming to Marian.

"If I am going to live in Sherwood Forest with you, I want a house. I am not sleeping in the mud." Marian bargains.

"But I like the mud... You stopped me for that?" Robin asks Marian.

"Well, when was the last time you did anything romantic for me?" Marian asks Robin.

"I protected you from that ravenous beast!" Robin Hood replies.

"NO. You got really drunk and punched a raccoon!" Marian bitches.

"Yeah! But I did it for you!" Robin retorts.

"It was the only Raccoon in England, Robin!" Marian scolds.

CHAPTER XV

The Greenhorn of Sherwood Forest

B ack at Nottingham Castle, it is night-time. Marian is sitting, distracted while her paid servant Sarah watches her. Marian doesn't have to pay Sarah, but she was always generous towards Sarah for some reason. Sarah is short but very feminine. She has long brown hair with green eyes like Marian. Sarah has a decent bust size, but while Sarah isn't as stunning as Marian, Sarah has that hot girl next door look going for her. Marian is sitting at the window looking towards the horizon.

"I know that look." Sarah remarks.

"What?" Marian asks.

Sarah giggles.

"You are somewhere right now." Sarah says.

"What do you mean?"

"You are somewhere. Somewhere that is not here."

"Sarah. Haven't you ever wanted something out of life? Something that can't be given. Something that you must take."

"I am here only to serve you, my lady. The question you are asking is for yourself. What do you want out of life?"

"To go into the forest. To live in the forest." Marian says.

"What is there in the forest that you want?" Sarah asks.

"Freedom. Adventure. Love."

"Those are all good reasons, my lady."

"But I would have to sacrifice so much. If I do it there may be no coming back. What do you think I should do?" Marian asks.

"I think that everyone must sacrifice much to obtain things like freedom, adventure, and love. But those three things make the sacrifice worth it."

"But what should I do about it?"

"Only what your heart tells you. That is all anyone can do." Sarah answers.

"I'll leave for the forest tonight. Follow me into the forest tomorrow night, Sarah."

"If it pleases you."

Marian fetches a horse then rides deep into Sherwood Forest. She arrives at Robin's camp. Robin and Marian embrace one another kissing passionately.

"I am here to join you and your merry band, Robin. I am here to be by your side in the forest."

Robin smiles.

"Nothing could ever make me happier, my love."

Marian wakes up next to Robin, she slides her fingers across his bare stomach up to his face. *He's so warm.*

Robin is having bad dreams, "No. N-no. No. uh. uh."

Marian puts her finger to his lips.

"Shhhhhhh."

Marian kisses him on the forehead so that Robin calms down. Marian begins cooking breakfast frying deer steak. She applies seasoning that she thought to bring with her. Marian flips the meat as it sizzles on the pan. Robin wakes up to the tasty odour of deer steak. He rises and walks over to Marian. He kisses her gently on the cheek. Marian turns her head to Robin.

"Good morning, handsome."

"I am glad you are here with me." says Robin Hood.

"Do you have my bow?"

"I put on a slightly longer string for you until you get back into the swing of things."

"Shall we have some target practice?" Marian asks.

"After breakfast."

Marian serves up the steak. They eat together.

"It is time for your next lesson. Write down the letters R-O-B-I-N-H-O-O-D." Marian says.

Robin Hood writes it down.

"What is it?" Robin asks.

"Your name."

"Robin of Locksley?"

"Robin Hood." Marian replies.

"Oh."

"Now write down your last lesson."

Robin Hood writes it down.

"Rob-in Hood. Thou shalt not kill." Robin reads aloud.

"You are learning." Marian says.

Robin takes Marian leading her to the Sherwood path. They find a scout hanging upside down. Robin and Marian aim their arrows at him.

"When are the taxes coming through?" Robin asks.

"I am telling you nothing!" The Scout shouts back.

Robin Hood looks to Marian.

"Shall we have some target practice?" He asks.

Marian shoots her arrow into the Scout's left nut.

"AAAAH!"

"No. No. That is not how we are doing things. Watch and learn."

Robin shoots his arrow narrowly missing the Scout.

"You're a worse shot than the woman, Hood!" the Scout says.

"Don't let him talk to you that way, Robin! Do something." Marian says.

Robin shoots an arrow into the Scout's right nut.

"AAAAH!"

"Where are the taxes?" Robin Hood questions.

"They are at the edge of Sherwood Forest. They are not coming through until I report the coast is clear!" The Scout says.

"I guess you can hang around here." Robin retorts.

Robin Hood spins around to Marian holding out his hand.

"Come with me."

The guards are standing by the carriage. Arrows zip out of the forest whistling through the legs of the guards. All the guards fall to the ground immobilized. Marian grabs the medallion a guard is clutching. Robin and Marian clamber onto the carriage driving it off into the forest back to the camp. Robin and Marian ride the carriage into the camp, the Merry Men unload the gold.

"The driver was carrying this medallion close to him. Do you think it is worth something?" Marian asks.

Robin Hood inspects the Medallion. He bites it.

"The Medallion is Bronze. It's worthless." Robin Hood says.

"Can I keep it then?" She asks.

"Sure, why not?" He says.

"This is so fun, going on adventures with you, Robin. What is the next adventure?"

"The next adventure is cooking lunch."

Cook your own lunch.

Marian smiles.

"Sure thing honey." She says.

Marian cooks Robin lunch.

"I hope the next adventure is better than lunch," Marian complains.

"The next adventure is much better. This adventure involves you scrubbing all of our pots and pans."

Cut off his thumbs and make him scrub the pots and pans.

Marian has trouble smiling.

"Whatever you say, sweetie." She says through clenched teeth.

Marian cleans all the pots and pans. Marian realises this sucks.

"There, it's finally done. Now, can we go on a new adventure that doesn't suck?" Marian asks.

"The next adventure is even better than all of my previous adventures. The next adventure is you doing all of our laundries." Robin Hood says happily.

"What?"

"Everyone else has done the laundry. It's your turn,"

Drown him in the washtub and take over the gang yourself!

Marian smiles. Robin pats her on the head so she gives Robin Hood the finger as he spins around to walk away.

Marian does all of Robin Hood and his Merry Men's laundry. It takes her all the time in the afternoon until it is evening. Robin Hood is with his Merry Men.

"Watch from the trees as I propose to Marian; then leap out and shout 'surprise.'"

Robin Hood puts the ring into his palm then closes his hand. Robin walks up to Marian.

"Marian it is time you went on the greatest adventure of your life. Will you..."

Marian slugs Robin really, really hard in the stomach; She Marathons back to Nottingham Castle. Robin is lying on the ground limp as all his Merry Men leap out of the trees.

"Surprise!"

Marian enters her chamber through the window and moves behind her dressing screen. She changes out of her green clothing back into her red dress. She emerges from behind her screen walking by the fireplace.

"I was just about to leave." Sarah says.

"Well don't." Marian grumbles.

"What happened in the forest?" Sarah asks.

"I don't want to talk about it."

"What about Robin Hood?"

"What about him?" Marian asks.

"You love him, don't you?"

Maid Marian is shocked by this.

"How do you know about that?"

"You spoke of love then left for Sherwood Forest the same night. Twenty-four hours later you return looking rather vexed. I am not stupid my lady. You are in love with the outlaw." Sarah says.

"I am found out. Will you tell anyone?"

"No. I am a servant my lady. I most of all understand the importance of a secret love."

"You are good to me, Sarah. I am glad you did not leave for the forest."

"Something told me you would be back."

"Have you told the person you secretly love how you feel?"

"I am not nearly as brave as you. Someday. Maybe someday."

The Sheriff of Nottingham bursts into the chamber.

"Where have you been all day?" The Sheriff demands.

"I have been in Nottingham all day." Sarah says.

"Not you! Marian. Where have you been?"

Marian points to Sarah.

"With her!"

"Oh! Well... just so you know some Knights Templar were robbed this morning by Robin Hood and the Lady in Green," The Sheriff says.

"Who is the Lady in Green?" Marian asks.

"I do not know. Since you have a history with Robin Hood, I just thought..."

"Thought what?"

Marian along with Sarah look at him with contempt and folded arms. The Sheriff smiles awkwardly,

"...Nothing! Pay me no mind! I shall find Robin Hood's whore soon enough."

The Sheriff of Nottingham exits through the door closing it behind him. Marian throws her pillow at the door. Marian sits down on her bed folding her arms.

"Robin Hood's whore indeed!" Marian snorts.

Marian pulls out her medallion deciding to finally read it. Marian gasps.

"This is the key to the release of the Lion Heart."

CHAPTER XVI

The Boys are Back in Town

Marian is in the courtyard feeding the pigeons. She has snow-white pigeons resting on her shoulder and hand. A voice emerges from the shadows.

"In all my years, I have never seen an angel live among the demons until now..."

Robin Hood emerges from the courtyard shadows causing the pigeons to fly off Marian.

"What do you want, Robin?"

"Why do you spend all this time in the courtyard feeding the birds? Why can't we just have sex?"

"But Robin... if I don't feed the pigeons, who will? Anyway, I have a gift for you..."

Maid Marian presents Robin Hood with a box. Robin opens it. He observes there is a pie inside.

"I have been waiting to give this to you for a while now."

"Why thank you Marian I don't know what to s-"

Marian shoves the pie into Robin's face. Robin spits out pie.

"Now that that's settled, listen to me very closely, Robin. There is literally a king's ransom being held in a haunted house near Sherwood. If you can steal it, I have set up a meeting on the shores of Sussex tomorrow night to pay for my cousin's ransom. Don't ask me how I did it, let's just say I have connections."

That night Robin is sitting underneath a tree, with many flags mixed with decorations in it, Marian lay on the grass by his side. Sitting upon a small hill, Robin Hood and Maid Marian gaze upon his castle.

"So, what was it like fighting in the Crusades?" Marian asks.

"The Muslim people call it Jihad... In Arabic it means struggle, it means Holy War in Islam, it is kind of an oxymoron. There is nothing Holy about committing atrocities in the name of a compassionate god. The Christians and Muslims alike have spilt blood in the Holy Land. Even if the Crusades stop tomorrow, the bloodshed will continue long after we are all dead. If the bloodthirst grows out of control it will consume all of mankind; all that will be left is nature. Man likes to tell himself how great he is without having to face his demons."

"Isn't there any hope?" Marian asks.

"I seem to have lost it. I have lost all hope in this world controlled by theocracy. Monarchies are willing to sacrifice everything to gain favour with this theocracy, yet I am equally doubtful about democracy. I don't know where hope lies anymore."

"Love." Marian says.

"What?"

"If mankind can learn to love as much as it has learned to hate there might be hope. Where there is love there is hope."

Robin Hood smiles. He and Marian passionately kiss one another. The green lights appear.

"Marian, it's those lights again, do you see?"

"I see them. Robin, come with me."

Marian grabs Robin's hand. They embark towards the lights.

"You want to follow the lights?" Robin asks.

"Are you afraid Robin?"

"I fear nothing."

"Come."

Robin Hood and Maid Marian continue towards the place of the lights. They see people in the woods carrying green lanterns. They follow to where the light is gathered.

"We are witnessing a rare moment in history, Robin. The forest god is dying. When he dies, so does the green light, then his religion. We are witnesses to the death of the old religion in England."

The green lanterns die out. Everybody leaves.

"It is done. England is now truly a Christian nation." Marian says.

"Maybe that is not such a bad thing..." Robin remarks. "Wait...What about the Jews?"

"Um...I think we killed them all while Richard was away."

"............Sucks."

THE MERRY MEN ARE LYING on their backs in the forest mud bitterly staring at the full moon.

"No women!" Says Mulch the miller's son.

"No women!" says Alan A. Dale.

"Where's Robin?" Asks Little John.

"With a woman..." Friar Tuck answers.

The Merry Men lay in defeat. "Uuuuuuuugggggghhhhh...."

Little John snaps.

"That tears it! I'm going to go get a woman!"

"Me too!" Alan says.

THE BOYS ARE BACK IN TOWN![14]

Little John is sitting at a bar table in Ye Olde Trip To Jerusalem. He's drumming the table with his hands. He could have been a Beatle in another time. Little John's jam is interrupted when he is served a pint of ale by a buxom waitress.

"Oh, my dainty little duck, if you join me in the alley, I bet I can make you quack in under three minutes..."

The buxom waitress slaps him.

THE BOYS ARE BACK IN TOWN!

Alan A. Dale is at the bar table wolfing down a lot of cookies.

"Are you going to pay for those?" Asks a glamorous female cook.

"With what?" Alan asks.

The female cook punches him in the face.

THE BOYS ARE BACK IN TOWN!

Mulch, the miller's son wakes up on the couch hungover, he finds a crossbow pointed right between his eyes by the home's owner. Neither of them says a word. The homeowner has his crossbow pointed at Mulch, the miller's son until he gets out of the house.

BECAUSE THE BOYS ARE BACK IN TOWN!

THAT EVENING, ROBIN travells through the foreboding woods. Coming to a decrepit haunting farmhouse in the woods, Robin walks up the creaking steps only to find that the door is locked. Robin starts picking the lock. Ink shoots out of the keyhole hitting Robin in the face.

"Gaaaah!"

Robin Hood resumes picking the lock, more ink shoots out of the keyhole hitting Robin in the face.

"AAAAAARRRRRGGGGGHHH!!!!"

Robin breaks down the door with his foot. Robin Hood spots a piece of string hanging from the ceiling with a sign that he can read.

"'Do. Not. Pull.' Oh yeah? I'll show you!"

Robin Hood pulls the string; is thus promptly pummeled into the floor by a giant boxing glove. Robin slowly claws himself out from under the boxing glove. Standing up, Robin Hood notices that the next door is slightly ajar. Opening the door, a small vat of molasses covers Robin. Robin Hood proceeds to trip on a wire falling down the stairs, landing in a pile of red feathers at the bottom.

It is at the bottom that Robin Hood finds the king's ransom. One hundred fifty-one chests of gold surround Robin Hood. The Emissary is standing on the shores of Sussex looking into the distance at the ship.

"The ship is waiting off the coast." Says the Deckhand.

"Funny that no one has come... you would think England might want its king back." Says the Emissary.

"Wait! What is that in the distance?"

"It kind of looks like... a giant robin!?"

Robin Hood shows up covered in feathers. "I have the payment for King Richard's release..."

"Only one chest of gold? The ransom is quite a bit higher than that," the Emissary remarks.

Robin opens the chest; it's full of purple. The Emissary moves his hand to touch the purple. Robin closes the chest pulling it away.

"It's not gold, it is yours, but King Richard must be released." Robin says.

"And released he shall be, but whom shall I tell him paid his ransom?" The emissary asks.

"Robin."

"Hell yeah! I called it!"

CHAPTER XVII

Double Robin Hood

That same evening in Nottingham Castle, the Court Jester is performing for King John, the Sheriff of Nottingham, Sir Guy of Gisbourne, with their guest the Lady Marian. The Jester's audience sits on chairs that rest on the stone dais.

"And for my next trick, I will saw the lady Marian in half!"

The Court Jester takes Lady Marian by the hand, He leads her to the box. He helps her inside. He shuts the box. Thusly he saws Maid Marian in half. He separates both halves, spinning them around as he juggles six swords. After sufficient time he removes the swords and puts her back together again. The Sheriff stands up pointing at the jester.

"He sawed Maid Marian in half and put her back together again! He's got the devil in him! Throw him in the dungeon then whip the bloody snot out of him!"

The castle guards throw the Court Jester in the dungeon then whip the bloody snot out of him.

THE NEXT MORNING THE Sheriff of Nottingham is in King John's quarters. The Sheriff is standing behind King John while King John sits sipping on a goblet of wine.

"I have thought of a way to capture Robin Hood," The Sheriff says in a muted tone of voice.

"...And what is that?" King John asks.

"We will play on Robin Hood's own vanity. He is an outlaw, so we shall crown a new King of the May Games. We will hold an archery contest with a golden arrow as a prize." The Sheriff answers louder.

"That is a stupid prize. This plan will never work." King John says.

"The winner will be presented a golden arrow with a kiss from the Lady Marian."

King John strokes his beard.

"Hmmm. Pimping out Maid Marian to catch an outlaw... it just might work."

IT IS THE DAY OF THE archery contest, a large crowd has gathered to watch the finest archers in all of England compete. There is a rumor that Robin Hood is somewhere among them. There is a series of targets on a range. King John, Maid Marian, Sir Guy, and the Sheriff sit on a Dais looking upon the tournament.

"The winner of this contest will be King of the May Games, receive the Golden Arrow with a kiss from the Lady Marian." Proclaims the announcer.

The archery contest begins. The archers let their arrows fly. Only four hit the bullseye.

"Mulch the miller's son, Robin Hood, the man who looks like Robin Hood wearing a cheap moustache, and the Silent Archer may continue...The rest are disqualified."

The Archers fire their arrows again. This time only Robin Hood and the man who looks like Robin Hood wearing a cheap moustache hit the Bullseye.

"Mulch the miller's son along with the Silent Archer are disqualified, only Robin Hood and the man who looks like Robin Hood wearing a cheap moustache may remain..."

Guy of Gisbourne snaps.

"Enough! We all know it's Robin Hood wearing a cheap moustache!"

Guy of Gisbourne walks up to him ripping off the moustache.

"OOOOOOOOUUUUUUUCCCCHHHHHH!!!!!!"

Robin Hood taps Sir Guy on the shoulder, Sir Guy glimpses Robin's face without the cheap moustache only a moment before the real Robin cold clocks Sir Guy. The real Robin Hood helps up the man who looks like Robin Hood. King John spits out the wine he is drinking from his goblet.

"There are two of them? Which one is the real Robin Hood?"

Robin points his finger towards himself.

"I am Robin Hood."

The man who looks like Robin Hood points towards Robin Hood.

"He is Robin Hood."

"You would like me to think that wouldn't you?" King John shouts with disdain.

"A test of skill will suffice," Robin Hood says.

"It really would." The lookalike Robin Hood adds.

"Robin Hood! Quit trying to get yourself hanged." Marian chastises.

"Don't worry about it, Marian, even if I lose King John will still swing us both."

King John folds his arms.

"Indeed."

"The two remaining archers will share a target. The target shall be moved another twenty paces." Proclaims the announcer.

The man who looks like Robin Hood fires his arrow hitting the target dead center. The Sheriff stands up. "No living man could beat that shot! He is Robin Hood!"

Robin Hood splits the arrow. The Sheriff sits down. "Bollocks."

"Robin split the arrow! Robin Hood wins!" The announcer shouts.

"That's not fair! I hit dead center first! He just shot it in the same place I did!" The lookalike Robin Hood says.

"Sudden death! The target shall be moved another ten paces!"

The entire crowd bursts into a murmur while Sir Guy of Gisbourne regains consciousness again. The man who looks like Robin Hood fires his arrow. The arrow hits the first circle around the bullseye. Robin closes his eyes regulating his breathing, he concentrates to feel his target.

Robin senses the wind blowing off his arrowhead. Robin opens his eyes, focusing sharp, then lets his arrow take flight. Robin hits the bullseye again as it splits his arrow once more. A hush falls over the crowd. Robin starts walking up the large wooden dais towards Marian giving her a knowing look.

"I'll trouble you for that kiss my lady." Robin Hood says.

Maid Marian goes to peck Robin Hood on the cheek but Robin Hood grabs Marian, dips her over then begins sucking face. Marian flails her arms about as Robin Hood is still kissing her. Marian's arms begin flailing in circular motions as a full minute has passed since they began kissing. Suddenly, Marian begins enjoying Robin's passion so much she raises her thigh.

"Enough of this farce! I hereby place Robin Hood under arrest for crimes against the Crown." Sir Guy shouts.

Robin Hood grabs the golden arrow off the pillow; He rams it straight through Guy of Gisbourne's right thigh.

"AAAAAAAAHHHHH!!!! SSSSSSS. AAAAAAAAAAAH-HHH!!!!"

Robin Hood tries fighting his way out but is subdued. Robin is put on his knees before King John with several swords pointed at his back.

"Are there any last words of the infamous Robin Hood before he is hanged?" The Sheriff asks.

"Marian..."

"Yes, Robin?"

"Did you catch last week's show of Punch and Judy? That was so us."

The lookalike Robin Hood steps forward. "Wait! I am Robin Hood!"

Mulch the miller's son steps forward. "I am Robin Hood!"

Little John steps forward. "No! I am Robin Hood!"

A man in a black mask runs up to the front of the crowd. "NO! I AM ROBIN HOOD!!!"

The man in the black mask mounts a black horse then rides off laughing maniacally into the distance. Robin Hood stares at King John; he smiles turning King John livid with anger.

"You're not Robin Hood! You're not Robin Hood! You're not Robin Hood!! And I think that was Rob Roy who stole my favourite horse!!!"

Robin Hood stands before King John. "He stole my horse too, let's get him!"

King John points at Robin Hood. "Shut up! You die first! Executioner! Kill Robin Hood!"

The Executioner wears a guard's uniform. The Executioner starts shaking his black hood. "I can't kill Robin Hood! He saved my buddy's life in Jaffa!"[15] The Executioner drops his war axe.

The Black Knight runs across the tournament field screaming his head off, as he is burning alive. Maid Marian points, screaming, "BUUUUUUUURRRRNNNING MAAAAAAAAAAAANNNNNNNN!!!!"

The entire place transforms into one giant mosh pit giving Robin Hood the chance he needs to escape. Robin is barreling through Sherwood Forest pursued by the Sheriff of Nottingham leading a garrison of soldiers under his command. Robin Hood zigzags his way through the brush trying to dodge the arrows being shot at him.

Robin Hood dives behind a bush entering into his burrow. Robin Hood observes a soldier standing outside his burrow. Robin listens.

A soldier's voice whispers loudly. "Where is he? Do you see him?"

"I don't see him. He could be anywhere." The second soldier's voice whispers back.

Robin Hood listens to a third soldier's voice.

"The way he dresses in green makes him look like part of the forest. Where is he?"

Robin Hood emerges behind the soldier standing outside his burrow. He uses his bow to crush the soldier's neck. Robin Hood whacks the bow against the nearby soldier's head, knocking him out. Robin shoots an arrow into the face of the third soldier standing in the distance. Robin Hood sprints past the trees as dozens of arrows whiz past his head hitting the tree trunks. Robin Hood gets to the spot he is running to, then spins around standing firm. The Sheriff leads his men on horseback riding towards Robin Hood, Robin draws his sword. This is the signal so Robin can spring his own trap.

Dozens of Merry Archers in the trees hit the Sheriff of Nottingham along with his soldiers in the crossfire. Robin Hood walks up to the Sheriff of Nottingham who has an arrow in the leg.

"My, oh my, how fickle the finger of fate is. I walk straight into your trap this afternoon, by evening you walk straight into my trap. We are the mighty trappers... Men, tie them up, gag them, it's time we celebrated..."

CHAPTER XVIII

A Celebration Gone Awry

It is generally agreed among historians that Robin Hood and his Merry Men never smoked pot. However, it is also generally agreed among historians that Robin Hood and his Merry Men never existed. But if Robin Hood and his Merry Men did exist and did smoke pot, this is probably what it would look like.

Robin Hood and his Merry Men are holding a Kegger. Little John is inventing the game of Ro Sham Bo with Friar Tuck. Friar Tuck holds two pitchers of ale, Little John kicks him in the nuts causing Friar Tuck to drop the pitchers, thus losing the game. Robin has his bow drawn with a lit joint in his mouth. Eight Merry Men surround him each with an apple on his head. Robin is blindfolded then spun around a few times.

"Remember kids, I am a trained professional." Mutters Robin Hood.

Robin Hood splits eight apples in six seconds. Everyone bursts into applause. Impressed, Maid Marian takes Robin by the hand, leading him away.

"Where did Robin go?" Alan A. Dale asks.

"Marian led him into the forest five minutes ago." Little John replies.

"Do you mean Maid Marian?" Alan asks.

"Not anymore..." Little John grumbles.

"WHHHOOOOOOOOOOOOOOO!!! Go, Robin!"

Robin and Marian are alone in the forest together. The light of the party is in the distance behind them as they venture deeper into the forest. Marian leads Robin to their old training area. The old target is still there. The stump Robin pulled his father's sword out of is still there too, minus a sword. Robin and Marian listen to the nearby river.

"What are we doing here?" Robin Hood finally asks.

"It is time for your final lesson. Read this."

Marian pulls out a piece of paper, handing it to Robin.

"Re-ward of 100 coin for the capture of the out-law known as Robin Hood Prince of Thieves."

Marian rolls over the piece of paper.

"Robin Hood is a champ-ion of the op-pressed, Hero of England-and the true love of Marian Fitz-water."

Robin lowers the paper realising Marian is smiling at him.

Robin smiles back at Marian. They embrace each other kissing. Robin begins kissing Marian on the shoulder, he goes up to her neck. Marian closes her eyes tilting her head back.

"It's my Birthday." Robin smoothly says.

Marian perks up a little. "Do you want me to give it to you now?"

Robin shakes his head. "No. I am going to give it to you. You see that tree over there?"

Robin points to a tree with a target carved into the bark.

Marian nods. "Yes."

"I want to see if the old Marian is back. I want you to bullseye the target."

Robin hands Marian a bow and arrow. Marian draws the bow with her right hand, firing the arrow into the center of the target.

Marian looks at Robin smiling. "The old Marian never left."

Robin throws his knife into the dead center of the target split-ting Marian's arrow. They go up to the tree. Robin pulls out his knife from the tree sheathing it. Robin pins Marian between him and the tree. Little John alongside Alan A. Dale listen to screaming. Alan looks at Little John. "I didn't know she was a screamer. "

Marian is sitting next to the tree. Robin walks towards Marian.

"Here. Let me help you..." Robin grabs Marian's dress ripping it.

"Robin! You have robbed my honour!"

Marian stands up then punches Robin Hood in the cheek.

Robin loses balance then falls down. Marian kicks the shit out of Robin Hood while he is down. Marian drags Robin Hood, she throws him a short distance into the river. Robin swims back to shore downriver. He walks back to where Marian was. Robin Hood follows Marian back to the base camp as the Merry Men start drinking and singing.

> *"Pass the ale and pour the wine,*
> *It's time to drink and finely dine,*
> *Pour the wine and drink the ale,*
> *It's time to be merry and to regale,*
> *In the morn, we'll commit more crime,*
> *We'll hit the roads and rob you blind,*
> *It is Robin Hood that we hail,*
> *The greatest hero of any Tale."*

Robin Hood leaps on top of the table holding a goblet of wine, he gives the most drunk and belligerent speech since the last time he got drunk and belligerent.

"Little John, my right-hand man, so good with his staff and his hands, you completely forget he never finished the second grade and is therefore illiterate."

The Merry Men laugh at Little John. Robin grows short.

"Don't laugh! More than half of you are illiterate dropouts! The lot of you are so badly screwed up I've been forced to church you up!

But since I can't manage to bring you to church; I've been forced to bring the church to you! That brings us to Friar Tuck! This drunk thinks God created the universe with a big bang, the earth revolves around the sun, get this... he doesn't think the earth is flat, he actually thinks it's round!"

The Merry Men laugh at Friar Tuck.

"The wise Socrates once said you can't go through life without the good, the good being pleasure, because without the good, the rest is not good enough!" Robin says.

Marian stands up. She points accusingly at Robin. "That's not what he said, and you know it!"

"Eat me!"

Robin Hood beats his chest.

"Finally, there is a fox in the hen-house men, its name is Marian! Sexy, foxy little Marian... You see that?"

Robin points to Marian's chest.

"That's mine! It belongs to me!"

"Her breasts?" Mulch asks.

"Her heart numb-skull. Oh yeah, one more thing... Earlier tonight, I fought the law, and the law lost! I have them tied up out back. Go kick the crap out of them for being different from us then toss them in the creek while I make out with my girlfriend!"

Robin Hood makes out with Marian for two full minutes. When the Merry Men return, Marian makes a proclamation.

"Happy birthday, Robin, this is from me."

Marian gives Robin Hood his birthday present. Robin Hood opens the gift. Robin looks incredulously at the gift. "Tights? "

"They are forest green and everything," Marian chirps.

"Tights, Marian?" Robin says in all kinds of crazy.

"I spent all week sewing them just for you." Marian says proudly.

"You got me tights for my birthday? I hate tights!"

Robin throws his goblet of wine.

"Get out! Get out! Get out right now! Get out all of you! I hate you all!"

Marian pulls out a knife. "You little black-hearted beast! I'm going to cut you!"

Little John grabs his hat. "Look out! Marian has gone crazy! And she gots a knife on her!"

A knife-wielding Marian chases Robin Hood around the party.

"Who gave that crazy bitch a knife?" Robin shouts.

They run around the table zigzagging around the party. Robin hops across the table quickly followed by Marian. Robin trips flying upside down onto the ground when Marian catches up to him.

Little John goes to take the knife, but she cuts his hand with a nice gash. She raises her knife at the surrounding men, so the other Merry Men back off.

Robin is on his knees shaking his hands before Marian. "Oh. God, please, I don't want to die."

"Run."

Robin Hood takes off. Marian chases Robin into the wilderness, through the foliage, across a ravine. Robin hides behind a bush, fearfully peering outwards, but he cannot see Marian. Robin Hood spins around as Marian slashes his arm with a knife. Marian drops the knife. She puts both her hands over her mouth.

"Robin, you're hurt!"

"Of course I'm hurt. You just cut my arm with a knife."

Robin is holding his hand over the gash keeping pressure on the wound, which was something he learned in combat.

"Wha- What- What should I do?" Marian asks.

"Go fetch a doctor, quickly!" Robin orders.

Robin Hood passes out. When he awakens, Marian is standing over him with the Quack Doctor.

"He's bleeding all over! What should we do?" Marian asks.

"It looks like it's only a flesh wound. We need to get the bad blood out before it becomes infected. Give me my leeches," The doctor says.

"You didn't bring any leeches," Marian answers.

"Then it's all over for him unless I amputate his arm!"

Robin has had enough. "The day I let a Quack Doctor amputate my arm over a recent flesh wound is the day I lose my mind! Marian, fetch a hot ember, bring a needle, along with those green tights, I have blood all over my clothes."

Robin Hood emerges from the bushes. He stands before his gathered men.

"Men, I may have gotten a little drunk and belligerent."

"A little?" A random Merry Man shouts.

Robin acts like he was stung. "It was only because today I have turned twenty-four, meaning I am to die in roughly ten years... only if one of you doesn't knife me in my sleep first. Friar Tuck, I have my eye on you." Robin points at Friar Tuck.

Friar Tuck opens his hands. "I am a man of God, Robin. You can trust me." A knife drops from Friar Tuck's sleeve. All the Merry Men laugh.

CHAPTER XIX

It's a Trap!

The Sheriff of Nottingham strolls through Nottingham Village with Sir Guy of Gisbourne. They are collecting taxes accompanied by a few guards. They walk out of one of the houses in Nottingham.

"We have collected taxes from everyone, Sheriff. It is time to return to the castle." Sir Guy remarks.

"That's the problem with you, Gisbourne. You don't know how to open new markets." The Sheriff scolds.

The Sheriff grabs a child heading to school while Sir Guy leads his men, rounding up the other children.

"Give me all of your lunch money!"

"Hey, I need that. My parents gave me that lunch money for my first day of school." The child says, his voice wavering with fear.

"A freshman huh? I know how to deal with freshmen." The Sheriff says coldly.

Sir Guy opens a small wooden box, there is a wooden paddle resting on a soft velvet pillow inside. The Sheriff of Nottingham grabs the wooden paddle spinning it in his hand a few times. The Sheriff starts wailing on the kid for about seven minutes. On the eighth minute, three arrows pierce the wooden paddle. The Sheriff drops the paddle spinning around. Atop the nearest home is the silhouette of a hood and cloak in front of a rising sun.

The figure launches straight up into the sky, landing on the ground. Robin Hood begins to bounce around the six guards like a human pinball, striking blows so fast, so furious that the soldiers have little time to react before they are knocked out. Robin saves the freshmen, but the Sheriff springs his trap. Many knights with crossbows appear.

The Sheriff of Nottingham has a complete shit-eating grin plastered onto his face. "Nice outfit, Hood. I will make sure to bury you in it. Gisbourne tells me you are good enough to dodge an arrow, but we have many arrows. Worse yet, you are surrounded by innocent villagers. Will you miraculously dodge all our arrows only to let innocent blood spill? Or will you stand perfectly still, and see the so-called Robin Hood legend through to its inevitable conclusion?"

Robin Hood looks around to see a gathered crowd and several men with crossbows surrounding him. Robin looks to the Sheriff and nods.

"Guards! Fire!" The Sheriff shouts with merciless conviction.

Robin Hood is pumped full of arrows. Robin Hood goes down. The Sheriff of Nottingham walks up to the collapsed body of Robin Hood.

"Not much of a legend after all, are you, Hood?"

Robin stands up screaming. Four guards rush Robin Hood. Robin punches two knights in front of him, elbows two knights behind him, finally he reverse-punches them in the face as their abdomens swing down.

The Sheriff is standing there completely stunned. "Wait, what? Oh shit! Gambeson! He's wearing a gambeson! Swordsmen!"

The swordsmen rush out. Robin dashes over to a pole at the market shop corner. He leaps to the pole grabbing it, he swings around sideways kicking a swordsman. Robin leaps upwards grabbing a beam, he kicks two more swordsmen. The crowd begins cheering. Robin notices the Sheriff grab his bow so he can break it on his knee. Robin observes the guards are regrouping. Robin unsheathes his sword and begins striding, sliding, and leaping. Robin is killing the shit out of the guards. Robin fights his way up the stairs to the top of the wall. Robin dodges arrows and strikes them out of the air with his sword. The crowd begins chanting.

"Robin Hood! Robin Hood! Robin Hood! Robin Hood! Robin Hood! Robin Hood! Robin Hood!"

Sir Guy looks up at Robin Hood fighting swordsmen on the wall. "He's a legend."

Robin gains two swords then finishes off the crossbowmen. Robin looks down, he notices that both the Sheriff and Sir Guy are gone. "I finally showed my hand. Now they know."

Inside Nottingham Castle, the Sheriff and Sir Guy are walking up the castle stairs. The Sheriff slams Sir Guy into the wall. "You're a grimy little pimp who will never amount to anything... wait a minute... are you wearing eyeliner, Sir Guy?"

Sir Guy looks away raising his palms. "Don't look at me!"

The Sheriff of Nottingham lets out a sigh. "King John is coming, so I am going to have to explain to him how Hood escaped... yet again. I am sure as hell not doing it sober. Servant girl! Where is my wine?"

KING JOHN ARRIVES BY Royal Carriage. The Royal Carriage is covered in arrows. King John arrives in nothing but his knickers.

"My king?" The Sheriff asks.

King John storms past fuming.

"Robin Hood dies!" He snarls.

King John gets dressed. He sits on his throne by the fire, tapping his fingers against the arm of his chair. King John, the Sheriff of Nottingham, and Sir Guy begin discussing Robin Hood.

"It's funny. Every time we think we finally have Robin Hood, he manages to slip through our fingers. Strange isn't it?" King John asks.

"I seem to remember the night Robin Hood broke into Nottingham Castle. He was reportedly wounded. Yet he seemed to be in perfect health later." Sir Guy adds.

"Yes, the following morning there was a black arrow found in Maid Marian's room. He stole her panties as I recall." The Sheriff says.

"Did you see the way he kissed her at the archery contest?" King John asks.

"Now that you bring it up, wasn't it Marian who caused the distraction that allowed the outlaw to escape?" Sir Guy asks.

"This means she has been acting as Robin's spy. Bring her here." The Sheriff of Nottingham orders his guard.

Marian is brought before King John and his lackeys. King John's face is boiling over in rage. "Maid Marian, you have been aiding, abetting, and acting as an accomplice to a known outlaw. Before we pass sentence on you, do you have anything to say for yourself?"

Marian decides this is the opportunity to finally say her piece. "Yes, I do! John, you are a usurper and a drunken swine of a ruler. Your two lackeys are as bad as you are. Sheriff, or should I say, Eustace of Lowdham, your duty is to protect the people, but you beat up school children for their lunch money on a daily basis. You are an evil amoral man; however, I find myself questioning why that makes me so hot for you? And you, Guy. Guuuuyyyyy... Every time I see you making kissy faces at me, it makes me want to puke!!" Marian finishes.

"Take her and imprison her in the castle dungeon!" The Sheriff barks.

"I can't wait until Robin Hood and his Merry band of twits and arrows get medieval on your sorry asses!" Marian shouts.

Guards escort Marian into the castle dungeon. They place her in her cell. The Court Jester witnesses this, so he frees himself from his shackles, then walks over to Marian's cell.

"Lady Marian, don't worry, I will rescue you."

The Court Jester begins to pick the lock. Ink shoots out of the keyhole into the Court Jester's face.

"Gaaaaah!"

Marian begins to plead. "Jester! Find Robin for me! Tell him what has transpired! Quickly!"

The Jester takes off. The Sheriff of Nottingham enters Marian's quarters, he starts ruffling through her underwear drawer. The Sheriff grabs Marian's panties, starts sniffing, then jams them into his pocket. The Sheriff puts his dirty mitts back into Marian's underwear drawer and feels some paper. The Sheriff pulls out a small note.

"Oh... oh no."

The Sheriff runs down the halls, he bursts into King John's chamber.

"Sire, I discovered a note in Lady Marian's chamber!"

The Sheriff of Nottingham pulls Marian's panties out of his pocket.

"That's quite a note you've found there!" King John remarks.

"Sorry, wrong pocket! "The Sheriff pulls the note out of his other pocket. "The note is from your brother! He'll be back by this evening..."

"What? How did Lady Marian receive a note from my brother?"

King John, Sir Guy, and The Sheriff find a pigeon at the window. The colour drains from King John's face. "Oh no."

The Sheriff points to the window, "The pigeons..."

"She has been feeding those stupid pigeons for years! No one even suspected." Sir Guy says with a sense of disbelief at how clever Marian actually is.

"There is no telling how much information she has sent or received. How much she knows...how much your brother knows." The Sheriff says frantically.

"Marian will be dealt with! What will we do about Richard?" King John demands.

The Sheriff grows excited, "Wait! The note says your brother will be taking the south road through Sherwood on his return."

"What if we lay a trap for him?" King John asks coldly.

"What kind of trap?" The Sheriff of Nottingham asks.

"What if we gather a dozen of the deadliest mercenary knights in England, what if we have them dress as Robin Hood? We send them to Sherwood Forest on the south road to assassinate Richard. The people will say the outlaw Robin Hood killed King Richard! We kill my brother and frame Robin Hood at the same time!" King John chuckles.

The Sheriff claps his hands together. "I love it!"

"Make it so, number one!"[16] King John orders.

Outside the chamber, the Court Jester is listening. After hearing all that was said he continues his escape. King John is willing to reenact Cain and Abel, killing both Richard then Marian to secure his power. The Jester tears through the castle and makes his way to Sherwood Forest, he needs to find Robin Hood.

CHAPTER XX

A Happy Reunion

Everyone is practicing combat except Robin Hood, Robin looks at Friar Tuck, then at his ring for Marian. Robin looks back at Friar Tuck approaching him.

"Friar. I wish to talk about marrying Marian."

Friar Tuck looks at Robin knowingly. He long suspected this was coming. "What are your feelings towards Lady Marian?" The Friar asks.

"I can give her my love, but she will be hunted like me."

Suddenly a Court Jester scrambles through the trees, frantically stumbling into Robin Hood at Robin's encampment. The Court Jester regains his balance and stands straight. "Robin! We have trouble at Nottingham! They found out Marian is working for you and have given her a sentence of death!"

"When will the sentence be carried out?" Robin asks with great worry in his voice.

"Midnight!"

Little John strolls over, intruding on the conversation. "Who is the funny-looking fellow you are talking to Robin?"

"This is my younger brother, Will Scarlet. While Marian served as my eyes in Nottingham Castle, Will served as my eye on Marian."

Robin hops onto a rock. "Men... I am going to Nottingham Castle to rescue Marian. I will lay siege to the castle in a one-man assault if I have to."

Will Scarlet pulls Robin Hood off the top of the large rock. "It's more complicated than that Robin! King Richard has returned from the Crusades, he is taking the south road through Sherwood, but our king's brother has found out! He has hired a dozen men dressed as you, they are sent to kill the king!"

"Then I only have a small window of time. I have to get moving." Robin bolts for it.

On the south road, it is becoming dusk. King Richard's garrison is upon the south road riding closer, much closer to the trap. More than a dozen Assassins are in Sherwood Forest, dressed in green, holding crossbows. They are in the midst of the trees next to the road.

"Isn't Robin Hood the best archer in all of England? Why did they give us crossbows?" Asks the mercenary.

"So, we will be more accurate. Besides, nobody is going to know it's not Robin Hood." The Assassin answers.

Back at King Richard's garrison, the knight leading the garrison points forward. "Look! There is someone in the distance."

Back at the trap, a sentry dressed as Robin Hood is on the treetop. Suddenly a sword pierces through his front torso several times until he falls down dead. Robin Hood sheaths his sword, grabs a tree branch, then swings down knocking off another of the Sheriff's men.

Robin Hood is hanging from a branch by his legs. An Assassin walking down the trail notices someone whistling from above. As he tilts his head up the last thing he witnesses is Robin Hood shooting an arrow into his face. Flipping off the branch, soaring to the ground below, Robin lands hard onto another impostor. Observing three bodies lying on the ground, Robin smashes the Assassin's head against the rock. Robin Hood gets up rolling an oncoming attacker onto their back. Pulling an arrow from his quiver, Robin stabs the impostor in the heart, he pulls the arrow back out then fires it into an impostor down the road.

Robin Hood dashes down the road, he ducks into the trees grabbing an Assassin from behind, Robin Hood breaks his arm then fires the crossbow into another treetop sentry. Two arrows hit the Assassin in the chest, killing him. Robin drops his human shield, drawing his bow, he fires two arrows in rapid succession killing two more treetop archers. Robin Hood climbs a tree firing his arrow at an impostor down the road, but the impostor moves out of the way keeping Robin's arrow from hitting its mark. The Assassin fires a shot-off with his crossbow.

Robin draws another arrow, spins his bow a quarter-counterclockwise, knocking the arrow out of the air. Once Robin shoots his opponent he drops from the trees once more. An Assassin gets the drop on Robin Hood from behind pointing a crossbow at the back of Robin Hood's head. Robin Hood kicks the Assassin in the pelvis applying 350 pounds of force, crippling the hapless mercenary.

King Richard's garrison enters the fray only to find bodies everywhere. Riding along the road, the garrison finds dead men garbed in forest green hoods, cloaks, and tights. Suddenly, a figure dressed the same way as the dead men, pops out, he fires an arrow straight at King Richard's head, but the arrow is snapped in twain mid-flight by another arrow. Robin Hood shoots the would-be Assassin dead.

"Lower your weapon or be destroyed!" Shouts the knight leading the Garrison.

Robin Hood's reaction to this order is to draw his sword then walk toward the garrison. All the knights in the garrison draw their swords. Without warning, Robin Hood spins around 540 degrees, throwing his sword in a spinning motion as it flies through the air.

Robin's sword decapitates the last Assassin who rides attacking by horseback.

"You have true skill with a blade, but now you have none, explain what is going on." Asks the king.

"I would do so gladly for my king. Unfortunately, you are not he." Robin says in a snide manner.

The knight leading the garrison steps forward, he removes his helmet revealing the face of the true King Richard. "Quite so, Robin of Locksley, only you could kill more than a dozen men with such ease."

Robin Hood looks around him then looks back at Richard.

"You call that easy?"

Robin Hood begins to kneel. "My Lord, your brother John, the Count of Mortain, has declared that..."

"I am well-aware of my brother's doings, Robin, thanks to Lady Marian. As for you, Robin, while it is a requirement, you do not need to kneel. From what I understand, Sir Robin of Locksley, I have you to thank for paying my ransom, as well as protecting my subjects while I was away when no one else would. You are a true hero of the realm." King Richard declares.

"I beg your pardon your majesty, but time is short. Your brother is going to execute Marian at midnight. I must save her." Robin Hood says.

"I will join you, Robin, so will every man in Sherwood under the order of King Richard the Lion Heart!!!" Richard shouts.

"My Lord!" Robin shouts.

CHAPTER XXI

Battle of the Two Kings

Thus, the forces of King Richard the Lion Heart, combined with the Merry Men, led by Sir Robin of Locksley, join to lay siege to Nottingham Castle. The combined factions gather outside the castle. The stars in the night sky twinkle above. There is nary a cloud in the sky.

Robin stands beside King Richard at the edge of the tree line looking upon the walls of Nottingham Castle. The Merry Men with the forces of the Lion Heart wait in the trees behind them.

"Fire a warning shot, Sir Robin!"

"As you say, my king."

Robin Hood fires an arrow that sails over the wall of Nottingham castle, straight into Guy of Gisbourne's right thigh. Sir Guy motions to the right thigh.

"AAAH! AAAH! AAAH!

"Fire another warning shot Sir Robin." King Richard says.

"As you deem fit my king."

Robin Hood fires another arrow that sails over the castle wall straight into Guy of Gisbourne's other thigh. Sir Guy motions to his left thigh.

"AAAH!"

Sir Guy motions to his right thigh.

"AAAH!"

Sir Guy motions to his left thigh.

"AAAH!"

Sir Guy motions to his right thigh.

"AAAH!"

"We need to get inside Nottingham Castle, but we only have an hour until midnight. Laying siege to the castle could take days." King Richard ponders.

"I suggest a Trojan Horse attack my King." Robin Hood suggests.

"What do you suggest we use as the horse?" King Richard asks.

Robin Hood smiles. "You are looking at him."

The guards in their towers search to find who is firing the arrows, but no one is there, all the guards can find are thirteen men dressed as Robin Hood. "Did you Kill the Lion Heart?" Sir Guy asks.

"Aye. We killed the Lion Heart." The false Robin Hood replies.

"Then why are you here? We already paid you for the job." Sir Guy shouts.

"We came for the reward." The false Robin Hood shouts back.

"What reward?"

"The reward for Robin Hood." The false Robin Hood takes off Robin's hood.

"Get inside now!" Sir Guy shouts.

The gate is raised. The party enters through the open gate.

"What's all this then?" A Nottingham Guard asks.

"Subterfuge." Robin Hood answers smugly.

King Richard removes his cloak, followed by his knights. Robin is cut free then handed his weaponry as Richard knifes the guard.

Sir Guy of Gisbourne's face has a look of horror upon it. "No. No!"

Robin Hood takes an arrow, draws his bow, then fires three arrows into a bell in the courtyard signaling the Merry Men to attack. Attacking from the tall grass the forces of Robin Hood and King

Richard storm the castle. The commotion brings out many castle-guards that Robin shoots dead. Robin Hood and Richard lead their forces into Nottingham, Sir Guy runs to the castle out of sheer fear adrenaline. Gisbourne enters the castle. He has a nearby guard to help him bar the door. Gisbourne growls to the guard.

"Do not leave this door alone."

"Whatever, I hate my job."

Robin climbs up the side of the castle by using the ivy growing up towards Marian's open window. Robin climbs through the window as he enters the castle. Robin makes his way to the door, opening it, but then hides behind it as a garrison of knights passes through the hallway. He exits Marian's room but is suddenly spotted by the guards. Robin shoots down dead eight different guards. He dashes down the stairs slaying his opponents, Robin spots the guard at the front door. He draws his bow but realises what he is doing, so he puts the arrow back into his quiver. Robin hides behind a nearby corner then shouts. "Help! Richard's forces are entering through the window at Lady Marian's quarters!"

The guard rushes from his post. Robin grabs him, slamming him against the wall putting his hand over the guard's mouth. Robin speaks to him, "Listen, I know you hate your job. Join me, help me unbar the door so our forces get through quickly, I promise you will live. If you oppose me, our forces will slowly pour into the castle the same way I came in, so I cannot promise that we will spare you. Do you understand?"

The Nottingham Guard nods his head. Robin Hood lets go of his scared captive. The guard helps Robin unbar the door. The door opens, the combined forces of King Richard's garrison and Robin Hood's Merry Men invade Nottingham Castle. The battle of the two kings is vicious and bloody. The combat is chaotic and messy. Suddenly everyone just stops as the Black Knight runs through the battlefield, still ablaze screaming in agony. After the Black Knight has left, the combat picks up again. The Sheriff of Nottingham bursts into King John's chamber. "The combined forces of Robin Hood and your brother, Richard, are inside the castle! What do we do?"

King John grabs the Sheriff slamming him against the wall. "Grab every man available and fight to the death because if I go down, I'm taking you all with me!"

Sir Guy appears amidst the combat. He wears the skull warpaint once again. "So, it boils down to a fight to the death, how utterly appropriate."

"Shut up and fight me!" Robin screams with a burning rage.

Sir Guy engages Robin Hood in mortal combat. The timing of the strikes is fast-paced, frenetic, while the motions of the swords have a refined fluidity to them. Their sword fight leads into the castle halls then down the stairs.

"You are surprisingly light on your feet today, Sir Guy. Remarkable for someone who has had so many arrows pierce their legs." Robin taunts.

Sir Guy stabs at Robin Hood, but Robin Hood dashes towards Sir Guy, ducking underneath the blade. Robin Hood hits Sir Guy in the stomach then quickly somersaults on the floor away from Sir Guy. Robin Hood rises glaring at Sir Guy. Sir Guy looks down realizing an arrow is piercing him. He looks at Robin Hood.

"Just what I thought. Gambeson." Robin hood quips.

"Gambeson over chain-mail." Sir Guy retorts.

Sir Guy pulls the second sword off the first. Robin begins sword fighting Sir Guy again. Sir Guy starts spinning both swords in a circular motion. Robin starts blocking the blows before Sir Guy reverses the direction of the swords. Sir Guy is using the Desert Rose technique as the swords spin upwards. Agony has the Desert Rose, Robin has sky. Robin leaps onto the side of a wall then immediately springs off of it stabbing Sir Guy in the shoulder. Sir Guy screams as his shoulder bleeds.

"A sword can get through." Robin Hood says.

Sir Guy does a charging flourish towards Robin Hood. Robin's gambeson is cut open by Sir Guy's sharp sword exposing his chest. He is disarmed. Robin Hood takes out his knife throwing it at Sir Guy's head. Sir Guy dodges the blade by moving out of the way. While Sir Guy moves out of the way, Robin picks up his sword from the ground. Robin Hood finally goes at it with Sir Guy of Gisbourne. Robin keeps swinging his sword wildly battering Sir Guy's sword. Finally, Robin Hood shatters Sir Guy's sword stabbing him in the heart.

The gambeson over mail Sir Guy is wearing stops the blade but Robin leaps delivering a flying spin kick forcing the blade through the gambeson, the mail, then Gisbourne's heart. Robin sets a cake by Gisbourne's dead body. "Sorry, Sir Guy, I should have told you, you were never up to the challenge."

King Richard finds his brother, grabs him, gives him a massive wedgie, then finishes by giving the Count of Mortain a mean noogie.

With Sir Guy of Gisbourne dead, Robin dashes down into the dungeon to save Marian. As Robin enters the lower dungeon, he faces the Sheriff of Nottingham.

"So, Guy failed to kill you, why am I not surprised? Just remember one thing, Robin... Down here, I am the Dungeon Master!"

Robin Hood finally faces the Sheriff of Nottingham in a sword duel with one another. Fencing each other throughout the dungeon, their swords cut through every lit candle until after some time, the only thing illuminating the room is an oil lantern. Soon, their swords crash into the lantern, drenching the weapons in oil. The swords clash together in the darkness. Sparks fly as the two combatants are trying to kill each other with fiery swords.

Two flaming swords are the only thing illuminating the darkness in the dungeon, spinning, clashing violently.

"If you are here for Marian you are too late. We executed her before you even got here." The Sheriff mocks.

Robin becomes enraged during the combat; Robin parries the Sheriff's fiery sword then manages to catch the Sheriff's cloak on fire. While the Sheriff is momentarily distracted by being on fire, Robin uses the opportunity to cut his head off. Robin stabs his sword into the ground leaning on it. Robin breaks down and begins to weep, Marian was dead. Robin Hood had failed the one person he cared most for. Robin begins considering falling onto his own sword when he is interrupted by a series of loud bangs. Someone is banging on a dungeon cell door.

"I am ready to face death!"

She's alive!

Robin Hood drops his sword, he rushes into Marian's cell to rescue her, Marian knocks Robin Hood's ass out cold with a large piece of stone from the wall. Marian rolls him over realizing it's Robin.

"Robin! You've come to rescue me!"

Maid Marian drags Robin Hood back up to Nottingham Castle where the victorious forces of King Richard await.

"Did Robin Hood save you, dearest cousin Marian?"

"He did! I love him my king! Marry us!"

"You're Married!"

Robin Hood wakes then sits up. "What happened?"

Marian is holding him in her arms. "Shut up and kiss me!"

Robin Hood kisses Marian. "The battle of the two kings is over. Richard has restored peace to the realm." Marian says smiling.

Everyone raises their swords. The Count of Mortain is brought before the Lion Heart. Prince John opens his arms stepping towards Richard. "Brother..."

"You're gone."

"But brother, when can I..."

"You're gone. Permanently. Get out."

A Merry Man grabs Prince John then starts dragging him away.

"Unhand me!" Prince John screams. The Merry Man quickly complies. Prince John straightens out his cape then straightens his shirt. "Peasant."

All the Merry Men grab Prince John, they carry him off laughing while he curses at them.

Robin exchanges glances with Richard, then they burst out laughing. Prince John is hurled into manure.

There is a large celebration in Nottingham. Richard pardons all the Merry Men, personally shakes their hands, he makes them the King's Foresters. A wedding is held for the Hero of England, Robin Hood, in the town square of Nottingham. Everyone in town and the surrounding lands crowd together to see it.

Robin walks down the aisle, Marian follows soon after. Will Scarlet hands Robin the ring. Robin places a silver and gold ring in-laid with silver and a large emerald shining on Marian's finger. Sarah hands Marian the ring. Marian puts a similar ring on Robin Hood's finger.

"You may exchange vows." The minister says.

Robin speaks first, "Marian Fitzwater, I have loved you ever since the moment you first kissed me on the shores of England. My father forbade our love. I went to war, I faced such hell, it's a miracle I'm back in one piece. I came back as an outlaw as I fell in love with you again. You gave me love, gave me compassion. I will love, cherish, and protect your kind heart until mine stops beating. The fact I am standing here, now, with you, shouldn't have happened. This feels like Destiny. I love you."

Marian speaks, "Robin of Locksley, Hero of England and the man who my heart belongs to. When I first kissed you, I knew one day we would be wed. God, look at me, I feel like a silly girl at my own fairy tale wedding. I know now that I am not just marrying the man I love, but I am marrying a legend. I am proud of it. I love you, Robin."

"You may drink from the wine chalice." The minister says.

Robin sips from the chalice. Marian sips the chalice.

"I now pronounce you lord and ladyship. You may kiss the bride." The minister says.

Robin dips Marian over kissing her with the fires of passion. Everybody in attendance goes nuts.

Richard walks up. "Well done, Sir Robin, magnificent show. Sir Robin, Lady Marian, meet me in Sherwood tonight."

Robin and Marian sneak out of the wedding celebration. They travell to Sherwood Forest together.

All the knights and Merry Men are in Sherwood. Robin and Marian stand beside King Richard.

"Hail King Richard the Lion Heart!" Robin shouts.

Everyone kneels.

"Hail King Richard! Long live the Lion Heart!"

"Thank you, Robin Hood, Earl of Huntington, thank you, Marian. All hail Robin and Marian! King and Queen of the May Games!" Richard shouts.

Everyone draws their swords raising them into the air.

"Hail! Hail! Hail! Hail!"

MUSICAL INTERLUDE DEEP in Sherwood Forest, a man is playing his piano singing a cheerful song.

"OH, we thought he liked girls, but he dances with wolves,
Someone I know has a crush on Kevin Costner.
Oh, we thought he liked girls, but he fancies Robin Hood,
Because someone I know has a crush on Kevin Costner.

*Oh, We thought he liked sports, but it turns out to be another type of
mariner,*
Because someone I know has a crush on Kevin Costner.
Oh, We thought he liked girls, but he dances with wolves,
Because someone I know wants his mail delivered by Kevin Costner.
Oh, We thought he liked girls, but at night he screams,
He's having a field of dreams about Kevin Costner.
Oh, I think Costner's okay, my friends don't think he's that good,
*But that doesn't stop someone I know from having a crush on Kevin
Costner.*
Oh I don't think he's okay, in fact, I think he's going insane,
The longer someone I know stays away from Kevin Costner.
Oh he dances with wolves but he still has a restraining order,
That says to stay far, far away from Kevin Costner,
Because there is someone I know who is in love with Kevin Costner."

Robin walks by but after hearing this performance he bashes the piano man's head against the keyboard really-hard five times and walks off.

PART THREE

IN THE LORE OF HISTORY MONSTERS EXIST

Dramatis Personae

Robin Hood-Assassin
Marian Fitzwater-Wife of Robin Hood
King Richard-King of England. Hero warrior
The Lord of the Darkness- A warlord in the east
Countess Carmilla Karnstein-tradesman in caramel plus ice cream
Jacques Mercardier- A French Mercenary
Eleanore of Aquitaine-Mother to King Richard
Locos- A Mad Hermit
Lara-Vampiric Concubine
Tara-Vampiric Concubine
Fara-Vampiric Concubine
Rick-Bill Collector
Wilbert-Bill Collector
Klaus Sanders-Saint Nick?
Charon-Boatman
Alucard-Son of a Dark Lord
Sarah-Servant to Maid Marian
Princess Haru- a strange royal
Famine-A horsemen
The Herald Pestilence-A horsemen
War-A horsemen
Death-A horsemen
Priest-one of Robin's Team

Unnamed

Screamers
Boy
Black Knight
Necromancer
Lycan Cult
Armies of Darkness

Zombies
King Richard's forces
Driver
Boat Captain
Skeletons
Annoying skull on the floor
Gargoyles
Monkey
Quack Doctor

CHAPTER XXII

The Quest

Robin is in the Holy Land. He is travelling with Assassins when Saladin's forces hit them. They fight their hearts out. The battle is small but tremendous. Robin engages in mass bloodshed, but the winds pick up, a sandstorm finishes the battle. He pulls out his bow starting to shoot arrows downwind in a 180-degree maximum kill zone. Robin spots someone coming for him, so he shoots him with an over-the-shoulder-trick-shot. Robin must have missed because the figure keeps running. He grabs Robin. Robin tries to get away but only ends up struggling with him.

The sandstorm dies down and it turns out to be someone dressed in a Knight's Tunic. Robin removes the Helmet.

"Priest? You've been promoted! Oh no."

Robin finds the arrow in Priest's abdomen. Robin holds Priest in his arms. Priest looks at Robin and speaks.

"You destroy all of us because that's who you are.

You destroy all of us because that's who you are."

Priest dies in Robin's arms. Pikes rise from the sand impaling everybody on the battlefield. Robin spots a dark figure walking through the rows of impaled bodies. Robin wakes up in his tent in a cold sweat. Robin puts his face down into his hands. "It was just a dream."

Robin begins to break down weeping.

England, 1199 A.D.

A black ship sails out of the mist arriving at the shores of England. A knight observing the arrival of the ship approaches on horseback, a figure in black robes emerges from the ship. It is the Herald of Darkness. The knight points his lance at the black-cloaked figure. The knight does not see his face. "Who are you, and what business do you have in England?"

"I am the Herald of the Lord of the Darkness. My master wishes to address his newest subjects before he delivers the day of reckoning."

"We are a proud people, and will not recognize any lord, save our king, and our almighty God!"

"God is dead, and soon enough your king will be too! My lord and master wanted me to bring gifts to England to prepare for his arrival."

"Gifts? What gifts? Tell me before I run you through, foul blasphemer!"

"The gifts of plague and death!"

Hundreds of rats pour out of the ship as the Herald of Darkness pulls a sword out of his robe running the knight through. The Lord of the Darkness steps off the ship putting his hand on the Herald's shoulder.

"Flawlessly executed. Come, I must prepare my speech for the masses."

KING RICHARD IS ON his horse riding next to Robin in a forest. King Richard has a red vest with three belts with lion head buckles. Robin has a green gambeson with a black outline around a red cross on his chest. They are riding through a forest path.

"My king, I need to know something."

"What might that be?" King Richard asks.

"After you were shipwrecked, you were captured by Leopold of Austria, you were put in a mock trial by the Holy Roman Emperor for negotiating with Saladin..."

"I'm not hearing a question yet."

"What did you say to clear your name? No one knows how you did that."

King Richard explains past events to Robin. Robin can visualize the events clearly. King Richard is before the Holy Roman Emperor, Duke Leopold, and a Jury out for blood.

King Richard grows angry with the bullshit, so he addresses the court, "You have some balls on you, abducting the King of England, putting him in this sham of a trial, well I've got some balls too! Let me give them to you..."

King Richard snaps his fingers. Three chests of Tennis Balls are brought in.

King Richard continues, "These are three chests of the finest Tennis Balls in England, you can all take them and shove them up your ass! Let me tell you something else, what goes around comes around, therefore when I am pronounced innocent, I will get out of here then personally make sure you will pay! I will make sure each-and-every one of you pay for this degradation!! I am Richard! I am the Lion Heart!!"

There is a long moment of silence then Duke Leopold starts to clap. The Jury begins clapping, then there is silence.

Robin realises Richard is not going to give him any more information.

"We are almost home after six years."

"I am well aware."

"I can see Marian again."

"I am aware of that too."

"Sometimes I wonder if she will even recognize me if I ever tell her of the things that I have done. Sometimes I wonder if I deserve her at all."

"Berengaria is waiting for me in England. England will want sons from me. England will need sons from us all."

"...And daughters." Robin adds.

King Richard raises his eyebrow. "Too true. When we return to England things shall be put right. Your payment is waiting for you for your many years of service, Sir Robin."

"I can't stop thinking about her." Robin says through gritted teeth.

"Wow, you got it bad." Richard says.

"The fact I am almost home to see her again is the only thing keeping me from planting an arrow through my head. I need to get back. I want to listen to her voice. Speaking of which, Marian told me that you are her great cousin. Is that true? Does my wife really have royal blood in her?" Robin asks.

King Richard lets out a sigh. "Yes and no."

"What does that mean?" Robin asks.

"She is a royal back-up. She is of royal blood, but it is bastard's blood. Should anything happen to all the royal family of England she will become queen as will her heirs. Say... What is that in the distance?"

"It seems to be a castle. Let us leave it be so we may return to our women and our country my king."

"I had better check this out."

King Richard rides up to the French Castle in the forest clearing. King Richard shouts up to the French Guard.

"Guard! I say, Guard! Can you hear me?"

"Oui monsieur."

"Tell your master that I, King Richard the Lion Heart, am going to lay siege his castle to claim the booty."

"Oui. The castle has the best booty in France. I myself have slept with them all five different times."

"Typical Frenchman," King Richard mutters. "I do not want your women! I demand you inform your master to surrender your castle booty. The treasure! Give me treasure or I shall besiege your castle! I will take it by force."

"Oui. I will inform him at once."

The French castle guard descends then rises again.

"He does not like it monsieur! He says I should fight you for it."

"You were only gone for a moment. You could not possibly have spoken to your master in that time frame."

The French castle guard looks to his left, then looks to his right, then looks at King Richard.

"Yes, I could."

"How?"

"I am the master of this castle."

"You mock me!"

A tomato is thrown hitting Richard on his tunic. "How dare you!"

"Go away, little English peasant king! Go back to your mud castle in the muddy English countryside. Leave the real men to make love to real women."

"I keep myself chaste only until I reunite with Berengaria, my Queen."

"You are but a little boy overcompensating to be like a man. You make me sad little boy-king, now go away."

"If you do not surrender your castle to me, I will take it by force!" King Richard shouts angrily.

King Richard has shit poured onto him.

"Eat shit and die little boy Englishman."

King Richard erupts. "It's war!"

It starts to rain blood. A bad omen.[17] King Richard rides away, he is soon joined by Sir Robin.

"Prepare the men to lay waste to the castle. By the end of this, I want that castle to be nothing but rubble."

Robin nods. "Consider it done."

Robin rides off. "Everybody, prepare for the final battle!"

Richard leads his forces into battle. King Richard's army is laying siege to the French castle. Arrows are flying everywhere. French Guards are falling over dead. Englishmen are killed by French cross-bows. King Richard is leading from the front as usual. He rears his horse screaming, "*Dieu et mon Droit!*"

Suddenly a boy shoots King Richard in the shoulder near the neck.

"That's for killing my father!"

Richard falls from his horse. The Captain of the Knights shouts. "Our king has been hit! Get the king to safety!"

The knights pick up King Richard transporting him to the tent.

Sir Robin, acting as Captain of the Archers, provides cover fire. The siege continues. They break the castle gate, Richard's army storms through taking prisoners for ransom.

King Richard lay bleeding on his bed. Mercardier stands at Richard's bedside with a Quack Doctor.

"What shall we do doctor?" Mercardier asks.

"He has an infection on his wound, he should be able to beat it; but we should get all the bad blood out first, I need to bleed the patient."

The Quack Doctor begins to bleed King Richard. The Lion Heart lay dying on his deathbed.

"Bring me, Sir Robin..."

IN NOTTINGHAM IT IS twilight. The Lord of the Darkness climbs the stairs of a wooden platform in front of a crowd. He gives a speech to the gathered masses.

"If I could have a year or two, I'll make something good. I'll do something... something good. Just one year. That's all."[18]

Someone in the crowd stands up. "Somebody give that man a year!"

The crowd begins to boo.

BACK IN FRANCE ROBIN Hood enters the king's tent. The king is talking to a tall man in a fedora and a short fat knight.

"Now go collect the bill."

Robin enters the tent. He crosses paths with the two bill collectors as he slowly creeps forward to his dying friend.

"You summoned me, my king?"

"I am dying, Sir Robin. The Crusade has ended. Not in failure, but without the capture of Jerusalem I feel I have failed God. There is still one last bit of unfinished business. We made a bloody mess of things in the Holy Land... Christians and Muslims alike. I suppose it is only natural that the mess we made led to the rise of great evil. Darkness is spreading like a plague throughout the lands. Robin, I've never told you this. There is another royal figure. In a land to the east. In a place covered by storms, there is a castle. It is the lair of a Dark Lord.

A warlord called, 'The Lord of the Darkness.' I need you to travell into his realm, infiltrate his fortress, then assassinate the Dark Lord. You must do this, Robin, or we will all be doomed. Soon, The Lord of the Darkness will be unstoppable. Kill him, Sir Robin; do whatever it takes, just kill him. This is your task, Robin ... your quest. One last thing. Do not kill the boy who shot me. Farewell, old friend."

King Richard's wound bleeds out. The Hospitaller checks his pulse. "King Richard the Lion Heart is dead!"

Eleanore of Aquitaine holds her son in her arms rocking his body as many tears are shed. Robin Hood looks at the dead body of his friend. "Mercardier, where is the castle's treasure?"

"There was no treasure." Mercardier answers.

Robin exits the tent to address the army gathered outside.

"Our king, my friend, has fallen in battle. Let's kill the little bastard who murdered him!"

Robin Hood exits the battlefield as a man on a mission.

The army kills the boy despite the king's wishes to spare him.

CHAPTER XXIII

Hello, Goodbye

Robin Hood returns to Huntington Castle on horseback. Robin marches through the entrance door of Huntington Castle as Marian wearing a red dress runs up hugging him.

"How is my great cousin's health, beloved husband?" Marian asks.

"King Richard has passed, my dearest wife. I was there in the room as it happened. I would attend the royal funeral with you, my love, I know how close the two of you were, but I must begin the Quest." Robin Hood says.

"The Quest?" Marian asks.

"The Quest. I must travell to a land of beasts and monsters to assassinate the Dark Lord."

"Let me help you, Robin."

"No, my love, it is too dangerous, besides, I need you to look after the people of the village in my absence. I just came here to prepare for the journey."

A pigeon flies into the window. Marian grabs the note attached to the pigeon's leg.

"Robin!"

"What is it, Marian?"

"An army of rats is headed straight for the village!"

Robin lowers his head, putting his index and middle finger to his temple as he closes his eyes. Finally, Robin Hood snaps his fingers.

"Marian, tell Sarah and the other servants to begin boiling the biggest vat of oil they can find. I am going to spread the word to all of the village to do the same."

Robin heads out into the village. Marian finds Sarah chatting with the others in the servant's quarters.

"Sarah, I need you and the other servants to help me find the largest vat we can begin cooking oil in."

"My lady, why do we need such a large amount? Are we going to repel an invasion?"

"An invasion of a sort, I am sure. I do not quite know what my husband has planned, but he always has good reasons for doing so."

"Where is Master Robin?" Sarah asks.

"He is off telling the rest of the village to do the same as he has ordered us to do." Marian answers.

Half an hour later, the army of rats descends on the village led by the Herald of Darkness. The rats enter the streets circling the Herald of Darkness.

"Behold, the gifts my master brings all of England! The pets of the Dark Lord shall release you from the suffering of life."

Every household in the village pours their vats of boiling oil into the streets. Robin Hood appears at the top of his castle with the English longbow, he fires a burning arrow into the streets. Fire erupts through the streets of the village, ending the plague that would have destroyed all of England.

Robin Hood goes down the stairs to his and Marian's quarters. Robin Hood grabs his hooded cloak, his sword, slings his English longbow and quiver across his back. Robin attaches an extra quiver to his right leg, then grabs three bags of gold. He sneaks through the stables. As he steps outside, Marian is there waiting for him.

"You did not need to come here to prepare for this journey, you came here to say goodbye, didn't you?" Marian asks.

Robin kisses Marian, then leaves. Robin Hood rides on a wagon with the driver and his son.

"Hey, son. Would you like a piece of cake?" Robin Hood asks.

"WAAAAH! Daddy, the bad man touched me!" The small child wails.

"Hey, nobody touches my boy there but me!" The driver yells.

"Wait! This is a misunderstanding. You see I'm the Hero of Ac...."

The driver punches Robin Hood in the head with the force of a heavyweight prizefighter.

Robin goes sailing from the cart onto the ground completely knocked out from the punch. A hooded figure in a green cloak arrives. Robin Hood wakes up at the dock. Robin walks up to the boat captain.

"A bag of gold for a trip on the boat." Robin says.

"Sure. Sure. Say how did you get the shiner?" The Boat Captain asks.

"Because I said I was the Hero of Ac..."

"You are the Hero of Acre? I judge you to be Robin Hood!"

"Guilty as charged."

"I will not take the Saviour of England's money. You keep it. I will not take a coin." The Boat Captain states.

"How is your business doing?" Robin asks.

"It's barely afloat."

"You keep it." Robin says.

"I take it that you are going off on a heroic quest to find a dangerous enemy to kill, like that time you killed Sibylla."

"I didn't kill her. That was a lie! How the hell do you know that?" Robin Hood asks.

"I was at Acre too. Deus Vult!"

"Deus Vult!" Robin answers.

Securing passage on a boat, Robin passes the Boat Captain, immediately heading towards his quarters. The captain turns his attention to a hooded figure in a green cloak.

"Fifteen coin a trip!"

The green hooded figure pays him then follows Robin Hood. The boat braves the English Channel arriving in France. Robin walks on a dirt road in the French countryside. A French Gang of Ruffians appears.

"Look! It is Robin Hood, Prince of Thieves! Let's kick the shit out of him and take his wallet!"

"NO! Wait! Wait! I'm a Hero on an adventure!" Robin protests.

"Look! It is a Hero on an adventure! Let's kick the shit out of him and take his wallet!"

The French Gang of Ruffians kicks the shit out of Robin Hood and takes his bag of gold. As the ruffians leave the scene of the crime a storm starts. Robin Hood is bleeding all over his clothes.

A hooded figure dressed in a green cloak appears. The figure rushes to Robin twirling the green cape over an unconscious Robin Hood. Lightning crackles in the sky. Red Lightning (Scientifically abbreviated as S.P.R.I.T.E. and E.L.V.E.S.) crackles downwards to earth. The hooded figure kneels and tilts Robin's head back with a hand that has black fingernails. A S.P.R.I.T.E. crackles in the sky.

The other hand with black fingernails heads closer, ever closer, to Robin's eyes.

CHAPTER XXIV

The Sword in the Swamp

When Robin Hood wakes in pain, he finds he no longer has any of his blood on him. Robin Hood continues his journey across the French countryside.

As he journeys, Robin runs across mutilated sheep remains. A French Farmer is standing there observing. "Bonjour."

"Hello." Robin says.

"Englishman? My English not so good."

"What did this?" Robin asks.

"Beast." The farmer says.

"Like a wolf?"

"No wolf. Beast. Beasts everywhere. You go."

"Okay." Robin says.

"Go!"

Robin Hood dashes away. Robin walks past several farms when he begins to understand that France is experiencing a famine.

Travelling several miles, Robin Hood sits down next to a giant tree, he falls asleep. A voice speaks to Robin in his sleep.

Sir Robin of Locksley, you have embarked upon a most perilous quest.

Whose voice is that?

My voice is that of the most powerful wizard in existence. Robin, if you expect to fulfill your mission, you cannot assassinate the Lord of the Darkness with mortal weapons. You must find legendary weapons or weapons made of true silver. There is a lost temple in the forest of eastern France... There you will find a treasure that will help you in your quest. Then, you must seek the help of the princess.

Robin Hood wakes up as it starts to rain. He runs his hands over the giant tree. "Was it just a dream?"

Robin Hood spots a little girl wandering through the countryside. He follows her to a location where hundreds of people are gathered at a tall column, there is a large amount of grain held in bags suspended on the side. Robin Hood shoots an arrow into the bags, causing the grain to fall. desperate farmers scoop the grain, Robin Hood gives an apple to the little girl who led him there. The little girl kisses Robin Hood on the cheek then runs away. A group of Frenchmen walks up to Robin Hood.

"Thank you, we can use the seeds in this produce to regrow our lost crops. Unfortunately, it won't do much good as long as the Dark Lord's Horseman, Famine is around. Strange for a Crusader to return from war with a cross on his chest. Perhaps your particular war is not over yet. I have been awaiting your arrival. My name is Jacques, I am Richards' liaison in these parts, by the way, you are more than welcome to stay in my chateau."

Robin stays in the chateau during the storm with his French liaison in central France. At the lodge, Robin Hood eats dinner with a small company.

"This is Klaus Sanders, he's from up north, then there is Countess Carmilla Karnstein, she's in the caramel plus ice cream busines." Jacques says.

"The country seems to be terrorized by large beasts." Robin Hood says.

"Oui Monsieur, pets of the Dark Lord." Jacques says.

"Murcielago." The Countess says.

"Murcielago? What?" Robin asks.

"We all call him by different names, but we always know who he is." Klaus says.

"Dracula." Jacques states.

There is a flash of lightning as thunder booms outside.

"He comes to our lands bearing gifts of plagues and rats." The Countess says.

"It is said he wears an iron helm as he commands his dark armies with a burning sword of doom." Klaus says.

"What are his armies?" Robin asks.

"His dark followers, the Screamers, his beasts, some even say he commands monsters. His armies are spreading throughout the lands. He conquers then converts. Resist, you will be killed. Even the Saracens are terrified of him. It is said to find the Lord of the Darkness, you must find the rose. The rose of the dead." Jacques answers.

"Listen I am about to leave in a few hours is there anything useful you can tell me? I am looking for some epic weaponry. Excalibur level type of weaponry." Robin says.

"Ah. If you want epic weaponry, they say there is a sword in a stone somewhere in the nearby forest. They say the sword is the key to the forest's mystery. Nobody has found that sword in over 300 years. It may not even exist." Jacques says.

Robin Hood gives a blank stare.

"Are you even listening to me?" Jacques asks.

Jacques realises everyone at the table is staring blankly towards him.

"What is it?"

A monstrous beast crashes through the windowpanes behind Jacques immediately eviscerating him. Robin Hood springs into action, shooting two arrows at a time Robin pumps twelve arrows into the beast over the next 4.5 seconds. By the time the beast kills the other two dinner guests, Robin Hood pumps so many arrows into the beast it appears to lay dead. A voice curdles from outside.

"The last remnants of food were meant to give you false hope. Taking the food has earned you your death! Come face Famine! Horseman of the Lord of the Darkness! Your doom is at hand!"

Robin Hood flexing mighty muscles lifts the castle's anvil. He carries it climbing the castle's watchtower. As he reaches the top of the tower, he cries out in exhaustion,

"Famine! I have a message for your Dark Lord! Listen!"

Robin Hood lets go so the anvil drops onto Famine, crushing the bitch. Robin Hood leaves the castle embarking into the forest of eastern France.

Robin Hood roams deeper, yet deeper into the woods before he becomes lost. Robin Hood decides to sit on a log so he can rest. As Robin Hood rests on the log, a magnificent White Hart appears before him. Suddenly, the White Hart takes off, Robin Hood follows.

Robin Hood tracks the White Hart through many rivers in the forest valleys. Finally, Robin Hood catches up to the White Hart. As Robin Hood approaches the White Hart, he notices a fire with some albino dancing around it, singing crazily. It is Locos the mad hermit.

"Dancing, dancing, dancing.
Dancing 'round the fire.
I know this whole forest,
Like a hare will know the briar.
They threw me out of town,
They think that I am dead.
But I will call them mad,
For they cannot dance upon their head."

Robin Hood applauds. Locos spins around.

"Who are you?"

"I am Robin Hood. I heard you singing. Who do I owe the pleasure of thanking for such a lively performance?"

"I am Locos. I am a mad hermit."

"I heard the lyric about how you know the forest. I am lost. I am wondering if you could lead me out of here. Can you be my guide?"

"Very well. I shall guide you out of this forest, but I have fits of madness sometimes, so I may just end up killing you."

"You've got to do you."

Locos leads Robin Hood out of the forest. While they are going across some wet rocks in a swamp Locos has a fit of madness then runs off leaving Robin Hood alone.

Robin slips, falling into the wet swamp. When he emerges, he finds he is in a graveyard covered by the swamp. The stones he was crossing were gravestones. Robin Hood spots a sword in the middle of all the 2/3 submerged gravestones. Robin wades to the sword. Robin Hood tries to pull it out but cannot. Locos leaps onto Robin Hood's back and tries to strangle him.

Robin falls backwards slamming Locos into the swamp. Robin Hood stands free of Locos and spins around. Locos explodes out of the swamp tackling Robin Hood, holding his head beneath the surface of the swamp water. Robin Hood stops struggling, his arms go limp then fall. Locos begins laughing maniacally. Someone in the bushes draws a bow.

A knife explodes out of the water piercing the mad hermit's heart. Locos falls into the water dead. Robin Hood emerges from the water gasping for air. Robin Hood stands up, retrieves his hunting knife, then walks back to the sword in the stone.

"This is so stupid. Nobody can pull this sword out! Wait. Nobody can pull this out! What if this isn't supposed to be pulled out? What if this is a key?" Robin deduces.

Robin Hood grips the handguard then finds that he can twist the sword. Suddenly a giant hole opens in the swamp, the draining swamp water carries Robin Hood into a newly created waterfall, and he falls through the ground.

The tall man sporting a fedora is walking through the forest graveyard with the short fat knight. The short fat knight starts to complain,

"It's been rainin' for hours, Rick. There's red and green lightning flashing in the sky all the time. It's unnatural, Rick."

"Awww... Quit your complaining."

"Can't we go to a nice little warm tavern and order a few drinks, please Rick? I want to warm my little toes by a warm fire."

"We have to collect this bill, Wilbert! Now, come on, don't act like you haven't marched a thousand miles before."

"Please Rick, My feet have calluses. My calluses have calluses. My calluse's calluses have corns, and those corns have calluses."

"Awwww. Enough of your bellyaching, you're worse than a Duck-billed platypus!" Rick says.

"I have an idea! Let's turn back!"

"We have to deliver the bill."

"The Platypus has the bill."

"The Duck-billed platypus."

"So, the Platypus has the bill?"

"We have the bill."

"What about the Platypus?"

"The Duck-billed platypus."

"So, if the Duck-billed platypus, then the Platypus pays the bill?"

"No, the bill goes to Dracula, he pays."

Why should he pay when the Duck-billed platypus?

The Duck is the Platypus!"

So, you're saying the Platypus billed himself?"

"Dracula gets the bill!"

"I don't think he'd want it."

"Of course He doesn't want it! But we have to give him the bill."

"Duck!"

The two characters hide behind gravestones as a Gigantic Platypus clambers through the graveyard.

ROBIN IS IN DARKNESS slipping on a water slide for thirty seconds, Robin Hood falls through the other side of the ground landing in a pool of water. As Robin Hood emerges from the pool of water, he finds himself in an ancient Forest Temple. A stream flows from the pool to a fountain in the center of the temple. The fountain consists of four pools, the water flowing from the top pours down to each pool. Several robins are sitting on the fountain.

Robin Hood walks past the fountain noticing a dusty mirror and a beam of light coming down near it. Robin wets his cloak in the fountain so he can wipe off the dusty mirror. He struggles as he forces it to reflect light into the back of the temple. It is there he finds an archer's target in the wall.

Examining the target closely, Robin Hood notices there is a hole where the bullseye should be. Robin Hood reads an inscription carved into the wall.

"Only a Hero... whose aim is true... can let his arrow fly... so he may pass through."

Robin Hood draws his bow, aims his arrow, then fires his projectile, the arrow passes through the bullseye of ten layered targets hitting a switch. A similar feat has not been accomplished since the times of Odysseus. The ten targets crumble revealing a passage.

Robin Hood takes the passage walking through the tunnel stepping on the crunching of crumbled stone. Robin steps into a room where there is a lake. In the middle of the lake, a ray of light shines on a small island. Robin Hood crosses a large log, he happens upon a treasure of three arrowheads made of true silver alongside a glowing gem. Robin Hood puts the three arrowheads and the glowing gem in his pouch. There is a large series of echoes resonating throughout the room.

"Crunching? No... Biting!"

A large creature explodes from the water's surface attacking Robin Hood. The log turns out to be a thirty-foot alligator. It bellows at Robin. The alligator attacks Robin Hood. He clambers onto the back of the alligator holding on frantically as the gator glides through the water. Robin Hood begins pumping black arrows into the creature's back and belly. He is thrown off landing in the shallows. Robin thrusts several arrows into the silt. He begins rapid firing. When the alligator charges Robin keeps firing while striding around the shallows.

Inside three minutes, the monstrosity lies dead floating in the water, filled with arrows of red and black fletching. Robin finds a ladder of rocks at the south end of the lake. Climbing it, he finds that he is behind a waterfall. Robin Hood touches the roaring water, suddenly without warning, Robin slips, thus he is washed into the Holy Roman Empire.

CHAPTER XXV

Princess Haru

Robin has a vision that across the realms, the dead are starting to rise from their graves. Suddenly, millions of bats cover the sky. There is a booming voice emanating from the dark stormy clouds,

There is not much time left for the earth... soon darkness will encompass everything, finally I, Dracula, will consume the world.

Thousands of bats fly down from the sky. Robin wakes up on the grass at sunset, His legs in the muddy soil, feet wet in the cold flowing water. The squishing of wet cloth soaks Robin Hood's back cushioning him from the hard earth. Robin stands, he begins traversing the forest, however, Robin does not comprehend he is in Darkwood, Robin is alerted to someone else nearby. When he peers over a bush, he gazes upon a member of the Ancient Greek Lycan worshiper cult.

Wild men who wear wolf skin, they worship the Arcadian King Lycaon, while also serving the Lord of the Darkness.

The wild man spots Robin, then attacks. Robin Hood kills the Lycan worshiper by shooting him in the heart. Infiltrating their encampment, Robin Hood spies a large group encircling a red-headed princess tied to a wooden post. A Lycan tribe member approaches the scared Princess Haru with a burning torch. The torchbearer is instantly killed as an arrow pierces his heart. The rest of the tribe zooms in on a hooded figure garbed in forest green holding a bow. The entire tribe attacks. Robin Hood climbs a tree then immediately begins firing arrows.

Robin Hood kills many wild men, but soon they overwhelm Robin with their sheer numbers. All the wild men carry axes, swords, hatchets, along with many sharp knives. Robin Hood pulls his last arrow, stabbing an enemy in the head with it who is climbing the tree before firing the same arrow through the head of another enemy climbing the tree. Putting the bow away, Robin Hood draws his sword, leaps down onto the ground then enters the fray of combat. Robin Hood fights intensely, chopping off limbs, stabbing, beheading. Robin Hood enters a Zen-like state of violent, glorious melee. After a while, the Lycan worshipers lay dead with arrows of green and red fletching stuck in the bodies. Robin Hood realises he couldn't have done this alone.

"You can come out now, I know you have been following me since England."

The hooded figure in a green cloak steps out from behind a tree.

"What a surprise, the Lady in Green." Robin says sarcastically.

The Lady in Green pulls her hood off revealing the face of Marian.

"Why did you follow me?" Robin demands to know.

"I will not stand by as the love of my life goes on a perilous quest alone." Marian answers defiantly.

"If you intend to join me in my Quest to assassinate the Lord of the Darkness, I must insist you take two of these three silver arrowheads."

Robin offers Marian two silver arrowheads from his palm.

"I have always been better than you at everything ever since we were children. I only need one..." Marian says.

"Well, take two of them anyway! It will make me feel better about this." Robin says frustrated.

"As you wish, beloved."

Marian takes the two arrowheads. Robin Hood and Marian untie the princess. The scared princess begins to struggle.

"Don't worry, you're safe now." Marian says soothingly.

"We're friends, we won't hurt you... what is your name?" Robin asks.

"My name is Princess Haru."

"I am Robin, this is Marian. We are pleased to make your acquaintance, Princess Harooooooooooo!"

Marian smacks the back of Robin's head.

"Quit hitting on the princess, Robin!"

"Yes dear."

"I owe the two of you my life. Is there any way I can repay you?" Princess Haru asks.

Robin charms the Princess, "I am looking for the rose of the dead. Do you know how I can find it?"

"The rose of the dead?" Marian wonders aloud.

"Why are you looking for the rose of the dead?" Princess Haru questions.

"Because it is key to the quest."

Robin smiles his boyish grin.

"The quest?" Marian asks rather puzzled.

"The quest?" The Princess asks.

"The quest." Robin Hood affirms.

Princess Haru takes a deep breath. "All right. To find the rose of the dead, you must travell through the Alps to find the Necromancer. They say he is a descendant of Merlin himself. He knows many things."

"Necromancer?" Marian asks.

"So, will this Necromancer tell us our fortunes?" Robin Hood queries.

Marian hits Robin in the back of the head.

"OW!"

"Don't be stupid Robin, of course he will!"

Marian looks at Princess Haru.

"He will tell us our fortunes, won't he?"

Princess Haru nods her head. Marian slaps Robin Hood behind the head again.

"OW!"

"See? What did I tell you?"

Princess Haru takes out a cloth with a glowing green gem.

"This gem has been handed down through my family for generations. Take it."

Robin Hood takes the glowing gem. He puts it in his pouch. Robin Hood and Marian collect all the arrows they can find from their fallen enemies.

"How did you know I had been following you?" Marian asks her husband.

"Most of my arrows have black fletching. I had noticed that someone had been assisting me in my quest... someone whose arrows have red fletching." Robin replies.

"How very observant of you. What is it with you and your black arrows?"

"It is my final judgment. The black arrow is so everybody knows they deserved it." Robin Hood says gruffly.

Princess Haru walks up to them.

"Friends... if you plan to find the rose of the dead, the Necromancer knows the only way to find it. Good luck on your Quest."

Robin Hood and Marian attach their arrowheads of true silver. They reembark on their journey. Unfortunately, as Robin Hood spins around he braces for The Lord of the Darkness' third Horseman, War, riding towards them. Robin takes an assassin's stance.

"Marian, take the Princess and run."

"Robin, I..."

"RUN!" Robin bellows.

Marian takes Princess Haru by the hand leading her away. War grabs one of his six hatchets then throws it at Robin Hood. Robin hides behind a tree, as the hatchet embeds itself in the tree trunk. Robin Hood dashes from behind the tree, he cartwheels away from an incoming second hatchet.

Robin Hood decides to stand still, making himself a target.

War throws his third hatchet straight for Robin's body. Robin Hood moves his body to the left as War's hatchet cleaves through Robin's cloak. War circles around and throws his fourth hatchet from behind Robin Hood.

Robin Hood, not liking that War is behind him, falls flat to the ground as the fourth hatchet sails over him. Robin Hood rolls over onto his back, cocking his head to the left as the fifth hatchet embeds itself where his head had been.

Robin stands up to face War like a man. War throws his sixth hatchet at Robin Hood, but Robin snatches it out of the air. Feeling the strong pull, Robin redirects the force by throwing it right back into War's head, splitting it open. A crimson river pours out of the Horseman's skull as Robin Hood walks up to the dead combatant.

"I only need one."

Meanwhile, Marian is leading Princess Haru into the woods. The deeper into the woods the two women get, the darker, the more haunting the woods become. Marian listens to the cry of the wolf. Marian realises that she and Princess Haru are being followed by a pack of wolves. Princess Haru points to a nearby cave.

"Take me in here."

Marian enters the cave with Princess Haru. Marian is terrified to find dozens of wolves in the said cave, she is terrified that they walk like men. Princess Haru walks up to two thrones sitting in the cave then sits in one.

"You can leave me here. I'll be quite all right, dear."

"You're surrounded by wolves that walk like men. How will you be all right? Every beast seems out of control!" Marian says in complete hysterics.

"The wolves are out of control! Every last one of them, save for the Wulfguard, who only serve my husband, and me."

A bewildered Marian walks back out of the woods, escorted by two wolves walking like men. Marian meets Robin, so they continue onward towards the Alps.

CHAPTER XXVI

Tatzelwyrms and Really Mean Squirrels

As Robin Hood and Marian near the Alps, Marian speaks.
"Robin, something is wrong, it has been twelve hours since the sun should have risen..."

"...And yet we are still in darkness." Robin Hood says completing her sentence.

Robin and Marian hear ungodly howling, they draw their bows as a vicious pack of beasts attack them. Robin fires twenty-two arrows in 16.5 seconds, while Marian fires thirty arrows with deadly precision in the course of 15 seconds. The pack of beasts lay dead on the ground before the two lovers. One of the beasts, not quite dead, lunges at Marian, but Robin slashes its throat in midair with his sword protecting his wife,

Robin turns his gaze to a huddled Marian. "Are you all right?"

"I'm fine, Robin, just a bit shook."

"Are you sure that's all?"

"I am cold... and hungry."

Robin Hood builds a fire to warm his wife. He cuts the meat off the dead beasts, cooking it to feed her. Robin and Marian lay together by the fire.

"What did you think of dinner?" Robin asks.

"Surprisingly tasty..." Marian answers.

"This storm has been raging since I arrived in France."

"This is weird. We have been climbing the Alps, yet it still hasn't died down." Marian says.

"I would say it has gotten worse." Robin says.

"Robin. Can I ask you a question?"

"Anything, my love..."

"Why are you doing this? This is not a Quest; this is a suicide mission."

"Because your cousin, my King, specifically requested me to do it. Because I am the only one who can do it."

"My cousin has passed. We could just turn back." Marian offers.

"Back in the Holy Land when I served King Richard, I was not just a soldier. I was an Assassin for the King. I have done terrible things in the name of England. This is my last job, after this, I'm done." Robin says.

"You won't turn back? Don't you want to?"

"Do I want to turn back? Yes. The reason I'm doing this is that I want the world to be a safe place for our children to grow up in."

"Our children? You want to have children?" Marian says in complete surprise.

"Maybe two or three, wouldn't you like children?"

"As long as one of them is a girl." Marian says.

"I would like that."

"Now I know why you won't turn back. You never turn back, Robin. You want to save the world."

A fairy lands on Marian's shoulder.

"Look, Robin! A fairy!"

There is a large WAP! as Marian crushes the fairy with the palm of her hand.

"Disgusting little thing..." Marian brushes the fairy off.

"But Marian...We could have flown there. It might have had some pixie dust."

"It might have had rabies, and you didn't protect me! Hmm... Rabies. All the more reason to get it the hell off of my shoulder!"

"Marian."

"Yes, Robin?"

"I am about to tell you something I haven't told anyone."

"Not even Richard?" Marian asks,

Robin shakes his head.

"Oh, God. You love Men. I knew it!"

"Yes! No! What? No! Is that what you think of me?"

"Well, what is it then?" Marian asks again.

"I spared Saladin's life."

"Who's Saladin?"

"Oh, come on... Don't you know anything about Holy Crusade? The Pilgrimage?"

"I wasn't allowed to fight. I'm a damsel, remember? Such is my lot, pure rot." Marian scowls.

"Didn't Richard mention Saladin?"

Marian shakes her head.

"Truly? You were in communication with him for years."

Thunder booms

"All Richard ever wrote was Dieu et mon Droit. Over and over. God and my right, all that kind of sentiment. He kept sending me lists of people. He referred to them all as used cart salesmen, He was going to repay them by visiting swift and righteous action upon them," Marian says.

"Richard had an enemies list?"

"Robin, Coeur de Lion's Royalty. They all have an enemies list."

"Am I on that list?"

"You were. However, Mercardier put you at the top of potential threats to the crown. You had a question mark. He considered you to be an unknown variable. I should know. I'm the one who burned the bloody thing. It was ash before you set one foot back on Merry Old England." Marian says.

"Things aren't so Merry anymore..." Robin Hood laments.

Purple Lightning strikes. Robin rises, shaking his fists at the stars. "Yeah! Come on! Bring it!"

Green Lightning crashes downwards.

"Is that all you got? Come on! Bring it!"

A Red Lightning storm showers bolts throughout the land. Robin is walking forward in fiery crimson flashes.

"I'm sorry, that's not nearly enough!"

"Robin!"

Marian grabs Robin Hood pulling him back from the precipice. They fall onto the ledge and watch as scarlet fire covers the earth.

"I'm tired." Marian yawns.

"But we still need to eat our salad." Robin replies.

"Robin..."

"Yes, Marian?"

"Spare the salad."

Marian falls asleep against Robin Hood, he puts his hand over his mouth and chortles mightily.

When Marian wakes up, she finds Robin has prepared a bag of food. He has kept the fire smoldering with heat for her.

"How long have I been asleep?" Marian asks.

"Six hours. The sun still has not risen. I am beginning to wonder if it ever will..."

A bright flash illuminates the land below. Dark Armies are marching through them.

"We're high up. It's a heavy storm, we might not have been noticed at all...it's time to get moving." Robin remarks calmly.

"Now? In this!?" Marian says frantically.

Robin spins around and looks her in the eyes.

"This isn't a game Marian! This is an assassination! We can't stay in one place for too long."

Robin Hood and Marian climb through the Alps as a storm rages on with the heavy torrent of rain bombing them with wet droplets only made worse by the sharp crackling of lightning. They are far above the ground freeclimbing a mountain, Marian loses her grip, but Robin catches her. The storm continues to rage on. Robin and Marian get to the top. Red and Green Lightning is going off like bombs in the sky. Red Lightning flashes revealing armies crossing through the mountains searching for spies.

Robin and Marian make camp in a cavern in the mountains. They hide as a squad of Skeletons carrying floating candles in their rib cages search the cavern. Robin is attacked by a Tatzelwyrm, a snake-like creature that has a cat's head with sharp claws. It gets underneath Robin's shirt.

"Don't worry, darling. It's only a Tatzelwyrm, it's known in these parts. Let's not antagonize it. Everything should be fine."

Marian grabs her sheathed sword.

"Don't worry, I'll save you, Robin."

"Marian, no. Wait!"

Marian wails on Robin, not hitting the attacking Tatzelwyrm a single time. The Tatzelwyrm scurries off as Marian drops her sheathed sword. Robin is face down on the ground when he slowly raises his index finger.

"One of these days, you will be the death of me, woman."

Robin sits on the cavern floor looking up at Marian. She smiles her red lips at him, they start laughing uncontrollably. They settle down. Robin Hood spins around followed by Marian, they face the Skeleton that is standing there watching them.

There is an uncomfortable silence that feels as though hours are going by. The Skeleton opens its jaw pointing at them with its raised index finger. It hisses as it leans forward before it lets out a Xena war cry. Robin and Marian shoot it with several arrows, but the Skeleton doesn't go down. Finally, Robin Hood shoots an arrow at the candle extinguishing the flame. The Skeleton collapses.

Several more Skeletons arrive. Robin and Marian make their way through the cave shooting the floating candlelight out of the enemy. The final Skeleton screams before it begins burning. The Skeleton transforms into a huge fireball barreling for them. Robin leads Marian out of the cave, into the rain. The Burning Skeleton emerges from the cave screaming while a gigantic bolt of lightning illuminates all the mountains. The boom of thunder is a crackling explosion. The heavy rain extinguishes the Skeleton. The single floating candle is still lit despite the heavy rain. The Skeleton peers down at the candle. It decides to charge Robin and Marian again. Marian fires an arrow extinguishing it. The Skeleton collapses in pieces.

Robin and Marian continue their journey. As soon as the couple manages to make it to the other side of the mountains, they find their path blocked by an enemy encampment.

"Here's what we can do Robin... we use our bows to take out the four sentries keeping watch, then we stick to the shadows to take out the others one at a time... "

"That is an excellent plan Marian, but I suggest we just clear out the entire encampment with one arrow."

"One arrow? Robin, I know you are good, but somehow I doubt you are that good."

"Marian, sometimes one extremely well-placed shot makes all the difference in the world."

Robin Hood grabs an arrow then draws his bow. Taking careful aim, he releases his shaft, and the arrow flies several hundred feet hitting a beehive. A swarm of angry bees descends onto the enemy encampment clearing the area of any living creature. Robin Hood and Marian walk calmly through the deserted encampment.

Marian looks around. "So, it has been seventy-two days since the sun should have risen. Things aren't so bad. The water is still water, the air is still air, nature is still nature. Isn't that right, Mr. squirrel?"

The squirrel throws a pinecone right between Marian's eyes.

"Don't worry Mr. Squirrel, I don't bite, much."

Marian chases the squirrel but is hit by a hail of pinecones.

"Ow! Ouch! EEK! Robin, save me!"

Robin Hood unsheathes his sword.

"I'll save you, Marian!"

Robin rushes to Marian's rescue, however, the hail of pinecones becomes a firestorm. Robin dashes away.

"Retreat! Runaway!"

"Robin! Wait for me!"

Robin Hood and Marian run away through the woods.

"Marian look! There is a light in the distance!"

Robin Hood and Marian stride towards the light while being pelted with pinecones by little six-inch bastards. Robin and Marian happen upon a homestead, they start banging on the door.

"Open up! Ow! Open up!" Robin Hood yells.

"I'm coming. I'm coming." The voice on the other end of the door says.

"For God's sake, hurry up!" Marian begs.

A pinecone hits Marian in the ass.

"EEK!"

The Necromancer opens the entrance to his domain. Robin Hood and Marian rush inside.

"You two were screaming as if the devil himself were after you..." The Necromancer quips.

"Not the devil... Just really, really mean squirrels." Marian says.

"I am the Necromancer. Feel welcome to stay here until you think the squirrels are gone."

Inside the Necromancer's lair, there are charts of the stars, leather-bound books of spells, with a crystal ball, which shows an image of the Timeless Clock. Marian peers closer into the crystal ball. She is staring at a large wooden grandfather clock that has a glowing green face with three hands but no numbers.

The clock opens a door to outer space. Marian is flying past the rings of Saturn. She strays into the three massive twisters of Jupiter. She is violently thrown about until she is thrown clear of the giant tornado, she lands in the second tornado where she is again violently thrown about before she gets thrown into the third tornado.

Violently shook Marian is sent flying past Mars, she swears she spots a face. As she flies past the moon as she notices multi-coloured lights on the far side of the moon.[19]

Marian enters the Earth's atmosphere flying down through the clouds, she is almost struck by Red Lightning. Marian falls into the roof of the Necromancer's residence before she falls out of her own iris flying into the wall. The Necromancer and Robin rush to her side.

"Marian! Are you all right? What the hell just happened?" Robin asks in astonishment.

"I saw other worlds, Robin." Marian answers.

"You gazed too deeply into the crystal my dear." The Necromancer says.

"A friend of ours named Princess Haru tells us you know how to find the rose of the dead." Robin says.

"Why in Merlin's name would you want to find the Rose of the Dead?" Asks the Necromancer.

"Because it is key to the Quest." Marian answers.

"Haven't either of you heard the story of the Questing Beast?" Asks the Necromancer.

"No." Robin says.

"No." Marian says.

"It doesn't end well..." The Necromancer says to both of them.

"I have to find it. Please. You're the only one who can help me." Robin pleads.

"Sigh. Very well. To find the Rose of the Dead, you must locate the Necropolis."

"The Necropolis?" Marian asks.

"A city of the dead that is located deep in the heart of Wallachia. If you can find safe passage through, you will find the rose of the dead. You're trying to find the Lord of the Darkness, aren't you?"

The Necromancer conjures the image of the Lord of the Darkness in a pool of water.

"How did you know?" Robin asks.

"Why else would you try to find the Rose of the Dead? He has been around longer than any of us. He is undead. Listen to me, it is said that the only way to defeat the Lord of the Darkness is to pierce his heart and his soul."

"How do you accomplish that feat?" Robin wonders out loud.

"The hell if I know. But before you find the Lord of the Darkness, you must find and obtain the Bloodstone before he does." Says the Necromancer.

"The Bloodstone? What is that?" Marian asks.

"In the beginning, there were the Dragons, then the Dragons created the stars with their great fire. Within the star systems lays the Celestial City. In the shining light of the Celestial City, the stones were created: The Sunstone, the Moonstone, and the Bloodstone. The Bloodstone is what The Lord of the Darkness covets most, it's the keystone. If Dracula obtains the third celestial stone along with the two others, he will fly from Demigod into something rivaling the Cosmic God, then it's GAME OVER."

"Where is the Bloodstone?" Robin asks the Necromancer.

"In the Dead House, where the river meets the forest. The Dead House is a place even I daren't go. It is in the Valley of Death. It feasts on the living. It is a place feasting on evil and fear. But there is a complication, to enter the Dead House you need the key, the key is not far, but it is in a tower in a heavily guarded castle."

The image of the Lord of Darkness notices the Necromancer spying on him, so he bites the Necromancer's hand.

"Robin, he looks awfully pale." Marian says.

Robin Hood pokes the Necromancer. The Necromancer falls over.

"He's dead..." Robin states.

"What do we do?" Marian asks.

"Let's sift through his pockets for any loose cash. He's not going to need it."

Marian and Robin roll the body then start taking all the valuables.

"Look, Robin! I found thirty pieces of silver!"

"Sweet! Now let's get a move on..."

Robin Hood and Marian travell to the nearby castle. Robin and Marian walk up to the castle's moat but the draw bridge is up.

"The Drawbridge is up. There is no other way in that I can think of, besides, there are only two of us. It's impossible to lay siege to the castle without an army."

"Robin, an army is approaching. Can we lay siege to the castle now?"

Robin looks at the army focusing his eyes on the flag with a Dragon on it.

"The enemy army is approaching. We are dead! We are so dead!"

"Robin, the castle moat is a river. See? There is a current in the water."

"So?" Robin asks.

"It means there is a sewer, a sewer leads inside the castle. Follow me."

Marian dives into the moat as does Robin Hood, they find their way into the underwater sewer, then climb out of the castle latrine. They get into the castle courtyard as giant fire-spitting bats spit fireballs at the gate. Robin grabs a castle guard then pins him to the ground. Robin puts a knife to his throat.

"Tell us where you are keeping the key to the dead house or I will slit your throat." Robin threatens.

"Go ahead! I do not fear death. He comes for us all eventually." The castle guard shouts defiantly.

Marian pulls out her knife, she puts it to his crotch.

"Tell us where the key is, or else I will sever what defines you as a man. If you don't, I can promise you will never pleasure anyone again including yourself."

"The northeast tower. Third floor!"

Robin Hood slits his throat. Marian stares at Robin.

"That was rather cold-blooded for even you, Robin."

"I have changed."

Robin Hood and Marian go into the third floor of the northeast tower. The castle gate is smashed open. The dark army floods into the courtyard. Robin and Marian find a locked chest on the floor.

"They are coming for us, Robin. It is only a matter of time."

"Give me your brooch, then lock the door."

Marian gives Robin her brooch, then she locks the door. Robin picks the lock with the brooch in ten seconds flat. He opens the chest, grabbing the key. Swords pierce through the door. There is a screaming sound outside the door.

"They are getting through the door. What do we do, Robin? What do we do?"

Robin sits down cross-legged.

"Wait to die." He says.

"That's not good enough!"

Marian stomps her foot on the floor rug, it causes a hollow sound. Robin gets up.

"Wait a second."

Robin Hood removes the rug revealing there is a secret door on the floor. Robin and Marian go below as the Screamers chop down the door with their swords. Robin Hood and Marian leap out of the second-story window into the moat below. The current carries them into the Valley of Death.

CHAPTER XXVII

The Dead House

Robin Hood and Marian move through the forest valleys, they climb to the top of the hill overlooking the Valley of the Dead House. They see massive battalions of men, beasts, and monsters, moving through the valley carrying white-hot spears and torches.

They listen to the constant beating of war drums. Robin spies The Banner of King Richard following the dark forces. Marian and Robin observe as the armies are drawn out of the valley to engage each other.

"The forces of light and darkness seem distracted. What would distract them from battle in this valley?" Marian wonders.

"The only reason they would not fight here is if they found something far worse than death in battle. They all know, let's move."

Robin and Marian go down into the valley where they see the Dead House. Robin Hood and his wife get closer to the Dead House. Giant, bat-like creatures swoop down from the sky, they begin hammering the ground with fireballs. Robin and Marian get to the Dead House clearing where they have clear sights. Robin and Marian draw their bows, firing towards the creatures killing them. The Dead House is on a hill as the autumn leaves fall. Red light emanating outwards.

"Marian, stay here. You are trembling. This thing feasts on fear and evil. You have a lot of fear in you. I'll go."

Marian grabs Robin's hand. "Robin, all the people you have killed over the years. What is the difference between good and evil there?"

"I wish I knew. If you hear screaming in there, do not try to save me. Run. Run away as fast as you possibly can."

Robin Hood climbs up the hill, he opens the Dead House door. Robin transforms into a silhouette bathed in radiant red light. Robin is inside the Dead House. Four Screamers appear floating out of the fireplace mantle holding swords, Robin fires his bow and arrow. Robin's arrows go right through.

"I can't kill you..."

The Screamers draw close to Robin, surrounding him. Robin drops to the ground as four Screamers pierce each other.

"...But I can make you kill each other."

Ungodly screams are heard by Marian. She follows Robin's instructions. She flees in terror. Robin is in the living room by the hearth. Suddenly, a Headless Knight bursts through the floor, taking a swing at Robin Hood. Robin draws his bow, shooting an arrow straight through the heart of the knight. The knight takes three steps back, then starts to rush Robin.

"Okay. That's new."

The Headless Knight attacks Robin. Robin uses the Headless Knight's momentum against him throwing him into the wall. Robin pierces the shoulders of this dead nightmare, pinning him to the wall. The Headless Knight walks towards Robin as the arrow's shafts slip through the wounds. Robin and the Headless Knight battle each other with their swords through the hall. The Headless Knight has Robin cornered in a small room. The Headless Knight rushes Robin again, but Robin throws him halfway through the window, cutting him in half.

Robin steps back into the living room only to find that he is surrounded by demonic creatures. Robin's shadow is on the wall, surrounded on both sides by grotesque monstrosities. The surrounded shadow draws a sword and lots of blood smatters the wall. Robin uses Marian's brooch to pick the lock on the chest.

Robin opens the chest obtaining the third glowing gem: The Bloodstone. There is an evil awoken, the Dead House starts laughing. Robin releases his sword. A hollow laughter is heard as madness begins to kick in. Robin Hood lifts the carpet, only to find a glowing light beneath the floorboards as well as a secret tunnel. Robin uses the tunnel but is washed out of the tunnel by blood. Robin Hood lays on the blood-drenched floor. A gigantic heart appears in the living room, slowly rising through the floorboards. The laughter echoes.

"Fuck this place!"

Robin drives the sword through the beating heart of hell. The hell heart explodes. Robin abandons the Dead House as it collapses in on itself.

"Marian? Where are you?"

The Horseman of Death silently drops from the trees above. He pulls out his two sabers, Robin Hood pulls out his sword as he spins around to meet Death in battle. Robin is on the defensive against a flurry of strikes. The swords are cutting through both the gambeson and the chain mail. Robin is cut a few times but is not badly wounded. Unfortunately, he is never given a chance for an offensive strike.

Robin finally manages to disarm Death of one of his swords by batting it out of his hand. Suddenly Robin Hood is more evenly matched with Death. Robin holds his sword out in front of him. His opponent does the same. They begin circling one another. Robin Hood manages to get a few cuts in, but in return is cut a few more times. Robin Hood anticipates his opponent. Robin stops circling.

"Come to me."

The Horseman of Death rushes at Robin Hood at terrific speed to deliver a killing blow. Robin steps aside letting him barrel past.

When the Dark Assassin spins around, Robin Hood kicks Death square in the ghoulies.

Robin is finally able to completely disarm Death of his sword, but then Death grabs Robin's sword from his hands. The Dark Assassin stands up with the blade pointed at Robin's neck. Robin Hood kneels before the English Steel. Death is a fraction of a second from running Robin through when three lightning-quick strikes in the shape of a Z occur in Death's body. Death explodes in blood and body parts, revealing Marian standing from behind with her sword drawn. Robin is looking at his wife in astonishment. "That was amazing! I have never seen anything like that before! What do you call that Z-shaped strike?"

"I call it the triple strike maneuver. I only used it to protect you, my love."

"... I am glad that you did."

THE LORD OF THE DARKNESS sits on his dark throne.

"So, all four of my horsemen have been defeated. It matters little... all of their combined might is barely a fraction of the power I possess."

The Lord of the Darkness climbs the spiraling staircase of his castle's dark tower until he reaches the top. The Dark Lord points his burning sword of doom towards the heavens so its fire shoots into the thermosphere, stirring the S.P.R.I.T.E.s and E.L.V.E.S.

This causes a red storm to brew, Red Lightning crackles downwards, scarring the Earth Mother. People across all the lands witness this dark event as terror fills their hearts. The Lord of the Darkness descends to the dungeon, finds a captive who he puts on a slab. He lowers the slab into the lava as many goblins hop around laughing.

Robin and Marian arrive at a river where the ferryman is waiting.

"I have been waiting for you, Robin and Marian of Locksley."

"How do you know our names?" Marian asks the ferryman.

"I know everything." The Ferryman answers.

Lightning crackles.

"Where would you like me to take you?" The Ferryman asks.

"Can you take us to the Necropolis?" Robin answers.

"I can take you there, but first you must pay my toll."

Marian pays the Ferryman so She and Robin can enter the boat. The boat takes off down the river on their journey to the Necropolis. Robin Hood glimpses into the river water, staring into the watery eyes of a woman of exotic beauty. She reminds Robin of Sibylla, but this woman has black hair.

Lightning strikes, illuminating thousands of human skulls on the bottom of the river. Robin places his hand over his belly, he senses movement in his gut, something is horribly wrong with the situation.

"Boatman, what river are we on?" Asks Robin.

"We are on the river Styx."

"That means that you are Charon..." Marian says.

"Correct..."

"Oh god..." Marian exclaims.

"There is no place for God where you are headed," The Ferryman says.

The boat enters some sort of fog. Robin Hood and Marian register ghostly faces in the fog. They both realise what they entered isn't fog.

"Please keep both of your hands and feet inside the boat the entire time, remember, feeding the dead is strictly prohibited, punishable, and enforced."

The boat exits the fog-like substance arriving at the docks of the Necropolis.

"Remember, if you ride upon the river Styx again, you automatically enter a chance to win an eternity on the log ride."

"I wanna go again! I wanna go again!" Robin shouts.

"Oh, very well." Marian says.

Robin and Marian ride the river Styx again.

Robin holds Marian at the front of the boat.

"Feel the surf on your face, Marian? Ride the wave! Ride the wave!"

The Boatman arrives at the dock of the Necropolis.

"I wanna go again! I wanna go again! I wanna go again! I wanna go again! I wanna go again! I wanna go...."

Marian smacks Robin in the back of the head.

"OW! Oh, right.... the Quest."

"Someday I will be back for both of you...." the Ferryman tells them.

The Ferryman takes off down the river. Robin Hood and Marian step off the dock. The Assassin leads his wife down the dark Gothic City streets.

"I feel like we are being watched from the shadows." Marian shudders.

Robin and Marian stroll into the city's square, where there is a cadaver impaled with a sword lying next to a broken-down fountain.

"If this is a city, where are the inhabitants?" Marian asks Robin.

The impaled cadaver rises to attack Marian, but she pulls the sword out of the body, beheading the cadaver.

"The dead are restless, Marian."

An army of the dead shamble towards Robin and Marian. Robin and Marian stride across a bridge. The lovers stride into a tower. They are surrounded on both sides of the tower staircase. Robin and Marian pull out their swords. The shadows of Robin Hood and Marian start hacking away; blood splatters across the wall. They get to the top of the tower after rising to the fourth floor. Robin grabs his rope, ties it to his sword, pierces the roof of the tower, then the lovers repel down the tower using their momentum to swing the rope. They land next to the circular chasm on the outskirts of the Necropolis. Robin Hood and Marian leap the chasm, landing on a large central pillar. The dead fall into the chasm. Robin peers over.

"Man. Dead men can't jump."

On the pillar there are twelve gargoyles in a circle, looking towards the center. In the center of the pillar lies a shrine adorned with a plaque. The statue of the thirteenth winged gargoyle sits perched on top of it. The center gargoyle seems to be holding something that is not there. Marian approaches, she examines the central shrine.

"This seems to be missing a few things." Marian comments.

Robin examines the shrine. He notices three small indentations on the plaque.

"I wonder..." Robin starts.

Robin Hood places the three glowing gems he collected in each indentation. A blue flame appears in the hands of the winged gargoyle. The flame rises, floating away from the Necropolis to a distant mountain.

The Gargoyles shockingly spring to life, they attack Robin Hood and Marian. The lovers fight the many gargoyles, but the Winged Gargoyle takes Marian by surprise, grabbing her, then carrying her off into the sky. A terrified Marian cries out, "ROOOOBIIIII-INNNN!!!!!!"

Robin Hood has a shot; He can't take it because Marian is too high up from the ground.

"MAAARIIAAAAANNN!!!!!"

Robin Hood draws his bow then spits and curses the remaining gargoyles.

"Damn you! Damn you all!"

Robin Hood slays the rest of the gargoyles with such ferocity, it's as if the gargoyles were no more dangerous than kittens to him. Robin Hood leaps the chasm to escape into the forest.

Many miles away, the Winged Gargoyle deposits Marian on the balcony of Castle Dracula. Marian, laying on the balcony floor, looks up, only to behold the dark majesty of The Lord of the Darkness. Remotely human, he is the most terrifying creature in history.

His smile consists of razor-sharp teeth. his blood-red eyes pierce. His pale terrifying face is completely devoid of emotion. He is a figure of malice and imminent doom that bears the symbol of the red dragon upon his dark armour, covered by his flowing black cape. The Lord of the Darkness stares into Marian's soul.

"Welcome to my lair."

Marian lets out a bloodcurdling scream.

CHAPTER XXVIII

As She Turns

Robin Hood makes his way to the distant mountain the blue flame travelled to. Making his way through the woods, Robin finds he is hungry. Robin Hood spots a little girl in a red hood with a cape skipping as she carries a basket of cupcakes. Robin Hood shoots past the little girl snatching the basket from her.

"Hey, those cupcakes were for my grandma! This is the eighth time this year! Curse your black heart, Robin Hood!"

Suddenly without warning, a werewolf in drag pops out of the bushes, grabs the little girl, pulls her behind the foliage before it devours her behind the bushes. Robin Hood is eating the cupcakes.

"Hey, these cupcakes aren't that bad."

Halfway up the mountain, Robin Hood finds a cave illuminated with blue light. Upon entering the cave, Robin Hood walks across the cavern towards the blue flame. Robin Hood out of curiosity touches the blue flame, it immediately engulfs his entire body.

MARIAN WAKES UP IN bed. She puts on a robe.

"What a long, horrible nightmare."

Marian walks across the room into the shadows. Marian bumps into something in the darkness. Unfortunately, that something has a name, and it is Lara. Her glowing green eyes are all Marian can make out through the darkness. Lara is Dracula's favourite because she is also the mother of his first child. She emerges from the darkness, dressed in black with red spikes adorning her dress.

"Who are you?" Marian asks.

"My name is Lara."

"What are you?" Marian asks.

"What I am is not nearly as important as what I am not." Lara replies.

Marian's voice trembles, "What are you not?"

"Alive!!!!!!"

Lara opens her mouth revealing sharp fangs. Marian clambers back.

"These are the others..." Lara says.

"Others?"

Two other beautiful women emerge from the darkness.

Their eyes are glowing green. All three of them are unnaturally pale. They are dead...but alive???

"How exquisite. A new toy..." Tara says.

"I want to play with her hair..." Fara adds.

Lara becomes wrathful. "HIIIIIIIISSSSSSSSSSSSSSSS!!!!!!!!!! The master wants her unharmed for himself."

"Who says we can't have fun with her first?" Tara asks.

"I DO!!!!!!!!"

Lara, Tara, and Fara back away from Marian, very scared for their lives. Dracula steps towards Marian.

"Come, walk with me. You must forgive Lara, Tara, and Fara. They are young, they are impulsive."

Marian, unable to help herself, walks with The Lord of the Darkness.

"I have heard rumors that someone from England has been coming to assassinate me, but never in several lifetimes could I imagine my Assassin to be as beautiful as you. Look here."

Marian follows Dracula to a book on a pedestal.

"This is a Limited Edition Necronomicomic. It's a book of demons and monsters. It took me a long time to obtain it. It's something I wanted for a long time, yet now I have it. I consider it to be the Holy Grail of my collection. What do you want?"

"I only want the darkness to end." Marian says.

"The darkness will never end. There cannot be light without darkness. But if you want to bring light to a darkened world, become my bride. Become an immortal symbol of light in the eternal darkness."

"I don't believe you." Marian says.

"Pretend to believe, think magic, wish mercy, and sin in paradise..."

The Lord of the Darkness grabs Marian by the back of her head, tilts her head back then begins kissing her with his serpentine tongue. Marian sheds her tears.

ROBIN HOOD APPEARS on a gigantic fountain surrounded by eight roaring waterfalls.

"So cold... the fire is so cold."

Robin Hood climbs up the various pools of the giant fountain to the very top. At the top of the fountain, Robin Hood finds a sword embedded in the fountain, a sword surrounded by stars.

"I shall call this *The Stormblade*," Robin says.

Robin Hood pulls The Stormblade out of the fountain, he swings it about with practiced precision. The sword shines with a magnificent blue radiance. Robin Hood sheathes his sword but is swept off his feet by the draining fountain water. Robin Hood washes down the fountain drain.

BACK AT THE LAIR OF The Lord of the Darkness, Marian and Dracula sit in a circular cushioned seat with a table in the center. They have a nice view of different tapestries depicting the constellations. Dracula pours a drink for himself and Marian. Dracula discusses things with Marian.

"You look like a nice lady and I don't wanna hurt you, but I will feast on your entrails if I have to."

"My, aren't you the lady killer..."

"The entire world will be enveloped in darkness, soon you, Marian, will be the sole reminder of the light the world once had."

"I never wanted this... I would never want this."

"Very soon the entire world will worship a Dark Lord."

"Why would they worship someone who tortures and kills them?"

"You worship the Crucifix which represents the promise of death, the ancient Hebrews worshiped a Deity idol of Ba'al which demanded human sacrifice, the Romans used the cross to kill people while the golden bull was another method of death. These are not religious iconography, these are instruments of torture and death. Symbols of torture and death have always been viewed by humanity as a means of salvation. Ironic, isn't it?"

Marian stares dumbfounded into her glass. "The irony isn't lost on me. What I find most frightening in what you say is that you are probably correct."

"Marian, do you know the secret of the universe? Life never should have happened. Our very existence is just a cosmic accident. History is a mistake. In the beginning, the heavens, the earth were created, when they are destroyed, it will probably never happen again. The fact that we exist on this earth, right here, right now, is a bigger miracle than any you will ever imagine."

"You speak foul blasphemy..."

"I speak it quite fluently." Dracula says rather proudly.

Marian motions Dracula towards her with her finger.

"Come over here. Give me some sugar, tiger..."

Marian begins making out with The Lord of the Darkness, while he is distracted, she pours lethal poison into his drink. After she is done, they stop making out.

"A toast..." Marian starts.

"To the dead." Dracula finishes.

Marian begins drinking with Dracula.

"This is really good wine." Marian comments.

"I never drink wine..."

"Really? Then what is this?"

"Blood."

Marian spits out the blood then tosses her goblet.

"You're really sick, you know that?"

"Enough of your insolence!"

Marian pulls out her knife as The Lord of the Darkness attacks her.

Kill him! Kill him until he's dead!

Dracula leaps onto Marian, she shoves the knife into his heart, he overpowers her.

I can't move!

The Lord of the Undead opens his maw revealing fangs to a petrified Marian.

I can't move! I can't move!

Dracula penetrates her neck flesh with thirty-two fangs. The Vampire drinks her blood.

Robin! You'll come! You'll save me! I just have to hol.....

After he is finished Marian lays dead on the table. Dracula raises his head screaming out of his blood-soaked jaws,

"Let slip the dogs of war!"[20]

The dogs of war are let loose. They chase Robin.

Things Robin Hood can do:

2. Robin Hood can be chased by the dogs.

Robin clambers up a wooden pole. At the top Robin Hood shoots the dogs dead with his arrows. Robin spies the castle in the distance. He storms in smiting the guards protecting the castle. There is a Screamer climbing across the floor. It is dragged down by chains tied to weights. It spots Robin before it lets out a scream, it starts crawling towards Robin Hood. It is crawling slowly. Robin rushes by it really quickly. The Screamer pounds its fist into the ground. Robin Hood dashes to the top of the tower finding Alucard waiting.

"You're too late. The princess is in another castle! Ah! Ha! Ha! Ha!"

Robin is perplexed. "Princess? I'm here to save Marian."

"Who's Marian?" Alucard asks.

"Shit!" Robin curses. The crawling Screamer arrives in the room extending its hand towards Robin Hood. Robin gives it a bag of gold, leaving the room first. The crawling Screamer begins to crawl away.

"Hey, you! Get back here!" Alucard shouts.

As the Screamer crawls away, it gives Alucard the finger then shortly disappears from the door frame.

Robin Hood journeys further until he must sit down to rest. Robin Hood looks above him staring at an impaled body. Robin finally collapses to the ground.

The sky has become red; Robin Hood is in the midst of thousands of impaled bodies. Robin has memories of all the times people told him about the rows of the dead. For the first time in a long time, Robin Hood is frightened. Robin Hood curls up in a ball and begins rocking back and forth. A mental image of Marian appears before him.

"*What is the matter, my love?*"

"I don't think I can do this... I don't think I can win this time... I'm not sure if I can save you. I'm nothing without you."

Marian takes Robin's hand and kisses it. Sitting down beside him, she puts her arms around him and speaks to him,

"*I know why you won't turn back. You never turn back Robin. You are a Hero, you want to save the world.*"

Marian takes Robin's hand and places it on his sword handle.

"*Just remember, Robin. Jesus saves souls, then redeems them for valuable prizes.*"

The red cross begins to emanate light. The cross becomes silver. Robin Hood tightens his grip on his sword, he continues onward marching through the rows of the dead. Keeping low, Robin Hood climbs a hill overlooking the castle. The harvest super moon lay above Castle Dracula.

Robin Hood witnesses Dracula emerge from the castle. He slides down the dirt ramp outside his front gates. Dracula sits at the table, overlooking the impaled. Dracula dines on human flesh; he drinks human blood. Dracula, quite drunk from the poisoned blood Marian slipped him, begins an exploration of his id.

"I really like wearing women's panties. They are so nice and soft, best of all, they never chafe. I also like petting the baby bunny rabbits. They are so furry and fluffy; I just want to hug each-and-everyone. I think I'll install a bunny farm out back. I want to see a Blackula in the closet of every white woman across Europe."

"I can't believe it; the guy is a friggin' terrorist..." Robin says in disbelief.

Inside the castle Marian lies in a coffin, her skin is completely pale. Her once brown hair transformed completely black with a small grey streak. Marian is dressed in a black dress with red spikes on it. Lara hovers over Marian. Lara turns her head to the right, making sure Tara and Fara are playing with their own experiments, two scared teenage girls.

Lara begins kissing Marian on the lips as she starts tearing off Marian's dress. Lara puts her head between Marian's legs then bites. Marian's eyes unexpectedly shoot open. They glow brightly green. Marian sits up.

"AAAAAAAHH!"

Marian realises that Lara is in the process of violating her body.

"You bitch!"

Enraged, Marian grabs Lara by the head pulling it back. Lara looks at Marian while panting. Marian flies out of her coffin.

"Time to go out the window..."

Marian drags Lara by the hair towards the window. Marian tosses Lara headfirst out of the window.

"That wasn't supposed to happen! You weren't supposed to kill Lara!" Tara screams.

"Marian threw Lara out the window! Run for your life, Tara! She's gone mental!"

Marian picks up a battle-axe off the wall. Tara and Fara run for their lives against a wrathful Marian.

"Armoury..."

CHAPTER XXIX

GAME OVER

Robin Hood has drawn his bow, he is about to let a black arrow fly into the Dark Lord's cranium when there is a loud crash followed by a large splash. Rushing down to the river below, Dracula finds the dead body of his bride, Lara. Lara's neck is snapped. Dracula cradles the body of his beloved Lara.

"NO! NO!!! NOOOOOOOOOOOOO!!!!!!!!!"

The Lord of the Darkness lets out a booming, inhuman shriek heard for miles. The cape of The Lord of the Darkness unfurls, revealing bat-like wings. He flies back up to the castle into the room with the broken window. Robin Hood dashes down the hill, past the table to begin picking the lock to the castle. As Robin Hood picks the lock, blood shoots out of the keyhole hitting Robin Hood in the face.

"Gaaah!"

Robin Hood stumbles down to the river Lara was cast into. Robin Hood notices some of the water is flowing into the rock. Robin Hood dives underwater. He emerges from a pool of water in a small cave. Walking through the small cave he spies an opening, stepping through the opening, Robin Hood enters the Dungeons of The Lord of the Darkness. Robin Hood is making his way through the dungeon when a skull on the floor begins harassing him.

"Hey! Hey buddy! You're gonna die here! I'm pretty sure I can pull some strings and have you buried in that suit!"

Robin takes the door out of the dungeon, closing the door behind him. The skull sits on the cellar floor.

"I'm lonely."

Robin walks through the dark corridors lit by torchlight. Robin tries not to notice that skeletal arms protruding from the walls are holding the torches. As Robin Hood steps through the corridors, the walls start bleeding. Robin Hood dashes up some steps at the end of the corridor, He emerges from a door to find he is on the side of the castle.

He spots several stone gargoyles sitting on the castle.

The stone crumbles, Robin faces off against six different gargoyles. The gargoyles begin flying around. Robin begins to shoot them with arrows. Three gargoyles are hit. The demonic creatures spiral to the ground. Three are hit but manage to land on the side of the castle to attack. Robin Hood unsheathes his sword in a quick draw attack cutting a gargoyle in half. Robin kicks a loose stone into the second gargoyle's face, stunned by the rock Robin Hood cuts off the gargoyle's wings shoving him off the side of the castle. The last gargoyle raises both of his hands.

"You know what? I don't even like this job. I don't get paid enough to deal with someone like you. I'm out."

The gargoyle flies away into the night. Robin re-enters a different part of the castle coming to a circular room with four torches. Four skeletons crash through the walls attacking Robin Hood. Each skeleton is holding a torch in one hand, with a saber in the other. Robin Hood unsheathes the Stormblade cutting the head off the first attacking skeleton. The other three skeletons surrounding Robin Hood strike.

Robin Hood blocks all three blades, he spins his right leg in a fluid 360-degree motion, tripping all three attacking skeletons. Robin

Hood uses the shining sword to destroy his fallen foes. Torches, sabers, and broken bones lay upon the ground as Robin Hood exits. He dashes into a hallway with six suits of knight's armour standing on each side of an archway.

Twin Faces of Thaleia and Melpomene hover over the Archway.

Suddenly, the six suites of armour spring to life to attack Robin Hood. Robin uses the sword to take on the six supernatural opponents. Robin goes into a sort of free-flow combat, cutting off the six steel sword hands like a hot knife through butter. Robin continues his combat by rendering all the armoured opponents limbless, he kicks them over just to add insult to injury.

Robin Hood walks through the door. He finds a normal rectangular room with a door on the other side. All that is between him and the way out is a monkey sitting in the middle of the room holding a ruby red ball. It's monkey ball time.

Robin begins to approach when the monkey screeches and throws the ball over his shoulder. The ball bounces off the second door back into Robin Hood's face. It falls onto the floor bouncing back into the monkey's paws.

"You little..."

The monkey throws the ball onto the floor in front of him so the ball bounces straight into Robin's own.

"AAAAH! NNNNG. RRRRRRGGGG! (Gasp!) What the Bloody hell is that thing!?"

Robin Hood draws his bow, but the monkey throws the ball back onto the floor in front of him in the exact same spot but this time the ball bounces off the floor into the ceiling above before bouncing off the ceiling flying straight through the arrow Robin fired at the monkey. The ball bounces off the floor rolling into the monkey's paws again.

"SCREEEEEECH!!!"

The Monkey throws the ruby ball sideways to his right as it hits the wall it bounces off into the opposite wall before it then bounces off the wall behind Robin and smacking right into the back of Locksley's head. Robin stumbles a bit before he picks up the ball lying beside him. He throws the crimson ball straight at the monkey, but the monkey catches it.

"Oh no."

"SCREEEEEEEEEECH!!"

Robin Hood pulls out a bottle of wine he purloined from Jacques' Chateau.

"We can fight, or we can party!"

The monkey sits there for ten seconds processing this information. The monkey throws the ball aside and Robin drinks wine with the monkey.

The monkey starts talking monkey talk. He has his arms out before freaking out. The monkey uses his archer's fingers to walk. The monkey screeches again then he puckers his lips before tapping his heart. Robin Hood has been watching the monkey.

"Yeah, they always want to be your friend, right after they take your heart and tear it apart."

Robin Hood hands the monkey the bottle. The monkey drinks two more times then passes out. Robin stands up. He never had a drop. Robin walks over to the door. The knob is a small brass wolf's head. He turns the knob. He turns the knob again.

Locked!

Robin Hood shudders in fear. He shakily kneels. He hesitantly picks the lock. He recoils putting his hands over his face. He sits there for six seconds. He slowly lowers his hands. He peeks then lowers his hand. Robin's arm trembles greatly as it slowly approaches the doorknob. The wolf doorknob bites his hand.

Robins bloody hand twists the doorknob opening the door. He glides through the doorway to enter a large room with hundreds of floating lit candles. On a lower level, Marian opens the door to the armoury to enter. Robin Hood is creeping through the grand room, he accidentally bumps into a few floating candles that begin moving away. Robin Hood touches a floating candle, it spins away slowly.

Suddenly, all the candles go out, Robin Hood is in complete darkness. Robin Hood feels something ominous growing.

"Perfect. You brought the sword right to me. You fool."

Dangerously, every flame jets upwards as blood starts raining down from the ceiling. Instinctively, Robin Hood ducks as a monstrous man-bat Dracula swings his burning sword from behind to behead Robin. At this point, Robin Hood has entered hell. Robin Hood pulls out the Stormblade grabbing the sword with both hands to block Dracula's powerful blow. For the first time, Robin Hood discovers how powerful The Lord of the Darkness really is.

Robin Hood grabs his sword handle with both hands, He fights for his very survival against a flurry of Dracula's powerful blows. Robin's shining blue sword spins and clashes together with Dracula's burning sword, causing dozens of candles to burst into floating hot wax, with others cut in half. Many candle pieces begin spinning in multiple directions as Robin Hood fights to survive.

Dracula's blows are so numerous, so powerful, Robin Hood is forced to the bloody floor. Dracula goes for the deathblow, but Robin Hood manages to roll out of the way of his killing strike. Robin clambers away, kicking lots of blood around. Dracula laughs demonically as the lights go out. Robin Hood is in complete darkness again. The candles jet upwards once more as blood pours down heavily.

A few candles fly towards Robin, but he cuts each of them in half. Robin Hood gazes upwards noticing Dracula hanging on the ceiling. Dracula drops from the ceiling, driving his burning sword towards Robin Hood, but Robin manages to roll away, only being slightly grazed. Robin lunges the Stormblade at Dracula's heart, but

Dracula is standing on top of The Stormblade before Robin can even process what happened. Dracula kicks Robin Hood in the head. The claws on Dracula's toes cut Robin's face. Robin Hood, stunned, drops his weapon.

Disarmed, Robin Hood thinks quickly, he uses the environment to his advantage. Robin Hood grabs two candles, he points the jetting flames at The Lord of the Darkness as hot candle wax burns his hands. Dracula is burning alive.

"AAAAAAAAAAAAAAAAAAAAA! HA! HA! HA! HA! HA! HA! HA!"

The flames consuming Dracula's body flow into his hand, The Lord of the Darkness shoots a projectile flame at Robin Hood from his left palm. Robin Hood barely manages to dodge the projectile, however white-hot chain mail is searing itself into the side of his torso. Robin cries in a blood rage, he guns straight for Dracula tackling him to the ground. Robin Hood uses fists lightning fast to pound in the Dark Lord's face. Dracula grabs Robin's shoulder, piercing Robin's flesh, Dracula hurls him across the room. Robin's torso is in great pain, as is his shoulder, there are slashes in his armour, he doesn't know if he is bleeding, blood is flowing everywhere. He tastes copper in his mouth. Robin Hood picks up the Stormblade as the lights go out once more. Robin Hood is in complete darkness for the third time. The candles jet upwards again as blood rains from the ceiling. Robin Hood tries drastic measures for drastic times. He copies Marian's triple strike maneuver, Dracula explodes into a swarm of bats that flies around the room, reassembling into The Lord of the Darkness on the other side. Robin is swinging wildly through all the blood.

Dracula silently rises from the blood behind him. Robin Hood spins around as Dracula grabs him, they go into the circular stained-glass window through a bolt of Green Lightning; emerging a moment later in a different part of the room from another bolt of Green

Lightning. Robin spins around with his sword but there is no one around. Robin begins losing his mind.

"Huh! Ha!... Ha!... Ha! HA! HA! HA! HA! HA! HA! HA! HA!   HA!   HA! AAAAAAAAAAAAAAAAAAAAAAAAAAAAA!!!!!!!"

The lights go out for the fourth time.

"Ha! Ha! I won't live much longer. Huh. Huh. Huh."

Robin is struggling to maintain control.

The candle's flames jet upwards again as blood continues to rain down in this hell. A grotesque, monstrous, Bat-Dracula spots Robin in his cloak and hood, he runs his burning sword of doom through the back of Robin's hood. Suddenly a blood-drenched Robin Hood attacks Dracula from behind, he begins stabbing the shit out of The Lord of the Darkness.

"DIE! DIE! DIE! DIE! DIE! DIE! DIE! DIE! DIE! DIE! DIE! DIE! DIE! DIE! DIE! DIE! DIE! DIE! DIE! DIE! DIE! DIE! DIE! DIE!"

After stabbing Dracula twenty-four times with the Stormblade, Robin drives The Lord of the Darkness to the ground. Robin puts his gambeson back on. Robin Hood understands he has only made his opponent angry. Dracula rips the Stormblade out of Robin's hands, grabs Robin by the throat, dragging him to the castle rooftop. Blood Red Lightning crackles around them as the castle roof is lit by harvest moonlight.

"What did you do to Marian?"

"I drank her blood. I drank her life away... any other last words before I cast you into the river, the way you cast my beloved Lara?"

"Yes, I do..."

Robin Hood points to the left corner behind the Lord of the Darkness.

"What the hell is that???"

The Lord of the Darkness looks behind himself. He witnesses the Black Knight still on fire, running through the distance screaming his head off.

"That's the coolest thing I've ever seen!!!"

"Look again!" Robin shouts.

Dracula looks behind himself again observing Marian on the right corner of the roof, holding crossbows akimbo. Marian fires the crossbows, two silver-tipped arrows fly into both of Dracula's eyes since the eyes are the windows to the soul (the brain). The Lord of the Darkness begins screaming violently.

"AAAAAAAAAAAAAAAAAAAAAAAAA!!!!!!!!!!!!!!!!!!!!"

Robin Hood pulls the silver-tipped arrow out of his quiver,

"SIC SEMPER TYRANNIS!!!"

Robin Hood stabs the silver arrow through Dracula's heart as The Lord of the Darkness continues to scream violently.

"AAAAAAAAAAA!!!!!   AAAAAAAAAAAAAA!!!!! AAAAAAAAAAAA!!!!"

The Lord of the Darkness spins around a few times, falls onto his knees, then collapses dead. Robin Hood leaves the cake next to the dead vampire. Marian is a bit crazed.

"Heh. Heh. Heh."

Robin hoofs it back into the castle as does Marian. They race down the hallways. Marian bolts left from Robin. Marian briefly halts at an altar in the hallway. The strange book lay there. Marian grabs the book before she continues towards the stairway with Robin. Robin and Marian meet at the grand staircase as stones are crumbling down. They flee down the stairs as they dodge falling debris. They exit the front gateway to run far away. Robin and Marian watch in the distance as Dracula's Castle explodes. Robin walks over to Marian. They embrace and kiss each other passionately. The first light of dawn appears for the first time in a long time. Robin Hood observes many fang marks on Marian's neck, Robin rubs his finger-tips across his wife's neck as tears stream down her cheeks.

"What happened to you? Your hazel hair is now black as night, the tone of your flesh is much softer in colour."

"Horrible things Robin. Terrible things. But the nightmare is over now. You are here, now we are together again."

A skeleton stands off to the side,

"Kiss!" He shouts.

Robin and Marian look at one another, nod, then attack the skeleton.

"Look, horses are running around wild." Robin says.

Robin Hood secures a horse for himself and Marian. Marian mounts Trigger to ride on the long journey home. They witness lava exploding from the surrounding mountains as they flee on their horses racing back to England.

IN THE LARGE PILE OF rubble, a stone starts wobbling before it tumbles off, a hand emerges from the rubble. The Lord of the Darkness crawls out of the castle ruins. He stands up. He brushes himself off.

"Hmmm. I'm dead now."

Rick and Wilbert arrive. Wilbert opens a scroll and begins to read,

"Dracula, we are bill collectors sent here to collect the two Gold Ducats that Richard The Lion Heart loaned you while on Crusade."

"Darn. I thought he forgot about that... Come on guys, I don't have two Gold Ducats on me. Everything of value I own is beneath that mountain of rubble."

Rick hands Dracula a shovel.

PART FOUR

IN THE RECESSES OF HISTORY LEGEND MEETS MYTH

Dramatis Personae

R obin Hood-Legendary Hero
        Marian Fitzwater-Legendery Heroine
Moonfang-The Wulf King
Princess Haru-Mate of the Wulf King
Ironsword the Conquerer-a legendary female warrior
The Gorgolac-Mother of the beasts
King Arthur-Legend
Morgan le Fay-Sorceress
Sir Mordred-Fallen Prince
Charon-Boatman
King John-King of England
Little John-Robin Hood's Lieutenant
Will Scarlet-Robin Hood's Brother
Jerry Springer-Host of trash TV
Priest-One of Robin Hood's Team
Isabella-Wife of Priest
Isaac Komnenos- Emperor of Cyprus
Dracula-Lord of the undead

                    Unnamed

Pirate Princess
Captain of the Archers
Minotaur
Black Knight
Witch Queens
Annoying Skeleton
The Robin's Man
Merry Men
Gryphon
Sea Serpent
Sea Dragon
Bootshine Boy

Driver
Archers
Phantom
Ninja Mouse
Audience

CHAPTER XXX

Love & Fire

I n the beginning, there was The Fox symbol. Lilith was exiled from paradise, taken to Mount Olympus where she waited on the mountaintop without food or water for three days and three nights. On the third night, a city of golden light appeared in the sky. A silver wheel descended from the city. Deus Ex Machina left the wheel, he observed the beauty of Lilith, he decided to take her with him into the machine, they left for the sky.

In ancient Greek times, Lilith returned to the world of man with her new nickname: The Gorgolac. She could not kiss men for they would die. She could not have children for she gave birth to monsters. She could not die for she was the first true immortal. Over the centuries the Gorgolac went mad.

ENGLAND, 1200 A.D.

Robin Hood and Marian arrive at the shores of England.

"Driver! I say, Driver! Can my wife and I catch a ride to Huntington Castle?" Robin asks.

"I do not give rides to those who touch children." The Driver answers.

"He. Heh. Heh. I... I mean...It's not true... Technically I never touched him... I offered him a cake. Besides! I am Robin Hood!"

"I do not give rides to Robin Hood's whores either."

Marian loses it. She clears the carriage grabbing The Driver.

"I. Am not. Robin Hood's whore!"

Marian throws him off his carriage. She rides off swinging around to pick up Robin Hood. Robin Hood and Marian steal the carriage. They ride to Huntington castle, They ascend the stairs to their quarters. Robin takes off his shredded Gambeson and mail; He puts on his green tunic instead. Marian walks behind her dressing screen, undresses from her torn red and black clothing, putting on her green clothing. Marian returns to watch Robin Hood sit by the open window on the third floor playing the ocarina.

"Could you be any more obvious? Everybody is going to know we are back if you keep playing that thing." Marian says.

Robin Hood begins to play his ocarina some more.

"What the frick is that?" Marian asks.

"An ocarina." Robin replies.

Marian points to the window.

"No, what is that?"

Robin peers out the window locating several lights below emanating from the forest. Men emerge from the forest holding burning torches. They gallop upon horses to set fire to the castle.

Robin loses it. "No! It's burning! Our home is burning down! My father's home! My father's father! NOOOOOO!"

Robin and Marian snatch their bows and quivers. They dash to the top of the castle away from the flames. They begin pouring arrows at the men on horseback. The men on horseback use shields to block the arrows.

"The flames rise. We can't stay here much longer," Marian says frantically.

"They have the advantage on the ground." Robin states calmly.

"We've faced worse, right?"

"True, but we have always had trickery or luck on our side."

"Is that a bad thing?" Marian asks.

"Only in moments like this when we have neither. We must go down."

Robin lowers a rope from the tower so Marian can climb down first. Robin climbs down right after she sets foot on the ground. The knights grab Marian, she starts screaming. Robin is grabbed, then immediately punched in the gut while held in place. Marian is thrown onto the ground as men start to gather around her. One man gets on top of Marian. Marian begins to fight back but her arms are pinned to the ground. Robin is struck across the face.

Suddenly, the captors are attacked. Robin is not sure who it is, but a large group of villagers swarms the soldiers. The swarm of villagers is led by Sarah. Sarah swings a large quarterstaff breaking it on the head of the attempted rapist knocking the soldier off Marian.

"Master Robin? Lady Marian? You've returned?"

"Sarah! What has happened to our country?" Marian asks.

"It's not safe for you here! King Richard passed leaving Prince John in charge."

Marian is horrified. "No..."

"King John hates you, both of you, when you left England, King John said you left to become servants of The Lord of the Darkness." Sarah continues.

"Did you believe him?" Marian asks.

"No! None of us who served under you believed his lies. We just were unable to stop him from doing this. You need to go... now!"

His face full of tears, Robin rides off into the forest with his wife. Robin and Marian are trotting through the old base camp, long abandoned and overgrown with thickets.

"Why are we in Sherwood, Robin?"

Robin Hood stops Trigger at a tree, he grabs Marian by the waist. He tosses a special rope over the tree branch attaching it to the horse; the horse pulls Robin and Marian up to the secluded hideaway.

"This was my anniversary gift to you Marian, a seasonal hideaway house in Sherwood Forest. The things we have been through together..."

"What kinds of things?"

Robin Hood begins lighting the candles.

"The way I have felt about you, ever since I can remember..."

Robin looks into a lit candle, which illuminates his face under his dark hood.

"What kind of way?" Marian takes off her husband's hood looking into his eyes.

"This way." Robin says.

Marian and Robin Hood unclothe each other as they continue kissing. Robin Hood and Marian make passionate, sensual love. Robin shoves Marian onto the floor establishing his dominance in the bedroom.

Marian lay naked on the floor as Robin stands over her.

Marian begins to crawl backwards away from Robin then motions with her index figure to come to her. Robin caresses Marian's flanks, rubbing his palm down her flanks to her leg squeezing the thigh.

Marian rolls Robin over as she lies on top of him. Marian leans over Robin, he starts pulling her hair, he keeps pulling on it until she lay on him, they kiss. Robin rolls her over again. Robin grabs her legs, and they start screwing against the wall.

After a while, Robin sits down with Marian on top of him. Marian grabs Robin's hand and pours hot candle wax onto it, causing him to squeeze Marian's delicate hand. Marian takes Robin's hand and places it over her chest so Robin can feel her heartbeat. "This will always be yours. My heart shall forever belong to you and only to you."

At that moment, Robin and Marian are connected on a deeper level than they ever have been previously. Robin gives Marian a love bite on the neck, for a brief moment, Dracula is in Marian's mind sucking her blood. Marian starts screaming, terrified beyond comprehension. She throws Robin off her. She lies sobbing naked on the floor.

"Is there anything you want to talk about with me?" Robin asks.

"No..."

"I love you, Marian."

"I know..."

Marian examines the scars upon Robin's body.

"What happened here?" She asks.

"A Nottingham guard shot me with an arrow... I nearly died."

"How did you get these burns?"

"I was severely burned when I fought The Lord of the Darkness in an attempt to rescue you."

Marian smiles. "And to think I ended up saving you... where did you get this scar on your shoulder?"

Robin looks away. "Jaffa."

"How?"

"It's the price I paid for saving a life."

"What about this long scar on your arm?"

Robin quickly glares. "That's where you cut me with a knife, you crazy bitch!"

Marian slaps Robin.

"After what you pulled in the woods that night, you deserved it, you wolf!"

Marian and Robin Hood start making out again.

"Robin, I have something to tell you. I saw you when I followed underground. You were phenomenal in your archery. No one has made a shot like that since Odysseus. Being with you is the only time I ever feel alive. Playing with you in Sherwood Forest when we were children, then the playing turned into training. We were good, then we got better. It got to the point where I felt you and I could take on an army by ourselves. Then you left for the Crusades, yet I couldn't follow, I was all alone.

I was sent to London to be with all the other noblewomen. I couldn't stand them, with their self-righteous attitudes. I gained more respect for my hard-working servant, Sarah, than I ever did for them. I felt like I was imprisoned by what society expected of me. One night I just ran, I ran so far, I went into the wild. I was alone in darkened woods, that night, I felt as if something was watching me, something with red burning eyes."

"lucifer?" Robin asks.

"Of course not!"

"Jesus?"

"Maybe... anyway, whatever it was, it felt like death. Then, when I felt I was about to be taken, I heard a woman singing a haunting melody. I followed it to a luminescent lake, where I witnessed a woman bathing in that lake. There was no moon out that night, but I saw her clearly. She had a pale beauty to her. I asked her if she was cold. She spun around addressing me by my full name: Marian Fitzwater.

She said it was no coincidence that we were both there that night. She told me she came from a realm beneath the water, then she spoke of the prophecy of the twin blades: the two were opposites of one another, but when united, the warrior that wields them would be unstoppable. She told me not to resent my place in the world, but to use it to my advantage. She disappeared beneath the water right before dawn broke. That morning, I went back to my residence, I was delivered my father's sword. He had been slain in the Crusade. I took Sarah, then moved to Nottingham Castle in my father's quarters, waiting for you. I waited for my twin blade."

Robin Hood stands up pointing.

"Look out! It's that ravenous beast again!"

A raccoon looks inquisitively from the windowsill before Robin Hood punches it. The raccoon falls to the ground below. Will Scarlet faces the treehouse from the ground. "Hey, I'm trying to walk here, can't you see I'm walkin' here?"[21]

"Will Scarlett! Is that you?

"Robin? Robin Hood? You're back! It really is you! We have an emergency!"

"What is it, Will?"

"When you left, Prince John took over. Little John, Allan A. Dale, and the rest of the Merry Men tried to organize a revolt."

"How did that turn out for you?" Robin asks.

"We tried our best and failed miserably!"

"What happened?"

"Most of them died fighting, the others were captured, they are due to be hanged." Will Scarlett says.

"Why are you still alive, and free?"

"As soon as the fighting started, I ran like a chicken with its head cut off..."

"Smart man, Will." Robin shouts back.

CHAPTER XXXI

The Inner-Circle

It is morning in Nottingham Town Square. Twenty not-so-Merry Men are about to be hanged by King John, in the very largest public display of mass hanging that could be remembered. The Hangman checks each of the Merry Men's bonds, he wraps a noose around each of their necks.

"I am not completely without mercy. Tell me where you renegade peasants have stored all the valuables you have stolen, so mercy can be granted." King John says methodically.

"Everything we have ever stolen was given to the poor as well to those in need, you chew-chomping dip-wit!" Little John shouts.

"A crime worthy of death!" King John says coldly.

"Are your souls prepared for what's to come, gentlemen?" The Hangman asks.

"Aye!!!!!" The Merry Men shout.

"So be it!" The Hangman says.

The Hangman disrobes, revealing himself to be Robin Hood. Robin pulls his sword out, spins his body throwing his sword spinning it three hundred and sixty degrees. The sword, spinning violently, cuts off three guard's crowns. Meanwhile, the Merry Men whose bonds Robin had cut, take off their nooses, Robin Hood pulls the lever, so the Merry Men fall beneath the platform, disappearing into the crowd.

While all of this is happening, the rest of the royal guard has been shot dead by deadly little Marian with her bow and arrows. Robin retrieves the Stormblade.

"Sic Semper Tyrannis!" Marian shouts.

Marian shoots the apple out of King John's hand, just to show that she can.

Robin, Marian, and the surviving Merry Men make it back to Sherwood Forest. That night, there is a Christmas Party near a snow-laden tree. Robin gives all his Merry Men presents.

"I got you guys something extra-special this year!"

The Merry Men open their presents, they all receive the dreaded red shirt from Star Trek.

"Redshirts for all of you! Merry Christmas everybody!"

The thumping of a loud heartbeat is heard.

"I like red." Mulch says.

The thumping heartbeat goes crazy.

A pigeon flies into Robin Hood's encampment. Marian grabs the pigeon; she finds a note.

"Robin, we received an invitation from Prince Wolfstonecraft of Darkwood." Marian says.

"We did?" Robin asks.

Marian begins to read the letter. "'Dear Robin Hood and Lady Marian, my fiancé, Princess Haru, told me of your bravery and exploits. You are welcome to join the two of us along with the rest of our inner-circle at Castle Wolfstonecraft.' Should we go?"

"Why the hell not?" Robin asks.

Robin Hood, Marian, Will Scarlet, Little John, Alan A. Dale, and the other seventeen Merry Men travell to Darkwood. The path to Castle Wolfstonecraft is treacherous, fraught with danger. Robin, Marian, and twenty of the Merry Men in red shirts hear growls from a vicious Gryphon in a field of mist.

Marian shouts to the rest of the survivors, "It's a Gryphon! They ask riddles just like a sphinx!"

Robin has his bow and arrow drawn. The Gryphon swoops through the fog. Robin's men bunch together in teams.

"Who. WHO. WHOOOOOOO."

The winged monstrosity wraiths through the mist.

"We face a monster of the mist." Robin Hood says.

Four of Robin's Men are bunched together.

"You. YOU. YOUUUUUU."

The Gryphon swoops down tearing open two of the Merry Men's torsos. The two remaining members of the squad are back-to-back. A silhouette approaches them in the mist.

"Who's there?" The Merry Men shout.

"Who's the boss?"

"Ho there, Master Robin," The relieved Merry Man says.

The silhouette reveals itself. It walks upon two legs, it has the tail and body of a lion, the wings the head, and the front talons of an eagle. The Gryphon screams.

The next four Merry Men wince at the hideous screams crying out in the fog. They notice a figure on two legs quickly approaching. The Merry Men line up in a firing squad and let loose a flurry of arrows. The figure emerges from the mist. The last remaining survivor is riddled with arrows. He topples over, dead.

"Wait, what?" the squad leader says.

There is a sharp flash of pain as the spines of each Merry Man are severed.

The Gryphon strolls among the paralyzed men.

"Riddle me this, what is the reality of being a soldier?"

A Merry Man coughs up bubbling blood. "We're expendable." he warbles.

"Very good. Now, who tastes the best?"

The Gryphon begins his feast.

Five of Robin's Men are bunched together the silhouette of the Gryphon glides through the mist above them. The team sends several volleys straight to the roaming aerial shadow. The Gryphon cries out, somersaults, and falls to the ground.

"Confirm the kill!" The squad leader shouts.

The remaining Merry Men swarm over the area the Gryphon seemed to crash into. There is an alarming scream erupting from the fog, The Merry Men scurry over to find one of them is now clumps of sticky meat. One of the Merry Men bends over to examine it. He rolls over the upper torso. The Robin's Man is shocked.

"Cumberbitch. Sumbitch killed Cumberbitch!"

"He always did hate that name," The other Merry Man says,

The Robin's Man stands up.

"Still, I won't miss his stupid jokes about the Scots." The Robin's Man says.

The Merry Man looks at the other. The other Merry Man is looking up.

"What is it?" The Robin's Man asks.

The Robin's Man spins around to witness the Gryphon carrying a headless fellow Merry Man. He glides earthbound casting the body on the two petrified brethren of his latest victim. The body lands on them with a large thud. Screams turn to gargling. The six remaining Merry Men bunch together.

"A donkey carries 20 bottles of milk in a cart, A Spanish Stallion carries 40 sticks of butter in his cart. Their drivers weigh exactly the same, both carts travell at one horsepower, they are two miles apart from one another, Where will they meet?"

"I could never handle word problems!" A Merry Man shouts before his head explodes.

"Neither could I!" Another shouts before his head explodes as well.

"Why does Helena meet with Blondel at 11:00 pm every Friday?" The Gryphon asks.

"I fucking knew it!" The Merry Man named Preston screams.

Preston takes off into the mist.

Three Merry Men are left bunched together. The Gryphon dive bombs, smashing into them.

Screams rupture throughout the mist. Marian is in a cold sweat, she glances over to Robin. Robin Hood's face is cool, calm, and collected.

"Who's the boss?" The Gryphon asks.

"Robin Hood's the boss!" Marian shouts back.

"Hey Gryphon! I have a riddle for you!" Robin screams.

"What is the riddle?"

"What flies, has no eyes, but hurts from here to hell?" Robin asks.

"Easy. An Arrow." The Gryphon answers.

"No. It's your head!"

Robin Hood shoots two arrows into the Gryphon's eyes killing it in the field of fog-covered snow. Finally, the company arrive at Castle Wolfstonecraft; Prince Wolfstonecraft greets the party at the castle entrance,

"Welcome to Castle Wolfstonecraft. I am Prince Lupin Wolfstonecraft, you must be Robin Hood, and you must be Lady Marian... My Lady, your beauty exceeds that of my fiancé's description. But who are these other fellows you have with you? I have not heard of them."

"These are my Merry Men. The big one is Little John, the one dressed like a court jester is my brother, Will Scarlet, the shifty-eyed looking one is Alan A. Dale." Robin says.

"They may enter the castle since they are your associates, but only you and your wife may enter the inner-circle," Prince Wolfstonecraft replies.

"I'm cool with that. Are you cool with that Marian?"

"I'm cool with that."

"Yeah, we're both cool with that." Robin says.

Prince Wolfstonecraft claps his hands together.

"Good. Good. I'm glad you're both cool with that. Follow me."

"So, I have been wondering, what is this inner-circle you speak of?" Robin asks.

"Since the fall of Camelot, there has been an inner-circle of legends. Devoted to filling the gap that King Arthur and his round table left, only those deemed worthy enough are to join. Robin Hood and Lady Marian, defeating The Lord of the Darkness cemented your status among our ranks."

"That's pretty sweet." Marian says.

"Let me go over the charter rules of the inner-circle of legends. Charter rule number one, you must become drunk and belligerent. Charter rule number two, you must become even more drunk and belligerent. Charter rule number three, failure to abide by the previous two charter rules is grounds for immediate expulsion from the inner-circle of legends."

"How exactly does this fill the gap King Arthur left?" Marian asks.

The married couple is led into a circular room with two women sitting on couches. One woman is clearly Princess Katherine Haru while the other woman has auburn hair, form-fitting armour, brandishing a large broadsword. There is a portly teenager with a brown cap, wearing peasant's clothing, shining boots in the hallway exit.

"I now would like you to meet another member, this is Ironsword the conqueror."

"I have heard of her, what is she doing in the inner-circle of legends?" Robin asks.

"So, you know of her. She has slain the nose goblin at Borgo Pass." The prince replies.

"So what? I have once slain fifty-four nose goblins inside of an hour!" Robin shouts.

Marian points accusingly at Robin Hood. "It's true! He made me sit and watch!"

"Also belonging to the league is my fiancé Princess Katherine Harooooooo!!!! Sorry... I kind of do that sometimes. Anyway, Katherine is one of the best hunters in the world." The prince informs Robin and Marian.

"What makes her so skilled at hunting?" Marian asks.

"She captured me..." The prince mutters.

Princess Haru becomes noticeably excited. "Marian! Robin! It is nice to see you both under much better circumstances this time."

Marian smiles. "I was not sure if I would ever see you again, Katherine."

Marian hugs Princess Katherine.

The prince points towards a fourteen-year-old boy. "Finally, over there is our boot shine boy..."

The boot shine boy pulls out a knife. "I'll friggin' cut you man..."

"Robin Hood wants ale!" Robin shouts.

Marian grabs Robin's shoulder. "I don't think that's a good idea honey, you get really belligerent when you drink."

Prince Wolfstonecraft hands a large mug to Robin Hood. "Here's a pint of ale!"

Robin Hood drinks the ale.

"Boot shine boy! Robin Hood wants to see his reflection by the time you're finished shining those boots! Do you get it, or does Robin Hood have to draw you a picture?"

"Don't you dare threaten him, Robin!" Marian chastises.

"When Alexander the Great visited the Oracle of Delphi, Alexander asked the Oracle who would defeat him. The Oracle inhaled strange gasses, then proceeded to answer in her usual incoherent manner, at which point Alexander grew short with her, He proceeded to smack the shit out of her. Finally, the Oracle cried out "No one can defeat Alexander!"" Robin Hood says.

"If you think you are right just because you have a dick, it doesn't mean you are right, it just means you are a dick." Marian says coldly.

"Then Robin Hood is the biggest dick alive!" Robin shouts.

Marian grabs her head. "Stop it! Just stop! I can't stand it when you talk in the third person like that!"

"Marian was irate... Robin could tell from her tone of voice and the half-crazed look in the eyes that it was that time of the month again."

"You son of a bitch!" Marian breaks Robin Hood's nose with her fist.

Robin clutches his bloody nose. "The nose! AAAH! The nose!"

Robin Hood, angry at a broken nose, takes it out on the boot shine boy by starting to kick him around.

"How was your journey here?" Prince Wolfstonecraft asks.

"More dangerous than before." Marian answers.

Prince Wolfstonecraft strokes his chin. "Yes, I thought as much. You both may have slain The Lord of the Darkness, but his armies of beasts and monsters are as numerous as ever... we really don't know why that is."

"I have something with me that might be able to help." Marian says.

Marian pulls out a book.

"Where did you get that Marian?" Robin asks.

Robin Hood continues kicking the boot shine boy around.

"I stole it from The Lord of the Darkness himself. He called it the Necronomicomic. It's a book of demons and monsters. I figure somewhere inside it must reference the source of these creatures." Marian says.

The inner circle gathers around the Necronomicomic. Robin Hood points to a page in the book. "There's the Loch Ness Monster! I told you I saw it once, Marian!"

"Just because the Loch Ness Monster is in the Necronomicomic, does not mean that it is real, Robin!" Marian responds.

Marian turns the page. "The Lord of the Darkness! He may have commanded the forces of darkness, but I doubt he's the source, right Robin?"

Robin Hood is sweating bullets looking at the illustration. "Ri-Right Marian..."

Marian turns the page. "The duck-billed platypus!"

Lightning flashes as Ironsword the conqueror gives out a shriek. Ironsword looks a bit embarrassed. "Sorry, it-it was the lightning."

"Riiiiight..." Marian says rather dryly. Marian turns the page. "The Gorgolac, also known as The Mother, or Lilith. It says she is a sorceress expunged from paradise who is as powerful as she is beautiful. She gave birth to The Lord of the Darkness, as well as all the other beasts and monsters that plague the world."

Marian closes the book. "It is abundantly clear about what must be done."

"What must be done?" Princess Haru asks.

"If there is going to be a future for the generations of mankind to come, we must travell to the source to face the terror of the Gorgolac." Marian states.

Robin Hood stops kicking around the boot shine boy. "Yes! For the children! How do we find the Gorgolac?"

Marian shakes her head. "I don't know... outside of this book, very little is known about the sorceress..."

Marian reopens the book. "Wait a minute. Two of the pages are stuck together."

"I curse your black heart, Robin of Locksley!" The boot shine boy shouts.

Marian rips the pages open.

"Good going, Marian! Now it's no longer a collector's item." Robin says.

"Great. Just great. It's only partly legible," Marian says.

Robin Hood grows angry. "You see what you did, you little bootlick?"

Robin kicks the boot shine boy again.

"Oof!"

The boot shine boy goes down. He lays on the floor where he kicks a little every few moments.

"What does it say, Marian?" Robin asks.

Marian keeps on reading. "Beware, the deadly Labyrinth of the Gorgolac. Only Knights of Avalon can find the location of the Labyrinth."

"Avalon? What is that?" Princess Haru asks.

"Avalon is the isle of apples." Marian answers.

"Otherwise known as King Arthur's final resting place." Robin adds.

Marian closes the book again. "Until the once and future King decides to return, of course."

Robin nods his head. "Of course."

The boot shine boy gets up off the floor.

"Does anybody here know how to find Avalon?" Ironsword asks.

Robin Hood shakes his head. "No..."

"Of course not!" Marian shouts.

"I don't know..." Princess Haru says.

"Don't look at me!" The boot shine boy says.

"I might..." Prince Wolfstonecraft comments.

"What?" Robin asks.

Prince Wolfstonecraft shrugs his shoulders. "Well, I know someone who might know."

"Who?" Marian asks.

"Sarah Cutter, the Princess of pirates." The prince answers.

"But she moves around so much... It is nearly impossible to find her. Besides, what makes you think she can find Avalon? Princess Haru asks.

Prince Wolfstonecraft addresses the princess. "Fortunately for us, this time of year she resides at her secret base at Cutter's Cove. Also, if she was able to find the sunken location of Atlantis, who here can say she can't find Avalon?"

"And so the Quest begins again. When it ends, no one knows when." Robin mutters to himself.

Robin Hood, Marian, Little John, Will Scarlet, Alan A. Dale, Prince Wolfstonecraft, Princess Haru, the boot shine boy, and Ironsword the conqueror depart castle Wolfstonecraft. They cross Europe, making the journey to Cutter's Cove.

WHILE CAMPING ONE NIGHT under a full moon, the party sits around the fire when everyone present experiences what sounds like over one hundred wolves howling nearby. The howling of the wolves is responded with the most powerful wolf cry ever heard by anyone in the party, everyone sits in silence.

"What in God's name was that?" Little John asks.

"I honestly don't know...Will, Alan, Little John, keep an eye out. I am going to check on Marian."

Robin Hood locates his wife in their tent.

"Marian, are you all right?"

"No Robin. Lately, I have felt very sickly."

"Should I stop our expedition party for you?" Robin asks.

Marian shakes her head. "I can continue. I am sure it will pass."

Robin wakes up, He steps into the woods by the camp. Robin Hood is about to drain the lizard when he spots Prince Wolfstonecraft chained to the tree.

"Hello." Robin says.

"Hello." The Prince answers.

"So." Robin says.

"So."

"The men got rather drunk and rowdy last night."

"Indeed." The Prince responds.

"Can I ask you a question?" Robin asks.

"Go ahead."

"How long have you been chained to that tree?"

"Just get me down already!" Prince Wolfstonecraft yells.

"Rodger dodger."

CHAPTER XXXII

Unexpected News

The travelling group arrives at Cutter's Cove. Prince Wolfstonecraft shouts upwards to the anchored boat, "Hello up there!"

Nine archers appear all wearing hooded tunics. The Captain of the Archers appears, he has tan skin with a black pointed moustache, any other features are hidden by his hood. He shouts downwards, "Choose your words wisely, for you will only have one chance to speak! State your business!"

"I am Prince Lupin Wolfstonecraft, these are my companions! Tell your princess, I have a mutually beneficial deal to discuss with her if she will grant us an audience!"

The captain of the archers disappears for a while, finally, he returns.

"My lady will grant you your audience!"

Robin, Marian, and everyone else boards the ship. They enter the cabin where the Pirate Princess sits seductively with her legs crossed on her throne. She has a long dark braid, tan skin, thin lips, brown eyes, a dress with stars complemented by crescent moons. Her blouse is tied into a knot instead of being buttoned up. Marian secretly admires this pirate's sexual audacity.

"What is the deal you wish to strike, Moonfang?"

"My companions and I wish to find safe passage to Avalon, so we may find the source of monsters then destroy it..."

The Pirate Princess snorts. "The legendary isle of apples... How is this beneficial to me?"

Robin Hood steps forward. "Monsters plague the earth, now more than ever! Don't you tell us you haven't had to deal with them too!"

"I'll admit, the constant warring between sea serpents and sea dragons has made crossing the oceans increasingly difficult. However, I refuse to grant you passage aboard my ship unless you have brought proper restraints with you."

"We have brought steel chains with us." Princess Haru says.

"Very good..." The Pirate Princess states.

"Why would we need steel chains?" Marian asks.

The Pirate Princess smiles.

"Why indeed? Very well, I will grant you passage to Avalon, but safe passage? Even I cannot guarantee that."

The ship raises anchor, it sets sail off to sea. Ironsword is surrounded by everyone in the crew's quarters which is a large wooden room. Ironsword in sitting in a wooden chair.

"Who wants to hear how I slew the Nose Goblin of Borgo Pass?" Ironsword asks.

"I do." Marian says.

"I do." Will Scarlett says.

"I do." Little John says.

"Hmmph. Very well." Robin Hood adds

"So... after I failed an attempt on the life of The Lord of the Darkness, I was locked up in his dungeons...

I was sitting next to a barred window with the light of the full moon shining through. My hands were shackled to the wall above my head. The Skeleton Guard was standing over me.

'You think things can't get any worse, but you would be wrong... soon the master will be down here to suck you dry, then you will be walled up to add structural support to the castle. How do you think he built this place?' The Skeleton Guard sassed.

'I need a release...' I said to him.

'Too bad! Here, nobody gets released! Not even in death!' The Skeleton mocked.

'No, you don't understand... I need some kind of release. I'm a huge necrophiliac and I really want to jump your bones.' I lied.

'Wowzers, you're a freaky bitch! What the hell, I haven't gotten laid in centuries...' The Skeleton shrugged.

Ironsword adjusts her chair. "The horny little creep." Ironsword scowls. "Now, Where Was I?...

I motioned him with my index finger. 'Come on over, tiger...' I seductively spoke.

The skeleton stepped close to my legs, I kicked the skeleton so hard it fell to pieces.

'Hey! You tricked me!' The skull on the ground shouted.

'Get over it.'

I pick up the keys with my feet, I skillfully unlock my shackles that are restraining me. I grab my iron sword then make my way to the nearest tavern.

I was sitting at a circular wooden table as I was surrounded by many people. I was astonished to find everyone drinking while being merry in dark times. A man strolled up to me.

'It has been a long time Ironsword.' A familiar voice whispered into my ear.

'Karak! My old friend. How is your family?' I shouted in surprise.

'Deceased.' He said rather bluntly.

'What is going on in this world where women and children are dying senselessly?' I asked.

'I want some payback.' Karak said.

'What do you suggest?' I asked him.

'I suggest we take out the Nose Goblin of Borgo Pass.' Karak said rather coldly.

'I'm game for it if you are.' I responded happily.

Me and Karak were hiding behind a large rock watching the Nose Goblin of Borgo Pass pick its nose by a dead tree.

'What is the game plan Ironsword?' Karak asked me.

'Alright here is what we do. You go out, distract the Nose Goblin, meanwhile, I sneak up behind it, then stab it in the back.' I explained.

'That does not sound very honourable nor heroic.' Karak said disappointed.

'History does not care how you do something as long as you do it.'[22]

'Okay, let's do it.' he said.

Karak popped out from behind the stone skipping towards the dead tree to talk to the Nose Goblin of Borgo Pass. 'You know, picking your nose is a disgusting habit.' Karak said.

The Nose Goblin grabbed Karak, it began punching him in the ghoulies repeatedly. Meanwhile, I sneak up behind the monster and impale it. The slain Nose Goblin fell over dead."

Ironsword is sitting forward in the English Oak chair which is facing the opposite way.

"And that is how I slew the Nose Goblin of Borgo Pass."

"Oh! Hmmm..." Marian cries out.

"What's wrong Marian?" Robin asks.

"I just thought I felt a presence, that's all..."

THE GORGOLAC IS IN the cave of echoes witnessing the ship entering the sea through a crystal encasing a dragon embryo within it.

"So... my son's murderers are coming to face my wrath. Let them come. They will be flies caught in the maze of the spider's web, completely helpless yet utterly terrified."

THAT NIGHT ROBIN HOOD enters his quarters, he finds that Marian is in tears.

"Why are you crying, my beloved?"

"I had another one of those dreams again..." Marian says.

"Tell me about your dreams; I know how important dreams can be..."

"I keep having this recurring nightmare that a one-eyed monster is coming for me in the darkness..."

Robin Hood mutters, "You bet your sweet ass it's coming for you."

"It's not just the nightmare, Robin... I don't know how to say... how to tell you... oh god..." Marian starts to cry again.

"Marian. After everything we have been through together, you know you can tell me anything."

"(Sniffle)... Robin. I think I... No. I know... Robin, I'm pregnant."

Robin Hood is covered with shock upon his face. "I'm going to be a father? This is the happiest day of my entire life!"

"But Robin... We are going after the Gorgolac. What if something happens?"

"Marian, my dear, beloved wife, I want you to know as long as there is a breath in my body, I will never let anything bad happen to you. As long as I'm part of the equation, nothing bad will happen to you. I will never forget that it was you that restored my faith in God. Now listen to me very closely. While I was serving in the Holy Crusade, I found the most valuable things there. I even found an object that has the power to change the world."

"Where is it?" Marian asks.

"I hid it in our French countryside farm. When all of this is over my love, I want you to have it."

Robin Hood gives Marian a key.

"Thank you, Robin. I have something for you as well."

Marian gives Robin Hood a dark blue shirt with stars making it look like space. She also gives Robin black tights with a black hooded cloak. Robin Hood cradles the clothes in his arms. "It's so beautiful. Where is the cross?"

"There is no cross. You are no longer a Crusader Robin, you are my husband. I have sown it just for you."

Robin Hood and Marian embrace one another; they begin kissing when a cry is heard.

"There is a sea serpent off the port bow!"

CHAPTER XXXIII

Giant Fire Spitting Bats

Off the ship's port bow, a sea serpent's neck rolls out of the calm water, it begins to bray. The Captain of the Archers leads his team as they shoot their arrows at the sea serpent to no avail. Robin Hood, Marian, along with the rest of the Merry Men scramble above deck to help fight off the beast. The serpent sprays bluish, electrical foam out of its mouth, which sends the team of archers into convulsions. The Captain of the Archers barely manages to not be hit by it. Robin Hood does not know what the bluish electrical foam is, nor does he know what convulsions are, but he does know he does not like any of it, so he pulls Marian away from an incoming blast.

Wrathful at the monster for attacking his wife, Robin Hood draws his bow, firing a black arrow into the soft green tissue of the sea serpent's right eye. The sea serpent cries out in a roar of pain. A roar of power and dominance answers the sea serpent's roar.

The wounded sea serpent is met by a savage sea dragon. The sea serpent entangles the sea dragon in a vicious struggle for survival. In this vicious struggle, the pirate ship is rocked by powerful waves.

"If this keeps up much longer, the creatures will destroy us as well as each other!!!!" Sarah Cutter screams.

The sea serpent sprays the sea dragon in the face with its bluish electrical foam. The sea dragon lets out a roar of pain. The sea serpent takes advantage, biting the sea dragon in the neck, goring it by ripping out a chunk of flesh. The gored sea dragon retaliates by biting the head off of the sea serpent. The headless corpse floats in the water.

The water turns red with the sea serpent's blood, as the sea dragon turns its attention to the nearby pirate ship. Marian shoots nine arrows into the sea dragon's wound as Robin Hood shoots six more. The Captain of the Archers only manages to fire three arrows. The sea dragon gives out a blood-filled roar before it collapses beneath the crimson tide.

"Is it dead?" Marian asks.

The bloody seawater churns for a few moments, then stills. Savagely, the sea dragon lunges out of the water attacking the ship.

"Enough of this!" Little John yells.

Little John steps forward hurling a spear into the open mouth of the sea dragon. The spear penetrates the roof of the sea dragon's mouth piercing its brain. The sea dragon collapses, it lays floating dead in the water.

Will Scarlett stares in amazement. "How on earth were you expecting it to do that, Little John?"

"When a fish dies, it floats in the water. When the sea serpent had its head bitten off, its dead body lay floating in the water. When the sea dragon disappeared beneath the waves, common sense dictated to me that it was still alive, so I grabbed a spear, then I waited." Little John replies.

Everybody on board begins clapping. That evening, Robin is changed into his blue shirt and black cape while everyone is on deck being merry. The Captain of the dead archers walks up to Robin.

"I wanted to apologize, Sir Robin. I thought of you as just another hedge robber; so I held you in contempt when we first met. I thought my team and I were among the best. But watching you and Lady Marian, using your bows and arrows, I came to the realization my men and I aren't even on the same level as you two. I was wrong to regard you with contempt; I want you to know I am man enough to admit it."

Robin Hood puts his hands on the captain's shoulders. "How about two pints of grog? I am sure we can get you something too."

The singing and dancing are interrupted by a most powerful wolf cry that begins the heart-stopping realization they have heard it before. Everyone listens to ungodly growling below deck. Robin and Marian trace the growling back to Prince Wolfstonecraft's cabin. Princess Haru is outside guarding the door.

"There is some kind of animal inside the Prince's cabin!" Robin yells.

"Stay back!" Princess Haru shouts.

Robin Hood rushes past Princess Haru.

"The door is locked!" Robin shouts.

The ungodly growling turns into savage blood lust. Princess Haru grabs Robin Hood pulling him off the door.

"I said stay back!"

"Marian, grab the princess! I'm breaking down the door!"

Marian grabs Princess Haru.

"No! You don't understand! It's for your protection!" Princess Haru shouts.

"Uhh. Robin, darling... I think we should listen."

"Quiet woman!" Robin Hood prepares himself.

Sarah Cutter is walking down the corridor. "What the hell are you guys doing? Wait! No! NOOOOOOOO!"

Robin Hood breaks down the door, then a seven-foot wolf lunges for Robin's throat. Just as soon as the werewolf can sink its jaws into Robin Hood's throat, it's suddenly halted by steel chains.

"Jeezus Effing Christ! That creature ate Prince Wolfstonecraft!" Robin screams.

"That creature is Prince Wolfstonecraft!" Princess Haru shouts.

"Oh. Okay. That makes much more sense. SIT!"

Robin Hood swats Moonfang the Wulf King across the nose. This sends the werewolf into a primal fury, causing Moonfang to break free from his chains. Moonfang, the infuriated Wulf King, chases Sarah Cutter, Princess Haru, Robin Hood, and Marian above deck.

"Swim with the fishes!" Alan A. Dale screams in terror.

Everyone on the ship dives overboard, leaving only Moonfang on board to mark his territory while he howls at the full moon. Come morning time Robin Hood is scrubbing the deck along with Prince Wolfstonecraft.

THE GORGOLAC IS WATCHING the ship enter the mists of Avalon through her crystal. "So they have finally come to the mists of Avalon... do not think you will find safe passage. There are monsters in the mist."

ROBIN HOOD IS ON DECK. "Now that we have entered the mist it is getting harder to see."

Squee.

"Did you hear that?" Robin asks.

"No," Moonfang replies.

"Listen..."

Squee. Squee.

"Whatever it is, it is getting closer," Moonfang says.

SQUEE! SQUEE! SQUEE!

"Do you see anything up there?" Robin shouts up to the crow's nest.

"No! The mist is too thick! I can't... Wait! I think I see..."

A giant fireball destroys the crow's nest. A gigantic bat creature swoops overhead. Robin Hood glimpses something monstrous riding atop the bat creature, but Robin cannot get a clear view. Robin Hood draws his bow and arrow.

"What's happening?" Sarah Cutter asks.

"We're under attack!" Robin shouts.

Several more bat creatures fly over spitting fire at the ship.

"They have some kind of firepower!" Moonfang yells.

Robin Hood listens to another squee, he fires an arrow at the position he heard it come from. Robin detects a faint splash a couple of seconds later. A giant bat-shaped creature swoops down carrying off the boot shine boy.

Robin begins shaking his fist. "Boot shine boy! You'll be avenged boot shine boy!"

Soon the reinforcements arrive on both sides of the ship. Arrows, spears, swords, and knives are used against the enemy's fireballs. The few bats that are killed are insignificant to the numbers that are left. The monsters climb aboard the burning ship to attack.

Robin Hood, Marian, Little John, Will Scarlet, Alan A. Dale, Moonfang, Princess Haru, Sarah Cutter, and the Captain of the archers receive many burns with many more scars defending themselves from the onslaught of attacks. The rest of Sarah's pirate crew dies in combat, Alan A. Dale is swooped off of the ground by a gigantic bat. He smashes his beloved lute on the bat, takes the neck of his beloved instrument, and pierces the skull of the bat through its ear. Alan falls towards the ocean before several bats swarm him, tearing his body apart.

A bat creature grabs Sarah Cutter, Robin Hood kills the monster riding atop the bat, however, the fire-spitting bat carries the Pirate Princess off into the mist. Robin Hood is knocked out by wooden shrapnel. Suddenly it is over, the monsters vanish into the mist, all that remains is a burning, sinking vessel.

Slowly but surely, the ship sinks beneath the waves as the survivors swim in the water, lost in the mist. Then there is darkness. In the darkness calls a voice, the voice is calm, soft.

"Robin of Locksley, your family, your name, your legend, are of greater importance than you know. Your life will be told and retold, it will be repeated throughout history. Your destiny is not of one who is lost at sea. Your destiny, your true destiny, is that of a hero. Soon you will have to face that destiny... awaken Robin Hood, or I will poke you with a stick."

Robin Hood awakens on the shore of a beach. He is promptly poked in the crotch with a stick.

"OW!"

Robin Hood is poked in the crotch with a stick again.

"OW! Quit it!"

Robin Hood is poked in the crotch with a stick again.

"OW! Quit it!"

Robin Hood is poked in the crotch with a stick.

"OW! I said quit it!"[23]

Robin Hood is rapped on the head with a stick.

"Son of a..."

Robin Hood looks up at his tormentor to behold an old man with a large grey beard. He holds a staff, wearing ragged clothes, eating a carrot.

CHAPTER XXXIV

Knights of Avalon

The old man stares down at Robin. "What's up Doc?"[24]
"Where am I?" Robin asks.

"You are on the shores of Avalon... come this way." The old man walks down a trail, Robin Hood shrugs his shoulders, then walks down the trail after him.

Walking down the trail, Robin spots a settlement of houses. He gazes upon three beautiful women standing around a cauldron.

"What fetching lasses, who are they?" Robin asks.

"That is my sister and her two followers... WITCH!"

"Incestuous, pig bastard tyrant!" The sister screams.

The old man's sister and her followers begin throwing exploding apples from the cauldron at her brother and Robin Hood.

"Runaway!" The old man shouts.

Robin Hood follows as the old man runs away. They dodge exploding apples. Robin continues roaming through the wooded trail with the old man.

"I haven't seen such spirit in such beautiful women since... Marian! Old man, have you seen my wife?"

"Perhaps. What does she look like?"

"She has a radiant beauty about her. Her eyes are like starlight, her hair is as black as the night sky. She is my wife." Robin says.

"Unfortunately, I only came across you. You were lying on the beach. So... you and this Marian were at sea?"

"There were others. There were my Merry Men and more. I don't know how many of them survived..."

"It's a big island you know... we can go on looking for them." The old man says.

Robin follows as the old man wanders further down the path. They take the bridge across a river when a familiar voice rings out from the left.

"Brother!"

"Will! Brother!"

The reunited brothers embrace.

"I'm so happy to find out you survived!" Robin says holding back tears.

"I wouldn't have if it weren't for Marian. I was pinned underneath one of those dead bat monstrosities as the ship was sinking. She freed me and told me to start swimming."

"Where is Marian?"

"She refused to leave without trying to save the others."

"Will... help us try to find more survivors."

Robin, Will, and the old man hoof it to the end of the trail, so they enter the woods. They see smoke rising from behind an apple tree. Coming around the tree, Robin Hood finds Ironsword the conqueror smoking out of an apple. Robin Hood points at Ironsword. "You! Yooouuuuuu!"

Ironsword looks at the small group, she begins to sit up. "Oh. You guys. For a minute I thought I might not live to see you again, but here I am and here you are, thanks to Marian."

"What happened? Where is Marian?" Robin demands.

"I don't know where Marian is, but I'll tell you what happened to me. The boat was on fire, I was stuck in a circle of flames, trapped. I cried out for help again and again. Just as my doom was at hand,

Marian came swinging through the flames hanging onto a rope. She snatched me away from a burning death. While we were swinging in the air the mast broke, Marian and I went sailing into the drink. We lost each other in the mist. I found myself here after I swam through the fog. I thought I would celebrate my survival by having a smoke. Nice seeing you guys, by the way."

Robin, Will, Ironsword, and the old man arrive at the other side of Avalon to find Little John making himself a new quarterstaff.

Robin puts his hands on his hips. "You look rather drenched, Little John."

"And if it weren't for Marian, I would be rather dead too! Ha! Ha!"

"What happened, Little John?" Robin asks.

Little John strokes his damp hair back. "The ship was sinking, one of its ropes got caught around my leg. I was being dragged to a watery grave. Suddenly Marian shot down before my eyes, she used her knife to cut the rope. We floated to the surface then I grabbed onto some driftwood. Marian swam off into the mist to look for you, Robin..."

Robin smiles. "There's a chance she's still alive."

Little John looks at the scar on his hand then looks at the desperation on his best friend's face.

"She saved my life, Robin." Little John says.

"And mine." Will Scarlett says next.

"Mine too." Ironsword adds.

Robin Hood lowers his head.

"Please, help me search for Marian."

The search party starts to scour Avalon. Robin witnesses a sorceress conversing with the dead. She has long black hair with blue eyes. Her build is slim, yet she has exotic beauty. She wears a flowing red dress with a golden bull near her waist, above the bull's head is a golden dragon with wings connecting to her shoulders, the serpentine head snakes its way between her breasts stopping at the cleavage. The dead are far more ethereal and indistinguishable from one another.

"I am searching for someone. Can you help me?" Robin asks.

The dead vanish then the sorceress spins around. "I am Morgan le Fay. I know all that was, all that shall be..."

Robin Hood perks up and smiles. "Will boot shine boy be avenged?"

"How about you show some concern for your wife, hmmm? She is laying over there."

In the distance there is a pedestal, laying on the pedestal is Marian, she is illuminated by rays of light.

"Marian."

Robin Hood rushes forward but is tripped by the Sorceress Morgan le Fay.

"By what right do you try to keep me from my wife?" Robin demands to know.

"You cannot move your wife lest life be lost."

Robin grows seriously concerned. "Is Marian injured?"

Morgan le Fay shakes her head. "Marian will be all right, I am talking about the life of the child."

Robin becomes alarmed. "No! If Marian lost our child, it would kill her."

Morgan le Fay puts her hand atop Robin's head. "What would you be willing to do to save your loved one?"

"Anything!" Robin shouts.

Morgan le Fay's hand brushes down the side of his head then grabs his jaw. She manually opens his mouth. She kisses Robin Hood.

"Good. There is a barrier to the north of Avalon. A barrier even I cannot penetrate. It is said that beyond this barrier lies the tree of life that grows golden apples. Pick one of these golden apples then bring it to me."

"How can I thank..." Robin starts.

"Don't talk. Go. Go!" Morgan le Fay says.

Robin Hood takes off through the woods at incredible speed. Weaving through the trees, leaping over fallen logs, making way through the brush, heading north until Robin travells to the edge of the forest. He finds a white wall diametrically long as he can see.

"The Barrier!" Robin exclaims.

Robin Hood beholds the sheer size of the wall, though he tries, he finds even he cannot scale it. Walking along the barrier Robin inspects the wall as he searches for a way through. Robin finally comes across a stone block with a circle of golden ancient marks.

"Nerty ot ontr h valano eher."

Robin Hood puts his index and middle finger to his head, he thinks. He thinks hard. Suddenly Robin Hood snaps his fingers, unsheathes the Stormblade, he spins the sword faster, still faster, until with all his skill, all his might, he pierces the center of the circle covered with ancient marks. Grabbing the blade by its grip Robin lets out a scream of exertion as he twists the sword.

The rune marks come into place.

"Entry to North Avalon here." Robin Hood reads aloud.

Avalon is bathed in light as the barrier is disintegrated. Robin walks past where the barrier once stood. He discovers a tower in the distance, to the side of the tower is the tree bearing golden apples. Robin plucks a golden apple, then he rushes back.

Robin barrels back to the pedestal with Marian's body resting upon it. Morgan le Fay is waiting beside it.

She is stunned by Robin Hood. "It is not possible... you actually managed to retrieve a golden apple."

"You said you could save them, so save them already..."

Robin Hood hands the apple to Morgan le Fay before he collapses onto the ground. The old man witnesses this as it occurs then begins shouting.

"No! You have picked the golden apple! You crossed the barrier! You do not know what you have done!"

Robin Hood raises his head then speaks as he recovers on the ground, "I have saved the two people I care most about! Who are you to lecture me?"

"I am Artorius Pendragon!"

The old man rips away the ragged suit revealing the visage of King Arthur! Robin Hood is brought onto his knees before the long-absent King.

"King Arthur... I thought you were long dead." Robin says.

"Time is different in this realm." King Arthur replies.

Morgan le Fay juices the golden apple, afterwards, she pours the shining amber liquid down the unconscious Marian's throat.

King Arthur continues. "By picking that golden apple you have saved your loved ones, but in the process, you may have doomed yourself. The golden apple is chaos."

"So be it."

"You really are ready to die for her, aren't you?"

"I am dead without her." Robin says solemnly.

King Arthur cocks his head. "Have you heard the story of the Questing Beast?"

Marian sits up. "I have heard it mentioned before."

"Marian! Thank God, you're all right!"

Robin rushes to her, hugging his wife.

"The last thing I remember is scouring the waters for you, Robin. Then I suddenly felt light-headed. I felt myself slipping into a dream."

"Sit down dear, sit down; I will relay the story of the Questing Beast to the both of you." King Arthur says.

Marian sits down. King Arthur relays the story of the Questing Beast.

"Back when I was a young man, I had a vision that England was infested with Gryphons, Giant Serpents were roaming the land, only later did I come to understand that my dream wasn't prophetic, but rather a metaphor for the problems besetting my kingdom."

Robin Hood interrupts. "No. No. Gryphons and Serpents are now plaguing England."

King Arthur is shocked by this news. "My dream actually became reality, Holy crap! Well anyway, when I awoke, I saw the Questing Beast. It had the head of a serpent, body of a leopard, and the tail of the lion."

"A Chimera." Marian says.

Arthur grows annoyed. "The Questing Beast... anyway, after it moved on, I witnessed King Pellinore was in pursuit of it on a quest to kill the beast. It was a quest that led to the downfall of King Pellinore and his entire bloodline. The lesson in these events is that if you are not careful in the pursuit of the quest, it can destroy you, as well as everyone you care about. Anyway, after King Pellinore departed, I grew short with a child, so I soundly beat the holy hell out of him."

Robin and Marian's mouths are agape in disbelief at the end of King Arthur's story.

Marian turns her attention to Morgan le Fay. "Sorceress, will there be any repercussions now that I have been given a new lease on life?"

Morgan le Fay is paying more attention to her nails than to Marian's question. "Yes, if by repercussions you mean swinging both ways."

Marian squints her eyes. "What was that?"

"Nothing..." Morgan le Fay says realizing she screwed up.

Marian turns her focus back to Arthur. "I have a question for you, King Arthur..."

"What is it dear?"

"England needs you now more than ever... why have you not come back?"

"I would if I thought I were truly needed, but I have found with each successive generation people like you, Robin and Marian, rise to the challenge of carrying the mantle of freedom and justice. So, you see, I would return, but I am not needed because there will always be people like you."

Robin Hood, Marian, Little John, Will Scarlet, and Ironsword the conqueror, gather at the shore. The remaining castaways hold a small funeral for their fallen comrades by burning the remaining pieces of the ship.

Robin Hood gives a eulogy, "Prince Lupin Wolfstonecraft may have transformed into a monstrous beast when the moon was full... but despite that, he was a good, honourable man. Alan A. Dale was the joy of all my Merry Men. He was brave honest and true-hearted."

Marian joins in, "Princess Katherine Haru must have been a kind, compassionate woman to accept and love both sides of the Wulf King... Alan was cool too."

"To our fallen comrades, pirate and royalty alike, may Alan and the others finally find rest." Will Scarlett adds.

The survivors take a bow of silence. King Arthur grasps the Stormblade, unsheathing it. He swings it towards Robin Hood's neck stopping at the right shoulder.

"Kneel..."

Robin Hood, Marian, Will Scarlet, Little John, and Ironsword the conqueror, kneel before King Arthur.

"Long ago I had a dream. I dreamt of a land ruled by justice and equality. I lived to see my dream nearly come true before it came crashing down before my eyes during the fall of Camelot. I see in every one of your eyes the rebirth of a long-dead dream, so I know in my heart the dream shall turn to reality. I say to you, kneel before me, and arise Knights of Avalon!"

The Knights of Avalon rise.

"How do we find the Labyrinth of the Gorgolac? Where do we go from here?" Marian asks.

King Arthur is horrified by this. "You're trying to find the Gorgolac? Jesus Christ!"

Robin grows exceedingly arrogant. "NO... I'm just a man."

"Honestly, I don't know how to find the Gorgolac." King Arthur says.

Morgan le Fay steps out of the woods revealing herself.

"The Labyrinth of the Gorgolac is beyond Avalon itself, her lair located in the Cave of Echoes at the edge of the Nether Land. To find it, you must travell past where the barrier was to the tower of Merlin. You must trigger the beacon."

"Why did you not tell me this before?" King Arthur scowls at his sister.

"It was not for you to know. It is the quest for the Knights of Avalon." Morgan le Fay says.

The Knights of Avalon travell past the barrier, past the golden apple tree then finally arrive at the tower of Merlin with the golden apple tree beside it. The Knights of Avalon enter the tower.

Inside the tower, there is a spiraling staircase, there is also a hole shooting down the center of the main floor. The Knights of Avalon explore the tower. There are many astrological charts spread about.

The Knights of Avalon are not impressed until they stumble across the armoury on the third floor. On the third floor the knights find "mystical weapons." Robin and Marian grab the only crossbows though they seem unusual.

Little John grabs a staff that separates into two billy clubs. Will Scarlet paws a bag full of metallic spheres. Ironsword the conqueror grabs a double-bladed sword that separates in two. The Knights find schematics of the tower belonging to Merlin. Going back to the main floor they find a lever on the wall. Will pulls the lever. A stone dragon rises from the water off the coast of Avalon, a green glowing ooze pours forth from the mouthpiece, creating a luminescent trail across the ocean, all the way to the Labyrinth of the Gorgolac. Robin witnesses this with the others after having just left the tower.

"We must follow to where the trail leads us." Robin Hood says.

Once the Knights of Avalon exit the tower of Merlin, they stand upon the shore. The Knights of Avalon peer into the fog rolling in from the ocean. Marian gazes into the fog.

"There is something in the fog..."

A small ghost Viking ship sails out of the mist landing on the shores of Avalon.

"Those of you that want to get off of this island, climb aboard!" Princess Cutter shouts enthusiastically.

Marian grins then throws her head back laughing. "You tricky little minx! How did you manage to find another ship?"

"During the battle with those giant fire-spitting bats, my previous ship began sinking. When I was carried off by that bat creature, I realised this was our only chance of not being marooned, so I crawled onto the back of this bat that was carrying me off then flew off in search of another ship...After twelve hours of finding nothing, I finally came across this ghost ship. Are there any more survivors?"

Robin stares at the ground. "No, unfortunately."

"Do you want me to take you home?" Sarah asks.

"Only after we see this through to the end!" Robin shouts.

"So be it!" Sarah answers.

Robin looks to Marian; he grabs both of her hands. He stares her in the eyes as he speaks, "Marian, I beg of you to stay behind. Where we are going, I don't think any of us will be coming back."

"You can't ask that of me, Robin... I refuse to be stranded on Avalon to spend the remainder of my days here! I will not stay another second on an island with the guy who had a kid with his own sister!"

Robin nods. "Very well, but I will take every precaution to ensure your safety."

King Arthur approaches Robin Hood with a large black kite shield with a golden dragon ornamenting it.

"Robin, as the first Knight of Avalon, I bestow upon you the Pendragon Shield. May it protect you."

Robin points to King Arthur as he walks back to the ship.

"See you later."

King Arthur watches Robin Hood trip backwards over the railing.

"Not bloody likely."

The long-absent king walks into the forest of apple trees to roam Avalon.

CHAPTER XXXV

Mordred

The Knights of Avalon board the ghost ship, setting off to follow the beacon. Soon the ghost ship exits the mists of Avalon.

The Gorgolac is watching them through the mystical crystal encasing a dragon within.

"There is smiting to be done. I'm going to smite you. I'm going to smite you. I'm going to smite you and you and you... I don't know who the hell you even are, but I will smite you too![25]

Green electricity shoots out of the Gorgolac's hands into the mystic crystal, causing S.P.R.I.T.E.s to come crashing down from the ionosphere. Green Lightning pierces the waters surrounding the ship. Then monsters riding giant fire-spitting bats attack. Robin breaks out his crossbow.

"Shoot them! Shoot them all!"

Robin and Marian begin firing arrows from their crossbows.

Many bats are downed. The monsters riding the bats begin to swim for the boat.

Marian looks around them. "They're in the water! Shoot them dead!"

Marian and Robin pierce the monsters in the water with many arrows. They expend their cartridges.

"I'm out of arrows," Marian says rather disappointed.

Robin hands her a cartridge. "Here are more! Make good use of them!"

The ship enters the mist. Marian dreads the cacophony of SQUEEs emanating from the surrounding fog.

"There are more of them, but I can't see them!" Marian shouts.

Robin counsels Marian. "Don't trust your eyes, Marian. Listen, then shoot!"

Robin and Marian shoot at the SQUEEs of the giant fire-spitting bats. Many splashes are heard.

Marian becomes alarmed. "Robin! Something is wrong!"

Robin waves his arm in the mist. "The mist has turned green."

"Robin, I can no longer see the beacon." Marian says.

"We have run ashore!" Sarah Cutter shouts.

Will Scarlett walks up to his older brother. "Robin... something tells me that you should have one of these..."

Will Scarlet takes one of the metallic spheres out of the bag handing it to his brother.

THE GORGOLAC PEERS into the crystal in the cave of echoes.

"The Knights of Avalon have made it to my shores... how brave! Let us see if they can withstand my army of the dead, led by Sir Mordred himself."

BACK ON THE SHORES of the labyrinth, the emerald mist descends into the mouths of fallen knights. Soon there is no longer any mist, but the army of fallen knights begins to rise, they march towards the ship.

Sarah Cutter is freaking out. "There has got to be at least fifty! There is only half a dozen of us! We're dead! We're dead!"

"No!" Robin shouts.

Sarah Cutter looks at Robin Hood. "What did you just say?"

Robin Hood stands drawing his sword.

"NO. Every event in our lives has led us to this moment! Heroes are not born... heroes are made when they are tested with moments such as these! Freedom? Justice? Equality? These are not ideas! These are the very birthright of every man and woman! These are the very rights worth fighting for, worth dying for. They think they can mess with us? They think they can mess with me?"

Robin spits.

"Rise, Knights of Avalon! Let us send these monsters back to hell... in pieces! DEUS VULT!!!"

Robin rushes headlong into battle. Will Scarlet, Little John, Ironsword, and Sarah Cutter draw their swords following Robin into battle. Marian stays aboard the boat providing cover fire because she promised Robin to keep as safe as possible. The Knights of Avalon are in the thick of battle, dismembering the risen corpses. Will Scarlet is stabbed through his right thigh then is overwhelmed. Will pulls a pin out of a metallic sphere.

"Will!" Robin shouts emotionally.

Will Scarlett looks at his brother with a sad expression. "I am sorry I failed you, Robin..."

The bag of explosives Will carries lights up like a Christmas tree, taking out a good portion of the battlefield. Robin Hood has a horrified expression on his face.

"Will! NOOOOOOOOOO!!!!!"

Robin Hood is furious. Fueled by rage, Robin Hood becomes the most dangerous opponent on the battlefield. Robin hacks his way to Sir Mordred through a wall of rotten human flesh. Robin Hood uses his shield against the mace of an opponent. Robin Hood leaps into the air stabs his opponent through its beating heart, then he pulls the blade out, the blade slides through the handle to the other side, stabbing another enemy.

Robin Hood and Sir Mordred clash swords swiftly yet brutally. Robin swings, Sir Mordred ducks. Sir Mordred swings, Robin Hood blocks. Sir Mordred punches Robin Hood then swings overhead to cleave Robin's head in two. Recovering quickly, Robin holds his sword out sideways, blade upwards, as Sir Mordred chops off his own sword hand. Robin Hood prepares to cut off Sir Mordred's head when Sir Mordred speaks,

"You will be lost in there for centuries. It has already been foreseen. HA! HA! HA! HA! HA!"

Robin Hood raises his sword, he looks down in pity. "Oh, damned knight, what be thy name?"

"Sir Mordred. I be thy king, so kneel before me and tremble."

Robin's face grimaces. "My fate is my own to make...And you're not the King!"

Robin Hood chops off Sir Mordred's head. The Knights of Avalon led by Robin Hood fight onward valiantly until the opposing army of the dead is crushed utterly.

Robin Hood turns his gaze to his victorious brothers and sisters in arms. "I have lost my home as well as my only brother... Knights, follow me into the Labyrinth so we can finish this once and for all. Marian, stay with the boat until we have returned."

"I think I would be more useful if I came with you." Marian replies.

"I know that, my love. I also know I would not be able to live with myself if anything were to befall you."

Robin Hood finds that a wall blocks where the entrance stood a moment ago. Robin pulls the pin off the metallic sphere, throws it, blowing open the entrance. The Knights of Avalon enter the Labyrinth, a maze-like network of caverns that leads to the cave of echoes; first discovered by the mad scientist Daedalus. There is a mass network of cave entrances.

Meanwhile, Marian sits on the boat alone undefended. An arachnid-like shadow descends upon Marian. Marian shoots her crossbow at her assailant but then lets out a terrified scream.

INSIDE THE LABYRINTH, Robin Hood leads the Knights of Avalon, however, they are lost.

"Where do we go from here?" Ironsword asks Robin.

"I'm thinking. I'm thinking." Robin replies.

"Think faster." Little John says.

Robin senses something, the distinct smell of something, something like rotten fruit but worse, it was...

Robin points to the only dark tunnel with cobwebs.

"That tunnel!"

"Why that direction, Robin?" Little John asks.

Robin slowly rotates his head to Little John with an expression of fear. It is a face Little John has never seen on Robin before.

"I can smell the fear... and the death." Robin says as he walks into the tunnel leading the way.

MARIAN IS WITHIN THE interior of the Labyrinth stuck to a giant web. The web is acting as a kind of trophy wall between two sections of the cavern. Marian has a view of the way in, to her right there is a stone altar with a large crystal, encased within the crystal is a baby dragon. Marian is within the center of the labyrinth; she is in the lair of the Gorgolac. The Gorgolac holds Marian captive. The

Gorgolac has black hair, piercing blue eyes, flat eyebrows, pale skin, with an exotic beauty about her. She wears a metal bikini under her silks. Marian looks upon the lavish beauty of the Gorgolac.

"When I first learned of the Gorgolac, I was expecting to find a hideous she-beast; not an alluring sorceress garnished in silk robes."

"My son loved the touch of my silks. I remember telling him 'It is the destiny of others to serve Mankind, but our destiny is to rule it. Then you, Marian, came along and murdered him... I should kill you right now... but I have something worse planned for you."

"What are you going to do to me? What are you going to do to me?"

"Bring out the Imp!" The Gorgolac shouts.

"The Imp is sleeping." The Minotaur informs her.

"Well, wake him up!" [26]

A Black Imp with one eye comes out of the darkness advancing towards Marian.

Marian has a look of terror. "NNNOOOOOOOOOOO!!!!"

CHAPTER XXXVI

The Last Temptation

Robin Hood is leading the last of the Knights of Avalon down the dark, winding tunnel when a nine-foot-tall Minotaur comes roaring around the corner, wielding a war hammer. The Minotaur deals a striking blow to Robin Hood, he is the first to go down. Ironsword the conqueror spins her duel-bladed sword cutting off The Minotaur's hands. This causes it to drop the war hammer. The Minotaur gores Ironsword with its horns. Pirate Princess Cutter cuts out one of the Minotaur's eyes with her sword. Angrily, the Minotaur slams her against the wall with his arms. Little John is driven out of his mind with fury.

"Monster!!!!!! I'll send you back to hell myself!!!!"

Little John grabs the Minotaur wrestling with the monster.

As the two tussle with one another, they edge towards a large pit that is miles deep.

Finally, the two of them are fighting at the edge of the abyss.

Little John positions his leg behind the Minotaur's, then pushes with all his might, tripping the monster into its doom. Unexpectedly the Minotaur grapples Little John's torso, pulling Little John into the black void of mutually assured destruction.

The Gorgolac is watching all that transpired intently through her crystal.

"Good. Good. They have all met their doom in the labyrinth... wait, wait, where is Robin Hood's body?"

The Black Imp crawls up Marian's legs biting her with its teeth when Robin appears silently out of the shadows. He stabs the Imp dead. Green blood spills out onto the floor.

His arm stretches forward, shaking badly. Robin pulls the sword, so the Imp is killed immediately. The little monster is lying limp on the floor.

Marian is surprised. "Robin!"

The Gorgolac is even more surprised. "Robin!"

The Imp is still dying. "Robin! Ack!"

The Gorgolac spins around, she begins speaking in a seductive, hypnotic way.

"You truly are a worthy hero, Robin of Locksley."

"You... you know my name?"

Marian begins shouting. "Robin! Kill it!"

The Gorgolac sashays towards Robin Hood. "You have travelled far; you have had to endure many trials..."

Marian begins struggling violently against the web. "For God's sake, kill it, Robin!"

The Gorgolac gently brushes away the Stormblade.

"You have suffered great losses. You blame yourself for deaths you had no control over. Worry not, Sir Robin, your hardships are over. You are a hero without compare, a hero that deserves a kiss from a beautiful woman."

Marian's face widens in fear. "Robin! NOOOOOOO!!!"

Robin Hood drops his weapon, embraces the Gorgolac, dips her over for a kiss when he gazes upon her silhouette. The shadow reveals her true nature. Robin drops the Gorgolac fast then leaps to his sword. Robin picks up the Pendragon Shield as the Gorgolac attacks. The Gorgolac begins laughing maniacally as four extra eyes open on her forehead.

The Gorgolac spins around then rushes towards Marian to finish her off. Robin Hood in his agile state leaps between Marian and the Gorgolac. The Gorgolac shoots green electricity from her feminine limbs into the Pendragon Shield.

The shield is starting to emanate smoke from a crisping surface. Robin Hood powers forward towards the Gorgolac, smashing her in the face with his shield. The Gorgolac wipes the blood off her face.

"Ha. Ha. I love men who like it rough. It's the ones with the fight in them who have the most blood!"

The illusion of the Gorgolac dispels, revealing itself as a hideous mutation, an arachnid-like humanoid. The Gorgolac separates her arms and legs into eight limbs. The Gorgolac rips the Stormblade out of Robin's hands, putting two of her arms around Robin's throat, she begins choking the life out of him. With her fourth leg she picks up the Stormblade then puts it into her fourth hand.

"Prepare to meet your maker, Robin. Know that you have failed when it mattered most."

Robin is disarmed, he has nothing left in him to go on fighting, he finds a strange peace with that. That's when he feels it, the light burning within him, the fire of the Grail. A cross appears upon Robin's blue gambeson emitting white light, this fire burns the Gorgolac.

"AAAAAH! It burns! What is this? What power is this?"

The Gorgolac climbs up a wall, retreating into the crevice. Robin strolls over staring up at the crevice.

"Faith."

Robin cuts Marian down. Marian immediately slaps Robin.

"You were going to kiss her!"

"Wouldn't you?"

Marian slaps Robin again.

"Where do we go?" Marian asks Robin.

"I got lost. I don't know. If I had to guess, if this is the Gorgolac's chamber, we may be in the heart of the Labyrinth."

"How do we find our way out?"

Robin starts looking around. "If these caves were fashioned like the one Daedalus built, then there is both a way in as well as a way out. We are between the way in and out."

"Let us go back the way we came." Marian says.

"Wouldn't be safe in any direction we go. Call me nuts, but I want to see what is on the other end of this labyrinth."

Marian points behind Robin. "Robin, the Crystal!"

Marian peers across the chamber into the Gorgolac's crystal with a dragon encased within. Marian is able to gaze across space and time. Marian watches another archer dressed in blue clothes, then there is an image of somebody steering a ship across the desert.

The images change again as she observes four people garbed in strange clothing, running from strange furry creatures. Marian witnesses a woman with purple hair on her knees before someone who resembles The Lord of the Darkness, weeping as the world burns.

Marian cannot watch any more after that because the dragon begins to hatch as the crystal cracks. There is a burst of maniacal laughter resonating through the labyrinth walls. Robin and Marian make a break for it. The Gorgolac reappears so Robin must defend himself with his shield. The Gorgolac shoots her webbing onto Robin. Robin is stuck to the wall.

"Marian, Run! Run, and don't look back."

Marian begins running. Robin Hood turns his attention to the Gorgolac and screams. The Gorgolac returns to her seductive human form.

"Robin. Robin. Robin. You have to admit, I got the better of you, just like my son did...."

Robin is staring down at her. The Gorgolac grows annoyed with Robin then points to her face.

"Robin Hood, my face is up here, not down there."

Robin Hood gazes back into the Gorgolac's eyes.

"...But now your precious Marian is nowhere to be found, and you can't move an inch."

"Good, because now you can have my surprise." Robin says.

"I like surprises." The Gorgolac replies.

"Doesn't everybody? You see the sword in my hand? I call it the Stormblade. The blade is just like my wife, it slides both ways."

The Stormblade slides through the grip piercing the Gorgolac through her brain. The Gorgolac drops dead. Robin starts to cut himself free. Marian is in the tunnel, huddled and crying. A hand places itself onto Marian's shoulder. Marian spins around finding to her surprise, Robin Hood. Robin Hood motions her to follow, Marian does so. Robin leads Marian safely out of the Labyrinth. Marian finds that the boatman is waiting on the edge of the Nether Land for them.

"I said that one day I would return for you both..." Charon says.

Marian and Robin Hood get inside the boat as they leave.

Moments later, the fiery Black Knight runs across the beach, into the Labyrinth. Once the Black Knight reaches the Gorgolac's lair, he is eaten by the newborn dragon. The combination of the Black Knight being on fire as well as the young age of the dragon begins a rare process of symbiosis. Fusing the two of them, they become the Knight Dragon. Marian, Robin, and the Boatman arrive at the shores of France. Marian climbs out of the boat.

"Robin, we made it."

"You made it...."

"What do you mean?" Marian asks.

".... I screwed up. I kissed her Marian, and she poisoned me. I endured long as I could, but I didn't make it out alive. I died in the Cave of Echoes stuck to a wall. I'm a ghost."

Robin is dead stuck to the wall in the center of the cave of echoes by webbing. There are crumbles of cake on the ground. Marian is in utter disbelief.

"No. Oh god no! Please come with me! Please. Please, Robin. Take my hand! Please, just take my hand!"

"I can't. I now find out what is on the other side. I hope we see each other again someday. Take my Ghostblade and shield to remember me."

Robin clasps his hands with his widow. She opens her hands to find the gold and silver wedding ring of her true love.

"Always know that I love you most of all."

"I love you, Robin Hood!" Marian shouts in heartbreak.

"I know."

Robin Hood floats off into the mist with Charon.

Marian arrives at a farm in the French countryside with her servant, Sarah. Marian enters the study. Marian finds purple silks are hanging from the walls, there is a chair with purple pillows, laying on a desk is purple goblets and bracelets.

She lifts a chest.

"Purple! I have never seen so much purple! Robin said he left me a great treasure inside of this chest..."

Marian turns her key opening the chest. She finds a piece of paper inside with an accurate illustration of the Grail. Below the illustration, there are the letters *MU*.

"He brought back a drawing of the Grail, Oh my God!"

Marian goes into labour.

1206 A.D.

Marian watches her children with Sarah. Marian and Robin's children Robin and Megan play with each other. Robin and Megan shoot arrows at a target with their bows. After the contest is over some children arrive.

A large boy calls to them, "Robin! Megan! Come with us! We're going to the forest to play Robin Hood!"

The children look to their mother standing in the doorway. Marian waves her children off.

"It's all right children. Go show your friends how to play Robin Hood!"

Robin and Megan run off with the other children. Marian puts her hand on the wall pinning Sarah. Marian smiles at her, Sarah smiles back. Marian closes the door. There is a knock at the door.

Marian rolls her eyes. "Now what?"

Marian opens the door. Priest is standing outside with Isabella.

"Is Sir Robin here?

Is Sir Robin here?" Priest asks.

"Robin Hood is dead." Marian says heartbroken.

"Sir Robin is Robin Hood? That doesn't surprise me. He was the one archer in Richard's army better than me. You must be the legendary Marian."

"I am hardly a legend."

Priest stares at her in awe. "Are you kidding? Everyone from England to Acre has heard the story of Robin Hood and Maid Marian."

"You flatter me, Priest."

"You know of me?

You know of me?"

"Robin considered you to be a brother to him."

"Tell me. Did you receive your father's sword that I delivered?"

Marian begins to break down then hugs Priest.

"Bless you. God bless you."

Isabella coughs a little. "May we come in?"

"Of course! We have much to discuss."

Priest and Isabella walk inside. Sarah shuts the door.

CHAPTER XXXVII

Reflections

M arian, Isabella, and Priest gather in the study. Marian rests in the red cushioned chair, Priest sits upon one end of the couch, Isabella on the other.

"What do you wish to know from me?" Priest asks.

"Who was Robin to you?" Marian asks.

"My commander, my friend, my brother.

My commander, my friend, my brother." Priest replies.

"Tell me of Robin in wartime, Priest." Marian says.

"Robin was quick, extremely so. He was cunning as a warrior,

Robin is the one guy I would not like to mess with." Priest says.

"Tell me why." Marian says,

"Years ago, we were spending time in Cyprus waiting with Robin's Prisoner

Marian's eyes pop.

"Robin took a captive?"

Priest nods his head.

"She was the Damsel of Cyprus," Priest says. "We waited in the castle that held the treasure. Robin stood by the windowsill gazing over the cliff-side to the thundering water below. Seawater brewing upon the rocks.

'The men who built this place must have been completely out of their minds... or completely desperate.'

Robin said.

Robin looked at me. 'Do you think we are out of our minds for joining in glorious battle?'

'Everybody involved is out of their minds, Robin.

Everybody involved is out of their minds, Robin.' I said.

'You cut me to the quick, Priest However we shall stand tall with righteousness and Holy Spirit driving us onwards. We rebel and abhor the indignation presented to our king; and gladly suffer the consequences as we apply hot irons up the rear of this jackass,

Cyprus praises Richard, Priest, As they should. Let us bask in the glory of the now. Let the respite from battle, the calm, the peace

wash over you like the ocean's waves. You must remember that is

the way the world should be. Why we fight. For the Holy Crusade, You cut me to the quick, Pries- Gaah! Now you have me doing it!'

Robin said

'For some strange reason, Robin kept staring at my chest..." Priest says to Marian.

"Robin always paid close attention to the chest of those he

considered a threat to his life. He once explained it to me this way, 'I have to look at them and be aware of their movements, why should I bother paying attention to their killer's eyes when that is the last thing I'll see?'" Marian recalls.

Priest continues recounting his tale,

"Robin turned to the Damsel of Cyprus.

'How do you think your Father will take the loss of the Treasure?' Robin asked her.

'I think my father's demeanor will be rather dour going forwards.' The Damsel remarked.

'BWA-HA-HA-HA-HA!'

Bishop scrambled into the room.

'Robin, we've got a Phantom!' Bishop frantically shouted to us.

'I bloody hate Phantoms! Disfigured fucks always use hidden passages. Priest, Bishop, we're going on a fox hunt. I want his mask.' Robin screamed.

Robin, Me, and Bishop split up to search the castle. The Damsel of Cyprus was paired with Bishop. I arrived at a split corridor. I spied a Byzant lying on the floor. I leaned over attempting to grasp it. Behind me, a corridor slid, and The Phantom emerged. Creeping slowly behind me, The Phantom raised his arm, ready to plunge the dagger into my back. A decorative suit of armour sprang to life seizing the blade.

The Phantom was grappling with the Haunted Armour but was put in a headlock. The dagger clattered onto the floor. I spin around.

'Jolly good show, Robin. You caught the sneaky SOB.' I said.

'War is a Jolly good time, Priest!' Robin said.

'It certainly led us to a jolly good time, Robin.' I said.

'Let us have a jolly good laugh.' Robin said.

'HO! HO! HO! HOO! HOO!'

'Jolly good!' Robin said.

'Jolly good!' I say, 'Should I take off his mask?' I asked.

'I want to see his face.' Robin stated rather <u>too</u> coldly.

I ripped off the mask. I swear Robin blinked twice. I swear Robin blinked twice.

'Old Man Isaac Komnenos? What are you doing dressed up as The Phantom?' Robin asked.

'I figured with the country overrun by Crusaders, and the coast-lined under siege by Richard's Forces, maybe I could plunder the Treasure of Cyprus, but you climbed into the castle so I dressed up as The Phantom to scare you away...' Old Man Komnenos said.

Robin kicked the dagger, it spun away.

'...And maim you. I was going for a vital organ or something...

And I would have gotten away with it too... If it weren't for you miserable kids!' Old Man Komnenos said.

'Sic semper tyrannosaurus.

Sic semper tyrannosaurus.'

'Damn straight, down with tyrant lizards,' Robin remarked."

'Priest...' Marian says.

"A castle mouse in a black domino mask scampered up, arched itself onto its hind legs, and gave us a thumbs up. 'Radical, Dudes!' The mouse shouted."

"Priest!" Marian shouts.

"What?" Priest asks.

"You are not telling me of Robin in wartime. You are telling me the legend of Robin Hood in wartime." Marian says.

"Very well. I arrived at the split corridor the stones were black and blue. I am clearing the area when I spied a Byzant lying on the floor. I leaned over attempting to grasp it. Behind me, a dark corridor slid, and The Phantom emerged. Creeping slowly behind me, The Phantom raised his arm, ready to plunge the dagger into my back. A mouse in a domino mask scampered up, leaped onto my head launching himself off my scalp, squeaked, 'Cowabunga Dudes!' and bit out The Phantom's right eye.

'Yeeaaarrrrrggghhh!'

The Phantom staggered backwards, pawing at his eye. The Phantom tripped over a foot sticking out of the corner behind him. The Phantom crashed to the floor like a sack of oranges while Robin was kicking the holy shit out of him. The fiend was feigning writhing on the floor in pain,

'Did you manage to obtain your Byzant?' Robin asked me.

'It's glued to the floor.

It's glued to the floor.'

'I hate it when they do that.' Robin said. 'Priest, Remove his mask.'

'Nooo!!' The Phantom screamed."

Priest is standing on the couch holding the pillow.

"I smack him in the back of the head like this for being immature about the situation."

Priest smacks the pillow, and it goes sailing past Marian's head.

Marian peeks at the pillow laying against the wall. Her head spins back with a smirk.

"Shut it freak!

Shut it freak!'

I removed the mask.

'He's hideous.

He's hideous.'

As I observed the monster, The Phantom's face was chiseled, he

sported a square jaw, a long Roman nose, a glaring blue eye, shoulder-length black hair, and a pulpy bleeding wound around his missing right eye.

'That's got to be one of the most disgusting things I have ever seen.' Robin said.

'I was an Adonis!' The Phantom protested.

'My second said, 'shut it freak!' Robin shouted.

Robin made his point by pointing the arrow's at the back of The Phantom's Skull.

'He might have a lovely singing voice.

He might have a lovely singing voice.'

Robin quickly glanced him over.

'Not every Phantom can sing, Priest.'

'Do you want the mask or not, Robin?

Do you want the mask or not, Robin?'

'Hand me the mask.'

I hand over half a mask to my friend. Robin stared at it before glaring at me like a dragon.

'It's broken!' Robin shouted.

'What did you expect, Robin? A mouse tunneled into his eye, God only knows if it's still inside or not, then you kicked the living shit out of this freak while he was on the ground, which was very un-sporting of you, Robin.

What did you expect, Robin? A mouse tunneled into his eye, God only knows if it's still inside or not, then you kicked the living shit out of this freak while he was on the ground, which was very un-sporting of you, Robin.'

Bishop returned with the Damsel of Cyprus in tow.

'Is that The Phantom?' Bishop asked.

'He claims he's an Adonis.' Robin replied.

'As does every man.' The Damsel quipped.

Scarlet blood trickled out of The Phantom's missing eye. A blood soaked rodent in a domino mask just burst out of The Phantom's face, scurrying down the hall, The Damsel of Cyprus screamed bloody murder as I took off down the hall after it."

Marian is looking Priest over.

"Can you prove that's what really happened?" Marian asks.

Priest hands Marian a small shroud of black cloth.

"What's this?" Marian asks.

"It belongs to that small-masked mouse avenger.

It belongs to that small-masked mouse avenger."

Marian throws it to the floor in disgust.

"EEEEEEEEEEW!"

Marian catches herself. She collects the shroud off the wooden floorboards, disappointed in how she behaved. She hands the mask back to Priest.

"You said you were Robin's second in the war." Marian says.

"I did what Robin told me, no different from Robin doing what King Richard told him." Priest says.

"How skilled are you with a bow, Priest?" Marian asks.

Priest smirks.

"It was 1190 A.D. Me, Bishop, and Pope arrived at the Crusader fleet. as we were walking towards the archery area The Captain of the Guard stepped forward.

'"Names?' The Captain of the Guard asked us.

'Priest, Bishop, and I'm Pope.'

'Occupations?'

'Archers,' Bishop said.

'Target is fifty paces away, anybody manages to hit the bullseye, they serve on the king's ship. Who's first?' The Captain of the Guard asked us.

Bishop stepped forward, he aimed, then fired. his arrow pierced the first ring.

The Captain of the Guard wrote this down.

'Who's next?' The captain asked us.

Pope stepped forward, he aimed, then shot his arrow which also planted itself in the first ring.

The captain wrote this down too.

The captain pointed to me next. 'You! Can you hit the bullseye?' he asked.

'If anybody can, it's him. Priest, aim for the center.' Pope said, it was flattering, really...

'The fly.

The fly,' I coolly remarked.

'I aimed and then fired... The arrow chipped the edge of the tar-get.'

'Did I hit it?

Did I hit it?' I asked.

The captain examined the target rubbing his fingertips across the surface. His eyes narrowed.

'Yes! You hit the Target!'

'Hooray! Hooray! Hooray! Hooray!' We shouted.

'You hit the edge of the target!' The captain interrupted.

'The fly?

The fly?'

'What fly? You washed out!' The captain said to me.

I aimed and fired at astonishing speed. My arrow sang with extreme velocity, planting itself nicely between the bullseye and the first ring.

'You made the cut! You're also the closest to the bull'seye.' The captain said.

'Has anyone hit the bullseye?' Bishop asked him.

'No. And I don't think anybody will...' The Captain replied.

Pope strolled up next to me. 'Did you really shoot that fly?'

'No, I obliterated it.

No, I obliterated it.'''

"You are good." Marian says.

"Not as good as Sir Robin, He's Robin Hood."

"He was Robin Hood alright."

"Tell me of his legend.

Tell me of his legend."

Marian sits there tapping her fingertips on the chair. She suddenly stops.

'Very well, this is a part of his legend nobody knows...

"Robin and I played in the forest at night like we were children again. As we rested in the moist grass by the flowing river, I ate a cake from Nottingham,

'Marian, where did you get that cake?' he asked rather intently.

'A merchant in the market gave it to me.'

'Did he look like he was from a different land?'

'Yes.' I replied.

Robin had a look of incredulity upon his face.

'What is it, Robin?' I asked.

'Someone wants you, or rather, me, dead.' He dropped on me.

'How do you know that?' I asked.

'You are eating a hashish cake, Marian.'

'What's hashish?' I asked.

'You'll find out soon enough,' Robin Hood laughed.

'Who wants us dead?'

'You'll find that out too.'

Robin strung his bow.

'How soon?' I demanded.

Robin Hood strung my bow.

'Real soon.' Robin Hood said.

Handing me the bow, Robin Hood drew his, I followed suit. The bush began to rustle.

'Back-to-back, now!' Robin cried out.

Robin and I were back-to-back. Crackling occurred within the brush.

'Robin, your men are too far away to run for help.' I whispered.

'I don't need my men, I need you.' Robin whispered back to me.

The Brush exploded. I was frightened out of my wits.

Robin fired twelve arrows. I fired eighteen. Three assassins were dead; unknown how many others there were. We were practically useless in absolute darkness.

The gurgling of water was heard nearby. I realised that Robin was walking us across the water. We halted dead center in the river. The clouds lifted their veil over the moonlight. I had the instinct we were surrounded by men from Robin's past.

'Come to me.' Robin said.

The seven assassins waded through the water to murder Robin Hood and me. Three assassins waded towards Robin Hood. Four-nasty looking assassins waded through the water on the other side towards Me. The water slowed them down and they had some distance to wade. The seven were struck dead by arrows within 2.25 seconds. As we made it back to the camp Robin Hood was keeping Me close to him. Our feet snapped the fallen twigs as we travelled upon the path to Robin Hood's base camp. Robin unsheathed his sword and sliced through three arrows.

'Get back against the tree.' Robin Hood commanded.

My feet and Robin Hood's crackled and snapped upon the fallen twigs as we put our backs to the trees. Several snap crackles and pops were heard when Robin and I killed the assassins. A twig cracked above, Robin Hood moved for his dagger and threw it upwards into the shoulder of his opponent. The assassin fell from the tree we were under. He grappled with the wounded assassin on the ground. He dragged him away from Me.

They start arguing. I didn't really hear much. Then Robin began growling, '...Mortain? Couer de Lion? Alamut? Veritas VERI-TAS!!!'

'You know!' The assassin pled.

I moved in to de-escalate the situation.

'Robin, Spare him.'

'I can't... not this one.' Robin said with a killer's tone.

'Thou shall not kill, remember?'

Robin released him and he began to leave. I put my hand on Robin's shoulder, 'I'm proud of you, Robin...'

'No.'

Robin drew his bow and sent an arrow flying through the back of the Assassins head. The assassin was dead before he even realised he had been struck. That was a sort of mercy given by my husband."

"That sounds more like the Robin I knew.

That sounds more like the Robin I knew."

"Do you know how to play Chess?" Isabella asks.

"No." Marian says.

"It's the game of kings," Priest continues, "Robin was a genius chess player, he was near King Richard's level." Priest says.

"Robin couldn't play chess to save his own life, and neither can I." Marian says.

"He May not have been the best on a board, but in real life? Robin was someone to contend with," Priest says, "I have learned the game; I will teach it to you. I would like to know something first."

"What's that?"

"Who was Robin Hood to you?"

"Robin Hood was a silly name I inadvertently gave him." Marian chuckles. "Robin of Locksley was a thief, a hero, and a Man!"

"He was the Sword of the Lion Heart.

He was the Sword of the Lion Heart."

"Robin Hood was the best of us, a Hero to the end. My Husband <u>was</u> the Sword of the Lion Heart, Robin's gone. Now, **I** am Robin Hood's Dagger!"

"With John having assumed the crown of England, we must bide our time and wait for the opportunity to strike. Until then, we must keep as low a profile as possible." Priest says.

"Si Vis Pacem, Para Bellum," Marian remarks.

CHAPTER XXXVIII

White Trash

Marian, the ghost of Robin Hood, the dead body of Dracula, and The Gorgolac are all on Jerry Springer.

Jerry Springer is on stage. The title appears knocking him over. He gets back up. "Today we have a real special episode: A famous outlaw who is a deadbeat dad to his wife and children because he is in fact dead. Marian Fitzwater, recently widowed single mother of two... And here is the rival family who says that Robin Hood and Marian ruined their lives. The formerly undead Lord of the Darkness, Dracula! Alongside him is his mother who has a real sore head because of the sword in her head, The Gorgolac! Robin Hood, you used to be a big deal around here what happened?"

"I sacrificed my body for Marian, I thought I finally earned redemption to enter the Kingdom of Heaven; but being dead means all I can do is talk to the dead body of Dracula all day."

Marian looks at Robin's ghost incredulously, "You sacrificed your body? I sacrificed my body to bear your children and you aren't even here to support me or raise your children."

"I'm a ghost! I died! I can't be there for you!"

A black woman in the audience stands up. "Robin Hood, the fact you left your woman alone to raise two children shows what kind of a father you are, Robin Hood! You may be a ghost, but we can all see right through you."

A southern cable guy stands up. "Robin Hood, you commie pinko son of bitch! It's people like you that made me vote for a corrupt piece of garbage! AMERICA! 'MEEERRIIICAAAAAA!"

Jerry Springer addresses the man. "Sir, we are filming in Nottingham, England today."

Priest and Isabella shout, "And God save the Crown!"

Jerry Springer snaps. "Shut it! Or I'll have all of you removed by force."

The dead body of Dracula speaks up. "Robin Hood put an arrow through my heart for the woman who put two arrows in my eyes! Ah! Ah! Ah! One arrow! Two arrows! Three arrows! Ah! Ah! Ah!"

"You put an arrow into a man's heart for the love of your life Robin Hood."

"Shut up Dracula. We are not doing this here on Jerry Springer!"

The Gorgolac points accusingly at Robin. "That green hooded ruffian put a sword in my head!"

Marian snaps. "Don't you talk about that way to my two babies' Daddy! You're the reason my husband is dead!"

"You two killed my son."

"Your son is a monster!"

The dead body of Dracula speaks up. "Go ahead and pierce my heart Marian! Wait! It's already pierced. Ah! Ah! Ah!"

Robin Hood's two children arrive on set. The two children rush to Dracula.

"Daddy! Daddy! Tell me a story!" Megan says.

"Robin and I both know that dead men can't have children! Anyway, I know for a fact that I am definitely not the father. Ah! Ah! Ah! 100% Dead sure! Ah! Ah! Ah! I'll take a lie detector test and pass because I don't have a pulse. Ah! Ah! Ah!"

Robin Hood grows angry.

"You son of the devil!"

Robin Hood tries to throw a chair but can't pick it up. The dead body of Dracula speaks up.

"What's the matter, Robin... You don't seem all there! Ah! Ah! Ah! Here is a little secret about Robin Hood, that isn't a sword he has down his tights! He has a big dick. Robin Hood used to go around beating gorillas with his big dick chasing them out of the forests. That's why you don't see gorillas in the forests anymore. Robin Hood chased them out. Now gorillas are in the one place they know they can't see a big dick. The mountain jungles in Africa! Ah! Ah! Ah!"

Jerry Springer is handed a sheet of paper.

"We have the test results From Dr. Acula. It says that Dracula is 100%, not the father. 101% 102% 103% 104%"

The dead body of Dracula speaks up.

"I am 105% not the father of the Count of sesame street. Vampires just like to count! 106% 107% 108% 109% 110% Ah! Ah! Ah!"

The Gorgolac pulls out a gun onstage firing three times into the air.

"I want to see my grandbabies!"

Marian grabs her children. "Keep that crazy bitch away from me and my babies!"

Jerry Springer is on the ground bleeding from a gunshot wound.

"Jesus! I've been shot!"

He crawls towards the nearest camera. The Audience begins to chant.

"JER-RY! JER-RY! JER-RY!"

Three-hundred-pound security guards wrestle the Gorgolac to the floor. As Jerry Springer is loaded onto an ambulance he speaks to Marian.

"Can I see you tonight after I get out of surgery?" Jerry asks.

Marian is examining her nails.

"Anything other than dinner and a movie will cost you ten mill."

"Do you take personal checks?" Jerry asks.

The Paramedics close the ambulance doors as the vehicle drives away.

PART FIVE

**IN THE PAGES OF HISTORY TYRANNY ALWAYS FO-
MENTS REBELLION
E PLURIBUS UNUM
THE MANY BECOME ONE**

Dramatis Personae

R obin Hood-An idea
      Marian Fitzwater-Outlaw Hero

Priest-Marian's Protector

King John-King of England. Prick

Rick-Bill Collector

Wilbert-Bill Collector

Philip the Bastard-Bastard son of King Richard

Archbishop Tuck-A heavier more powerful Friar Tuck

Baron Robert Fitzwalter-Uncle to Marian Fitzwater. Part of the barons

William Marshall- Advisor to the Royal house of England

Isabella-Wife to Priest

Sarah- Servant to Marian

Charon-Boatman

Baron Eustace De Vesci-Part of the barons

Earl of Gloucester- Part of the barons

Lord Dominos-Member of a dark cult

Alucard-Son of Dracula

Lord Artie-A survivor

Lance-A survivor

Queen Isabella of Angouleme-Wife to King John

Anthony of Mastrantonio-A frisky creep

Unnamed

Hellhound

Bear

Disillusioned Sheriff of Nottingham

Monkey

Dark Knights

CHAPTER XXXIX

GAMBIT

July 1185

It's daylight, Marian has her bow drawn, her arrowheads are blunt but dripping with red dye. He will have green. The roar of the waterfall splashing on the rocks cancels out any noise that might give him away. The trees are nearby, she rushes to them. Robin hops out bow drawn.

"I beat-yaaaahh!"

Robin is yanked high off the ground upside down. Robin hangs there swinging. Marian winks and shoots Robin in his scrotum.

"Ow!"

"You Lose! I beat you, Robin!"

"That wasn't fair!"

"Who said war is fair?" Marian asks.

"Then why do they call it warfare?" He retorts.

The two young lovers ponder whether war is fair or not.

Robin eventually passes out. Marian cuts him loose.

25th of December, 1200 A.D.

"Sic semper tyrannis!"

King John is sitting on the throne eating his apple. He is observing a hanging going horribly wrong when a woman's voice rings out the moment before an arrow flies through his apple. The arrow causes apple sauce to explode. The sauce is covering John's face slowly dripping off of his nose.

Robin Hood! Robin Hood again! It's always Robin Hood!

King John slowly wipes off the applesauce from his face. He can't lose control in front of his subjects. It's not kingly. He stands up to start walking to his carriage. As he steps off the dais, Robin Hood dashes up, kicks him in the Jimmys, then runs off.

King John is writhing on the ground. A royal guard arrives shortly afterwards.

"Are you all right my king?"

King John gets on to all fours before he explodes. "I'll kill Hood! I'll kill him...and everybody he loves!"

King John arrives at the Royal Palace. He is given Five Gold Ducats by the Fedora wearing Rick and Chain-mail wearing Wilbert. He sits on his throne stewing things over.

"Hood. Hood. Hood. If I could get close enough to Hood I would kill him myself. If I could get close enough to Hood..."

King John has an epiphany.

"Bring me the Friar of Nottingham!... And a Fedora!"

The next morning Friar Tuck is brought before King John.

"I am under the protection of the church..." Tuck says fearfully.

"Did you have a Merry Christmas?" King John asks, smiling beneath his fedora.

"Yes. I heard your Christmas was merry as well, despite your efforts."

King John smiles. "In the spirit of Christmas, I have a gift for you."

"What kind of fiendish gift do you plan to give?" Tuck asks.

"A recommendation for promotion." King John answers with the devil's grin. Tuck will always swear he saw a tooth sparkle.

October 1214 A.D.

"Check and Mate."

Marian loses another game of chess to Priest.

"I can't win at chess!" Marian shouts.

"You have to think several steps ahead of your opponent. You're much better at this than you think." Priest says.

Isabella rushes in.

"Sarah, Lady Marian! Sir Priest! King John has been defeated at Bouvines! He has returned to England humiliated!"

"This is our chance. We must act quickly to succeed." Marian says.

"What do we do?"

"I'll arrange to meet our contacts in England."

Marian writes a note and strolls to the pigeon cage. She attaches the note to a pigeon before she releases the avian aviator.

The four retire to their quarters for the night. The next morning Marian finds a pigeon carrying a confirmation. Marian and Priest pack their things. Their quivers, their bows, their arrows, and their armour. Isabella kisses Priest. Her skin seems a bit too pale.

"What about me?" Sarah asks.

"I may not return from this adventure, Sarah..."

"Like Master Robin...."

"Take care of Isabella."

They ride all day to arrive at a dock while the sun sets. Marian secures passage to take an old boat back to England.

They reside in the boat cabin, lightning crackles as heavy rain pummels against a wooden door. Marian and Priest sit at a table as they listen to the raging storm.

Marian is wary of Priest. Still wary of his demon after all these years.

The two odd companions land in England.

CHAPTER XXXX

SEEKING COUNCIL

Marian and Priest rough it through the countryside as they are pelted mercilessly by a torrent of dihydrogen monoxide. They travell to Baron Fitzwalter's Castle.

They are let in by the Fitzwalter's servant. They are led by candlelight up the stone steps of the stairway. The two enter a large roof and the two meet the Nobles of England.

They sit in a circle around the room. Marian and Priest stand in the center facing Baron Robert Fitzwalter.

Fitzwalter speaks, "We do not care that you come from royal blood, cousin. The only reason we are meeting with you right now is that you are Married to Robin Hood."

"Yes."

Baron Eustace De Vesci pipes up, "We made a lot of money off of Robin Hood. He was great for business. But moreso, he was a huge pain in the ass to King John."

"He stole from you." Marian says.

"He took a small sum from us but we made much more from the powerful economy he created." The Earl of Winchester says.

"King John got rid of that economy as soon as he took power. He is bleeding the country dry. His taxation for his french campaigns is crippling us, worse yet, there have been no military gains at all." Baron Fitzwalter says.

"He has created his own Royal Courts to redirect fines from the guilty into his Treasure Chest. That money was to be paid to us!" Baron Eustace De Vesci argues.

"He increased the fee we Barons must pay to him when our Daughters wed. Our sons must pay him when they inherit our lands. Some of us do not have children. Us without heirs must give our lands to other nobles, however, King John has kept such lands for himself." The Earl of Gloucester says.

"We all have the same question." Baron Eustace De Vesci says.

"What's the question?" Marian asks.

"Where is Robin Hood?!" The roomful of barons demand.

Marian gulps.

"Robin is... Robin Hood... is... Heh. Heh. He. He has been delayed. I am here in his stead to write down your grievances with the crown. Robin Hood will address it later." Marian says.

Baron Robert Fitzwalter explodes, "That is entirely!!!...acceptable."

"Where is my niece?" Marian asks.

Robert's eyes water. "Matilda."

"Uncle." Marian says.

Robert Breaks down. "My Matilda is dead."

The grieving father buries his face into his hands sobbing.

Marian learns the true grievances of the Nobility.

"John had designs on my daughter, Maid Matilda Fitzwalter. After being spurned by a Fitzwalter, King John poisoned her, my cousin." Robert wails.

"You two are cousins?

You two are cousins?"

"half-cousins." Marian says.

Baron Eustace De Vesci speaks, "Next time you come here, we had better meet with Robin Hood. You may go now."

MARIAN AND PRIEST ARE led outside and are surprised the rain has ceased. They walk to the nearest town and it is a sorry sight. The town is broken down, the markets are barely there, people are in poverty. Marian and Priest must hear out the grievances of the peasant class.

The merchants are the first to speak with them.

"King John is destroying our livelihoods. He has been greatly increasing our taxes over and over." The bee-keeper says. "Do you want to buy some honey?"

They back off.

They speak to the Potter, "We can barely afford to pay the Barons for the commodities we sell. How would you like to purchase some discounted pottery?"

The two back away until they bump into the farmer's produce table. They turn around and face the farmer.

The Farmer speaks up, "We are selling at the maximum price. We cannot increase it any further without pricing ourselves out of business. We have to sell more, more each day!"

"Where's Robin Hood?" Asks a peasant sitting in the street.

Marian takes her bag of gold and throws as many coins as she can to the peasants and merchants. Marian closes her bag and the two odd companions continue onwards. Marian is writing down her notes.

"Where do we go now?" Priest asks.

"To the Church." Marian answers.

"I am not sure if that is the best place for me to go." Priest gulps.

CHAPTER XXXXI

PERIL OF FAITH

They go to see Archbishop Tuck. Marian and Priest are walking down a red carpet through the church. Stained glass windows are towering over them. Marian looks upon windows depicting Moses, Jesus Christ, while Priest looks upon windows depicting A Silver Saucer, the final window is an interpretation of the Grail, It is a golden chalice adorned with Rubies.

Priest is nine years old when he breaks into the church pantry. He pulls out a metal drum. Priest opens the drum and finds Sherbet Ice Cream inside. Priest grabs a spoon and starts eating the Ice Cream. As he is halfway through the Sherbet he is suddenly seized by the arm. It is one of the Fathers. The Father heats up the brand. Priest is branded with another cross.

"Motherfuckery!
Motherfuckery!" Priest shouts.

Priest realises he is still in the Church standing next to Marian.

Priest is horrified, he kneels making the sign of the cross.

Tuck does not like Priest. he snaps his fingers and two knights of the order escort Priest away.

"Forgive him for that, Tuck." Marian asks.

"He must ask forgiveness himself. It has been far too long since our last meeting. Come Marian, let us parliament."

Tuck and Marian sup together.

"I see you haven't lost your looks, nor your figure, Marian." Tuck says.

"I see you haven't lost your girthful sense of humor, Tuck." Marian replies.

"I think you mean mirthful."

"If you insist... OW!"

"What is it, Marian?"

"Something bit me!"

Marian peers underneath the table but finds nothing. She raises her head to the table and finds a fat orange cat eating her supper. Marian's eyes perk up.

"Kitty!"

Marian pets the cat.

"Tuck, since John's defeat in Bouvines, we have set out to neutralise him."

"MMM-HMMM... And I suppose Robin Hood intends to commit regicide?"

Marian glances around the room, then back to Tuck.

"Tuck, can I tell you something confidential?"

"We are engaged in Parliament, everything we discuss will never leave these walls."

"Robin isn't coming back to England."

Tuck is taken aback.

"What!? Why???"

"Because Robin Hood isn't coming back to life."

Tuck stares blankly.

"Tuck?"

Tuck's expression is total Space Cadet.

"Tuck, we need your support if we are to take on the crown."

Tuck's expression sours significantly.

"Excuse me, Marian, I have matters to attend to. My final answer is no. You can show yourself out."

Tuck lifts his heavier frame and exits the room. Marian is left to her own devices.

Tuck is unwilling to help Marian, the wife of his former friend and ally. It's crystallised to Marian, Tuck has become corrupted by power. Sneaking through the Church archives Marian manages to learn.

PRIEST IS BEING HELD in a private room.

The hashish is presented to Friar Tuck. Tuck glances at it, glances over to Priest, then glances back to the hash. Tuck tosses it to the floor.

"No.

No."

"Show me. I want to see it." Tuck says.

Priest's shirt is ripped off. Crosses are branded all over his body. The brands have faded over the years.

"You truly are the Cursed Crusader."

Tuck steps on the hash smearing it on the floor with his heel.

"No!

No!"

"No. No. No! No!" Tuck mocks. "Could it be that after all the holy brands of the cross were bestowed upon you, despite you serving in the Crusades, despite two decades in the Holy Land, you are still possessed by a demon profaning our Church? Well, to best save you, maybe it's time to go back to basics."

The two knights grab both of Priest's arms. Tuck reveals the brand of the Cross.

MARIAN IS PERUSING the church archives. She is searching for any dirt she can find on King John. She tears through charts, scrolls, and loose papers. She finds nothing! She looks through the bookshelves. She notices four books are sticking out from a bookshelf, she removes the book quartet to find a fifth book tucked behind them.

Marian holds the book in her hands, she wipes off some dust. Marian starts to read. The book has to do with the Crusades and the Holy Church of Rome. She keeps flipping through the pages. She finds the insignia of the Order of the Dragon. Dracula's name is present, however, it's crossed out. Somebody wrote Dracula's Name backwards like it's supposed to send him back to the eighth dimension or something equally stupid.

She copies down The insignia. Priest streaks past the exit.

"Somebody grab the giant naked man!" Tuck shouts.

Several Guards quickly follow. Marian exits the archives and pursues the naked Priest in the church.

TUCK BRANDISHES THE hot iron menacingly, Priest is fearful, but quickly remembers he is no longer a small child, he's a Badass Crusader. Priest pulls one of the knights holding him close to him so that Tuck brands his subordinate instead. The Knight screams.

"It sucks, I know."

Priest throws the branded knight into Tuck and sends the other knight flying into them. Priest bolts for the exit, but his trousers rip on a loose nail in the door.

"Somebody grab the giant naked man!" Tuck shouts.

The two knights rise and are quickly in pursuit of the Naked Crusader.

Priest is streaking through the corridors, making it to the exit. He steps to the side and clotheslines the two hostiles. Marian rushes past his arm clearing it from beneath.

Marian is that short, or Priest is that tall, or both in tandem.

The first thing they do is make serious distance from the church. The second thing they do is locate the nearest tailor.

AS MARIAN CROSSES THE countryside she keeps glancing at Priest's naked frame. She knows she shouldn't but cannot help herself. They find a Tailor. Luckily the Tailor's Wife is the first to answer and she is a fan of their newest customer.

"Oh...Oh my. Please come inside, we are glad to serve you." The Tailor's Wife says.

A RECLOTHED PRIEST makes his way to the forest and constructs his new bow.

"Where now, Marian?

Where now, Marian?"

"We seek the Order of the Dragon, Priest. We must go to where Crusaders gather."

The odd pairing travel to Ye Olde Trip to Jerusalem.

THE BASTARD ARRIVES. Philip Planteganet leads an elite guard known as The Dark Knights. Tuck addresses The Bastard.

"It took you long enough."

"Take that tone with me Holy Man, I'll take something from you." Philip says.

"What does that even... Nevermind. Listen, the reason I called you here is that Marian, the Lady of Huntington has returned." Tuck says.

"Where's Robin Hood?"

"Somewhere hard to find, yet all too easy."

Philip raises a finger.

"What does that even me- You know what? Nevermind. Hood's Woman will talk. She has always been his weak point." Philip says.

"Philip!" Tuck shouts.

"Yes?"

"She has The Cursed Crusader as a companion."

Philip breaks into a cold sweat.

" I... I didn't... He exists? No! You're toying with me, he's a fairy-tale. A bedtime story to frighten children. He can't exist."

"She has The Cursed Crusader as a companion, they intend to commit regicide."

Philip gulps down his fear and puts his game face on.

"The demon is dead."

CHAPTER XXXXII

FOXING IT OUT

Marian begins her quest to locate the Dark Cult and destroy them all with the assistance of Priest.

They are in Ye old Trip to Jerusalem, they find many Crusaders drinking and looking miserable. A young lord named Dominos sits at a table. Young Lord Dominos has the Signet Draconus on his shirt. Marian and Priest stroll up to the young lord pretending to be waiters.

"Hello." Marian says.

"Hello."He replies.

"Would you like some drink?" Marian asks.

Priest and Marian get him proper smashed by serving him cocktails of the leftover ale, wine, and grog. Lord Dominos is a bit tipsy.

"This is strong. What is this drink?"

"I call it a Graveyard." Marian says.

They serve Lord Dominos a few more. Young Lord Dominos spills it.

"Yeah, I belong to a secret organization, We are called the Order of the Dragon, we were led by Dracula, but now that he is gone, We are being led by his son Alucard. We're the real power behind King John, Without us, He would be strong, But capable of folding under pressure. We have sects of sorceresses, dens of warlocks, and a few of those sick fucks that dance naked in front of their pets."

"Dracula disappeared?" Marian asks.

"Right after the one episode of Jerry. You were great by the way."

Marian turns to Priest.

"Priest, We're dealing with the remnants of an organization, We have to take a detour on our way to King John."

"Jer-ry! Jer-ry! Jer-ry! Jer-ry!" Young Lord Dominos chants.

Marian and Priest shadow Lord Dominos by laying on top of his carriage. The carriage stops on a bridge and the young lord steps out. The young lord strolls down to the Brooke, following it into the forest. Marian and Priest leap off the carriage scrambling after him.

They keep to the brush the pine needles prickle against Marian's delicate skin. they keep their distance but they are trailing the young lord.

Marian stares around their environment. She recognizes the waterfall and the surrounding forest.

Lord Dominos jumps out from behind the large Brookstone and rushes Marian. Priest has his bow drawn but he can't get a bead on the attacker. The young man has the look of the devil in his eyes, but Marian stands there, arms folded, unimpressed. The little spitfire is suddenly pulled upwards. He hangs there by his foot swinging upside down upon a snare.

"It's time to play a little game called: YOU LOSE!" Marian shouts.

Marian sings an arrow past Lord Dominos' head.

"AAAAAH!"

"You Lose!" Marian shouts.

Priest steps up.

"You lose!

You lose!"

Priest sends an arrow through the throat of young Dominos. The dead lord hangs there with an arrow completely piercing through his throat. The crimson-coated arrowhead is slowly dripping blood.

"Priest! What the blazes are you doing?"

"What Sir Robin would do.

What Sir Robin would do."

"We're not doing this like Sir Robin! We're trying to do this Robin Hood's way!"

"His screaming was giving away our position.

His screaming was giving away our position..."

"He was Bait."

"Bait?

Bait?"

"Now we must brave the fox's den for our prey."

They slowly creep towards the roaring waterfall and a Hellhound explodes out of the waterfall roaring. The Dark Canine Spectre is barking furiously, Priest shoots an arrow through The Phantom Hellhound's head. The Hellhound's fur arches its back, hairs standing up, the Demonic Dog's eyes glow red as it starts to glow blue.

The Demon Dog runs at the Two Adventurers.

Run. Demon Dog. Run.

The Two Adventurers Scream.

Scream. Two Adventurers. Scream

See the Demon Dog run.

See the Two Adventurers scream.

The Order of the Dragon sits in a circle at a table. They are deep in a cave behind a waterfall, a place no adventurer would ever think of checking.

Alucard rises from a green pool in the corner side of the cave, streams of water pouring off of his lithe naked body, and puts on a robe in full view of the Lords. He puts on the traditional black ceremonial cape and walks over to The Order of the Dragon and sits down at the head of the table.

"Report." Alucard says.

"There are rumours the Spirit of Camelot stirs. That could present a potential problem."

"The Dark Knights can easily deal with the Spirit of Camelot. Not an issue."

"The Dark Knights are currently under the command of Philip Planteganet." Lord Blackmoore says.

"Oh. yes, I don't like the idea of loaning out my personal guard; even if they are currently foxing the rumoured whereabouts of Robin Hood." Alucard sneers.

"The whereabouts of Robin Hood are currently a mystery, we are combing his old hunting grounds for clues, we even checked the recently discovered outlaws camp. Arch-Bishop Tuck is to thank for revealing that little secret." Lord Blackmoore says.

"By the way, Where is Robin Hood? I haven't seen him in over a decade. In fact, nobody has! Has anybody actually seen him lately?" Alucard asks.

A blood-soaked corpse bangs furiously onto the table...

A dead Hellhound.

"What the hell is this?" Alucard asks.

"A slaughter!"

Marian and Priest enter the room from the tunnel directly above the Order. Marian breaks out her bow, her compound bow.

"Let's go, Priest!"

They slaughter fourteen men in under seven seconds. Only Alucard is left. He smiles to a point that's unsettling.

"You can't kill me! I have fifty hit points! I'm invincible! HA! HA! HA! AHA! HA! HA!"

Fifty hits later, Alucard is dead.

He spins around several times and lands on the ground. A coffin rises from the rock and absorbs Alucard's body and sinks into the fresh soil of the grave. A headstone appears and a single white calla lily quickly grows over the grave.

"Seriously? Seriously, Holland? I mean, Jesus... the whole Zelda thing was laying it on a bit thick, but this is too far. What's next, Dancing Bears?" Marian asks.

Go Jump in the bay and kill all the fish, wench![27] Marian ceases obstinance and continues acting out the demented author's insane rantings.

CHAPTER XXXXIII

VERITAS

The saucy waitress at Ye Olde Trip to Jerusalem saunters up to the platonic couple.

The waitress sets down two pints of ale.

"We didn't order these," Marian says.

"Compliments of the house, it's about bloody time somebody stood up to the jerk who's writing this."

The waitress walks away demurely. Marian is having a celebratory drink with Priest.

"We took out a large piece of the Chessboard, Priest!"

"Marian.

Marian."

"Yes?"

"The Hashish is wearing off. The demon is taking hold once more.

The Hashish is wearing off. The demon is taking hold once more."

Marian is shocked. She scoots her chair away, she is wary of Priest as a large man grabs her. Marian is struggling when Priest rises up to look down on the little man.

A small man molesting My brother's widow!

"That's my best friend's wife!

That's my best friend's wife!"

Anthony of Mastrantonio lets go of Marian, he stares up at Priest, they lock eyes in a staring contest. Anthony is projecting daggers from his eyes. Priest has a look in him that disturbs the attempted rapist. Priest has the look of conviction with ill intent; the devil blazing hellfire out of his eyes. The eyes of the grabby s.o.b. quickly glance to the table. The big guy named Anthony of Mastrantonio goes for a knife on the table. Priest grabs his arm promptly pulling him down to the floor. Tony gets back up. He angrily backhands Priest. Enraged, Priest looks at his victim's chest. The Cursed Crusader gives the civilian an epic Crusader-style beat down. Priest blocks a blow and rolls Tony onto the floor.

"Get up! Get up! Don't be a bitch! I said Get up!

Get up! Get up! Don't be a bitch! I said Get up!"

"What the hell is wrong with you? I'll kick your crazy ass!"

Anthony scrambles to his feet then attempts to kick Priest in the head but only hits his rock-hard pecs.

"Ow!"

Priest grabs Anthony's leg and swings him onto the bar table.

Priest grabs both of Tony's legs sliding him off the table and onto the floor. Priest picks him up and knees the guy in the Solar Plexus. Priest drops the guy. Priest leaps onto him and punches the man repeatedly in the face. Priest is grabbed by the guy he knocked the bloody spit out of and his head is slammed against the table twice.

"Priest! No!"

Priest lies on the floor still but breathing normally. Anthony stands back up groggily. He doesn't look as damaged as he should be. He also has a rather vexed demeanor about him. Marian has the knife in her hand. Marian looks at Tony's chest. She throws the knife down into the wooden table.

"Pick it up." Marian says rather passively.

"What's your game, woman?"

"I want you to pick it up." She says coyly.

"No...."

Marian unleashes her inner bitch.

"Listen, you arrogant peasant, You messed up in the worst way in all of England."

"How did I make an error?

"You crossed Robin Hood's Dagger... Either you pick it up, or I will."

Priest awakens on the floor. The guy springs for the knife. He firmly grasps the knife, Marian tilts her body back to avoid the knife. She swings her legs kicking the man in the left arm. He has the knife in his right arm, Marian has something special planned for the right arm. He thrusts the knife, Marian sidesteps the blow, he thrusts the knife again, Marian sidesteps the second blow. This continues five more times until Marian sidesteps for the last time grabbing his arm. Marian jerks the arm as she pummels his ribcage with several dam-aging elbow strikes. Anthony of Mastrantonio is on the ground in shock with a dislocated arm and several broken ribs.

The Nottingham Guards arrive at Ye Olde Trip to Jerusalem, sur-rounding Marian and Priest.

The Deputy surveys the scene, "Men, get this man to the Hospi-tallers. You two are under arrest."

Marian is shackled alongside Priest, both are promptly trans-ported into a prisoner wagon. Priest rocks his head back and forth violently. A storm brews. Light rain patters onto the prisonwagon.

"How long?

How long?"

"How long since what?" Marian asks.

"Since you were knighted.

Since you were knighted."

Priest steadies his head against the iron cage bars. Marian lowers hers.

"How did you figure it out?" Marian asks.

"That look in your eyes. I recognized it.

That look in your eyes. I recognized it."

"It occurred on Robin's last adventure. We were made Knights of Avalon."

"Avalon? Did Robin find the Grail?

Avalon? Did Robin find the Grail?"

"From what I observed, I think the Grail found him."

Priest and Marian sit in silence for the remainder of the trip. The only thing breaking the silence is Priest knocking his fist on the bars.

When the carriage stops the Nottingham Guards open the doors of the Carriage, the two Prisoners explode out of the cage and are ready to tear everybody apart. Instead, a net is quickly thrown over both of them, they are ignominiously dragged to a Nottingham Dungeon pit, and tossed in like rank trash.

Priest starts freaking out. Priest has lost full control of his body and is violently shaking on the floor. Marian is against the wall terrified out of her wits. She decides she must try to soothe the demon. Marian slowly walks over, she bends down on her knees and starts massaging Priest's back with her fingernails. Priest gradually calms down. She continues to soothe the demon. She slowly massages Priest with her hands relieving a lot of tension.

"Priest, tell me, what is it like to kill in Holy Crusade?"

"My feelings on the matter amount to nothing. Nothing matters except the Crusade.

My feelings on the matter amount to nothing. Nothing matters except the Crusade."

"Yes. But what's it like to kill in it?"

"I have participated in horrors you could not fathom. So many men dead for their God. Why does he require it?

I have participated in horrors you could not fathom. So many men dead for their God. Why does he require it?"

"To take back Jerusalem."

"Must we have endless slaughter or can we achieve peace?
Must we have endless slaughter or can we achieve peace?"

"Peace is in the afterlife like the Church says. I observe you do not find peace in your sleep. What do you dream?"

"I dream of Fire. What do you dream of?
I dream of Fire. What do you dream of?" Priest asks.

Marian blushes.

"You would think me silly."

"Tell me, I won't laugh.
Tell me, I won't laugh." Priest says.

"I dream of Sherwood Forest. Just me and Robin. I have dreamt of it ever since Robin passed. It's strange..."

"I've seen stranger things.
I've seen stranger things." Priest says.

King John arrives.

"Marian? Marian, what are you doing here? No. No. There has to be some mistake. But that is inconsequential, for I have you trapped. I'll let you out when you decide to sleep with me."

"I will never sleep with you, not even for coin doubled exponentially across a chessboard you cheat!"

King John is enraged, The King of England reveals a state secret to Marian, "I wish for you to know that your truest love, Robin Hood, cheated on you with Queen Sibylla, He fucked her to death. I am privy to this information as an actual Royal, besides, I have already had to pay three years' worth of income to pay for Richard's release. Figures I still have to clean up his mess."

John walks off leaving her stunned and heartbroken.

"Priest, is it true? Did Robin truly sleep with Sibylla?"

"There were rumors about it. It wasn't until Robin mentioned Queen Sibylla was alive a year after they said she died that I realised the rumors were true.

There were rumors about it. It wasn't until Robin mentioned Queen Sibylla was alive a year after they said she died that I realised the rumors were true."

"Why did Robin do it?"

"I don't know why, all I know is that I wouldn't have my wife, and Sir Robin never would have returned to you if he hadn't.

I don't know why, all I know is that I wouldn't have my wife, and Sir Robin would have never returned to you if he hadn't."

"No."

"Marian, I..."

"NO!!!"

Marian begins pounding her fists onto Priest's chest. Marian begins to cry. Her eyes are flowing streams, Priest holds her in his arms. Marian hugs Priest, Priest does the same. Marian presses her lips against his, He drinks into her lips. He's enthralled in them. His eyes shoot open then he pulls away.

"I can't do it. God knows I want to, but Sir Robin was my brother.

I can't do it. God knows I want to, but Sir Robin was my Brother."

"I am his Widow!"

"That's why I'm getting you out of here.

That's why I'm getting you out of here."

"How?"

"Allow me to demonstrate for you.

Allow me to demonstrate for you."

Priest's Muscles ripple as he pulls the grating off of the middle of the opening.

"It's too small for me. Maybe you can climb through it, Marian.

It's too small for me. Maybe you can climb through it, Marian."

Marian climbs on top of Priest squeezing through the opening. Marian stands up, walks over to the keyring, unlocks the dungeon door then starts to walk out. She then looks at the cell grating on the floor. Then spins around and walks off. Marian recalls a conversation she had with Robin years ago in Sherwood Forest.

"So as I was saying, this guy, Priest, a hell of a shot. He's huge, powerful, deadly, all-around a true badass! I'm glad he's my brother in arms because he's the one person I would not incur the wrath of."

"He's possessed by a demon, Robin."

Robin Hood glares at her. "What did I say? demons do not save people!"

Marian nods her head. "demons do not save people."

"He saved so many prisoners, so many women, with his bare hands. He would have been one of my best Merry Men."

Robin Hood looks away.

"He should have been."

Marian finds herself back at the exit staring at the broken cell grating. She walks over and unlocks the cell. Priest climbs out.

"I am afraid of you Priest, but after this, I trust you with my life."

Marian and Priest walk through the strangely deserted castle and enter the courtyard, where a small army of Archers are ready to shoot them both dead. Suddenly, the Sheriff of Nottingham appears.

"Let the prisoners escape!"

The Archers put down their bows.

"Why?"Marian asks.

"I hated my job so I took the Sheriffs. I have to pay back Robin Hood for sparing my life. Where is he anyway?"

Marian thinks quickly, "Oh. Um... He's out there doing his thing."

The Sheriff of Nottingham smiles, "Of course he is. Let me know if he needs us."

CHAPTER XXXXIV

SPIRIT OF CAMELOT

Tuck is sitting on the Church Dais, the man's wracked by guilt, the memory of Robin Hood will not stop tormenting him. The dark room becomes illuminated as lightning crashes.

Robin Hood appears in the flashes. "Why did you not help my wife?"

"My loyalty is to the church, not to outlaws, nor their widows."

Robin Hood clasps onto Tuck's shoulder. "You used to be an outlaw yourself. We did much good together." Robin squeezes his friend's shoulder.

"You never returned!"

"Have I not? Then how is it I am in your head?" Robin Hood asks.

"You are my conscience in the form of an old friend."

"Then, as your conscience, may I remind you who gave you the power you now wield?"

"No. No. Please don't," Tuck pleads.

"You made a deal with King John."

Tuck sits broken upon his Dais.

MARIAN AND PRIEST ARE marching up the hillside of Camelot. The elements are showering them as they march up the hill. It rains in the snow.

The two come across a haunted Camelot. There are rumors that the Round Table still meets here. Priest and Marian shall see. They creep through ancient castle ruins.

"Camelot is in disrepair. In a few hundred years, this castle will be nothing but stones on the ground." Marian remarks.

"This place smells rank.

This place smells rank."

They step silently through the dark hallway. The two duck into a room as soon as they spot a light approaching. A man in black with a blue cape carries a lit candle as he patrols the hallway past them. As soon as the coast is clear, the two allies traverse the darkness. They take a left at the window by the end of the hall. They come to the edge of what was once a balcony.

The two friends peer into the room below and witness 100 men sitting at a round table. A leak is dripping water onto the table.

They have arrived at the meeting of the Knights of the Round Table.

"Lance, any news from Sir William?"Artie asks.

"He awaits the coming of Robin Hood! He is ready, Lord Artie."

Priest gazes in wonder.

"I never thought I would gaze upon the visage of King Arthur Pendragon.

I never thought I would gaze upon the visage of King Arthur Pendragon."

Marian squints.

"That's not Arthur. That's not Arthur at all!"

A sentry clasps onto both of their shoulders. Marian and Priest grab onto both hands and throw him into space before descending into freefall. The sentry lands on the Round Table.

Everybody at the table is surprised.

"Anybody moves, and they are the first to die!" Marian shouts.

They hold hostage the knights of the round table.

"What do you want from us?" Artie asks.

"First, who are you? Who are you, really?" Marian asks

Artie sighs.

"We are the surviving Jews of England. We took Camelot as our refuge. We sent out agents to procure the provisions we need to survive." Artie replies.

"So what now?" Marian asks

"As for now, all we want is to live in peace with our fellow Englishman. You know, everybody keeps blaming us Jews for the death of Jesus Christ. Did not the Jews hire a lawyer to defend Jesus? The only reason he died was that the lawyer was running late." Artie says.

"Wow. Really?" Marian asks.

"Wow. Really?" Lance asks.

Artie slugs his elbow into Lance's gut.

"Oh, yes. Assuredly." Lance says.

Artie continues, "We have no reason to hate one another... in fact... we should be allies."

"If we are to be allies, you must come out of hiding. We must fight for England! England is the Covenant Land, is it not?" Marian asks.

Artie and Lance glance at one another. They ponder this proposal.

Artie continues, "As it is, I have information for Robin Hood."

"Robin Hood is busy fighting so that our presence is allowed." Marian says.

"I guess I can share the information with Robin Hood's wife. William Marshall has evidence on King John, But he will want to see Hood himself. He waits for Robin at the beginning." Artie says.

CHAPTER XXXXV

MARSHALL

May 1215 A.D.
Marian and Priest follow the clues to William Marshall.

Marian arrives at the charred remains of Locksley Castle. Marian winds her way to Robin's father's room.

Robert's room, our entire lives living here, we never dared enter Robin's fathers room. For all we knew Robin's father is still sitting in his room. The room was surely diseased, but fire purifies all things, even souls; possibly the souls of petty, arrogant, stupid blokes like the elder Earl of Huntington.

Marian kicks down the charred remains of the door. She strides in and realises that the portrait of Robin's Father still hangs upon the bed, perfectly un-singed.

Marian fumes, steams, then boils over.

She screams and hurls her dagger at the old piker. The dagger sails right between the bastard's eyes. The knife passes through the painting and the Earl sticks his silver pointed tongue out at Marian as if to mock her.

Marian is losing it before she realises the silver pointed tongue is, in fact, a steel pointed dagger. Marian climbs and walks across the blackened bed-frame. The lady of Locksley Manor tears down the painting and finds a cavity in the stone wall. Two tickets to the May Games lie there.

PRIEST AND MARIAN GIVE their tickets to the ticketeer so they are permitted to enter the May Games.

"What's with the Tickets? The May Games are free!" Marian complains.

"Not anymore. Not until the crown can pay the debt of The Lion Heart's release." The Ticketeer says.

Marian and Priest enter the May Games.

Marian and Priest pass the many young people celebrating love. The kids are dressed as King Arthur and Queen Guinevere, Sir Lancelot and Elaine of Astolat, Merlin and Nimue, General Julius Caesar and Queen Cleopatra, Robin Hood and Maid Marian.

An old man is in the wooden ring beating the bloody spit out of every opponent.

The two allies approach the ring. The old man takes notice and meets them halfway.

"You are the one named William Marshall?" Marian asks.

"Step this way. We need to speak in private."

"That way is the ring.

That way is the ring."

"That's because my time isn't free, if you want me to spend it, you're going to have to earn it."

Priest steps into the ring.

Priest takes a swing at the old man. He kicks Priest's shin out from under him, grasps Priest's throat, choke-slamming him to the ground.

Priest gets back up.

"Round two." the old man says.

Priest punches twice. The old man dodges twice. He punches Priest many times, but the old man's hands ache, Priest is fine. The old goat sacks Priest. Priest goes down. The old man walks away.

Marian is sitting on the bench.

"Priest, don't be a bitch! Get back up!"

Priest stands up.

The old man stops in his tracks when he hears a voice,"Round three.

Round three."

The old man steps back into the ring. Priest shows mercy to the old man and throws him a quarterstaff.

The old man tries to strike Priest, but Priest blocks him with the forearm. He gives the old goat a chop to the head. The old man stumbles backwards and Priest advances. The old man stops, reverses course battering Priests head. Priest isn't hurt but he's now all piss and thunder. Priest grabs the quarterstaff and tosses it. Priest grabs the old man and tosses him. The old man tumbles across the ground landing in a classic Spider-Man pose. He stands up, chortling as he walks over.

"I've only known two real men in my time, Richard the Lion Heart and Robin Hood. I am joyous to meet the third."

Priest salutes William

"Deus Vult.

Deus Vult."

"A Crusader! Nice to see a fellow fighter. Did you attack Zara?" William asks.

"I refused. Zara was not part of the mission. I believe in what I do.

I refused. Zara was not part of the mission. I believe in what I do."

"A true believer! It seems rather rare these days without a man like Robin Hood to inspire people."

"We heard you can prove King John murdered his nephew, Arthur." Marian says.

"I may. I may not. I want to speak with Robin Hood." William says.

"Robin Hood is not here. He sent me to collect the proof while he tries to stop Prince John." Marian says.

"Robin Hood is dead isn't he?" William asks.

"No. He is just out there and he... he... he's dead. He's dead! I saw it all...."

Marian breaks down crying.

"Jesus.

Jesus."

"How did you know?" Marian asks.

"If Robin Hood wanted to stop Prince John, he would have seen me himself years ago."

William hands over the Document.

"This is a signed document by Eleanor of Aquitaine attesting that John murdered Richard's nephew Arthur to consolidate his power." William says.

"The problem is that Robin Hood was just a man. No more. No less. With this, we can make him permanent." Marian says.

Marian presents her notes. William reads it over, he grins like a Cheshire Cat.

"We will still need Robin Hood to pull it off." William says.

Marian and William look at Priest. William dresses Priest in four in one chain-mail covered by green gambeson.

Priest is dressed as Robin Hood. Marian looks at him sideways.

"He doesn't quite look convincing."

"We need a mask." William says.

Priest puts on a mask.

"Well?"

"I can see it." Marian says.

"What will you do now?" William asks.

"E Pluribus Unum.

E Pluribus Unum."

"From many, one." Marian states.

CHAPTER XXXXVI

FIERY, BUT MOSTLY PEACEFUL

William Marshall is present in the Royal Court of King John. John is surrounded by a small army. The Bastard is among them.

"What's your report, Marshall?" King John asks.

"There are several reports that Robin Hood has finally revealed himself, Sire."

"I'LL TAKE TWO APPLES." A commoner requests.

"That'll be four-coin with a five-coin tax." The farmer says.

"We're taxed too high!" The commoner shouts

"Where's Robin Hood?" The commoner's wife asks.

Priest hops up onto a house roof disguised as Robin Hood.

"My Fellow Englishman, I am Robin Hood! I have come to help with your tax problems...."

Priest quickly covers his mouth.

"How?" the farmer asks.

"Burn it down! Burn it down! Burn it all down! Burn it down! Burn it down! Burn it all down!"

"ROBIN HOOD IS CREATING an uprising, sire." Marshall reports.

THE MASSES TEAR DOWN statues of King John, The guards are in their barracks when a severed statue head of King John is thrown through a window.

"Tyrannis Rex!
Tyrannis Rex!"

"Tyrannis Rex! Tyrannis Rex! Tyrannis Rex!" the mob shouts.

"HE'S LEADING AN INSURRECTION? This shouldn't be as surprising as I find it. I should've seen this coming." King John says.

"Robin Hood isn't just tearing down statues m'lord," Marshall says.

King John glares at him.

"My Lord..."

"What else is he doing?" John asks.

"He's committing arson."

"A few villages can be sacrificed to maintain power...." John says.

"He's committing arson on the tax records, sire." Marshall informs him.

MARIAN AND PRIEST LEAD the peasants to burn down the tax records. They burn them down from village to village across England. The mob fires burning arrows into the tax record archives. Hundreds of thousands of Byzants burn in the records. The mob rages to Nottingham.

KING JOHN LOSES IT.

"That grimy hedge-robbing thundercunt!"

Marshall continues, "You see King John, you spent so much time dividing the people, turning them against each other, you gave the people time to catch on. They're uniting behind Robin Hood."

"And my bastard nephew could not find Robin Hood, even with the full assistance of the crown and other resources. Useless." King John sneers.

"I don't know how he evaded capture. It's as if he didn't even exist until now." Philip the Bastard says.

"A convenient excuse for sheer incompetence." Marshall cracks.

"I'll send you out the third story window you keep talking, old man!" Philip hisses.

"I spanked your father in combat; by Mary, I'll spank you thrice as hard, boy!" William roars.

"Enough! Philip... take the Dark Knights and join with my other forces. Do it for king and country." John snaps.

"I do it for profit." Philip Planteganet says.

"Fine, whatever." John says.

CHAPTER XXXXVII

COALESCENCE

The mob floods into Nottingham. They bear torches. The Sheriff comes out of the castle and confronts the mob with his men. They place themselves between the tax records and Robin Hood's Mob.

"Hey, Hey, Hey, Whoa. I can't let you burn down the tax records, Robin Hood. It's my job to protect those records for King John and...And...And I hate my job! Burn it down!" The Sheriff says.

The mob rages around England. Chaos reigns the day as civilians tear down statues of King John. The tax records burnt to ash.

THE PEASANTS GATHER outside Baron Fitzwalter's castle, as Robin Hood steps inside. Marian visits her cousin.

"We have been taxed so much to offset the cost to Free Richard. When will enough be enough?" Robert asks.

"Robert, Robin paid for Richard in full personally." Marian says.

"You surely jest me, Marian, Robin was a minor lord, he was not very..."

"Robin came back from the Crusades with more purple than you could ever dare hope to witness. John has been taxing you unfairly for years."

"Can you prove this?" Robert asks.

Marian shows him her purple bracelet.

"We must rise, Robert. We must demonstrate to John the full power of our nation."

"E Pluribus Unum.

E Pluribus Unum." Priest says with zeal.

The barons in the room gather around Robin Hood, touching the Legend.

Baron Eustace de Vesci stands. "Robin Hood, No. With these Nottingham Guards and English Peasants, we stand no chance against John's might. We would need the Spirit of Camelot to prevail."

Robin Hood motions for them to follow right before he spins around and dashes through the exit. They all follow Robin Hood down the musty castle steps.

They walk outside and pass through the mob, the crowd parts for Robin Hood. The Barons arrive at the edge of a forest.

The Knights of the Current Round Table step forward.

"The Knights of the Round Table 2: Cruise Control is behind Robin Hood, No longer in spirit, but in the flesh, blood, and English Steel." Lance says.

Robin Hood raises his sword.

"The many are one!

The many are one!"

The crowd quickly whips into a frenzy.

"The many are one! The many are one! The many are one! The many are one! The many are one!"

The First Baron's revolt begins. Revolution begins.

CHAPTER XXXXVIII

REVOLUTION

15th of June, 1215 A.D.
Civil war breaks out. Marian, Priest, along with Robert Fitzwalter lead the First Baron's Revolt to London.

"Sword, bear my temper; Heart, be quite chill, Priest, pray for the enemy, my broken heart shall kill." Marian says icily.

Philip the Bastard leads the Dark Knights. Mass violence is achieved before a bear wanders through the battlefield. Everyone flees from the bear. The bear roams through town. Hijinks ensue. The Bear eats the beekeeper's honey. The bear walks up to a knight and snarls. The knight jumps out of his armour and scrams.

The Bear rises up and bellows. Everybody on the battlefield is scared witless.

The Bear starts doing The Robot.

"Dang, the Bear has moves.

Dang, the Bear has moves." Priest remarks

The Bear grabs Priest and starts to waltz around the abandoned battlefield. The Bear rests its head onto Priest's shoulder, Priest breaks down crying. Streams pour down Priest's crimson cheeks as they dance a perfect waltz.

The Bear drinks some grog then exits the battlefield. Priest is huddled in the market rocking back and forth.

The Baron's War resumes.

Marian is killing with hell's fury. The corner market erupts. Something new blasts its way into history. King John unleashes The Crown's Cannons upon the Baron's Revolt. Explosions rock London. Several more blasts hit the revolutionaries. Marian can't find Priest, she hastens through the smoke and flame towards the cannon fire. She stops and pulls out three arrows, lighting them on the fires burning on the ground.

PRIEST AWAKENS NEAR the Corner Market, flour and produce are everywhere. Priest witnesses Marian committing suicide, She is attacking several cannons with only three burning arrows. Priest searches with his eyes and comes across sacks of flour strewn about.

Marian is dashing towards certain death and she knows it.

"Marian!

Marian!"

Marian knows who it is and she smiles devilishly.

"Marian, Shoot!

Marian, Shoot!"

Three sacks of flour are thrown at several cannons. Marian's three arrows hit their mark, she kills the cannoneers by blasting them old school. She flies past the cannoneer's dead bodies. Rushing up the stairs she gains a clear vantage point.

Marian sings death upon her enemies. The other cannons cease; Marian continues to sing death. She pierces many the hearts of men. The baron's cheer. The Dark Knights quickly dart out of the shadows to apprehend the barons. Philip the Bastard climbs over the edge of the wall. He grabs Marian, taking her by surprise. Luckily Marian was inhaling when she was restrained. Marian exhales as she drops with all her weight.

Philip is not expecting this, allowing Marian to escape his grasp. Marian sweeps his legs so he lands on his back. Marian is on top of him trying to plunge a knife into his throat. Philip grabs Marian's wrist forcing her to ram her fist into her once perfect nose.

Marian tumbles off of the Bastard. She is stunned.

Philip the Bastard clasps onto the knife. The Bastard rises.

"Tell me where Robin Hood is, wench!"

Priest bear hugs Philip Plantagenet. The Bastard sticks Priest in the thigh. Priest releases Philip the Bastard. Philip spins around glaring with hate.

"Robin Hood!" Philip roars.

Priest limps; blood trickling from his thigh.

"Philip, Don't do this!; for God's mercy, don't do this!" Marian pleads.

Philip spits."Profit be my god!"

Philip tackles Priest, knifing him several times. Priest is mostly protected by the gambeson and four in one chain-mail link. Philip the Bastard raises the knife for his final blow.

A tall lanky knight sporting a cream-colored Fedora arrives. His Fedora is accentuated by a Zoot Suit of the same color. He is accompanied by a short fat knight in Bluish Chain-mail.

The short fat knight un-scrolls his message, "Philip Planteganet, also known as Philip the Bastard, also known as the illegitimate child of our beloved King, Richard The Lion Heart, also known as the cheapskate who owes me sixty gold pieces!"

"Those dice were loaded!" Philip shouts.

"They weren't the only ones." Wilbert says.

Wilbert raises his hand to his mouth exhaling loudly.

"Are you going to pay this man his gold?" Rick asks.

"Stay out of this Stretch; or I'll bust your' nose bloody, buddy!" Philip says.

"You can't talk that way to me!" Rick shouts.

"Says you, Stretch Hawkins." Philip says.

"Who's Hawkin' Stretch?"

"You."

"Wilbert. Break his glass jaw."

Wilbert socks Philip in the jaw. Philip growls at them.

"It's a jaw made of iron." Wilbert moans.

Philip towers over Wilbert.

"Whatever you do, Don't pop me in the weasel." Wilbert says.

Philip kicks Wilbert in the groin popping his weasel. Wilbert collapses like a sack of rocks.

"Just what I thought... That the best you got?" Philip asks.

"I'll show you the best I've got!" Rick shouts.

Rick walks over to Wilbert.

"Get up, Wilbert." Rick coaxes.

"Leave me, I'll sleep here."

"I said get up!"

Wilbert stands up.

"I dare you to try that again!" Rick shouts.

"I sure wouldn't." Wilbert whimpers.

"Shaddup, you! Alright, Philip, do that again." Rick says.

Philip pops Wilbert in the weasel again.

"Timber!" Rick shouts.

Wilbert falls over.

"I bet you don't have the balls to do that again. Get up, Wilbert."

"Rick, He does that again, I won't have the balls." Wilbert moans.

Philip raises his Gold Ducat into the sky and proclaims, "Sit tibi, Christe, datus, quem tu regis iste ducatus."

Rick strolls up, "Pick a number between seven and forty-two, I bet you all the money you owe Wilbert and King John, that I can tell you the right number." Rick says.

"Okay, I picked a number." Philip says.

"Which number is it?"

"Sweet sixteen."

"Sorry but the right number is five." Rick says.

"But you said to pick a number between seven and forty-two." Philip says.

"Yeah, and you trusted me, the guy who wants your money. The right number is five. Now pay up."

"That's not fair!" Philip says.

"Life's not fair, Why are you yelling at me about it?" Rick asks, "Now pay up."

Philip the Bastard pays up.

"Fortuna Favet Fortibus." Rick says with a smile.

Wilbert and Rick leave with all of Philip's money.

"A pox upon your cold greedy heart, King John." The Bastard screams.

London falls to the rebels.

CHAPTER XXXXIX

CHECKMATE

15 th of June 1215 A.D.
Marian and Priest ride to southeast England, west of London. The two siblings in spirit behold King John's six-story castle in rural Runnymede. The two archers enter the chessboard. The first floor has a checkered floor. Marian and Priest begin shooting the garrison of guards (pawns). It's a slaughter.

The second story has a checkered floor as well as the garrison of Archers (Rooks.) there are whizzing arrows flying in every direction and Marian dodges arrows. Priest's Gambeson is pierced a few times. As time goes on, less whizzing arrows are flying around. the whizzing stops.

The third story has a checkered floor upon which the Knights stand. The Dynamic Duo has few arrows left. Nowhere near enough.

The Ghost Blade manifests itself back into Marian's hand. She and Priest go to town on the knights. Priest is unleashing hell upon the enemy as Marian fights with her sword and her Ghost Blade. The Ghost Blade cannot be broken. The Ghost Blade cannot be stopped. The same is true for Marian.

The fourth story has checkered floors as well.

The fourth story has Knights with Pawns backed up by Rooks. Marian is put through each and every one of her paces. She is supremely lethal. All men fighting in the room find Marian's broken

389

heart kills. Priest is fighting his own heart out. he is throwing knights into archers and stabbing guards with zeal. Priest is into it when he is stabbed.

Marian is slaughtering wholesale as she turns her head she glances at Priest falling to his knees. An archer has his bow drawn; arrow pointing at Priest's forehead. Marian blocks her opponent's blade with her steel and throws the Ghost blade across the room into the Archer. The Ghost Blade re-materializes in Marians grasp, and she runs through her opponent without ever penetrating his armour. Marian slaughters the rest with her ethereal sliding sword.

Marian moves to the fifth floor only to find more checkered flooring. She comes across a monkey holding a ruby red rubber ball. The monkey is throwing the ball around the room in crazy accurate trajectories. Marian is dodging the ball like a master. The monkey throws the ball at her head. She tilts her head to her left as the ball sails past bouncing off the wall behind her. Marian tilts her head to her right as the ball sails past her head again, straight into the monkey.

The monkey is knocked into a back flip landing on his butt.

Marian makes it to the sixth floor, The Queen of England is waiting for Marian. Isabella of Angouleme has auburn hair, a perfect nose, and is rather busty. She reminds Marian of herself.

"I am Queen of England, My blood is pure. Not the bastard blood of an outlaw's harlot." Isabella shouts.

Marian gets into a cat fight with Isabella of Angouleme, the Queen of England, they're scratching and clawing at each other.

"I command armies! My beauty is the greatest in the land!" Isabella shouts.

The queen has her hand on Marian's face.

"Shut up!" Marian shouts.

The queen struggles wildly as Marian removes the offending hand from her face. The two ladies bear hug each other. The queen slams Marian into the wall. Marian collapses onto the floor.

Isabella attempts to kick Marian, but Marian rolls across the floor, out of the way. The queen kicks stone face instead of Marian's face. Isabella finds the reverberations of pain are intense. She curses unladylike. Marian stands up, she spins around to face the queen. The queen backhands Marian. Marian wipes the blood from her broken skin. Marian takes an Assassin's fighting stance.

"What makes you think you can beat me?" The queen shouts.

Marian stares at Isabella's chest. She throws a left hook at Marian's face. Marian deflects the blow, sailing her fist straight into the queen's once perfect nose. Isabella clutches her nose cursing up a storm. The queen swings wildly. Marian grabs her arm, rolling Isabella onto her back.

"Bigger tits." Marian snaps back.

"AAGH! Bitch!" The queen wails.

Marian kicks Isabella of Angouleme across the face knocking her out. The queen loses the cat fight.

Marian enters King John's royal quarters to put the king in check. Marian has her bow drawn with a black arrow pointed at the king sitting on his throne.

"Checkmate."

King John's eyes narrow beneath his fedora.

"You think you have beaten me?" King John asks.

"Sic Semper tyrannosaurus." Marian shouts.

King John's eyes go wild. He stands up, rushing Marian. Marian shoots King John in the heart. He steps back a few times, but John rushes her again tackling her before she can get a bead on him. Close quarter moving targets are much harder to shoot. Marian tried to kill King John, but worse she also shouted he is a tyrant lizard who is finally getting his. King John is furious, so he starts going True Romance on Marian's ass, beating the hell out of her.

"Did you think Robin Hood is the only one who wears gambeson?!" King John roars.

King John pulls out his flask. He grabs Marian's jaw forcing it open.

"Here Marian, have some medicine, it helped Matilda."

He raises the flask to her mouth to pour in the poison.

Priest arrives wounded in the doorway still dressed like Robin Hood in a mask. King John becomes terrified of the wounded Priest so much that he becomes distracted. This gives Marian the chance to knock the flask to the floor, as well as the opportunity to kick John in the gut. John smacks her enraging Priest. Priest dashes up and slams John into the stone wall.

"I've endured years of hell because of men like you!

I've endured years of hell because of men like you!"

He throws John onto the ground and starts stomping the crap out of him while the king is down. Priest's Commanding Officer taught him well. Marian has to shield John with her body.

"Stop! You're losing control again!"

Priest stops. Priest picks up King John, shoves him onto his throne pinning him there with a table. Marian immediately plops down the articles of the barons.

"What is this document?" King John asks.

"A list of rights for your subjects." Marian says.

King John reads over it.

"This represents a permanent Robin Hood." King John says.

"Exactly." Marian says wryly.

"What if I refuse?"

"We tell all of England you murdered Richard's heir." Marian says.

"Prove it." King John says.

"We can.

We can."

King John turns his head and looks up at Priest. "I'm sorry, who are you again? I'm pretty sure Robin Hood would have killed me by now."

"I am a Crusader who fought alongside Sir Robin.

I am a Crusader who fought alongside Sir Robin."

"Fine. Whatever. Even if you could prove it, nobody can do a damn thing about it."

Marian whispers in an ice-cold tone, "Either you sign it and continue to rule, or I have my friend here kill you now so I can take over by succession. I'll sign it myself."

King John signs what will become the Magna Carta.

He is prodded onto the balcony looking over the revolting Commoners standing side by side with the Nobility. Crusaders, Nobles, Peasants, the Ill-Desired, and all other of his subjects are gathered below. The Bear in the crowd sports a rainbow afro while he holds up a sign reading: JOHN 3:16

John begins announcing the existence of the Magna Carta, including all the rights afforded to all of his subjects. He continues for a while since there are 63 Clauses.

"...No freeman shall be taken, imprisoned, disseised, outlawed, banished, or in any way destroyed, nor will we proceed against or prosecute him, except by the lawful judgment of his peers or by the law of the land. There will be a Parliament made up of a House of Commons and House of Nobility. The purpose of which is to keep the Crown in check and give the people a voice. No one will be taxed who does not have representation in the Parliament, and a fedora for every..." John grows angry. "No."

Two arrowtips brush the back of his neck drawing blood.

"And a fedora for every man in England." John croaks out.

William Marshall speaks up from the gathered crowd. "Excuse me, King John. Would you say this is a permanent Robin Hood?"

King John becomes flush and furious, but two arrows digging into his neck back makes him regain composure. King John lowers his head in defeat.

"Yes. Yes, I would."

And the crowd goes wild! The Bear in the crowd sporting a rainbow afro holding a sign reading: JOHN 3:16 eats a random guy.

CHAPTER L

CHECKERS V CHESS

Marian and Priest are escaping from the castle grounds but Priest collapses. Marian shakes Priest, Priest is unresponsive.

Arch-Bishop Tuck arrives with Crusaders riding upon white horses. King John runs up to the unconscious Priest.

"Kill them! Kill them now!"

"These men answer to me, not you!" Tuck shouts.

Arch-Bishop Tuck smiles at the fact he finally has Priest at his mercy.

"Kill them, Tuck!" King John screams.

Marian tilts her head upwards to Tuck.

"Tuck... Don't do it."

"I have to, He is possessed." Tuck says.

"He is one of Robin Hood's men! He is the Cursed Crusader!" King John spouts.

Tuck snaps his fingers.

"Hospitallers! See to this man immediately."

The Hospitallers pick up Priest so they can transport him to the Hospital.

King John is in a panic, "What are you doing? He's possessed! He is not Robin Hood! He is only one of Robin Hood's men!"

Arch-Bishop Tuck loses his cool.

"I am one of Robin Hood's men! Priest is a Crusader who served his God! His place in Heaven is assured, You, however, are speeding towards a very warm place."

Rick and Wilbert arrive as the Hospitallers carry off Priest.

"Wowzers! Was that Robin Hood? I always wanted to meet him."

"I keep telling you, Wilbert. Robin Hood's a fairy tale, a cruel construction of random facts to discourage the children from trying to obtain further gains. It's a sick world that does it, but it's not my job to fix it." Rick explains.

"King John, We have arrived with all the tax money you squeezed out of England." Wilbert says.

"Show me the Money!"[28] King John shouts.

"Before we do, we want our 35% of the Gold Simoleons,we won it fair." Rick says.

"Those cards were marked!"

"Nobody accuses my lucky deck of being marked! Pay up, you skinflint!"

"You dare talk that way to me? I'll break you in the balls." King John says.

"I dare you to back that up! Go on Wilbert!"

"Rick, ol' buddy, ol' pal, couldn't you take my place?"

"If you don't go right now, I'll murderize ya!" Rick threatens.

Wilbert meanders sorrowfully to King John.

"Oh, my King, can you please grant me mer-"

King John sacks Wilbert.

"Huh. It didn't hurt that time!" Wilbert says.

"Sic Semper Tyrannis!" Wilbert shouts as he breaks John in the balls.

King John falls to his knees.

"We served Richard at Cyprus too." Wilbert quips.

Wilbert turns to Rick.

"What do we do now? I just kicked the king in the ghoulies." Wilbert asks.

"I suppose we take our money."Rick says.

The two start to take their money. Rick snaps his fingers,"Hey! I know... Why should we only take our 35% when we could take it all!?" Rick exclaims.

"What do we do with the extra money?"

"We give it back to the people!"

"Why not? It's what Robin Hood would do." Wilbert says.

"Fortuna Favet Fortibus." Rick says.

"Say, Rick, you keep spoutin' 'Fortuna Favet Fortibus,' what does that mean?" Wilbert asks.

"Fortune favors the brave, my friend, Fortune favors the brave," Rick answers.

The two buddies saunter off to do good.

Rick spins around. "Waitaminute. That was Arch-Bishop Tuck! That cheapskate owes me two sovereigns. I've killed men for less."

"You've killed men for one sovereign?" Wilbert asks.

"Yes, in the Crusades. Same as you. Now lets after him, follow the money Wilbert, always follow the money." Rick says.

The two buddies haul off. Marian stands there, still observing.

"Wow, those two characters somehow managed to beat King John at checkers while we were all too busy playing chess." Marian states.

ROBIN IS ON PRIEST'S patio in Acre taking no joy in the sunrise.

Priest walks out and joins Robin. Robin is rather morose.

"Out with it." Priest says.

"I should be married right now." Robin says.

"What do you mean?" Priest asks.

"I shouldn't be here, I should be married. My Father wouldn't allow it. I'm twenty-two. I have been denied love seven years now." Robin spews.

"So that's why you're here, you ran away.

So that's why you're here, you ran away."

"We're all running from something Priest. We all pray it never catches us."

PRIEST BECOMES CONSCIOUS. In The Chapel Hospital, a Knight Hospitaller is tending to Priest. He looks upon his wife Isabella, she is so lovely, Her eyes are like starlight, her eerily pale skin, her black as night...hair. It isn't Isabella.

"Marian? where is my wife?

Marian, where is my wife?

Marian breaks down and hugs Priest.

"I'm so sorry, Priest, I am so, so sorry. Isabella caught a fever and passed." Marian cries. "My Sarah shared that fate..."

Marian is there to witness Priest becoming one of the order.

Priest is known for the rest of his years as the Father battling a demon within him. After a few months of bad faith negotiations, open warfare breaks out between the rebel barons and the king and his supporters in summer of 1215.

On the 18th of October 1216, John dies of dysentery at Newark Castle, The war began over Magna Carta but quickly turns into a dynastic war for the throne of England. Louis VIII has to give up his claim to be the King of England by signing the Treaty of Lambeth on the 11th of September 1217. Marian vanishes into history.

THE END

EPILOGUE

1220 A.D. Marian stands on the shores of England watching the sunset. A man she has never seen before creeps up behind her. They both watch as the sun sets together. The sun disappears beyond the horizon.

"I've been expecting you for years." Marian says.

"You know why I'm here?" He asks.

"Sibylla."

"I'll Make it quick." He says.

"Thank you."

Marian is stabbed through the heart. She stands there and watches as the Assassin leaves cake and departs. She feels a sense of euphoria. She smiles then laughs. She feels like she's nineteen again, in fact, she is nineteen again. Then she recognizes that boyish tone.

"Marian?"

Marian slowly turns around.

Robin Hood is standing before her holding out his hand. She takes it. The Boatman Charon takes them.

Where are we going, Robin? Heaven?

"No. We have been selected for something special, we are to dwell in the realm of ideas."

Robin and Marian are bathed in light as they are taken to the collective unconscious by the Boatman Charon.

Robin Hood and Maid Marian now live in Sherwood Forest together in happiness for all time.

ROBIN HOOD ENDURES

AFTERWORD

I bet you didn't see that ending coming when you started this book. I never intended to write this story. Originally, I had an idea to write a Legend of Zelda movie trilogy. When I ran the concept by Elliott, one of my best friends at a game show themed party he was holding, he said it sounded like a great idea, but it would be difficult to get the rights from Nintendo, "Why don't you do your own thing?" I took the advice then filed the story for the Zelda trilogy in the back of my mind (where it still resides to this day.) I won the game show that night. Cut to a couple of years later, I discovered The Adventures of Robin Hood starring Errol Flynn, co-starring the lovely Olivia De Havilland. I was also watching season seven of Smallville, I saw that Green Arrow had returned, I felt the universe was trying to tell me something. I remembered my Zelda story, I began to think how Link was wearing green, wielding bow with sword. Robin Hood wielded a bow with sword, the wheels in my head began to turn, what if Link was Robin Hood? It could work, best of all I did not need to obtain the rights to Robin Hood.

I started researching Robin of Locksley, writing down notes over the course of the year. I remember in December of 2008, I was saying goodbye to my Grandfather Jay Evard Welch, as I sat by him on his deathbed, I pulled out my laptop and started to write "The Legend of Robin Hood" Over the course of 1 and ¼ of a year. I completed a 200 plus page story in three acts. I went to film school, graduating with high marks and honors. I started to pitch the idea to Hollywood, but no one took me seriously except for Silver Pictures owned by Joel Silver.

They read the script, when they finished, they said it was not something that they normally do, but they also gave me some advice, "Put it away for a couple of years and then come back to it." So I gave up on trying to get it made, abandoning the project for a few years. I focused more on my other creative endeavors before I came back to the project. Unfortunately, my computer crashed but my files were saved. During my six months unplugged from the Net I had almost no distractions, my creativity skyrocketed. I went back to my Robin Hood project with a vengeance and heavily rewrote it for the better. I also decided I would do something nobody else did with Robin Hood, I would focus on his time in the Third Crusade.

Initially, I had no idea what happened during the Third Crusade. I decided to research it, it probably wasn't that exciting, maybe there was a battle or two that I could expand into an interesting story. I began researching the beginnings of the Third Crusade, Richard's conquest of Cyprus, the siege of Acre, Arsuf, Richard's negotiations, the march towards Jerusalem, when I got to the Battle of Jaffa, I realized something, this was the best action movie that has never been made. I learned Europeans had a complete, balanced, healthy diet unlike everyone else, so the Crusaders were bigger and stronger than anyone else at the time. Imagine an army of Captain Americas. I also realized my understanding of the Crusades were just a series of misconceptions. I wrote a complete story in six months and spent another year obsessing over all the details trying to make it as historically accurate as possible. I personally know what parts happened and which parts did not. As I wrote this story, I eventually became an expert on the first four Crusades and an expert on Robin Hood himself. I hope that when you read this you will go out to learn about the Crusades yourself.

I realized that the story I have written is so important and personal to me that I would refuse to compromise on the story during the filming process. The script was nearly 300 pages long at this point and it would take multiple movies to tell in its entirety, but the script was very much in the style of classic literature, so I decided to transform it into the book you hold into your hands. I realize the length of time the story took since I began it is twelve years and I learned many things I never intended to learn. I think the quality shows in the work.

I always say that if you compete with Howard Pyle, Michael Curtiz, William Keighley, Kevin Reynolds, Mel Brooks, Foz Allan, Dominic Minghella, and Ridley Scott, you better have made something damn good. Hopefully, I did.

During the summer of 2018, as I was writing this book I began to dream that I was fighting in the Crusades myself. One Crusade dream is fine, but three months of fighting is far too much. Over those few months of dreams, I became increasingly miserable; dreading the time I had to get some sleep. Finally, after finishing this story I began having my old dreams of being chased by dinosaurs again. Never have I been so happy to be chased by a pack of Velociraptors into the path of an oncoming T-Rex than after those few months of battles.

I spent years getting all the details on the Crusades correct. July 1st to August 11th of 2021 I wrote the last twelve chapters of this book and rushed it off to publication. I want to give my readers a complete story.

The name of this book has changed over the years. It started as The Legend of Robin Hood, it became Tales of the Adventurous Robin Hood, then it became Assassin of the Cross. Each act has a title in my journals. Act 1 is Assassin of the Cross, Act 2 is The Legend of Robin Hood, Act 3 is Robin Hood vs. The Lord of the Darkness, Act 4 is Knights of Avalon, Act 5 is The Assassin's Dagger.

Assassin of the Cross is a fairytale/parable about America. I used European History/legends then began mixing them with Japanese Anime. If you boil it down to its core elements. I see the book as a loose adaptation blending Zelda/Rurouni Kenshin/Robin Hood/Beowulf. The third act I imagined when my friend Tyler described *Eaters of the Dead* to me.

I have made friends along the way as well, including reconnecting with my Aunt Cathy, befriending Don Rosa, and beginning an association with Jennifer Roberson. If you are interested in books like this one, I would suggest *The Archer's Tale*, *Vagabond*, and *Heretic* by Bernard Cornwall, as well as *Lady of the Forest* and *Lady of Sherwood* by Jennifer Roberson. I included a lot of my research into the story you have read. According to a dozen years of research, I do believe there was an original Robin Hood, after researching this subject from 2008-2020 I may have found the original Robin Hood.

Henry the 2nd, King Richard's father who was alive in England on March 5th, 1133 A.D.-July 6th, 1189A.D. Yeoman had many roles in medieval society, but during King Henry's reign Yeoman were the archer bodyguards for the king. There are stories they wore green tunics. According to Robin Hood Legend, Robin or Robert Hode was a Yeoman. Henry the 2nd died naming Richard his warrior son king. In 1190 Richard led the Third Crusade to reclaim Jerusalem and ended up reconstructing the ruins of the Holy Land. There is the possibility Robert Hode was Richard's Bodyguard, they could have had a close relationship. J.R. Planche published his paper, *A Ramble with Robin Hood*, in 1864. Planche believed Stukeley had confused the name Fitzooth in place of Fitzodo, a family whose name appears in Dugdale's *Baronage*. This family apparently became lords of Loxley, a village in Warwickshire. Planche believed Robert Fitz Odo, lord of Loxley Manor from the reign of Henry II until 1196, was the original Robin Hood. Planche discovered evidence that Robert Fitz Odo was still alive in 1203,

As for Marian, this is Matilda Fitzwalter's story, as told by Edward Brayley in "The Graphic and Historical Illustrator" (1834): Matilda was the daughter of one Robert, Baron Fitzwalter, castellan of Castle Baynard, and one of those who opposed King John and forced him to sign the Magna Carta. Aged 18yo, she was among many neighbouring nobles who were invited to a banquet hosted by Prince John. There were three days of jousts and tournaments which entertained those assembled. The young Matilda was the "queen" of the event. On the fourth day, a mailed knight entered the field, vanquishing all those who came before him and enamouring the fair Matilda, who duly awarded him a fine collar of gold. He left as he had arrived.

During the events, Prince John found himself also smitten by Matilda's charm, and "basely endeavoured to take her for a mistress. Her father's indignation so enraged the Prince, that he attacked Baynard Castle, taking advantage of the king's absence in the Holy Land. Her father slain, Matilda escaped into the nearby forest, coming upon none other than the knight. No longer clad in his mail, but dressed in "Lincoln Green", he revealed himself to be one Robin Hood, outlawed Earl of Huntington, and insisted on keeping both her and her honor safe from the Prince.

However, Prince John discovered her escape and attacked the foresters – in the the battle, the Prince met the fair Matilda (now in male attire) and engaged in battle. She put up a "stout defense" and as such, the Prince was obliged to withdraw.

Matilda married Robin, who upon Richard's return, was restored to his lost earldom, and she became Countess of Huntington. When Robin was outlawed by King John, she joined him. Following his death, Matilda took refuge at Dunmow Priory – which had been patronized by her family.

King John, learning of her refuge, sent the knight Robert de Medewe to the priory with a small token – a poisoned bracelet. Robert was received by Matilda, who though no longer in the fresh bloom of youth, still could flutter the heart of a hardened warrior. Robert hastily left – not as a result of his mission but due to his growing passion for Matilda. Absence did not curb his desire, and he returned to the priory. He was greeted by the sounds of a funeral dirge echoing through the church. There in the chancel, on a bier of flowers, was the lifeless body of Matilda.

The poisoned gift had "eaten its way to her bone, and the fiery poison had dried her lifeblood". Robert flung himself upon her corpse and could not be persuaded to return to court. He instead gave up his knightly ways for the cowl and became an Augustine monk. This would cause His wife's father Robert Fitzwalter to go to war with King John. In the following years, the stories of giving the middle finger to the man may have continued to occur. In 1225 A.D. a Robin Hood is caught by the Sheriff of Nottingham Eustace of Lowdham, the outlaw's name was put down in records as the first known instance of the name Robin Hood. This would be among the first of many. I subscribe to The Multiple Robin Hood theory. I have spent time looking for the originator. I have assembled the evidence, I submit that the pieces are there, they fit together to form the basis of the Robin Hood legend.

I realize the records may not match; however, I think someone like King John the first would be someone to attempt to erase him from history. King John may have the power to change history much like Augustus Caesar had the power to manipulate time. That, or the pieces are random information gathered and coalesced through history and oral tradition. In either case, the troubadour's felt this hapless lord and his poor Matilda would make a good story.

I wrote this book for that twelve-year-old boy who spends countless days looking for this book. I can't be the only one looking for this story as a kid. Robin Hood is awesome!

Robin Hood now has lived in story for hundreds of years and is everyone's favourite outlaw, because he robs from the rich and gives to the poor. He robs the tax collector and gives to the Tax Payer, He also pays his merry men. I do not know how they actually feel about that name.

Signed,

Holland Timmiins

P.S.

One of my beta readers has this theory that the rest of the book is a hallucination Sir Robin is having as he lays dying in a ditch, still in the Holy Land. I totally subscribe to this theory as a strong possibility.

P.S.S.

Fuck Monotremes! Their entire existence is an abomination in the eyes of the natural order!

Glossary

A*bdallah al-Aladil* Brother to Salah Ad-din. He had designs upon and succeeded Saladin's rule.

Abubu Ali al Ad-din's long-suffering second in command.

Acre Port city in the Holy Land. South of Tyre. North of Arsuf.

Agony The assassin who trained Robin. Also called Sir Guy of Gisbourne. A knight who survived Saladin's Massacre at Hattin near the end of the Second Crusade. Trained at Alamut after the fall of Jerusalem.

Alamut It means the eagle's teaching. It's the fortress of the assassins at the top of a mountain in Iran.

Alan A. Dale Minstrel who served in the Crusade, later becoming one of the Merry Men.

Ali al Ad-din Cousin to Salah Ad-din. Ali al Ad-din is a Sultan of a country across the vast ocean of desert. Some say he rose to power by dealing with the Djinn. Nearly everyone agrees Sultan Ali al Ad-din is a hero.

Al-Janah Brother of Al-Mastoob. Stood up to Saladin at the battle of Jaffa.

Alucard Dracula's first-born son. Desperately wants his daddy's approval which he will never get. Despite this, there is still a princess out there that needs to be rescued.

Anthony of Mastrantonio A soldier that gets a little too frisky. His descendant plays the woman who hospitalised him.

Archer Captain of the Archers in Richard's army before being replaced by Robin.

Arsuf A forest in the Holy Land in between Acre and Jaffa.

Artorius Pendragon Proper name for King Arthur.

Ashkelon Another city in the Holy Land south of Jaffa north of Egypt.

Assassins Named after the Hashish they smoke. They follow the old man of the mountain.

Avalon Resting place for King Arthur.

Balian of Ibelin Valiant Hero Crusader during the fall of Jerusalem at the end of the second Crusade.

Berengaria of Navarre Wife of King Richard, Queen of England.

Bishop An archer that was part of Robin's team in the Holy Land. Brother to Priest and Pope. Friend/ brother in arms to Robin Hood. Hothead.

Blacula A blaxploitation movie character. Slave to Dracula.

Blondel King Richard's favourite lute player. The story is told that Blondel went from castle to castle across Europe singing a particular song that only Blondel sang to Richard in private. Blondel sang underneath the Kuenringer Castle, the imprisoned Richard replied with the second verse. Richard knew He had been found.

Bouvines A village community in the Nord department of northern France located on the French-Belgian border located between Lille and Tornai. It has been host to the Battle of Bouvines. A coalition of forces went to war with Philip Augustus II of France. On July 2nd, 1214 John was defeated at La Roche-aux-Moines, near Angers. A second decisive battle was fought at Bouvines where France was Victorious and won back English lands. King John's Authority weakened allowing the First baron's war.

Byzant A coin made of gold or silver. Minted in Byzantium.

Captain of the Archers Leader of Sarah Cutter's Private squad of archers.

Carmilla Camille An associate of Richard's French liaison Jacques. Master tradesman of Caramel plus Ice cream. Possibly a vampire who sold out Dracula to Jacques who informed Richard. Based on Carmilla the vampire.

Castle Dracula The only castle taller than six stories which would have been structurally improbable in the medieval period.

Castle Moonfang The castle home of Prince Lupin Wolfstonecraft of South Germany.

Charon The boatman who ferries the dead to the afterlife.

Christine Former captive. Daughter of Isabella, foster daughter of Priest.

Conrad of Montferrat Crusader King who is the most qualified to sit on the throne of Jerusalem. Eliminated by the Assassins. King Richard is rumored to have ordered the assassination.

Count of Mortain Royal title of Prince John.

Cutter's Cove A secluded Cove that Sarah Cutter anchors her ship in once a year.

Cyprus Island nation located in the Mediterranean. Important strategic location for launching Crusades.

Damascus North of Tyre in the Holy Land.

Damsel of Cyprus Daughter to Isaac Komnenos, emperor of Cyprus. Returned to England with Berengaria and Joan. Name unknown.

Dark Knights An elite force of knights that are the personal guard for Alucard. The knights are named after Batman who ripped off the Knight of Darkness himself, *The Shadow*.

Death An assassin who serves Dracula. One of Dracula's four Horsemen.

Dieu et mon Droit French, Translated it means: God and my right.

Deus Vult Latin for "God wills it." A Crusader's motto.

Dracula Crusader, brilliant tactician, psychopath. Also called the Lord of the Darkness or Murcielago. Belonged to the Order of the Dragon created by the Church. The remains are currently missing.

Duke Leopold of Austria A leader in the Crusades. Hated Richard so much he held Richard captive, ransoming him back to England.

Eleanor of Aquitaine The former Queen of England, mother to Richard, Joan, John, along with seven others.

E.L.V.E.S. Elves are extremely brief disks of dim light that appear at around 100 km. Sometimes they appear with sprites, but usually not. Elves are also low-frequency radio emissions. The name stands for "Emissions of Light and VLF from EMP Sources." They were first observed in 1994. They can be red or green.

Eustace De Vesci Eustace was important in the Magna Carta's creation, and was one of the 25 barons appointed to see it carried out. he was excommunicated with the other Barons in 1216. On the way to do homage to King Louis of France he laid siege to Barnard castle. An arrow pierced his head during the siege.

Eustace of Lowdham Also called the Sheriff of Nottingham. Robin Hood's traditional nemesis.

Famine A general in Dracula's Army. One of Dracula's Four Horseman.

Fara Vampire bride of Dracula.

Fitzwater Crusader, Father of Maid Marian.

Friar Tuck A friar who is an advisor to Robin Hood. Tuck helps distribute Robin's stolen money.

Gambeson Padded armour made with several layers of linen. Gambeson can stop an arrow depending on how sharp it is, even a sword cannot pierce it.

Garden of Delights A secret room rumored to be located somewhere in Alamut. Used by the old man of the mountain to fool assassins to think that they enter paradise if they killed for him.

Geoffery of Lusignan Brother of Guy of Lusignan. When Acre was reclaimed on July 28th, 1191 Geoffrey was awarded the title of Count of Ashkelon, despite Ashkelon still being in Saladin's hands at that time.

Gold Dinars Currency used by the Turks in the Holy Land.

Gorgolac Greek name given to Lilith.

Grail The Chalice Jesus Christ used during the last supper. Heavily featured in Arthurian lore.

Guy of Lusignan Husband to Queen Sibylla. Guy has a loose claim to the throne of Jerusalem.

Helena Unfaithful wife of Preston, she's been sleeping with Blondel since Robin Hood's wedding day. Preston is beginning to suspect, but she thinks he's oblivious to the fact the kid isn't his. Helena has mysteriously vanished after Preston caught her in mid-coitus with someone that's not him.

Henry of Champagne Henry the 2nd Count of Champagne, nephew of King Richard arrived in the Holy land in 1190 to join the siege of Acre. While he supported Conrad's ascension to the throne over Guy, after the assassination of Conrad of Montferrat the High Court, composed of the most important barons and bishops of the realm, named Henry, King of Jerusalem

Holland Timmins The hack who wrote this book.

Holy Sepulchre Burial tomb of Jesus Christ located in Jerusalem.

Hospitallers Knights who cared for the sick as well as fought in the Crusades.

Huntington Castle The three-story castle home of Robin Hood. Sits on a hill overlooking Locksley village.

Imshi Arabic for, go away! be off!

Inshallah Arabic for: If Allah wills. In other terms, it means: God willing.

Ironsword the Conqueror A female wandering warrior. Part of the inner circle of legends. She has had many adventures, often coming into conflict with her arch-nemesis, an evil VCR played by Tom Cruise.

Isaac Komnenos False emperor of Cyprus. Rose to power by making a deal with Saladin.

Isabella Former captive at Acre, mother of Christine, wife of Priest.

Isabella of Angouleme Isabella was renowned for her beauty, and is called the "Helen" of the middle ages. She was betrothed to Hugh IX de Lusignan when John chose her to be his second wife. They were married at Bordeaux on August 24, 1200, when she was only about 12. It was a different time.

Jacques Richard's French liaison.

Jaffa Port city in the Holy Land west of Jerusalem.

Jerry Host of the trashiest program ever, it was maddeningly difficult to book him for a show, much less in Nottingham England circa the 13th century. Former Mayor of Chicago, he resigned after a scandal involving a prostitute and a personal check. He went on to host his own show dealing with the problems of America's White Trash for years. Jerry lives the American dream.

Jerusalem The prize city of The Third Crusade. Site of the Holy Sepulchre.

Joan Sister to Richard, John, and seven others.

Katherine Haru Also known as the crimson beauty for her blood red hair. Princess, Hunter, true love to Moonfang.

Klaus, Sanders Associate of Richard's french liaison Jacques. From up north of Scandinavia. Based on the Greek Bishop of Myra, Nicholas, Patron Saint of Children.

Lady in Green Marian's name when she is active in the field alongside Robin Hood.

Lara Vampire bride of Dracula.

Lilith Biblical figure that gives birth to monsters. Mother of Dracula. Also called the Gorgolac.

Little John One of the Merry Men. Robin Hood's right-hand man.

Lord Dominos A little punk brat based on Lord Courtley in Taste the Blood of Dracula (1970)

Lord of the Darkness Another name for Dracula AKA Murcielago. Cleaned up the bodies from the Crusade and added them to his army. The vampiric demigod attempted to kick start the Day of Reckoning ahead of schedule.

Lupin Wolfstonecraft Prince, leader of the inner circle of Legends. Also called Moonfang. Body washed ashore in Japan under a full moon. Lupin's head was severed by Yoshi Gyaku and fashioned into a werewolf mask by a clan of demon samurai that worship evil.

Mamelukes African slave soldiers that serve Saladin.

Marian Fitzwater Robin Hood's true love. Also known as the Lady in Green. Best archer alive.

Masked Ninja Mouse A character based on an urban legend of a mouse that wore a mask and practices Ninjitsu! This Mouse appeared around the time of Teenage Mutant Ninja Turtles craze. While the Cheese Muncher's existence is debatable; that masked rodent hero may or may not have protected an entire airport. Respect!

Mategriffon Richard's wooden fortress in Sicily during the occupation. It was constructed on a hill with a view of all of Messina. The name loosely translated means "Curb on the Greeks." Possibly constructed with sticks and blankets.

Matilda Fitzwalter The historical daughter of Baron Robert Fitzwalter. Wife and Mother to Sir Robert Fitz Odo. There are conflicting stories about both of them, but their stories surround the Magna Carta.

May Games Games people played during the May Day festival. People often dressed as figures like Lancelot along with many others. The festival was looked down upon by the royalty in charge.

Melpomene One of the nine Mousai (Muses). In theatrical circles, Melpomene is attributed the tragic mask alongside her sister Thaelia. According to some of the stories, the half-bird, half-woman Sirens were born from the union of Melpomene and Achelous, the river god.

Mercardier French mercenary, leader of Richard's mercenary forces. Fiercely loyal to Richard.

Merry Men Name was given to a group of bandits that follow Robin Hood.

Moonfang Prince/Werewolf. Also known as Lupin Wolfstonecraft.

Morgan le Fay Powerful Sorceress. Half-sister to King Arthur, mother to his child, one of the four Witch Queens.

Murcielago Spanish for bat. Also, another name for Dracula AKA The Lord of the Darkness.

Necromancer A sorcerer that deals with the dead.

Nottingham Castle Located on the hill near Nottingham. Serves as a residence to the Sheriff of Nottingham, Sir Guy of Gisbourne, Marian Fitzwater, sometimes Prince John. The castle is heavily patrolled by a guard that hates his job.

Old man of the mountain Leader of the Assassins, sometimes ally of the Crusaders, an enemy of Saladin.

Order of the Dragon A military organisation modeled after those of the Crusades. It was to fight "the Enemy" essentially any force of anti-Christendom. It's a society whose members carry the *signum draconis*, but assign no name to it.

Pendragon Shield The shield Arthur carried at the end of the Grail Quest.

Philip Faulconbridge AKA Sir Richard Planteganet AKA Philip the Bastard. the son of Richard The Lion Heart, appears in a William Shakespeare play The life and death of King John.

Philip the second of France Crusader King who led his forces on the Third Crusade. Left the Third Crusade for Richard to handle after the fall of Acre in 1191.

Plague A general in Dracula's army. One of Dracula's Four Horseman.

Pope Archer in Robin's team in the Holy Land. Brother to Bishop and Priest. Friend/brother in arms to Robin Hood.

Preston A merry man named after my cousin Preston, who I often refer to as the Queen of the Harpies, why? No particular reason. I once left a message calling him that repeatedly. He loves it.

Priest Second best archer in Richard's army. Part of Robin's team in the Holy Land. Brother to Bishop and Pope. Husband to Isabella, stepfather to Isabella's daughter Christine. Friend/ brother in arms to Robin Hood. Third-best archer alive. Has Tourette's syndrome.

Prince John Brother to King Richard the Lion Heart. Also known as the Count of Mortain and eventually King John. Enemy to Robin Hood, therefore, the oppressed. Prince John offered to lead the Third Crusade. King Richard led the pilgrimage to Jerusalem instead. John kicked Longchamps out so he could usurp the crown. When John was banished by Richard, their mother forced them to reconcile.

Purple A rare red purple colour in medieval times therefore it was valued more than gold. Primarily located in Sicily. The rare colour is created by rock snails known by the name *Murex*.

Richard the Lion Heart Warrior, king, The leader in the Third Crusade, Robin Hood's friend/mentor. A Crusader King, Richard was one of the most brilliant tacticians of the medieval era. He employed military tactics that wouldn't be seen again for centuries. He lived by the sword and died by it. A true warrior.

Rick Bill Collector, the only man in the entire story wearing a fedora. Ancestor of Bud Abbott.

Robert Fitzwalter the Father of Matilda Fitzwalter, Robert was the driving force of the first Baron's War.

Robert Hode Robin's overbearing father. Former archer, protector for King Henry the second, King Richard's father.

Robin Hood Robin, Sir Robin, Robin Hood, Trickster, Crusader, Assassin, Hero, Outlaw, Lover, Legend, the second-best archer alive. Just as good a shot but is .25 seconds slower than the best.

Saif adDin Brother to Saladin. Saif helped negotiate the peace treaty at the end of the Third Crusade.

Saladin The leader of the Muslim forces in the Holy Land. Also called Salah Ad-din. Career military commander. While interested in conquering Crusader territory it is known The Crusades were a sideshow next to the three-ring circus of the Islamic world during that time period. Saladin was far more interested in these times conquering his fellow Muslims. He was good at it. This is due to the long lasting strife between the Sunni and The Shia. Saladin's death has long been a mystery. Initially it was thought to be a stress induced heart attack. Stephen J. Gluckman, MD, professor of medicine at the University of Pennsylvania School of Medicine theorizes Saladin most likely died of Typhoid. If that's true, when Saladin destroyed the cisterns, he sealed his own fate.

Salah Ad-din Proper name of Saladin.

Sarah Marian's servant. Secretly in love with Marian. Sarah's a huge Punch and Judy Fanatic.

Sarah Cutter Princess of the pirates. An acquaintance of Moonfang.

Sherriff of Nottingham Robin Hood's calculating nemesis. Sir Guy of Gisbourne's superior. Also called Eustace of Lowdham. Is part of a group of dark followers of Dracula.

Sherwood Forest Robin Hood's base of operations in England.

Shish Kebab A delicious Middle-Eastern dish comprised of various meats, marinated and cooked on a skewer, often alongside vegetables. In 1980's American Youth vernacular it also means Bullshit.

Sinbad A later addition to *1001 Arabian Nights,* Sinbad is a legendary Arabic captain who encounters the supernatural. He went on seven voyages. He would have gone on a voyage to Mars but the uncreative cheapskates in Hollywood refused to fund Ray Harryhausen's final Sinbad Projects.

Sibylla Queen of Jerusalem, wife of Guy of Lusignan. She usurped the crown after Baldwin the 4th the Leper King died. After she usurped the crown and went against the baron's wishes, she married Guy of Lusignan crowning him King of Jerusalem. She doomed Her Kingdom. After Saladin took Jerusalem, Sibylla, Guy of Lusignan, Balian of Ibelin, regrouped at Tyre. The Archbishop of Tyre departed for Europe. Sibylla was instrumental in launching the Third Crusade. Robin knew this. Everybody knew. Sibylla died in real life possibly July 25, 1190 A.D. during the Siege of Acre.

Sic semper tyrannis Latin for: thus always to tyrants. The meaning: tyrants get what's coming to them.

Sic semper tyrannosaurus: Latin for, Thus always to Tyrant Lizards. The Meaning: Priest screwed up the phrase.

Sigerson A high ranking Crusader, who believes he has an authority that in fact, he does not wield.

Sir Guy of Gisbourne Robin's nemesis since the incident at Damascus. Also called Agony.

Sir James of Abbott The only Christian soldier to die at the battle of Arsuf. Was referred to as a pillar of the army by King Richard.

Sir Mordred Son of King Arthur and Morgan le Fay.

Sir Orlock A knight Robin Hood saved at Jaffa. Sir Orlock is friends with an executioner.

Sit tibi, Christe, datus, quem tu regis iste ducatus Latin phrase that translates to "O Christ, let this duchy, which you rule, be dedicated to you."

Si Vis Pacem, Para Bellum Latin phrase that translates to, "If you want peace, prepare for war."

S.P.R.I.T.E. Transient luminous events or TLEs are similar to lightning. The most common TLE is the sprite. Sprite is an acronym for **S**tratospheric/mesospheric **P**erturbations **R**esulting from **I**ntense **T**hunderstorm **E**lectrification. They normally are coloured reddish-orange or greenish-blue. Sprites occur a fraction of a second after strong lightning strikes. This happens at a soaring altitude of nearly 100 kilometers in the ionosphere. This appears as a flash of red light directly above large storms. The lightning is theoretically purple too.

Stormblade A blue sword that is the equivalent of Excalibur. Made of star metal.

Tancred of Lecce Illegitimate cousin to King William the second of Sicily. Imprisoned Richard's sister Joan.

Tara Vampire bride of Dracula

Templars Order of Knights in the Crusades. Bankers, Badasses all around. Order destroyed during the inquisition on Friday the 13th, 1307.

Thaelia Eighth-born of the nine Mousai (Muses), the goddesses of music, song, and dance. Thaelia means to flourish. She presided over comedy and idyllic poetry. In theatrical circles, she is symbolized by a smiling mask alongside her sister Melpomene.

The Finger Essentially it means, I can still shoot you. Archers would show their middle finger to the enemy to show that the archer can still shoot, hence the gesture became offensive.

The Phantom A character appearing in an unrealistic story, while also appearing in a slightly more realistic version of the story. The

Phantom is based on a lower monster class, do not underestimate him.

Timeless Clock The Grandfather Clock that contains Time, Space, and the multiverse.

Trigger Name of Marian's Horse. Also, the name of the Horse carrying Maid Marian in *The Adventures of Robin Hood (1938)*, Trigger went on to be Roy Rodgers' horse.

Tyrannis Rex Latin for Tyrant King

Veni, Vidi, Vici A famous quote by Julius Caesar. It translates to, "I came, I saw, I conquered."

Veritas Latin translation, "Truth."

War A general for Dracula's forces. Also, one of the Four Horseman for Dracula.

Wilbert Bill Collector, a friend of Rick. Ancestor of Lou Costello.

Will Scarlett Brother to Robin Hood and one of his most trusted Merry Men.

Zara A major snafu of the Fourth Crusade; When the Crusader army arrived, Sicily built them boats. As payment for the boats, The Doge of Sicily, Enrico Dandolo suggested the Crusaders turn Mercenary, and siege the nearby port city of Zara. Zara was a catholic city in the Dalmation Coast. The Crusader army split at Zara, some walked away while others attacked. Zara foreshadowed the same army's assault on Constantinople around 1203–04. The Crusader turned Mercenary turned Marauding army sacked Constantinople in the first successful siege of the city in over a century.

DELETED SCENES
Deleted Scene 1

2002 A.D.

ELISHA GREY is a seventeen-year-old girl. She has black hair and wears a black sports bra, black sports pants, and a red trench coat. She walks into a castle library in the North Cascades. It is called Castle Bloodcraft.

"Hello?"

"Hello. Vampiressa responds."

"I am looking for a book."

"Everybody has a book here."

Elisha Grey notices the librarian's fangs. This librarian has pale skin, long black hair with a white streak of hair, she has a slender feminine body covered by a black silk dress adorned with protruding red spikes. Elisha tries not to choke on her next words.

"I need a book on the Third Crusade for my high school research paper."

Vampiressa motions with her hand. "Follow me." Elisha and Vampiressa walk up a long staircase. They come to a shelf on an upper floor. Vampiressa pulls out a book. Vampiressa hands it over to Elisha. "This is your book."

Vampiressa gives the book to Elisha. The book is bound by black covers but there is a green cross on the front cover. In the corner there is a drawing of a tribal fox.

"Assassin of the Cross. Cool."

Author's Note:

This is a wrap-around section I decided to remove even though it introduces Elisha Grey to the reader, as well as establishing her relationship to Vampiressa.

Deleted Scene 2

Robin: I intend to join the Crusade to reclaim the grail in Jerusalem. I head out tomorrow. Marian: You scorn me Robin. I am so sorry.

Robin: For what?

Marian: I am going to have to kill you now.

Robin grabs his things as Marian grabs her bow. Robin runs down the road in his underwear as his woman fires arrows at him.

Marian: Quit making it hard to hit you Robin. I am a scorned woman so I must destroy you!

Robin grabs the bow and quiver off of Marian, kisses her, and runs off.

Author's Note:

I removed this scene because this made Marian unsympathetic from the start. Big thank you to Jenna Moreci and Galatea Tao for helping me make her a lot more likable.

Deleted Scene 3

Richard comes across a group of peasants practicing falconry. The Raptor lands on the arm of the Peasant.

"Magnificent bird," Richard says.

"Thank you sir," the peasant says.

"Give me the Raptor," Richard says.

"Why?"

"Because I want the bird," Richard says.

"Well, I want a dirty limerick about my life," The Peasant says.

"Give me the Bird!" Richard shouts.

The peasant flips the bird at Richard. Richard takes his sword and lops off the offending hand. The peasant screams as he drops to his knees. He clasps his stump. Richard takes the falcon. The other peasants begin to grow angry. They extend their middle fingers towards Richard. Richard hands the falcon to Mercardier before he rides off annoyed. There is clanking metal striking wet, Robin walks by a patchwork of bloody pieces of meat on the side of the road.

Richard is on horseback leading his army towards Messina when he draws his sword. King Richard raises his sword in the air. "We go to war with the usurper King Tancred of Lecce! By God's calves I shall reclaim my sister!"

Author's Note:

I went a little too far with the massacre of civilians, I decided to alter it.

Deleted Scene 4

King Richard stands before Isaac.

"Come with me to the Holy Land with your army. Together we can fight Saladin."

Richard holds out his hand in friendship. Isaac holds up his index finger. "Hold that thought." Isaac runs off and goes to a mountain fortress in the distance. King Richard strokes his red beard.

"I think I have been tricked."

Robin chimes in, "You were tricked my king. You were."

"Tricks are for kids! Ah! Ha! Ha! Ha!" Isaac laughs in the distance.

Richard is wroth with anger. "I am going to burn this shit hole to the ground!"

Author's note:

Tricks are for kids went a little too far. I altered the scene.

Deleted Scene 5

The former captives take off their burkas and throw them to the ground.

. King Richard: Archer, tell your men to pick up the burkas and put them on.

Archer: It will be done. Archers! Put the burkas back on!

The archers pick up the burkas and put them on the enemy. The enemy is paraded down the street to their cells. The Crusaders and former slaves watch in silent contempt. The last prisoner enters the dungeon then the Crusaders and former captors celebrate.

Author's note:

Biased history from the Victorian era suggested Richard massacred women and children at Acre. There is zero evidence that ever happened. I decided to try to explain a historical question of how people came to believe Richard killed women there. I turned this solution into a Guantanamo Bay type scenario, I ultimately removed the concept for the reason listed in Deleted Scene 7

Deleted Scene 6

Robin feels something dark rise up inside of him. Robin spins Sibylla around, bending her over. "No. Tonight you will find his name is Mister Robin, and He coMes frOm beHInd..."

"You like talking in the third person during sex? I would think that was rather strange, but Guy has called me mommy more than once during sex."

Author's Note:

This scene was supposed to set up Robin's penchant for drunkenly talking in the third Person. I used a phrase my African college buddy Behailu used to say to me because I move like a ninja. Ultimately, I decided to change it back because I felt it was making light of Robin's greatest sin. Don't feel too bad for Sibylla's treatment, she had already been dead for a year before Richard arrived in our reality. I altered it.

Deleted scene 7

"I collected the ransom for the Princess. Everybody gets 50,000 gold coins."

Robin distributes the money. In the morning the prisoners are gathered and put on their knees. The hijabs are pulled off. King Richard's army pull out their swords. Robin pleads with King Richard.

"You can't be serious."

"The enemy shall see how serious I am," King Richard says.

Author's Note:

I decided I was becoming like George Lucas with the Star Wars Prequels. I was becoming so obsessed with answering the small historical details of the story, I was leaving the audience behind. I decided to remove the Guantanamo Bay type scenes. Richard's massacre was an unexpected move. Strategically brilliant, morally wrong. He is historically condemned for it, but Saladin's Massacre at Hattin is conveniently forgotten by those that condemn Richard. It is also forgotten by the self-styled critics of history that massacres happen all the time, especially in the medieval time period. Despite this, I couldn't let Richard walk away unpunished. I altered it.

Deleted Scene 8

Robin starts learning to bake a cake. Robin keeps messing with his formula until his cake is as delicious as Mrs. Bakker's. Robin and Agony stand in the center of the courtyard.

An Assassin shouts "Welcome to Top Cake! Where only the best chef will win. Welcome the Judge, the old man of the mountain!"

The old man tastes the different cakes. The old man of the mountain tastes the cake of Robin's instructor.

"Well?"

"You have outdone yourself this year. The prize will surely go to you after I taste Robin's cake." The old man of the mountain tastes cake that is exactly like Mrs. Bakker's cake. The old man of the mountain's eyes pop. The old man of the mountain places his hands on Robin's shoulders.

"Where did you learn to bake cake like this?"

"I spent several days trying to remember Mrs. Bakker's cooking lessons from when I was a boy."

"You win this year."

Every Assassin in the courtyard goes nuts.

The man with the painted skull shouts, "Hey! What about my cake?"

The old man of the mountain turns to him. "Oh. Your cake sucks."

Author's Note:

I decided Top Cake was too much. I removed it. I'm not getting paid to include the cake in my book, I just really like Mrs. Bakker's cakes.

Deleted Scene 9

Salah Ad-Din: While Richard has been away these past eight months I have been planning an invasion to conquer all of Europe. Once the three years are up we shall conquer and enslave all the Christians.

Abdallah al-Aladil: Unfortunately we have seen large numbers of our forces attacked by an invisible enemy.

Salah Ad-Din: I don't understand. We had a peace treaty with the Crusaders. Why would they violate that?

Abdallah al-Aladil: It does not act like a Crusader. I think this is the work of some new kind of Assassin.

Salah Ad-Din: This terror came from Alamut?

Author's Note:

I really like this scene, It shows the story from Saladin's perspective. The scene factually displays his battle plans for after the truce ends though he was gunning for enslaving all of Europe not just the Crusaders. Unfortunately, I had to cut the scene, due to the fact the story is told in third person limited during the first act. Robin is nowhere in this scene. I cut it.

Deleted Scene 10

Back in the castle, it's night-time in the year 2002 A.D. Elisha Grey closes the book.

"Awesome account. I have my final source."

Vampiressa checks in on Elisha.

"Is everything in order?"

"Yes. Can I check out this book?"

"The book is yours. I own the film adaptation."

"Thanks!"

Elisha is home writing her paper. Elisha begins to read off of her computer screen, "The Crusades, there is a reason it is referred to as a series of religious wars. You cannot judge this historical period by modern day standards. You have to think about it from the perspective of those who were there. After 400 years of constant attacks Christianity faced a crisis it had to solve. That is where Pope Urban the second came into the picture. Pope Urban gave a speech."

South Whidbey High School History Teacher: You just destroyed your 4.0 GPA with this paper.

Elisha Grey: How? I was Historically accurate. I provided eleven different sources.

History Teacher: You came to the conclusion that the Crusaders saved Western Civilization and you did not justify Muslim aggression against the West.

Elisha Grey: What about the historical significance of 9/11 during the Crusades?

History Teacher: Remember tower seven?

Elisha Grey: Gulf of Tonkin?

History Teacher: You just forgot the most important lesson.

Elisha Grey: What's that?

History Teacher: Never question the narrative. You got an F.

Elisha Grey: Fuck!

There is a sign outside the walls of Jerusalem. The sign reads: "Welcome to Jerusalem Land! The Holiest place on earth! Get a free Grail at the Sangreal gift shop. Kart track coming soon."

Author's Note:

I removed this wraparound mainly because I was going into False Flag attacks. As good as this scene was, this book is not about 9/11, False Flag attacks, nor the bullshit with Tower 7. The Third Crusade is the new Act One. Briefly considered to be labeled Act Zero.

Deleted Scene 11

In the NORTH CASCADES it's 2006. It is a stormy night, and in the mountains there is a lavish castle. Something that is reminiscent of the opening of Bride of Frankenstein. A wayward traveler enters the castle to get out of the storm. "Hello?"

Lightning flashes and there is a Woman behind her.

"Welcome to the Library of Castle Bloodcraft. This is a special Library."

"What is Your name?"

"Vampiressa the Mistress of shadows. May I inquire as to what your name is?"

"Claire Grey"

"American?"

"Whidbey Island, Washington. What's so special about this library?"

"An American from Whidbey by the name of Grey. Interesting. Very interesting. Here, follow me through the castle. I have to show you something."

The two walk through the shelves, catacombs and up stairways traveling by candlelight. Vampiressa turns towards Claire.

"It has been a long time since we've had a visitor."

Vampiressa turns back. They rise up the floors of the castle until the librarian finds the book she seeks.

"Everyone who visits here has their very own book. That is what makes this castle library so special. This book is yours, read it until the storm passes." "'Tales of the Adventurous Robin Hood.' Cool cover."

Claire opens the book and starts reading as lightning strikes.

Author's Note:

The third wraparound introducing Claire Grey. This is how Claire first meets Vampiressa establishing their friendship. Ultimately, I felt it was breaking the flow of the story, so I removed it.

Deleted Scene 12

The leader of the group Sir Guy of Gisbourne suddenly becomes aware of this hooded newcomer.

Sir Guy of Gisbourne: You dare interfere with justice?

Hooded figure: What crime could have been so grave that it requires seven armed men on horseback to kill a helpless child?

Sir Guy: This helpless boy has killed one of the prince's deer.

Hooded figure: No man or child deserves to be lynched... especially for something as trivial as killing a deer.

Sir Guy of Gisbourne: Well, I have no problem killing you as well as the whelp.

The hooded figure lets fly six arrows in eight seconds hitting all six men on horseback in their faces. Sir Guy of Gisbourne flees like the coward he is.

Author's Note:

This scene was from an earlier draft. Gisbourne should not see Robin in person at this point in the story. I cut that.

Deleted Scene 13

Maid Marian: So please tell me Prince John, is there any news from the Holy Land about my cousin King Richard?

Prince John: Everything is going fine my dear child, but you really shouldn't concern yourself with such ugly affairs.

Maid Marian: And what should I concern myself with?

Prince John: Why...Finding a good man to marry of course. Why take Sir Guy of Gisbourne for example. A braver or more trustworthy man cannot be found.

The Sheriff of Nottingham coughs.

Prince John: Besides the Sheriff of course...

Suddenly Sir Guy of Gisbourne bursts into the hall terrified out of his wits.

Sir Guy of Gisbourne: Hooded. Alone. Six men. All dead.

Sheriff of Nottingham: Quit your babbling Sir Guy and tell us what happened.

Sir Guy: Six of my men and I were on horseback when someone arrived and shot all six of them dead in eight seconds with a bow and arrow.

The entire court bursts into debate upon hearing this news.

Prince John: Are you telling me that a lone man on foot killed six armed soldiers on horseback armed with nothing but a bow and arrows?

Sir Guy: I beg forgiveness your majesty, but I have never encountered anyone so skilled with a bow and arrow.

Maid Marian under her breath: Robin...

Sheriff of Nottingham: Who was this mysterious assailant?

Sir Guy: I do not know. He wore a hood.

Maid Marian breathes a sigh of relief and starts to sip her wine when a voice cries out: Salutations to Prince John usurper of the throne!

Marian spits her wine out as a mysterious Hooded Figure enters the great hall.

Prince John: Why look. Look, Sir Guy... It's your friend from the forest!

The Hooded Figure: Long have I fought in the Holy Land in service of the good people of England... And how are my efforts repaid? To return home where the rich get richer, the people are impoverished, and injustice runs rampant across the land due to common thugs like Sir Guy.

Sir Guy of Gisbourne: Curb your tongue and show us the traitorous face you cowardly hide under that hood!

The Hooded Figure pulls off the hood revealing the dashing figure of Sir Robin of Locksley.

Robin Hood: I'm neither coward nor traitor Sir Guy!

An onlooker cries: It's Sir Robin's Hood!

Prince John: So. Sir Robin of Locksley is back from the Crusades... Tell me Sir Robin, what do you plan on doing now that you have killed six of my men?

Robin Hood: I am going to use every resource at my disposal to become a Prince of Thieves. I am going to systematically bankrupt the system, forcing good King Richard home to reclaim the throne. None of you are prepared for the level of violence I will unleash on your sorry butts!

Maid Marian seems to faint at the sheer audacity of Robin's statement.

Robin Hood: I will strike like a shadow and disappear just as quickly Exacting a death for a death. From this moment onward the rich are no longer safe...

Prince John: Seize him!

Robin ducks beneath a table as a spear is hurled. Several guests feel something bump against their legs. Robin rolls out from under the table. Robin spots Prince John and starts gunning towards him. Prince John cowers in terror as Robin leaps up onto the table in front of him. Robin crouches to Prince John's level, briefly making eye contact with one another, Robin launches himself through the stained-glass window into the moat below. Robin makes it to the treeline by the time the castle guards ride out on horseback. As the guards ride into Sherwood Forest they are quickly shot by a camouflaged Robin sitting in one of the trees. Robin takes a horse and sends other horses running off in many directions. Rearing his horse Robin Hood rides off into the darkness of the forest.

That night Robin sleeps in a tree and has a horrible nightmare or is it a premonition? Robin Hood is back in battle killing in the Crusades. After a while he runs out of people to kill and is left last man standing in a valley of the dead... suddenly hundreds of pikes rise out of the ground impaling the Dead. Robin is scared but cautious then he realises there is something walking through the rows of the dead.

Robin Hood wakes up screaming. Realizing where he is he looks around and sees that the horse is gone.

Robin Hood: Of course the horse is missing.

Author's note:

This is the original opening for the book. This is a far more jokey version of the story. I knew why Robin Hood was acting this way, but my writer's group had no idea why Robin Hood is behaving like this, he seemed so out of character. I decided to answer the question I already knew, how Robin Hood can do what he does, I answered why, with a mostly historically accurate backstory of the Crusades, I added the stories that are attached to the history. I had Robin Hood train as an Assassin in Persia. I decided to replace the Castle Scene with the May Games. The castle scene was good, but I felt it was too derivative of Errol Flynn. Marian and Robin Hood were King and Queen of the May Games. Their story was used by Medieval Troubadors to create the concept of romantic love, as well as the importance of wooing a lady. The May Games provided a more original and historically fitting opening. I cut it.

Deleted Scene 14

Robin Makes his way through Sherwood Forest for hours until he comes across a river. There is a large man standing on a log guarding access to the other side with his quarterstaff. Robin gets onto the log.

Robin Hood: Make way big man.

Big Man: Only if you pay the toll...

Robin Hood: This river runs through my land. I refuse. What's your name big man?

Robin cuts off a sturdy branch.

Big Man: Little John.

Robin Hood: Let me get this straight... your name is Little John?

Little John: I'm aware of the irony.

Robin Hood: Have at you.

Robin Hood delivers a flurry of attacks towards Little John, Suddenly Robin and Little John are rapidly exchanging blows while staff fighting with furious martial precision. After two minutes of intense fighting Little John manages to break Robin's staff in two. Robin begins stick fighting his opponent. Robin and Little John begin an insane exchange of strikes and counter strikes. Robin keeps smacking his sticks into Little John's face, which is making him angry. Little John finally manages to trip Robin Hood off the log.

Little John: HA!

Robin Hood is falling off the log manages to catch a branch underneath. Using the momentum of his fall Robin swings under the log and back up over to the other side knocking Little John off in the process.

Robin Hood: HA!

Little John falls into the water and begins drowning.

Little John: I can't swim! Help! Help me!

Robin Hood throws a rope to Little John and pulls him up.

Little John: You saved me... It's not every day I meet a man who not only bests me in combat but also saves my life. Forget the toll. I want to know your name.

Robin: I am Robin of Locksley.

Little John: It's you! You're the outlaw everyone is talking about! You're Robin Hood!

Robin Hood: Robin Hood? Hmmm. Robin. Hood. Robin Hood. Ha! I love it! It rolls off the tongue.

Little John: I'm sorry Robin, but taxes have become so high that it forces decent folk like myself into a life of corny medieval stereotypes.

Robin: You truly have my sympathies friend. Decent folk shouldn't have to live like that. But If you would like to help I think I have a good plan to change things.

Author's Note:

I often kept an eye out for a log laying high across the river in my local park. One day I walked by a waterfall and I visualized Robin Hood and Little John fighting there. I dropped the scene I had written to instead write a new one taking place at the top of a waterfall. Everyone can agree Little John is still a Corny Medieval Stereotype.

I cut it.

Deleted Scene 15

There is a knock on Marian's door. Marian opens it and Robin Hood is standing there dressed as a royal cook.

Robin Hood: I am the Royal Cook. I am here for my kiss.

Porn music starts to play.

Maid Marian: I didn't order anything.

Marian closes the door and the porn music stops. A few minutes later there is another knock on the door. Marian answers it and Robin Hood is standing there disguised as a Royal Massage Therapist.

Robin Hood: Hello, I'm the Royal Massage Therapist. I am here to give you a massage.

Porn music starts to play.

Marian: I didn't order a massage.

Porn music stops.

Marian: Come on in.

Porn music continues to play. Marian is lying down while Robin gives her a massage.

Marian: HHHNNNNN. You really give a good massage.

Robin Hood: That's good to know because I'm not really a massage therapist.

Marian opens her eyes.

Marian: Robin!

Porn music finale.

Author's Note:

I realize that the story becomes far more sarcastic before it turns Sardonic, but the Cook disguise and 1970's Porno music was too much, even for the second draft. I cut it.

Deleted Scene 16

Announcer: Yes, fellow reader there is no creature on earth as evil as the duck billed platypus. It is a fact that the duck billed platypus is more evil than Dracula.

Dracula: RAWR!

Little Billy: Oh, I don't think the duck billed platypus is that evil.

Announcer: Oh no little Billy? Have you considered the fact that the duck billed platypus is venomous? That is an evil trait! The duck billed platypus uses its snout to find things! That's evil too! The duck billed platypus builds dams and is in league with the angry, angry beaver! It is biding its time to take over the world! That's also Evil! It is one of the five existing species of monotremes, mammals that lay eggs, that's really evil! And that is why the duck billed Platypus is the most evil creature on the face of the earth.

Author's Note:

This is a Semi-Psychotic Rant about Monotremes. This is also to show that Dracula is not the most evil being on the planet, the problem is I didn't want to reveal Dracula this early, He's a surprise for Act Three. I don't know why I railed so hard against Monotremes, three out of five of them are extinct. I cut it.

Deleted Scene 17

Robin Hood pulls the string and is pummeled into the floor by a giant boxing glove. Robin slowly crawls out from under the boxing glove. Standing up Robin Hood sees that the next door is slightly ajar. Opening the door a small vat of molasses covers Robin. Robin Hood proceeds to trip on a wire and falls down the stairs landing in a pile of red feathers at the bottom. It is at the bottom that Robin Hood find's the king's ransom. One hundred and fifty-one chests of gold surround Robin Hood. Robin travels south towards the Isle of

Wight. A farmer reading the bible spots Robin crossing the country-side.

Farmer: My word! A gigantic bird... Cyrus! Grab your crossbow to protect your mother!

Cyrus comes out of the house wielding a crossbow.

Cyrus: Yes Father! Lord, let my aim be true!

Cyrus fires an arrow that embeds itself in Robin Hood's back-side.

Robin Hood: Goddamn I hate getting shot in the ass all the time!

Isle of Wight

Emmissary: Funny that no one has come... you think that England would want it's King back. Deckhand: Wait! What's that in the distance?

Emissary: It kind of looks like... a giant Robin!?

Robin Hood: I have the gold for King Richard's release...

Emissary: Only one chest of gold? The ransom is quite a bit higher than that.

Robin Hood: One hundred and fifty of my merry men are following me and each of them carries a chest of gold. But King Richard must be released.

Emissary: And released he shall be, but whom shall I tell him paid the ransom?

Robin Hood: Robin.

Emissary: Hell yeah, I called it!

Author's Note:

The boxing glove and ink are part of a game I play in all of my writing. I call it spot the Duck reference. I felt that Cyrus was too American for the story. I also felt Robin Hood was a prick for taking three years worth of gold from the English Tax Payers to pay for Richard's ransom when Robin Hood possessed more wealth than all of England combined. After I had him pay with Purple I altered the scene.

Deleted Scene 18

Doppleganger:

Wait! I am Robin Hood!

Mulch the Miller's son: I am Robin Hood!

Little John: No! I am Robin Hood!

Man in black cape and red mask: I am Robin Hood!

Man in black cape and red mask swings his rapier wildly into the air. He mounts his black horse, and rides off laughing maniacally into the distance. Robin Hood spins to King John and smiles, turning King John livid with anger.

Prince John: You're not Robin Hood! You're not Robin Hood! You're not Robin Hood! And I think that was the scarlet Pimpernel...

Author's note:

This was me experimenting with including other storybook characters in my Robin Hood Story. Earlier the Scarlet Pimpernel was El Zorro. Neither fit the time period. Eventually, I took the repeated suggestion of Rob Roy to heart and included him.

Deleted Scene 19

Robin Hood comes behind the soldier standing outside his burrow and uses his bow to snap the soldier's neck. Robin Hood whacks the bow against the nearby soldier's head, knocking him out and shoots an arrow into the face of the third soldier standing in the distance. Robin Hood runs past the trees as dozens of arrows hit the tree trunks. Robin springs his own trap as dozens of merry archers in the trees hit the Sheriff of Nottingham and his soldiers in the crossfire. The camera man dies in the crossfire and a Merry Man picks up the camera and continues filming. Robin Hood walks up to the Sheriff of Nottingham who has an arrow in the leg.

Author's Note:

I felt when this project was in an earlier film form, I felt that this would be a very dangerous project to film, With all the characters killing in medieval warfare; I figured every once in a while the camera man would die. The person nearby usually picks up the camera and keeps filming. When the project changed into a better book form Some gags wouldn't make as much sense.

Delete Scene 20

Dawn

The Sheriff of Nottingham and Sir Guy of Gisbourne are collecting taxes accompanied by a small garrison of men.

Sir Guy: We have collected taxes from everyone, Sheriff. It is time to return to the castle.

Sheriff: That's the problem with you, Gisbourne, you don't know how to open new markets.

The Sheriff grabs a child heading to school, while Sir Guy and his men round up the other children.

Sheriff: Give me all of your lunch money!

Child: Hey, I need that! My parents gave me that lunch money for my first day of school!

Sheriff: A freshman, huh? I know how to deal with freshmen...

Sir guy opens a box, and there is a wooden paddle resting upon a velvet pillow inside it. The Sheriff of Nottingham grabs the wooden paddle and spins it in his hand a few times. Then the Sheriff starts wailing on the child's backside for about seven minutes. On the eighth minute, three arrows pierce the wooden paddle. The Sheriff drops the paddle and turns around and looks atop the nearest home. A hooded figure garbed in black leather armor and a forest green hood and cloak. Behind him is the rising sun. The figure seems to launch straight up into the sky and lands on the ground.

Robin Hood's Voice cries out: Yield!

Robin Hood begins to bounce around the six men like a human pinball, striking blows so fast and furious that the soldiers have little time to react before they are knocked out. Robin knocks a few of Sir Guy of Gisbourne's teeth out, then Sir Guy blacks out. Robin Hood aims two arrows right at both of The Sheriff's eyes.

Sheriff: So what are you going to do Robin? Murder someone in front of the very eyes of impressionable schoolchildren?

Robin Hood: No!

In a lightning fast maneuver, Robin Hood fires both of his arrows into both of the Sheriff of Nottingham's feet.

Sheriff of Nottingham: AAAAAAA! AAAAAAA! AAAAAAA!

While The Sheriff is momentarily distracted with two arrows in his feet, Robin Hood picks up the paddle, spins his body around and smashes the wooden paddle against The Sheriff's ass.

Sheriff of Nottingham: Me arse! You've destroyed me bloody arse!

Schoolchildren: HOORAY! YAAAAAAAAYYYYYY!!!!!

The schoolchildren, once threatened, proceed the kick the snot out of The Sheriff and his men while they are down. Robin Hood pulls out his own paddle and spins it a few times.

Robin Hood: Now that that's been taken care of, it is my turn with the freshman.

Author's Note:

This is the original scene, even Robin Hood won't let a freshman go, I escaped that fate luckily. I was rewriting heavy portions of the book and decided this could be a better scene. It turned into a trap set for Robin Hood that sprung into the birth of his legend. I wanted a sort of Keith Allen Sheriff of Nottingham in the revised version of this scene. In my humble opinion, Keith Allen is the real star of the BBC Robin Hood (villains often are.) He keeps referring to him as Hood, We are at status quo here. The giveaway is that Robin is wearing black leather armour with a green hood and cloak in the original scene. Listening to lectures by Shad M. Brooks, I realized that leather armour was shit, and that gambeson was better. I decided that Robin has gambeson in this scene. The existence of gambeson has influenced other parts of the story too.

The eye shadow in the new scene is a film joke.

Deleted Scene 21

Will Scarlet pulls Robin Hood off the rock. "It is more complicated than that Robin! King Richard has returned from the Crusades, he is taking the south road through Locksley Village but our king's brother has found out and has a dozen men dressed as you hired to kill the king!" "Then I only have a small window of time and have to get moving." Robin bolts for it. At the south road it is becoming dusk. King Richard's garrison is upon the south road riding closer and closer to the trap. More than a dozen Assassins are in the village dressed in green holding crossbows. They lay in wait hidden throughout Locksley village. "Isn't Robin Hood the best bowman in all of England? Why did they give us crossbows?" Asks the mercenary. "So we will be more accurate. Besides nobody is going to know it's not Robin Hood," The assassin answers.

Back at King Richard's garrison, the knight leading the garrison points forward. "Look! There is someone in the distance."

Back at the trap a sentry dressed as Robin Hood is on the roof. Suddenly a sword pierces through his front torso several times until he falls down dead. Robin Hood sheathes his sword and leaps soaring down landing on top of one of the Sheriff's men. Robin Hood gets up and rolls an oncoming attacker onto his back. Pulling an arrow from his quiver, Robin stabs the impostor in the heart, pulls the arrow back out and fires it into an impostor down the road. Robin Hood runs down the road, and ducks around the corner, then grabs an assassin from behind, breaks his arm and fires the crossbow into another rooftop sentry. Two arrows hit the assassin in the chest killing him. Robin drops his human shield, draws his bow and fires two arrows in rapid succession, killing two more rooftop archers. Robin Hood climbs a house and fires his arrow at an impostor down the road, but the impostor moves the door in the way keeping Robin's arrow from hitting its mark. Swinging the door shut the assassin fires a shot off with his crossbow. Robin draws another arrow, turns his bow a quarter counter clockwise, knocking the arrow out of the air. Walking along the edge of the roof Robin gains a better vantage point then shoots his opponent. he drops from the roof once more. An assassin gets the drop on Robin Hood from behind pointing a crossbow at the back of Robin Hood's head. Robin Hood kicks the Assassin in the pelvis applying 350 pounds of force, crippling the hapless mercenary. King Richard's garrison enters the fray and finds bodies everywhere. Going along the road, the garrison finds dead men garbed in forest green hoods cloaks and tights. Suddenly a figure dressed the same way as the dead men pops out, and fires an arrow straight at King Richard's head, but the arrow is snapped in twain mid-flight by another arrow. Robin Hood then shoots the would be Assassin dead. "Lower your weapon or be destroyed!" Shouts the knight leading the Garrison. Robin Hood's reaction to this order is to draw his sword and walk toward the garrison. All the knights in the garrison draw their swords. Without warning, Robin Hood spins around 540 degrees, throwing his sword in a spinning motion and flying through the air. Robin's sword decapitates the last Assassin who came attacking on horseback. "You have true skill with a blade, but now you have none. So explain what is going on," Asks the king. "I would do so gladly for my king. Unfortunately, you are not he," Robin says in a snide manner.

The knight leading the garrison steps forward and removes his helmet revealing the face of the true King Richard. "Quite so, Robin of Locksley. Only you could kill more than a dozen men with such ease."

Robin Hood looks around him then looks back at Richard. "You call that easy?"

Robin Hood begins to kneel. "My Lord, your brother John, the Count of Mortain, has declared that..."

"I am well aware of my brother's doings Robin, thanks to Lady Marian. As for you Robin, while it is a requirement, you do not need to kneel. From what I understand, Sir Robin of Locksley, I have you to thank for paying my ransom, as well as protecting my subjects while I was away when no one else would. You are a true hero of the realm," King Richard declares.

"I beg your pardon your majesty, but time is short. Your brother is going to execute Marian at midnight and I must save her," Robin Hood says.

"I will join you Robin, and so will every man in Sherwood under the order of King Richard the Lion Heart!!!" Richard shouts.

"My Lord!"

Author's Note:

I decided that since the Assassins wore green outfits the same as Robin Hood's. It would make more sense for the battle of the Assassins to take place in Sherwood Forest. A forest environment would be deadlier than a town. This action scene pays homage to the final shoot out in For a Few Dollars More. I cut it.

Deleted scene 22

The guards in their towers look to see who is firing arrows but no one is there. All the guards can see are bushes and a cart being pulled by a man. The guards lower the drawbridge and raise the gate. One of the bushes begins to move around to the back of the castle. Casting off his camouflage disguise Robin begins to free climb up the castle wall.

Nottingham Guard: What's all this then?

Cart Man: Delivery of flour to the pantry.

Nottingham Guard: That is an alarmingly large amount of flour.

Cart Man: Your telling me! I had to drag it here! Bloody horses are on sick leave.

Once Robin reaches the top he round house kicks a guard off the wall, catches an arrow on fire from a nearby torch, draws his bow, waits for the Cart Man to get clear and shoots three burning arrows consecutively into three lanterns lighting them and causing them to fall onto the cartload of flour. The resulting explosion takes out the castle gate leaving Nottingham Castle open to attack.

Author's Note:

This is an early draft scene where I was toying with the idea of a gigantic flour explosion. I cut it.

Deleted Scene 23

Richard Pardons Robin Hood and all of his Merry Men. Deep in the Sherwood Forest, in the green of Robin Hood's Camp, A target is hung onto a tree branch. Everybody takes their turn to bullseye the target. Robin Hood is rather bored by this. Finally, Robin can show everyone his stuff. He slides an arrow between his fingertips. He feels the breeze. He focuses on the target. He draws his bow with years of practiced skill and misses the target by a mile. King Richard has his men hold Robin Hood down as a wooden box is presented to King Richard. Richard opens the box and a wooden paddle with holes drilled into it lies upon a velvet pillow. Richard The Lion Heart grasps the paddle and does his kingly duty by paddling the shit out of England's favorite bandit laughing maniacally as he does it.

Author's Note:

This was an alternate ending I had devised, I like the idea of King Richard punishing Robin Hood for his criminal ways at the end. I like it as a finale to the Robin Hood story, but I found it too similar to the Merry Adventures of Robin Hood by Howard Pyle. I made the new ending more triumphant. The song that follows the end of this act is not about Kevin Costner. Who it's actually about I will only disclose to Mr. Costner privately.

Deleted Scene 24

Villager: Count Dracula, you want to take over the world... Why do you want to be Sheriff of Nottingham?

Dracula: If you are going to take over the world you have to start somewhere.

Author's Note:

I figured the speech Dracula gave to the masses was enough, this question and answer afterwards ruined the mystique of Dracula. Dracula is the only character I have written so far who was pure evil, but became funny when he was dead. In 2011 he has been slapped with seven sexual harassment lawsuits. He's the bad guy so of course he's a racist moron with delusions of deification. I cut it.

Deleted Scene 25

Inside the castle, Marian lies in a coffin, her skin is completely blue. Lara hovers over Marian. Making sure that Tara and Fara are playing with their experiments. Lara begins kissing Marian on the lips. Marian's eyes unexpectedly shoot open, and she sees that Lara in in the process of violating her body. Enraged, Marian grabs Lara by the head and gets up out of her coffin.

Marian: Time to go out the window...

Marian tosses Lara headfirst out the window.

Tara: That wasn't supposed to happen! You weren't supposed to kill Lara!

Fara: Marian threw Lara out the window! Run for your life Tara! She's gone mental!

Tara and Fara run for their lives against a wrathful Marian.

Marian: Armoury...

Author's Note:

This is the original scene. Lara, Tara, and Fara are a combination of Donald Duck's nephews, Huey, Dewey, and Louie, as well as Daisy Duck's nieces, April, May, and June. Dracula's castle is supposed to be sexually perverse. In 2008 two girls kissing was considered somewhat taboo, a dozen years later and society has slipped further into degeneracy and the kiss is no longer considered risqué. I had to up the ante by going between the legs. This isn't a slight against lesbians, I love lesbians, and they love me, it's just that Western Civilization is engaging in decadence and degeneracy. In less than a dozen years society will slip further into degeneracy. Good thing to know that I will have had a hand in it this time.

Deleted Scene 26

Dracula's blows are so numerous and so powerful, Robin Hood is forced to the bloody floor. Dracula goes for the deathblow, but Robin Hood manages to roll out of the way of his killing strike. Robin clambers away on the floor, kicking lots of blood around. Dracula laughs demonically as the lights go out.

Robin Hood is in complete darkness again. The candles jet upwards once more as blood pours down heavily. The Second Cameraman starts breathing heavily and makes a break for it. Dodging burning candles, the Second Cameraman looks up and sees Dracula hanging from the ceiling above.

Second Cameraman: Jesus Christ!

Dracula drops downward and the camera drops. The camera records Dracula feeding on the cameraman, ripping out chunks of flesh as the camera lens is covered in blood. A skeleton picks up the camera, wipes the blood off the lens, hisses into the camera, and continues filming.

Author's Note:

I felt at the time that not enough people were dying during the Swordfight between Dracula and Robin Hood. I decided that the Camera Man was the logical choice for Dracula to literally tear to pieces.

Deleted Scene 27

Robin Hood:

What happened to you? Your hazel hair is now black as night and the tone of your flesh is much softer in color.

Maid Marian:

Horrible things Robin. Terrible things. But the nightmare is over now. You are here and now we are together again.

Skeleton Cameraman:

Kiss!

Robin And Marian look at one another nod and attack the skeleton cameraman from a third person perspective.

Robin: Look, horses are running around wild.

Robin Hood secures a horse for him and Marian to ride on the long journey home. They witness lava exploding from the surrounding mountains as they flee on their horse racing back to England.

Epilogue:

Steps to kill a vampire:

Step One: Stake it

Step Two: Cut its head off.

Step Three: Stuff its mouth full of garlic.

Step Four: Burn the body at a crossroads

Step Five: Bury head at crossroads

Step Six: Apply Holy Water to ashes.

Step Seven: Pray

Step Eight (optional): Urinate on ashes to diss the bloodsucker.

Author's Note:

The Author is well aware Robin Hood cannot kill Dracula. Anybody familiar with the Dracula Legend knows that Dracula returns to terrorize Bud Abbott and Lou Costello.

Author's Note 2:

The epilogue to the Dracula section was unnecessary once I decided to introduce the bill collecting duo. Besides, nobody knows how to kill a vampire, Nor do most know vampires can walk in daylight. The everyday vampires suck you until you're dry, but Goddamn if they're not useful when you need them in court.

Deleted Scene 28

Marian turns the page of the Necronomicomic.

Marian: The cookie monster!

Boot shine boy: That monster is the bane of my existence! It somehow manages to raid the cookie jar every night!

Author's Note:

I like the Cookie Monster, But I felt it broke the rules of my universe. Rule #1 Monsters exist, Ones that are said to exist in legends, and the newer ones such as the Cryptids. Rule # 2 If it can exist it does, what is fiction is fiction, But the Legends and Myths of old are all true. Cookie Monster does not and cannot exist in the story. I cut it.

Deleted Scene 29

Robin Hood: Prince Wolfstonecraft, I am wondering something...

Prince Wolfstonecraft: Yes, what is it Robin Hood?

Robin Hood: Why do you wear that wolf's skin around you? It reminds me of the wild men who served The Lord of the Darkness.

Prince Wolfstonecraft: In my last encounter, the Dark Lord shattered my sword and defeated me, I became enslaved to his dark will. Those wild men are an abomination and should be wiped out! They believe if they kill me and eat my flesh it will give them the power of transmutation. I wear this wolf's skin because it was once my father! You can choose to believe this or not but I was raised by wolves... it was Princess Haroo who found me and taught me the ways of man... I will never forget that it was man who killed my father... That's why I will always wear his skin.

Author's Note:

This gave away the secret of Moonfang before it should have been revealed. I cut it.

Deleted Scene 30

Marian: Sniffle... Robin. I think I... No. I know... Robin, I'm pregnant.

Robin Hood: I'll go fetch the coat hanger...

Marian: Robin!

Robin Hood: I mean, I'm going to be a father? This is the happiest day of my entire life!

Author's Note:

I don't think coat hangers existed back then, so it doesn't make any sense. Anyway, this scene is blatantly Pro-choice. I cut it.

Deleted Scene 31

Robin Hood goes above deck to talk with the Pirate Princess Sarah Cutter.

Robin Hood: Do you have any idea where we are going?

Sarah Cutter: The Direction we are currently sailing means that we should be entering the Super Sargasso Sea right about now.

Robin Hood: I thought I knew the names of all seven seas, but I have never heard of the Super Sargasso Sea. How do you know where to find it?

Fish start falling from the sky, flopping around on the main deck.

Pirate Princess: That's how...

The Gorgolac is witnessing the ship enter the Super Sargasso Sea through a crystal encasing a dragon embryo within it.

Author's note:

I like the scene, but nobody knows what the hell the Super Sargasso Sea even is. I cut it.

Deleted Scene 32

Marian arrives at a farm in the French countryside with her servant Sarah. Marian enters the study and grabs a chest.

Marian: Robin said he left me the greatest treasure in the Holy Land inside this chest...

Marian turns the key opening the chest finding a piece of paper with a zero on it.

Marian: He brought back an effing hole? Oh. Oh. Oh God!

Marian becomes so upset she goes into labor..

Author's Note:

Math joke. Get it?

Deleted Scene 33

In Castle Bloodcraft, it is morning. The storm is over and the light is shining through the window.

Claire Grey: "'We spoke of the many tales of Robin Hood throughout the night. That is the story of the legendary heroic outlaw Robin Hood as I knew him, signed Marian of Locksley'. Holy crap! This book is legit. It's all true!"

Claire rushes down the steps of the castle to find Vampiressa standing in the morning light of the castle entrance.

Vampiressa: There is a book for everyone, dear Claire. Know the trickster nature of the Fox. For it is that trickster blood in the book that flows through your veins. Keep the book and add your story to it.

Claire Grey: You're standing in sunlight. Shouldn't you be dead?

Vampiressa: Why would sunlight kill me? I'm already dead.

Claire takes the book and exits the castle and walks out into the woods. There is a pagan tribal fox on the key chain attached to her backpack.

Author's Note:

This is the last scene in the book. Again, just like with every scene I cut, it dragged the momentum of the story down. Besides, it killed the mood the reader has after reading the Nottingham episode of Jerry.

Deleted Characters

There is also a character named the Scion of Magi, he is a descendant of Merlin and Nimue. I changed him into a necromancer in the Dracula section and wrote the character out of the part with the inner circle and their quest. He was too much for the book, the book that ends up turning into a mild episode of Jerry Springer, the Scion of Magi was just too much. Still... I like to think he is roaming around in my head, doing who knows what in my subconscious, while residing in my imagination just waiting to be used again. A salute to the characters that did not make it! To Calidad, Abdul, Fritz, Kong, Monica, and the Scion of Magi!

BONUS STORY
Moonfang The Wulf King
Written by Holland Timmins

A GREAT BATTLE HAD been waged between two kingdoms. After the North Kingdom had fought the South Kingdom to a stalemate the two armies withdrew, the rivers ran red with blood.

At the great wood, the White Hart, the embodiment of the forest spirit, begins to drink from the river. As the White Hart drinks, it tastes something strange in the water. Suddenly the entire river turns red with human blood, the White Hart begins to smother itself in it. Finally, the forest spirit lifts its head from the river of blood, but by that time it had gone mad... so from that day onward, the Great Wood was known as Dark Wood. Soon after that fateful battle, the wicked King Wolfstonecraft of the South Kingdom had a son under the full moon.

Twenty years later.

Princess Katherine Archer Haru is the greatest hunter the Northern Kingdom has ever seen. She has red flowing hair complementing her blood-red lips. Her royal hunting party accompanies her as they creep through the heart of Dark Wood. One of her escort whispers to Katherine, "You have heard the stories just as I have. Why must we travel so deep into the heart of Dark Wood when we could just as easily bag our game at the borders? "

Katherine responds, "Because the largest game lies in the heart of Dark Wood, look at the size of that buck then you will see I am right."

With that Katherine draws her bow, aiming aided by the light of the full moon, but before she can let fly an arrow, a large wolf pounces upon the buck bringing it down. A royal guard nudges Princess Haru. "Looks like the wolf claimed it first, my lady."

"Quiet, my target has changed; I am now taking that wolf as my prize."

Katherine shoots her arrow into the wolf. Upon closer inspection, Katherine gasps.

"I have made a terrible mistake. I see now that it's not a wolf, but a man in wolf's clothing."

A guard quips "Worry not Princess, it is only a savage."

Princess Haru panics. "It is still a man! Now pick him up, we are bringing him back to the castle grounds to save him. I have some questions about him..."

The following week they nurse the man back to health.

Once he was able, the man follows Katherine wherever she goes. First on all fours, then on two legs. Two weeks before the next full moon he started to form words. Katherine begins asking him questions.

Katherine Haru asks him, "Who are you?"

"I am a leader."

Katherine asks him again, "What is your name?"

"In your tongue, I am called Moonfang."

"You say you are a leader... of what?"

Moonfang tells her who he is, "I am the Wulf King. I have command of all the wolves the world over."

Katherine looks at him skeptically. "I somehow doubt that... why do you wear a wolf skin?"

"It is the skin of my father, the original Wulf King. He raised me until a human killed him."

A voice rings out, "Wolves are in the courtyard!"

The two wolves stand on two legs before terrified Knights. The wolves start roaming the courtyard. The wolves start howling.

Moonfang leaps to the window letting out two howls. The two wolves get back onto all fours heading back to Dark Wood.

Another voice rings out, "The wolves are retreating!"

Katherine is astonished by what has transpired. "You have control over those evil beasts?"

Moonfang laughs. "Wolves are not evil. They in fact are very social animals. The two in the courtyard were part of the Wulf Guard sent to find me. I merely informed them I was safe, so they should head home. To be fair, thanks to the past twenty years of deforestation I am unsure if we will have a home much longer."

Katherine presses him for more information.

"I want to know more about Moonfang the Wulf King."

Moonfang tells her more, "Katherine, you and I have much in common. We are both leaders, we are both great hunters at heart. As the leader of the wolves I protect Dark Wood, but in order to do that, I must have all the skills to do so. I am intrigued by human combat, there is almost an art to it, even though I would prefer to rip my enemy's throat out. The next full moon we shall travel to the caves together, where I shall show you everything you want to know about me."

The last two weeks are spent with Princess Haru tirelessly practicing the art of combat. The more they practice, the more their connection grows. Soon Moonfang is learning sword techniques from the best knights in the kingdom. At last, the final day comes where Moonfang announces he must return to Dark Wood. He requests that the Princess be allowed to accompany him for one night. At first, King Haru will not accept but the princess convinces the king to let her go.

As Katherine follows Moonfang through the forest, they travel deep into the heart of Dark Wood, they pass several prowling wolves, which begin to follow them. As night falls, they arrive at the caves. Moonfang takes off his father's skin.

"You have shown me the secrets of combat Katherine. I shall show you the secret that I keep, as I step into the moonlight behold my true form..."

Moonfang steps into the moonlight. Katherine lays before the werewolf standing in front of her,

"I have heard the stories about you. Something neither man nor beast, living in the heart of Dark Wood. Something else that can communicate with animals. I thought you were only a story to scare children from wandering into the forest. Now I finally know all the stories are true."

THE NEXT MOMENT MOONFANG the giant werewolf sniffs, lets out a powerful roar, bounding out of the caves. A carriage of the South Kingdom is traveling through Dark Wood when Moonfang attacks. He kills the guards, carries an old woman in his arms back to the caves. Moonfang sets the old woman down, spins then bounds back out of the cave.

Katherine Haru tends to the old woman. "Who are you?"

"I am Lupin's Mother..."

Katherine asks, "Who is Lupin?"

"He is the one who saved me."

Princess Haru is astonished by this revelation.

She whispers, "Moonfang?"

Crying the Old woman recounts her past, "I used to be the queen of the southern kingdom but when I gave birth to the one called Moonfang he was a werewolf. The King went mad, he saw it as a sign that nature conspired against him, so he declared war on nature itself. He swore to begin that war by killing his own son, my son, Lupin Wolfstonecraft. I could not bear it. If Lupin could not live safely with humans, I reasoned he might have had a chance of finding peace if he lived with the wolves."

Katherine, while dreading the answer, says "You didn't..."

Queen Wolfstonecraft collapses pounding her fist into the cavern stone. "I had no alternatives. My son would have been killed if I hadn't. It may not matter anyway, soon Dark Wood will be gone, then my Husband will have clear access to attack the Northern Kingdom."

Moonfang is watching from the opening in the cave where the moonlight pours in. He takes off sprinting through the woods moving silently in the shadows. Moonfang approaches a stone altar with a sword embedded in it. Whenever Moonfang comes near the sword under the light of the full moon, he transforms into a human again, but only near the sword. Many times, he has tried, tried so hard only to fail to free the sword. At last, Moonfang seizes the hilt of the sword, braces his legs, he taps into an inner strength in his human side that he does not know he has. He wrenches mightily, he collapses exhausted onto the ground. When he regains enough of his strength to stand, he finds the blade has loosened barely an inch. Again, Moonfang grasps the sword feeling its weight as the sword easily slides out of the Alter.

That night, Moonfang, Princess Haru, along with Queen Wolfstonecraft tell King Haru of King Wolfstonecraft's intentions. His plan to destroy Dark Wood completely in order to wage war on King Haru. At dawn, King Haru sends his forces to war against the Wolfstonecraft Kingdom. The two armies meet in Dark Wood, blanketed by the morning mist. The scent of pine mixed with morning dew permeates the air. The opposing forces do not have much visibility in the mist, but what the soldiers cannot see, the hunters can smell. When Wolfstonecraft's soldiers become isolated in the mist, wolves pounce on them tearing their throats out. The soldiers in both armies are terrorized by the growls of the wolves, the sound of their victims screams, all behind the shifting curtains of mist. In the halls of Castle Wolfstonecraft, the king sits alone, silent on his throne.

A voice rings out from the darkness. "Stand up to face me, you cur!"

Moonfang steps out of the shadows. He approaches the king with his blade drawn.

The king demands an answer, "How did you get in here?"

"My army of wolves dug a tunnel underneath your castle... I came through the kitchen. You have hunted my kind, you have hunted me, for far too long, it is time for me to put an end to your cruelty. You don't even know who I am, do you?"

King Wolfstonecraft laughs, "Sure I do! You are that bastard son of mine I had with that bitch called your mother. Tell me, why do you wear that skin of the wolf I killed?"

Moonfang angrily responds, "He was the alpha male, the closest thing to a friend that I have ever known. Now I represent the alpha, so I must destroy you who represent the omega."

King Wolfstonecraft is puzzled, "So you want a representational battle?"

"No, I prefer to rip your throat out, but I am willing to take what I can get."

King Wolfstonecraft becomes angry, "Get this!"

King Wolfstonecraft draws his sword beginning to battle his son, Moonfang the Wulf King. The sword combat between the two of them is an intense, merciless affair. King Wolfstonecraft fights in a refined sword combat style, while Moonfang fights back in rough guerilla combat style. The sword fight takes them across the great hall, up the grand stairway through the halls of castle Wolfstonecraft, to the top of the tower. Below the tower, all three armies are engaged in battle with one another. At the tower's top, King Wolfstonecraft uses a sword flourish driving Moonfang to the stone over the mortar.

Moonfang rests on his elbow, he tries to do a forward lunge, but King Wolfstonecraft parries the blow disarming Moonfang. King Wolfstonecraft kicks the sword over the side of the tower. He stands atop Moonfang with his sword pointed at his son's neck.

"Do you have any last words before I run you through?"

Moonfang looks right up at him smiling.

"Yes, I do. There is a solar eclipse happening right now. You're fucked."

The moon finishes covering the sun. Moonfang transforms into his true form as a werewolf. Moonfang bats away his father's sword, ripping his father's head off with his jaws, casting it into the battlefield below. Moonfang stands upright, bellowing a bloodthirsty roar, signifying the arrival of Moonfang the Wulf King. All the other wolves on the battlefield stand upright then begin howling alongside their King. No soldier on the battlefield that day ever killed another wolf again. That day, Lupin Wolfstonecraft took his place alongside Katherine Haru, uniting the two kingdoms with nature, it was what he was born to do. After that, the White Hart forest spirit was sane once more.

THE END

BONUS STORY
THE IDEA OF A HERO

During World War Two there was a writer. He had written great works of fiction in every genre. One day his house was destroyed during a German Blitzkrieg. All of his work was destroyed. He should have been distraught, but he simply smiled. He was happy to start from scratch for he had what really mattered. He had the idea.

In the realm of ideas the archetypes lived. A new one was born: The archetypal hero. His name was Fox. He was born in fire, a voice tells him to leave the fire, to go forward. So he did.

He went through a large graveyard arriving at a courtyard, there lay the sword in the stone. Fox tried to pull out the sword but could not no matter the effort. He left the sword behind.

"Some Hero I am..." thought Fox.

Heading back through the graveyard a skeleton crawled out of a grave. The skeleton walked towards Fox, Fox felt fear. The skeleton spoke to Fox, "I am the skeleton. I am the physical idea of man's fear of death. I represent fear. Are you afraid?"

"Yes!" Fox shouted cursing himself for admitting it.

"Good!" The skeleton replied, "For I am just the beginning."

The Skeleton transformed into a ghost. The ghost floated up to Fox. Fox felt a shiver up his spine. The voice spoke in a haunting tone, "I am the ghost. I am the spiritual manifestation of Man's fear of death."

The ghost put his hand on Fox's shoulder, Fox screamed.

"I am nothing. Evil shall consume the realm of ideas. Soon all shall suffer greatly." With that the ghost vanished.

Fox ran out of the graveyard He arrived at a church coming across a crescent moon, a six pointed star, both are on opposite sides of the cross. The Idea of God appeared before Fox.

"I am the Idea of God."

"What is God?" Fox inquired.

" I am, I am also whatever people need me to be." God replied.

"I need counsel." Fox said.

" I am that too."

" I am told that Evil is coming to consume all. What can I do to such a thing?" Fox confessed.

"Be wary of Evil, but do not fear it, lest it consume you." God counseled.

Fox left with his answer for all the good it would do him. He still did not know what to do. Fox wandered into a forest soon becoming lost in it. He was drawn to a fire in the forest, Fox came across another Archetypal Hero with a woman beside him.

"Who might you be?" Fox asked both of them.

" I am Robin Hood." The Hero in green replied.

"And I am his true love Maid Marian." The Beauty responded.

"What is love?" Fox asked this for he did not know.

" Love is Happiness, love is contentment, love is joy, all at once." Robin Hood answered.

"Is that how you feel?" Fox responded.

"Yes. But it is also something you must give to another." Marian replied with a smile.

"Excuse me, but you do not look like ideas. Not quite." Fox said.

"We were once flesh and blood but were transformed into ideas to both represent and explain love to others." Marian replied.

"How long have you loved?" Fox asked.

"For as long as we can remember." Robin responded. "Now give me your wallet."

Fox was led out of the forest by the loving couple, but there in the greenwood they remained. Fox traveled further before he spotted a Darkness. A blackness that was consuming everything. The blackness enveloped the Hero Fox. Fox was surrounded by darkness as was everything else. Fox was huddling but unexpectedly stood erect.

"Are you the Idea of Evil?" Fox shouted.

"I am Evil!" The Darkness boomed, "Are you not afraid?"

"No," Fox said calmly.

"Then you are a fool."

"I am a Hero!" Fox shouted back.

"Then where is your sword?" The darkness demanded.

"If I were to strike you down would I not become what you are?" Fox asked.

"You would," The evil chortled.

"Then I need no sword. I already have what I need."

"And what is that?"

"Love."

"Love? What is Love? I do not understand," the darkness roared.

"Love is something precious. Something I give to you freely and unconditionally. I love you."

The dark evil recoiled.

"No! No! Take it back! Take it back!" The Evil pleaded.

But it was too late. The evil was vanquished by Fox's love. Fox went forward, he reached the sword in the stone. Fox pulled on the hilt, it slid out easily. Fox had proven himself worthy, for Fox was the Archetype of the Hero in the realm of ideas.

If you like this book please write a review.
or recommend it to a friend

Contact the author at
hosersneedemail@gmail.com
Also from the Author
From B-list to A-list:
The evolution of the genre picture

[1] Mendola, Luigi. Richard 1 Lionheart in Sicily. Best of Sicily Magazine. Internet, 2011

[2] Real Crusades History. Third Crusade podcast. Richard The Lionheart's conquest of Cyprus. Scott Amis. Dr. Stephen Donnachie. J Stephen Roberts. Dr. Helena Schrader. YouTube.com, Internet.

[3] Real Crusades History. Third Crusade podcast. Siege of Acre. J Stephen Roberts. Dr. Helena Schrader. Scott Amis. Dr. Stephen Donnachie. Youtube.com, Internet.

[4] Real Crusades History, Third Crusade podcast. Battle of Arsuf. J Stephen Roberts. Rand Brown. Dr. Stephen Donnachie. Dr. Helena Schrader. Youtube.com, Internet.

[5] Real Crusades History. A Letter of Richard the Lion Heart from the Third Crusade. J Stephen Roberts. Youtube.com, Internet.

[6] Real Crusades History. Third Crusade podcast. Diplomacy of the Third Crusade. J Stephen Roberts. Dr. Helena Schrader. Youtube.com, Internet.

[7] Real Crusades History. Who were the assassins. J Stephen Roberts.

[8] Real Crusades History. Third Crusade podcast. The march on Jerusalem. Rand Brown. J Stephen Roberts. Dr. Helena Schrader. Dr. Stephen Donnachie. Youtube.com, Internet.

[9] Holt, J.C. Robin Hood. Book. Written by Professor Sir James Holt. Thames and Hudson publishing, 1982 P. 120-122

[10] Real Crusades History. Third Crusade Podcast. Battle of Jaffa. Rand Brown. J Stephen Roberts. Dr. Helena Schrader. Dr. Stephen Donnachie. Youtube.com, Internet.

[11] Richard the Lion Heart as quoted in The conquest of Jerusalem and the Third Crusade. Book. P. 179

[12] al-Din, Baha. Islamic Scholar. Battle of Jaffa, 1192

[13] Ephron, Nora. My Blue Heaven. DVD. Directed by Herbert Ross. Warner Brothers, 1990

[14] Lynott, Phil. The boys are back in town. Thin Lizzy, 1976

[15] Unknown Source.

[16] Roddenberry, Gene. Star Trek the next generation. DVD. Paramount, 1987

[17] Bilyeau, Nancy. The Strange Death of Richard the Lionheart englishhistoryauthors.blogspot.com. Internet

[18] John, Nicholas ST. King of New York. DVD. Directed by Abel Ferrara. Lions Gate Films, 1990

[19] SGT. Wolf, Karl. U.S. Airforce. The Disclosure Project. National Press Club, 2001

[20] Shakespeare, William. Julius Caesar. Stage play, 1599?

[21] Hoffman, Dustin. Midnight Cowboy. DVD. Directed by John Schlesinger. 20th Century Fox, 1969

[22] Alexander the Great cutting the Gordian knot 333 B.C.

[23] Groening, Matt

[24] Blanc, Mel. Bugs Bunny, A Wild Hare. DVD. Directed by Tex Avery. Warner Brothers, 1940

[25] Smith, Kevin. Zack and Miri make a porno. 2008

[26] Tarantino, Quentin. Pulp Fiction. Blu-ray. Directed by Quentin Tarantino. Miramax, 1994

[27] Barks, Carl. Parrot Joe from Singapore Walt Disney Comics & Stories 65. Dell Comics. 1946

[28] Crowe, Cameron, Jerry Maguire, Tristar Pictures. 1996

About the Author

Holland M Timmins has worked in modeling, advertising, radio, film, and stand up comedy.

He occasionally rants about rectangles when he isn't ranting about something else.

Holland resides in the Pacific Northwest chilling with bigfoot and other cryptids. He was possibly abducted by Aliens